Also by Melinda Salisbury

The Sin Eater's Daughter

The Sleeping Prince

Melinda Salisbury

SCHOLASTIC

First published in the UK in 2016 by Scholastic Children's Books
An imprint of Scholastic Ltd
Euston House, 24 Eversholt Street,
London, NW1 1DB, UK
Registered office: Westfield Road, Southam, Warwickshire, CV47 0RA
SCHOLASTIC and associated logos are trademarks
and/or registered trademarks of Scholastic Inc.

ISBN 978 1407 14764 2

A CIP catalogue record for this book is available from the British Library.

Printed and bound by CPI Group (UK) Ltd, Croydon, CR0 4YY
Papers used by Scholastic Children's Books are made
from wood grown in sustainable forests.

1 3 5 7 9 10 8 6 4 2

www.scholastic.co.uk

For James Field. For, amongst other things,
getting opening-night tickets to *The Cursed Child*.
Thank you, Strdier.

Tallithi Sea
T A L
Tallith City
Scarron
Tremayne
T R E G E L L
Newtown
River Penaluna
Tremearne Sea
Tressalyn
River Penn
Pender

Prologue

The night guard on the East Gate reached to scratch the sudden sharp itch at his throat. As his legs gave way beneath him and he crumpled, he saw his fingers, slick with blood, black in the dim glow from the lamp that lit the gate. He was dead before he hit the ground.

The golem stepped over his body.

The second guard turned, lips parted to scream, or swear, or beg, his sword rising to meet the creature, but too late. A silver flash through the air and the guard collapsed, his blood mingling with that of his colleague.

The lumpen, blank space where the golem's face ought to be was tilted towards the sky, as though sniffing or listening. It passed through the gate, its misshapen head knocking the lamp, sending it swinging, casting nightmarish shadows over the thick stone wall. As the oil spilled and smoked, and the flame guttered, the golem trod a trail of bloody footsteps through the gate and into the slumbering royal town of Lortune, dragging a club as long as itself in one hand, a large double-headed axe in the other.

Moments later a second golem followed, an axe and club of its own clutched in its twisted hands. Its weapons had yet to be christened.

The two creatures moved forward, slowly but steadily, their gait rocking and lilting, the motion more reminiscent of ships on the ocean than anything that moved on land.

The Sleeping Prince followed them.

In contrast to the monstrousness of the golems, the prince was beautiful. His silvery-white hair reflected the moonlight, flowing down his back like a waterfall. His eyes, when the light of the lamp caught them, were gold: like coins, like honey. He was tall and slender, and moved with a grace that made each step look like the beginning of a dance. In each of his hands he carried a flat, curved sword, the gold hilts adorned with symbols from a long-dead world, but he had no plans to use them, or to bloody himself at all this night. If all went as he expected, he wouldn't need to. Tonight, the swords were mostly for effect, so that anyone who happened to be awake – an old woman with pains that kept her from sleeping, or a small boy woken from a terrible dream – might look from their window and witness his magnificence, as he walked through their town. He wanted to be seen – not by everyone, not yet, but certainly by a few. He wanted the rumours to spread of how he walked unchallenged into the city and took it. How with only two golems he invaded the town of Lortune and its castle, killing no one, save for those paid to keep Lortune from being invaded. He wanted the townsfolk to whisper behind their hands of how regal he looked as he strolled past their homes. He wanted them to remember that he could have had them all killed in their sleep but he hadn't; he had spared them. His people.

He wanted his new people to think well of him. Eventually, at least. His father had told him there were two ways to rule: through fear or through love. He could not expect the Lormerians to love him, not yet, but he could make them fear him. He could easily do that.

He followed his golems through the silent streets, casting a critical eye over the dirt pathways and roads, the stains from sewage flung from windows on to the pathways, the buildings that huddled in the shadow of the castle, cramped and dirty, looking more like outbuildings than prosperous merchant houses and businesses in the capital of the land.

His lip curled with distaste as he peered into the windows of some of the homes they passed, with their utilitarian furniture, their drab decor. He looked up at the castle of Lormere, a thick, square keep, flanked by four towers, dark as its occupants slept. Ugly, like the rest of town. But better than no castle at all. . .

The golems did their work again on the Water Gate, the least secure of the entrances to the grounds of Lormere castle, even with the extra guards assigned by the new king. This time, eight bodies – four armed sentries at the gate and four more stationed atop the battlements – had fallen, forever silenced. The Sleeping Prince had been forced to join in the fight this time to end it quickly, engaging the men on the gate while his monsters slashed and lunged at the archers positioned twenty feet above them on the walls. The arrows had bounced off the clay hides of the golems; if they'd realized they were being shot at, they gave no sign as they harried the men until they fell, before crushing their skulls into the earth.

There was blood on the Sleeping Prince's golden tunic and he wiped at it, smearing it across the velvet. His face darkened and in response to his mood the golems swung their clubs and stamped, their movements agitated. He stalked past them, striding along the path that led through the outbuildings, through the kitchen gardens to the castle that loomed up ahead of him.

Then, impossibly, a horn split the night apart. He spun back towards the Water Gate and broke into a run, the lumbering footsteps of the golems behind him. On the ground a white-faced guard, clearly not as dead as he ought to be, was breathing frantically into a horn, his eyes bulging with each blast. The Sleeping Prince plunged one of his swords into the man's chest, the blow stopping his heart, and the horn, in its tracks.

But it was too late. As he turned back to the castle, he saw lights flaring in windows that had been dark moments before. He heard new horns sounding the alarm, heard the shouts of men, and he sighed. He reached into his pocket and pulled a sheaf of parchment and a writing stick from it. Frowning thoughtfully, he scribbled some words, then tore the paper in two. He gestured to the golems and they each held out a hand, allowing him to place the torn parchment on their palms. For a moment it rested on the surface. Then the clay-flesh turned liquid and the paper sank into it, reforming around it until the paper was concealed within. The shouts became louder, closer, and the whip-thud of arrows began to pierce the air.

The Sleeping Prince sighed. Then he and his golems began to walk silently towards the commotion. The Sleeping Prince swung his swords and smiled.

In the Great Hall of Lormere castle, the king of Lormere stood in pale cream breeches and a billowing white shirt, the laces of his boots uneven, watching the Sleeping Prince warily. The Sleeping Prince in turn eyed his opponent, his head angled with curiosity, his own clothes now torn and soaked red, his beautiful hair tainted with gore. His eyes burned in his blood-splattered face, fixed upon the king. Behind him lay piles of bodies: soldiers, and guards, and any servant who had been foolish enough to try to defend their king, sprawled like broken toys across the stone floor. He'd left a trail of corpses marking a macabre path, beginning at the Water Gate and winding through the gardens and hallways to here, where the battle would climax.

On the opposite side of the Great Hall, near the door leading to the royal solar, lay one of the golems, inanimate. Its arm had been severed by a lucky guard, weakening the alchemy controlling it, giving a second guard the chance to remove its head. In a fit of delicious irony, it had crushed its destroyer as it toppled in a final act of retribution. The second golem stood in the doorway of the Great Hall, waiting for any final guards who had yet to join the fray.

There were none.

The king held something in his hands: a metal disc on a chain, which he brandished at the Sleeping Prince as though it were a gift. The Sleeping Prince smiled indulgently.

"If we could talk," the king said urgently, his face pale, his hair a frenzy of dark curls around it.

"No talk, Merek of Lormere," the Sleeping Prince said, his smooth, calm voice a contrast to his maniacal smile. "Your men are all dead. Your castle and kingdom are mine. The only words I'll hear from you are your pleas for mercy."

Merek's dark eyes flashed. "I assure you, you won't," he said. "I won't die begging." Then he lunged.

The Sleeping Prince stepped to the side and raised one of his swords, arcing it through the air until it found its sheath in the unprotected breast of the new Lormerian king.

King Merek made a soft sound of surprise, turning his eyes to the Sleeping Prince, his disbelief childlike. Then those same eyes fluttered closed and he slumped to the ground. The Sleeping Prince watched him, his expression unreadable.

He stepped over the king's body and crossed the hall,

mounting the steps to the dais. Behind the long wooden table, the sigil of the House of Belmis hung, a shield emblazoned with three golden suns and three silver moons on a blood-red background. With a snort of disgust he tore it down and walked over it, to the high carved seat at the centre of the table. Slumping into it, he ran a finger over the carving, his lip curling once more. Cheap, peasant craftsmanship. He deserved better.

And now that Lormere was his, he would have it.

Part One

Chapter 1

I keep my eyes fixed on the door ahead as I approach it, not looking at the soldiers on either side, doing my very best to seem bored, even a little vacant. Nothing special here, nothing worth paying any mind to. Just another villager, attending the assembly. To my immense relief they don't even spare me a glance as I step out of the drizzle and into the run-down House of Justice, and I exhale slowly as I pass them, some of my tension easing.

It's no warmer inside, and I pull my cloak tighter around me as I walk to the chamber where Chanse Unwin, self-appointed Justice of Almwyk, will brief us on the latest word from the Council of Tregellan. Rainwater drips from my hair, down my nose, as I look at the rows of wooden benches and chairs lined up to face the podium at the front of the room; far too many seats for the remaining villagers to fill. Despite how few of us there are, the room stinks and I wrinkle my nose at it: unwashed bodies, wet wool, leather, metal and fear, all creating a soupy, musty perfume. This is what despair smells like.

Those of us who are still clinging to life here are wet and shivering. Bitter air and autumn rain have seeped through our thin, threadbare clothes, and into our skin, where it feels as though they'll remain for the whole of winter. The soldiers lined up neatly against the walls, on the other hand, are bone dry, and look warm enough in thick green woollen tunics and tough leather breeches, their watchful eyes roving throughout the room.

There is a scuffling behind me and I turn in time to see them stop the man behind me and force him against the wall, patting him down and examining his cloak and hood before releasing him. Heat rushes to my face as I look away, pretending not to have seen.

Ducking my head again, I slink along the back row, taking a seat on a bench a good six feet away from my nearest neighbour. She grunts, possibly a greeting, though more likely a warning, and her hand rises to touch a charm hanging on a leather cord around her neck. I peek at it from the corner of my eye, watching the gold disc gleam between her gnarled fingers before she tucks it away inside her cloak. I know what it is, though I doubt it's real gold. If it were real gold someone would have had it off her neck by now – Gods, if it were real gold, *I* might have had it off her neck. At least if it were gold it would be worth something.

My friend Silas laughed when I told him the villagers were wearing charms to protect themselves from the Sleeping Prince, and I laughed with him, though I secretly thought it wasn't all that strange to put faith in eldritch magic, under the circumstances. Crescent moons made of salt and bread are hung on almost every door and window in the village; medallions etched with three gold stars are tucked inside collars. The Sleeping Prince is a thing of magic, and myth, and superstition. If I'm generous, I can see why it seems natural to try to fight back with magic, myth and superstition. But I know, deep down, that no amount of cheap tin pendants will keep him from coming if he wants to. No salt-strewn thresholds, or holly berries and oak twigs hung over windows and doors, will stop him if he decides to take Tregellan. If a castle full of guards couldn't stop him, a metal disc and some shrubbery isn't likely to.

Before he came back, hardly anyone in Tregellan would have put their faith in something so irrational; it's not the Tregellian way. There might be the occasional crackpot who still believes in the Oak and the Holly and paints their face and their arse red with berry juice every solstice, but that's not how most of us live. We're not Lormerians, with their temples and their living goddesses, and their creepy royal family. We're people of science, and reason. Or at least I thought we were. I suppose it's hard to remain on the side of reason when a five-hundred-year-old fairy tale comes to life and lays waste to the castle and the people in the country next door.

Be a good girl, or the Bringer will come, and then the Sleeping Prince will eat your heart, that's what girls in Tremayne were told. He was a fairy-tale monster, a story to make us obedient, a cautionary tale against greed and autocracy. We never dreamed that he'd wake up. We'd forgotten that he was real.

I turn away from the woman and begin my catalogue of who's left in Almwyk, accidentally catching the eye of one of the soldiers, who nods at me, causing the ever-present tightness in my chest to squeeze a little more. I nod back curtly and break the eye contact, trying to stay calm, resisting the urge to pat my pocket and make sure the vial is still there.

I'm really not cut out for drug smuggling. I checked the vial at least six times on the way here, despite the fact I didn't see a single other soul, let alone have someone come close enough to pick my pockets. Then again, you can't be too careful in Almwyk.

Almwyk, by and large, isn't the kind of village where you're friendly with your neighbours. Here asking for help or showing weakness of any kind is likely, at best, to result in being laughed at. At worst, it could mean a knife in your kidney if you ask the wrong person at the wrong time. Before the soldiers came it wasn't uncommon for a body to be hauled into, or out of, the woods, and we all turned a blind eye to it. You learn quickly to be blind here.

The derelict cottages that make up Almwyk are the home to the desperate and the damned: those who lost their real homes and lives in other parts of Tregellan for crimes

14

they'll never, ever confess to. People always say that in times of great need, like war and disease, communities come together, support one another. Not in Almwyk. As the war has crept closer the cottages have slowly evacuated, and those remaining have descended on them, ripping out whatever they can for their own needs. I bet it's a matter of time before occupancy isn't an obstacle to the scavengers, when the instinct to grasp at anything that might make surviving easier will be stronger than basic courtesy. Even now I glance around the room, noting who remains, who is the likeliest threat.

It's a game I like to play sometimes, trying to guess the crimes of the people still here. The worst criminals – murderers and the like – evaporated the moment the soldiers arrived, which leaves the middling dregs: the debtors, drunks, addicts, gamblers and liars. The poor and the unlucky. The ones who can't leave because there is nowhere else for them to go.

This isn't a place people come to live; it's a place people come to rot.

I bunch my fists under my ragged cloak and watch my frozen breath hover in the air as I exhale, before it scatters, mingling with everyone else's, adding to the damp fug in the room. The thick glass windows are rimed with condensation, and I hate the feeling that I'm breathing in my neighbours' breaths, hate knowing that even the air I breathe these days is second-hand, or stolen. I can hardly breathe as it is.

When it seems everyone who's coming has arrived, sitting dotted around the room like the last of the raisins in a sad plum pudding, Chanse Unwin – surely the realm's most ironic Justice – strides into the room, chest puffed out, scanning every face. When his eyes land on me he half smiles a greeting, and my skin crawls as his smile rearranges itself into a concerned frown, or a parody of one. He looks so sweaty that I'm surprised the frown doesn't slide clean off his face.

He's flanked by the two grim-faced, green-coated soldiers who were manning the door outside, and they're joined, unusually, by their captain, a red sash across his barrel chest. When six more soldiers follow them and position themselves around the edges of the space, the atmosphere in the room ripples and tightens.

Instantly I sit upright, alert as a hare, and around me every single one of my neighbours does the same; even the woman who grunted at me when I sat down unfurls from her crone-like hunch to glower over at Unwin. As my hand glides to my belt to check for my knife, I see other hands moving to boot tops and waists, all of us wanting the reassurance that we're armed.

Whatever this meeting is about, Unwin clearly expects the news to be taken badly, and my heart sinks because there's only one thing he could possibly say at this point that would make us mutinous. The already scant air feels as though it's congealing in my throat.

Chanse Unwin looks around the room once more, taking

us all in, before pressing his palms together. "I have news from the Council in Tressalyn," he says, his voice unctuous and self-satisfied. "And it is not good. Three nights ago the Sleeping Prince's golems attacked the Lormerian town of Haga. They destroyed the two temples there, and once again left no survivors. They slaughtered anyone who refused to bend the knee to him, some four hundred souls. This attack follows the sacking of the temples in Monkham and Lortune, and brings his army within fifty miles of the border between us and Lormere. Based on this pattern, the Council believes he'll march on Chargate next."

At this everyone turns to their neighbour with raised eyebrows, petty local arguments and generations-old feuds forgotten as they begin to murmur to one another. I don't look at anyone. Instead I squeeze my fingers around the hilt of my knife and take a deep breath. Chargate is on the other side of the trees; it's Almwyk's Lormerian counterpart. It would put the golems merely hours away from us, the other side of the wood.

Unwin clears his throat, and the whispering dies away. "The Council concludes that its attempts to negotiate with the Sleeping Prince have failed. He has outright refused to sign a treaty of peace with Tregellan and will not deny that he plans to invade." His gaze flickers briefly to the captain, who smirks and glances at one of the other soldiers, making me wonder how much Unwin truly knows of what he's reporting, and what he's merely been told to relate. "Because of this," Unwin continues, "the Council has sat in emergency session,

17

and unanimously decided that we have no choice but to declare a state of war in Tregellan."

He pauses dramatically, as if expecting us to make some protest. But we say and do nothing, remaining stony-faced and silent, saving our reactions until he gets to the crux of the matter, the part that affects us, and warrants fifteen of the newly mustered Tregellian army's finest in a room where we barely outnumber them.

Realizing this, he continues. "Last night the Tregellian army sealed the border from the River Aurmere to the Cliffs of Tressamere. Including the East Woods." He pauses and the whole world narrows to this room, to these words. *Don't say it.* I concentrate as hard as I can. *Don't say it.*

"All trade and traffic between here and Lormere is prohibited from now on. The border is closed. Anyone caught trying to cross it will be killed on sight."

We draw in our breath as one, taking all the air from the room.

"Given its strategic position, the village has been requisitioned as a barracks and base of operations for the garrison defending the border. Almwyk is to be evacuated. Immediately."

No. There is the tiniest fragment of a moment in which the news filters into the brains of the occupants of the room.

Then all hell breaks loose.

Chapter 2

I found out about the meeting when Chanse Unwin rapped on my door before the sun had risen this morning. I'd finally fallen asleep an hour or two before dawn, and I'd been dreaming of the man again. This time we were standing on the bridge over the river, near my old home in Tremayne. It was summer; silver fish darted in the clear water beneath us, and the sun beat down on us, making my scalp warm. I was dressed in my old apprentice's uniform. The dress was blue and clean, the many pockets of my apron full of small vials and plants and powders. I could smell them, the herby, pungent tang of rosemary and willow bark and pine: scents that meant home and knowledge, work and happiness. I reached into one of the pockets and let my fingers drift through dried leaves as I listened to him speak.

He was tall, thin, cloaked and hooded despite the warm

weather, and he stooped as he spoke, his body curved towards me, making us a circle of two as he told me some tale, his hands moving gracefully through the air to illustrate his story. The words were lost immediately, in the way they often are in dreams, but the feelings they evoked remained, and I knew his words had been chosen to make me laugh – really laugh – deep, creasing belly laughs that had me clutching my stomach with the pain of so much joy. He smiled at my delight and it made it all the sweeter.

When I finally stopped laughing, I turned to him and watched as he rummaged inside his cloak. He pulled out a small doll and pushed it towards me, sliding it over the stone of the bridge. I reached out, taking it, my fingers brushing against his. I heard his breath catch and it made my stomach ache in a different sort of way.

"What is it?" I asked, looking at the tiny figure.

"It's you," he replied. "I like to carry you with me. I like to keep you close. To watch over you."

Then he took the doll back, plucking it from where I'd held it cradled in my hand and replacing it carefully in the folds of his cloak, while I watched, my heart beating double time inside me. Though I couldn't see his face, I could tell he was looking at me and I blushed, which prompted him to smile softly, his lips parting, his tongue moistening them.

The thumping of my heart grew louder as he moved closer, until suddenly it became the insistent banging of the front door, and I was yanked out of my summer dream to hear rain beating against the wooden shutters. The pain in my stomach wasn't from laughing but from hunger, and the dream drifted away like a broken spiderweb. I was both heartbroken and relieved. It was bittersweet here in Almwyk, in winter, to think of Tremayne in the sun.

Stretching as best I could, I hauled myself up from the pallet on the floor, pulling one of the blankets around me as a makeshift cloak, and hit my knee against the table leg with a hollow crack that knocked me sick. I took advantage of the relative privacy to swear violently while the rapping on the front door continued, rhythmic as a pulse.

When I opened it, Chanse Unwin stood there, pale, fleshy lips split into a grin as he looked me up and down. My skin prickled as his eyes roamed over my blanket-draped body.

"Errin, good morning. Have I woken you?"

"Of course not, Mr Unwin." My answering smile was all teeth.

His grin widened. "Good, good. I would hate to think I'd inconvenienced you. May I speak with your mother?"

"I'm afraid she's not here."

He peered behind me as if he expected to see her hiding there.

"Not here?" he said, nodding towards the sun peeping through the trees of the East Woods. "But the curfew is barely ended. Surely I would have seen her had she just left."

"I can't understand how you didn't," I said blandly. "She left a few moments before you knocked. In fact, I thought at first you were her returned, having forgotten something."

21

"Hence answering in a state of undress." He leered at me, taking the chance to drag his gaze up and down my form again.

I pulled my blanket cloak closer. I'd overheard enough gossip at the well to know Unwin has been in Almwyk a good twenty years. For all his veneer of respectability, the rumours say that he ended up here for the same reason we all did – he was out of options and unwelcome anywhere else. It's said that he created Almwyk from the ruins of an old hunting village of the royals, and began to regulate it, first as a black-market hub, then as a village, to make it turn a profit for him. By the time officials came to investigate, he was doing his best impression of repentance and atonement, offering shelter to the needy for a pittance and keeping them in check. Justice of Almwyk.

"I'm surprised you opened the door; I could have been anyone. These are desperate times, people with nothing to lose ... soldiers miles from their homes, their girls. Refugees out for what they can get."

I said nothing. I couldn't. But I suspect my face said everything I was too wary to say aloud.

"You might feel full of compassion for these people now, but when they're cold, and starving, and then night falls..." Unwin leant in. "You have no protection." He looked up at the empty lintel of the door, before pulling a handful of berries and a gold disc from his pocket and holding them out to me. "Against mortal men, or the Sleeping Prince."

I didn't believe that Unwin had faith in the idea of charms

and amulets any more than I did, but I kept it to myself. "You're very kind, but I wouldn't like to leave you vulnerable."

"I'd be happy to come inside and wait with you until your mother returns; that way we can both benefit from the protection I'm offering."

It took a lot of effort for me to remain polite when I replied. "Thank you for such a generous offer, but I'd hate to steal your time and I have a few errands of my own to run this morning. In fact I really must get on. Goodbye, then." I began to close the door, but he wedged his foot in the gap.

His eyes narrowed further, until they were slits above his florid cheeks, and he put his amulet away. "Everything is all right here, isn't it?" he said slowly. "I don't suppose you've heard anything about your brother? You can trust me, you know. I am a friend to you. And your mother. I'd be happy to help, if you'd only ask."

"It's fine, Mr Unwin. Everything is fine. My mother likes to keep busy, that's all."

"Clearly. It's surely weeks since I saw her last. Moons, even. Though I'm sure she'll be eager to attend today's meeting."

My stomach cramped with dread. "A meeting?"

He clapped a hand to his forehead theatrically. "Have I not yet said? My, how you distract me! I've had word from the Council in Tressalyn. They've sent a messenger with an important announcement. I'm at haste to call everyone to the House of Justice to hear it."

"Then you must let me keep you no longer."

His face twisted into a grimace of annoyance and I knew I'd gone too far; I never have been much good at holding my tongue. But within seconds he mastered himself. The broken veins on his cheeks danced as he contorted his lips back into a grin.

"You're too kind. Too diligent by far; it's unusual in a young woman. Perhaps not to everyone's taste. I admire it, though. I find your directness refreshing. I'm sure you value it in others, too, so I shan't beat about the bush or offend you by being unclear. I'm also here for the rent. You still owe me two florins from last moon. I thought I'd save you the trouble of bringing it to me, seeing as I had to deliver my own message to you."

"Of course," I replied. "I'd not forgotten. As it happens, now I think on it, that's the errand that took my mother away so early. It seems you're at cross purposes here."

"I fear so," he said darkly. "Still, I trust I'll see you both at the meeting, and you can give me the four florins afterwards."

"Four florins? The rent is two."

"Interest, Errin. Sadly I've had to borrow money to cover your late payment. I have obligations too, you know. So I'll need a little extra from you this time. You understand, I'm sure. Not many landlords would let a tenant stay on without paying the rent. But, as I said, I'm your friend." His smile was sickly with triumph. "I want nothing more than to aid you."

I fumed. He was lying, taking advantage in the worst way because of the hole I'd dug for myself. He knew I could barely afford the two florins I already owed.

"That won't be a problem, will it? Because you can talk to me if it is. We can negotiate." He licked his lips, and immediately I was grateful for my empty stomach.

"It's fine, Mr Unwin. I'm sure my mother has it under control."

Unwin's smile faltered and an ugly expression flickered across his face. "The meeting starts at three sharp. Until later, then." He reached for my hand and pulled it to his lips, bowing to me.

Giving my body a final sweep with his eyes, he turned away and I closed the door, leaning heavily against it as I listened to him walk away, unable to suppress a shudder.

Four florins. There was one still hidden in the pot. The last of what we had, kept back for emergencies. Thank the Holly for Silas, I reminded myself. I'd have to find him before the meeting. With luck he'd have another order for me and offer payment up front.

But the temporary relief was cut short at the sound of more banging. This time at the other door. The one that led to the bedroom.

When I opened the bedroom door, I narrowly missed being hit in the head by the object flung at me from the dark room. I ducked, but not quickly enough. The enamel chamber pot had hit me in the shoulder and urine had soaked the blanket still wrapped around me, seeping through it into my tunic. My mother was crouched on the bed, her teeth bared, her eyes feral, tinged with red as she poised to leap at me.

"Mama?" I said quietly.

I barely closed the door in time. The second the lock clicked, she slammed against it. I leant against the door as she started pounding it, then walked shakily into the kitchen.

Too close.

I waited until the sun was fully up before I returned to my mother. I found her wedged between the bed and the wall, curled up and staring silently out past me.

"Mama?" I said softly, moving slowly towards her, keeping a clear path to the door in case she was still mostly beast; I've been fooled by her before.

I lifted her gently until she was standing, trying not to wince at how insubstantial she felt in my arms. The rushes on the floor rustled softly as she dragged her feet through them, and I made a note to seek out the soiled ones and replace them. In truth they all needed replacing, but money is as thin on the ground as the rushes on our floor. I braced her against the battered rocking chair and collected fresh water and a cloth.

It doesn't matter how many times I do it; it always feels strange to clean her. Her skin was papery, shifting as the cloth dragged over it, fragile as a moth's wing. The scratches on her forearms are healed, leaving a map of silvery scars that gleam in the candlelight. Those I dabbed at with extra care, even as I tried not to look at them.

When I raised her arms to put a clean nightgown on her

she held them up obediently, allowing me to move her as though she were a doll.

I prefer it when she's violent.

Once upon a time there was a young apprentice apothecary who lived on a red-brick farm with a golden thatch roof, surrounded by green fields. She had a father who called her a "clever girl" and gave her a herb garden all of her own, and a mother who was whole and kind. She had a brother who knew how to smile and laugh.

But then one day her father had an accident and, despite her efforts to save him, he died. And so did all of her hopes and dreams. The farm – the family's home for generations – was sold. Her mother's brown hair greyed, her spirit dulled as she drifted towards Almwyk like a wraith, uncomplaining, unfeeling. And her brother, once impulsive and joyful, became cold and hard, his eyes turned east with malice.

If someone had told me six moons ago, before I watched my life slip through my hands like water, that my mother would be cursed, locked away, and drugged by my own hand, I would have laughed in their face. Then I would have kicked them for the insult and laughed again. I would have sooner believed in fairy tales coming true. Of course, we all believe in fairy tales now. The Scarlet Varulv has slunk out of the pages and lives with me in this cottage. The Sleeping Prince has woken and sacked Lormere, an army of alchemy-made golems behind him as he murders his way across the country. Stories are no longer stories; characters run rampant through the world these days. All I'm waiting for is Mully-No-Hands to knock on the window, begging to come in and warm himself, and my life will be complete.

Actually, no, that's not what I'm waiting for.

The newly declared king, Merek of the House of Belmis, was killed before he had the chance to put the crown on his head, as were all those who refused to swear fealty to the Sleeping Prince, all those who tried to stop his march to the throne.

I saw King Merek in the flesh, a little less than a year past, when he was still a prince. He'd been riding through my old home of Tremayne with a retinue of equally shining and proud young men. Lirys and I exchanged impressed glances, our cheeks flaming so red that my brother scowled at us, and then at the prince atop his white horse. Prince Merek was handsome, almost too handsome, his dark curls framing his face, bobbing as he nodded here and there to acknowledge those throwing flowers and coins into his horse's path. Tregellan might have done away with its own royals, but we were happy to celebrate the future king of Lormere. He looked how a prince should look.

Before the soldiers came, I used to talk to the refugees hurrying through here on their way to Tyrwhitt. They told me how the king's head, crowned with a crude wooden band, now sits at the centre of a row of them, mounted on spikes over the main gate into Lortune town. I know better than to be sentimental, but I can't bear the idea of his handsome, hopeful face slack and staring over a kingdom he'll never rule, surrounded by the heads of those who stayed loyal to him to the last. I don't know if one of those heads is Lief's.

I've asked every hollow-eyed refugee that I've managed to speak to if they've heard anything about a Tregellian being killed by the Sleeping Prince, or whether a head with hair and cheekbones like mine sits above the gates alongside the king's. Whether they've heard of a Tregellian being captured and held. Or even hiding somewhere. I've spent hours walking up and down the length of the woods, waiting for him to come striding out, grinning manically, not even a little sorry for making me worry.

Because I can't believe my brother is dead. Lief would have done anything to stay alive; he wasn't the kind to throw himself on his sword. Had the Sleeping Prince told him to bend the knee to save his neck, he would have done. He'd have knelt, and bided his time until he could get out. He was clever – is clever. He must be trapped somewhere, perhaps ill, or wounded, or merely waiting until it's safe to run.

Family first, Papa used to say, whenever we fought. He'd remind us of his grandmother spiriting her sons away from the old Tregellan castle the night the people rose against the royals and killed them. Our great-grandmother had been a lady-in-waiting of the queen, and the wife of the head of the army. When she'd heard the people at the gates, she'd abandoned her post, taken her children and run. Run from her old life to begin again in safety. Other people come and go, but family is for ever.

Lief did the same. He moved us to keep us alive. He had to go to Lormere because we had nothing. We sold everything to cover our debts when we left Tremayne. This hovel, this draughty, dirty, cramped little hut, and the apathy of our neighbours are the last things protecting me and my mother while we wait for Lief to come home. Now it's going to be taken from us too. Now we'll have nowhere to hide.

And we need something to hide, because when the moon starts to round out and become fat and heavy, my once-gentle, steady and loving mother turns into a monster with red eyes and hooked hands who whispers through a closed door all the ways she'd like to hurt me.

But at least when she has the beast in her she can see me. She can hear me. When she's my mother I'm a ghost to her. Like my father, and my brother, except I'm still alive. I'm still here.

Chapter 3

Seventeen furious villagers are on their feet, shouting and shaking their fists, some clutching their amulets, some waving them, their protests unintelligible, save for the swearing. The room, which felt so large when I first entered, now feels stifling and dangerous, and I shrink in my seat, my hand going to the vial in my pocket. The soldiers shout for order, imploring people to sit down, and to listen. Unwin is slamming his fist on the podium, demanding silence, but I've already tuned it all out, my ears buzzing with the sound of my own rushing blood, my fingers gripping the edge of the bench.

I can't leave Almwyk. I have no money; I have nowhere to go. I have to wait for my brother; he might not be able to find us if we leave. But mostly, I can't leave because of my mother. Because I have no way to get her out of the house without her being seen. And she can't be seen. Not as she is.

The soldiers finally restore order but the atmosphere is mutinous, mutterings rumbling across the room like thunder. Unwin looks down at us all with false pity in his eyes.

"I understand you're upset to have to leave your homes," he says smoothly. "The decree from the Council says that you'll be welcomed as a priority at the new refugee camp outside of Tyrwhitt if you have nowhere to go. No questions asked. Just make sure to have your papers stamped by myself so they know you're Tregellian, and not seeking asylum from Lormere."

"Camps won't keep us safe," a voice pipes up from the middle of the room, Old Samm I think – an irrepressible gambler, but nice enough. "We can't be expected to survive winter in tents, let alone a winter under attack if the Sleeping Prince comes."

"By all means, you're free to go elsewhere in the realm if you wish," Unwin sneers. "The camps are merely an option for those who have nowhere to go, and no desire to be jailed for vagrancy. Or anything else."

Again the atmosphere thickens with threatened rebellion. He knows that none of us would live here if we had anywhere else to go.

"So that's it?" Old Samm continues. "We're to be thrown out, unprotected?"

"This is war," Unwin says with an air of drama, glancing around at the soldiers, trying to make eye contact with them. I like them a little better when their faces remain stony, refusing him the approval he's looking for. "This is war,"

Unwin repeats. "There are no easy roads from here on. We all must make sacrifices. Almwyk will be the base from which the whole of Tregellan is defended by our finest soldiers."

"How will they protect us from golems?" Old Samm says, and Unwin looks to the soldiers again to help him. But it's too late; the mention of golems sends a tremor through the room and suddenly everyone is back on their feet. "How are they supposed to defend us against monsters that can't be killed? They're ten feet tall and made of stone. Boy soldiers won't stop them." His words begin a flood of other voices, all of them terrified.

"I heard the Sleeping Prince can turn a man to stone by looking at him. Is it true? Is that how he makes his army? Are they people he's bespelled? Will our amulets protect us?"

"We don't have any temples; surely he'll leave us be?"

"I heard he's demanding a tax, paid in young women, and that he'll eat their hearts," a female voice calls, shrill with fear.

"Well, you'll be all right then, you've not been young for a good thirty harvests," someone bellows back at her.

"Does the holly work for ever?" another voice shouts. "Do the berries need to be fresh? If I wear the juices, will that help repel him?"

"Can't we offer him something? Do we have nothing he wants?"

The noise level rises again as people shout their questions, pleading for answers or yelling abuse, and the soldiers step forward menacingly, hands on the hilts of their swords. But the villagers will not be cowed. Their voices get louder and louder, they stand on their chairs, and I can't take it any more. I climb over the back of the bench, skirt down the side of the wall and out of the door.

I pause to lean against the pillory outside the House of Justice, my heart beating so fast I feel nauseous, my skin flushing warm and then turning cold. Above me the sun is starting to dip down towards the horizon, and dread curdles inside me. It'll be dark soon. I need to make my mother her sedative. I need to find Silas and get the money for Unwin.

I need my father and brother to be here.

No. I push that thought away as my heart trips over itself. Not now. I have things to do.

But my body doesn't obey me, and fear makes a corset around my ribs as I walk blindly back towards the cottage, ignoring the stares of two passing soldiers, marching towards the woods.

I can't breathe.

When the soldiers have passed I stop, pressing the heels of my hands into my eyes, trying to calm down. My brain spits out thoughts so fast I can't cling to them; could I drug her into sleep to make the journey? *Journey where? You have nowhere to go, nothing, no one.* Could I keep up the pretence that she's ill, something contagious? *We're at war; we're really at war.* How much longer could we stay here? *We can't; he's less than fifty miles away.* We have nowhere to go. *We have to leave; we can't leave.* How will Lief find us? *We can't leave him behind.*

Four hundred souls were killed in Haga, added to the three hundred in Monkham. We don't even know how many died in Lortune, or in the smaller hamlets and towns across Lormere. When Lief left for Lormere it felt as though he'd travelled half a world away, but now it's no distance, the East Woods a flimsy barrier that an army of golems could trample with ease.

I imagine the heads of people I know mounted on spikes along the outskirts of the West Woods. Unwin. Fussy Old Samm, sour-faced Pegwin with her mutterings and dark looks.

Silas.

My hands lower to cover my mouth, and then I see him, as if thinking about him summoned him into being. Loitering in the shadows at the side of my hut, out of sight of the soldiers, shrouded in his customary black cloak. Silas Kolby. As always, his face is hidden by the hood that hangs so low it leaves only his mouth visible. It's a mark of how strange life in Almwyk is that my single friend is a boy whose face I've never actually seen, and that that seems completely normal to me now.

It's his height that allows me to recognize him; he's a good eight inches taller than I am, and I'm tall enough for a girl. His feet are crossed at the ankle as he leans against the wall with an air of studied nonchalance that I can see straight through. He raises his head at the sound of my footsteps and my mouth suddenly dries.

"I've been waiting for you," he says in his low, ragged voice. All of him is ragged: his patched cloak; his shabby gloves, the fingertips thin and worn; his scuffed boots. His words always seem to catch on my insides, like a goose grass burr, or a torn fingernail dragged across silk. His voice sticks. "How was the meeting?"

My voice is thankfully steady when I reply, though my heart still beats like the wings of a bird against a cage. "If you'd come, then you'd know."

"Alas, I had other plans. Skulking. Creeping. Avoiding discovery and possible arrest. The usual."

"How did you even know there was a meeting?"

"Skulking. Creeping. I just said that, pay attention." When I raise my eyebrows at him, my lips pursed, he smiles and continues. "I overheard a pair of soldiers moaning about having to police it. Were there many of them there?"

I try not to return his smile, and fail, as some of my anxiety recedes. "We practically had one each."

"Was it that bad?"

"It was that bad," I say, my smile fading, the knot inside my heart returning and tightening. "Golems marched on Haga last night and destroyed the temples there. Four hundred people were killed."

His mouth opens, but he says nothing, waiting for me to continue.

"The Council think he'll move for Chargate next. It's not that far from here, fifty miles at most. We're at war, officially." I take a deep breath. "They've closed the border."

Silas nods, chewing his lips thoughtfully before he speaks. "It was bound to happen, sooner or later."

"Sooner, it seems."

His mouth becomes a line and he speaks hesitantly. "What about Lief?"

I shake my head, glancing at the forest involuntarily. I don't believe Lief is dead. I *know* he isn't. But it's not something I want to talk to Silas about. He knows Lief was in Lormere, and that he hasn't come back. The way he speaks about him, gently, distantly, tells me he's less optimistic than I am. I don't think we need to talk about it.

I look around before I reach into my cloak and pull out the vial of hemlock draught hidden there. "Here. I brought it to your hut on my way to the meeting. You weren't there," I tell him.

"It's not my hut any more. I had to move again," he says. "I'm in the one by the old pigsty now. Gods know for how long though."

He holds out a gloved hand for his potion and I drop it into the palm, watching his fingers curl over it, making it disappear. Then it vanishes into the folds of his cloak, to be replaced with gold coins. I open my hand as he does, so he can drop them in; we don't touch, Silas and I, not even like this, not even during the simple taking of a coin or a vial.

"Thanks." He nods, peering around.

When he pulls his hood down further, preparing to leave, I blurt, "Do you need anything else?"

He shakes his head, his lips pursed. "No, thanks. With the border closing I expect the situation will change."

Silas has placed a fair few orders with me over the

last few moons, wildly varying his requests from the most innocent remedies to the deadliest poisons. I've recorded each and every order in my apothecary log: what it was, how much of it, and the cost. He pays three gold florins for the illegal ones, and four silver centas for anything else. I have no idea what he does with them; he won't tell me, nor will he tell me how he gets the coin to pay for them. If I'm honest, he never tells me anything. I've tried asking outright, and I've tried tricking him into it. He always shakes his head ruefully, giving me a close-lipped, inscrutable smile, and tells me if I ask no questions, I'll be told no lies.

I shrug, as though I don't care either way. "You should probably get going," I remind him. "The meeting was practically over when I left. It was risky to come here."

"I didn't have a choice, Errin. I told you, I had to move; you wouldn't have known where I was if I hadn't come to you." He smiles. "I was careful, don't worry, I always am. Besides, I needed to know what the meeting was about."

"And if I hadn't left it early?"

A slight twitch in his jaw as his smile falls away. "I suppose I'd have some explaining to do."

His tone strives for nonchalance, but his body gives him away. He's tightly held, coiled like a snake, ready to flee, or strike if he has to. He's nervous about being here, being exposed, despite his words, and I feel a perverse thrill in my stomach that I can read him like this. For three moons I've been feeding him parts of my life: about my father dying; about Lief's determination to support us and then his disappearance; about my apothecary work; in fact everything except for my mother's condition, in the hope it would prompt him to reply in kind. That's how it's supposed to work, a secret for a secret, and a story for a story. Instead he takes my tales with a nod, as though we're at some kind of confessional, the corners of his mouth turned up or down depending on what the story is about. He never comments or judges, instead listening and absorbing and never telling me anything personal in return.

But I've discovered that you can learn a lot without words. And what I've learned is hard won, because – though he's the closest thing I have to a friend here, and as far as I know, I'm his – I have no idea what he looks like beneath his hood. It sounds impossible. It ought to be; how can you call someone a friend, know them for so long and not know what they look like? Yet I don't. I don't know what colour his eyes are, or his hair. I know his mouth, and the point of his chin, and his neat teeth. Once I even saw the end of his nose when he tipped his head back to laugh. But that's all. From our first meeting, to today, he has always, always been hooded, gloved and cloaked, and he's never removed them, never even pushed them aside, whether we're indoors or out. When I asked him why, he told me it was safer like that. For us both. And to not ask again.

Mysterious boys are not as enjoyable in reality as they are in stories.

The obvious reason would be that he's hideously disfigured in some way, but something about the way he carries himself makes me think that can't be it. In my mind's eye he's dark haired and dark eyed, his hair brushing his shoulders, but in truth I don't have a clue. The few times I have managed to peer up into the ever-present hood I've seen the glint of an eye, before he's pulled the hood lower, the rest of his face shadowed and hidden.

Despite that, I can tell when he's worried, or anxious, or angry, or pleased. I've learned to read his lips and his shoulders and his hands, the way he holds himself. He leans forward when he's relaxed, his head tilting to the left. He taps his fingers on whatever surface he can find when he's agitated: tree stumps, his own legs, his arms if they're crossed. When he's amused, two dimples form on the left of his mouth, none on the right. He rubs his tongue along his front teeth when he's thinking. I can see the things he doesn't say, because they're written all over him.

"Is there anything else I should know?" Silas crosses his arms, cutting across my thoughts and pulling me back into the here and now. "From the meeting?"

The panic returns like a wave washing over me, and my stomach lurches as I remember what Unwin said. "We're to be evacuated. With immediate effect. We're all to go."

"Go where?" he says.

"The refugee camp at Tyrwhitt, if we've nowhere else," I say, even though I know we can't go there.

I can feel his eyes on me, the fingers on his left hand tapping his arm with haste, his bottom lip pulled between his teeth, in what I've come to look on as his "thinking face".

"Do you have to?" he says finally.

"The village will be turned into a barracks." I have to force the words out past my tightening throat. "There'll be a proper regiment here. Generals, archers, pike men, cavalry; they'll requisition everywhere. There won't be anywhere for us to stay." I look away from him, breathing deeply, trying to stay in control, to fight off the terror that's rising again, choking me. I feel suddenly warm, feverish. Dizzy.

I imagine my mother tearing through a refugee camp, slashing at children, pulling old men and women to her and sinking her teeth into them. I imagine the blood. The screams and the horror. Axes and swords and hacking, trying to stop her. The inevitable spread of the curse, even if they killed her. Me, orphaned, or dead alongside her. Fire...

"Errin?" Silas says quietly, and I force myself to look at him, pushing my cloak open a little to allow cold air to seep beneath it. The chill calms me, leaching the heat from my skin, and I take a deep breath. Silas waits quietly, chewing his lip.

"Sorry," I say after a moment, when the fear has faded again. "What will you do, about the evacuation?"

"Nothing," he says.

"But you can't stay, they're requisitioning everywhere. All of the huts will be used."

"I have to stay."

I open my mouth to ask for the hundredth time why, but snap it shut again at the sound of boots marching towards us, the sucking sound of wet mud pulling at leather. Without

41

stopping to think, I push my front door open, grabbing Silas by the cloak. He makes a garbled noise, his hands rising to keep the hood against his face as I swing him into the room and close the door after us as quietly as I can, keeping an eye pressed to the tiniest sliver of a gap.

I breathe a sigh of relief when the pair of soldiers I passed earlier stride by without even looking at the cottage, their faces grim and their voices too low to hear. "I said you shouldn't be out there," I say, turning back into the room and blushing when I see Silas looking around, taking it all in.

I've never let him inside before, because of Mama, because no one can know what she is. In the books they burn the Varulvs at the stake, and the houses their families live in. With the families locked inside, to kill the infection. Four moons ago, I'd have thought that archaic, and impossible. But now ... now people wear amulets and nail good bread to their doors. And people like me steal it when we can. Bread is bread.

I follow his gaze, looking at the shelves with their meagre contents: my faded smocks with their mismatched buttons; the blankets dangling from the makeshift washing line in the vain hope they'll dry before my mother's next incident; my pallet and thin blankets on the dusty floor; the battered table that acts as its canopy. I see the fireplace with its single scarred and empty pipkin hanging over a pile of ash in the grate. No trinkets, no knick-knacks. No gleaming pans or hearty broth steaming gently. It looks like it was abandoned years ago; it looks worse than some of the huts he's slept in.

I cannot stand it when he turns to me; my face feels alight with shame. I wonder what he sees when he looks at me. Brown hair turned darker with grease, wound around my head in braids to keep it from my mother's grasping hands, crescents of black dirt under my fingernails, lips chapped. It's no wonder that he... I cut that thought dead.

I don't need to see his face to feel the pity that radiates from him, and it ignites my temper, humiliation and rage building a fire in me. "You should go now," I say rudely, pulling the door open.

Chanse Unwin stands there, his fist raised to knock.

He looks from Silas to me, his eyes widening. I turn to look at Silas, horror digging sharp fingers into me as the lower part of Silas's face turns chalk white.

Chapter 4

Unwin's expression might be amusing if I weren't so terrified. His eyes bulge as he gapes at Silas. I see him cataloguing the worn boots, the loose threads dangling from his cloak, his battered gloves. He looks him up and down, two, three times, before his gaze settles on Silas's hidden face.

"You left the meeting early," Unwin says finally, turning to me, his voice glassy and dangerous. "I saw you go. I thought we had an agreement to meet afterwards."

"Forgive me," I say. "I was afraid there'd be trouble; I didn't want to get caught in it."

"It was nothing I couldn't control. I am the nearest thing to a Justice here, after all," he says, looking back at Silas. "Which leads me to ask, who are you, exactly, my good sir?" He says "sir" as though it's a dirty word. "Where are you from? I don't recall seeing you here before."

Silas lowers his head so only his chin is visible. "I was just leaving," he mutters. His fingers are blurred, tapping a rapid tattoo on his arm as tension rolls off him.

"You'd better get going." I shove Silas past Unwin, stepping out of the house and between them.

Unwin's face starts to darken and he sucks in a deep breath. It prompts Silas to move, disappearing around the corner of the cottage. Unwin watches him go with an ugly expression.

"Evacuation plans," Unwin snaps suddenly, turning back to me. "That's what you missed. There's a caravan leaving the village at first light, for the camp near Tyrwhitt. You're to leave with it."

Dread fills me. "I can't."

"Why?"

"My mother is ill. Very ill. I daren't move her." The lie falls from my lips before I've had time to think it through.

"That's funny, because this morning your mother was out and about, looking to pay her dues, you said. And now she's at death's door?"

"She was. She had to return before she could find you; she should never have gone out, it was foolish." I know I'm babbling but I can't stop. "Now she's resting, but she can't be moved. I'm not sure what it is but . . . I wouldn't want her near anyone." I lower my voice. "It might be contagious. And in a caravan, and then a camp . . . it could spread like wildfire. And I couldn't nurse her there."

I understand too late that I've talked myself into a trap, only noticing when I see something akin to victory in his answering smile.

"Well, doesn't this bring us neatly to a proposition I have for you."

"A proposition?" I repeat.

He looks over his shoulder, glancing around before lowering his voice. His tone is cajoling, sickeningly intimate. "If you wished to stay here, I could make room in the manse for you. For you both." His smile is all teeth.

"What?"

"I saw your face when I mentioned evacuation. I know you have nowhere to go, nowhere to turn. Your father and brother dead."

"Lief isn't dead. He'll come back."

The look Unwin gives me is pitiless. "You have nothing, my girl. And I'll be staying on here, working with the army. I can't go into the details, but I'm inviting you both to stay too. For a price, of course."

"What price?" Sweat breaks out along my shoulders and cools, chilling me.

"I was thinking we could come to an arrangement. Between us. One that's mutually satisfying."

His pupils are dilated, his voice low and breathy, and I understand what he means, what he wants. That he thinks he can ask me for it and he'll get it, because he thinks we have no choice.

I fight to keep my expression blank, to keep my hand

from flying through the air and hitting him. "That's very kind, but we must refuse."

"Refuse?" He blinks. "Refuse? How can you refuse?"

"We do have somewhere to go. We have family in the north. We're expected. As soon as Mama is better, we'll go. That's what worried me, Mama being ill and delaying us. Not that we were destitute."

His eyebrows rise higher and higher with every word I say, and then he bares his teeth at me. "You'll go nowhere before you've given me the money you owe. Six florins now."

"I. . ." I begin, but Unwin cuts me off, his tone whip-cruel and vicious now.

"*I. . .*" Unwin mimics in a high-pitched voice. "You what, Errin? Another excuse? Another witty retort?"

"I. . ." But my words have all left me, as fear of him – for the first time real fear – pins my tongue in place.

"Oh, will you spit it out." He leans forward, his saliva speckling my face. "You were all full of clever words this morning. Where are they now? Hmm? No snappy comeback? No snide remark? Where's my money, Errin?"

"Here." Suddenly Silas is there again, rounding the corner and thrusting his hand out to Unwin, who turns to him as my jaw drops. He came back. He came back. "How much is it?"

"I'm here for her debts, not yours, whoever you think you are," Unwin sneers as I gawp at Silas.

Before I've recovered myself Silas speaks again, moving his lanky frame between mine and Unwin's, as if he's preparing to shield me. "Six florins, did I hear you say? Of course." He smiles at Unwin with a wide, beaming grin that I'd never have believed he was capable of as he thrusts a handful of coins at him, forcing Unwin in his surprise to take them. "There. All paid."

The three of us stand in stunned silence; it seems to me that none of us can believe what has happened.

"Remove your hood," Unwin barks at him suddenly. "Who are you? Show yourself."

"If you'll forgive me, I'll keep my hood up," Silas says calmly. "I was badly burned in a fire some years past. The burns never truly healed – it's not a pretty sight."

It's clear Unwin doesn't believe him. "I'll bet I've seen worse, boy." He reaches out as if to yank the hood down, and Silas steps back as I suck in a sharp breath.

"I'd rather you didn't." Silas's voice suddenly radiates menace, all pleasantness lost to a rumble of threat.

"Where are your papers?" Unwin snarls. "Where are you from? You don't even sound Tregellian to me. What's your business here? Who are you to her?"

"He's a family friend," I say at the same time Silas says, "Cousin."

I feel my skin heat again but it's nothing, nothing compared to the violent purple blotches that bloom on Unwin's cheeks, then spread across his face.

"Though I've always thought of him as a cousin," I say swiftly. "We grew up together. It's to his family in the north that my mother and I are going. He's here to help us pack.

And to escort us when Mama is better. Aren't you?" With every fibre of my being I will him to go along with it.

"That's right." Silas smiles at me – a mischievous smile, lazy and wide – and my entire body burns with such intensity I'm surprised I don't burst into flames. He takes my hand in his gloved one and I feel my heart shudder, and then stop. He's touching me. Voluntarily.

"I'm here to help my dear cousin. We're close." I hear him speak, but it sounds far away, buzzing in my ears, my mouth dry.

Unwin's eyes narrow to slits so thin I can't believe he can see out of them. He looks back and forth between Silas and me. "I see," he says slowly. "I see."

"If that's all – Mr Unwin, was it?" Silas says, and I can hear the relish of victory in his words. "We simply have to get on. Lots to do," he says smartly, pulling me to the cottage door and pushing us both through it, before closing it in Unwin's face.

My heart is beating so fast it feels as though it's vibrating, but as soon as we're inside he drops my hand. The swiftness of the rejection stings, and I move to the window to hide my hurt, peering through the cracks in the horn slats at Unwin, who is staring at the door, outrage etched across his face. When I turn back to Silas he's seemingly staring at his hand, though it's impossible to tell with his stupid hood covering his face. His posture seems stiff with unhappiness, and the set of his mouth, the stark, humourless line of it, makes my stomach clench unhappily.

"Well, that was clever," I snap. "Tell me, how does your neck support the weight of so much idiocy?"

Silas's head jerks upwards. "Excuse me?" he says, his voice rising with bewilderment.

"You. Why not stick your knife in his gut? It would have been less antagonistic."

He takes a deep breath. "I was trying to help."

"By winding him up?"

"I don't like bullies. And I didn't like the way he spoke to you. Or looked at you. I couldn't stay out of it, Errin. I couldn't."

That takes the wind out of my sails, my heart giving a great lurch in my chest before I recover. "You should have left when you had chance," I say, but the sting is drawn.

"I know." He speaks softly, his voice a hoarse whisper. "But I wasn't going to stand there and listen to him talk to you like that."

My stomach twists in a way I don't like one bit. "I can handle it," I say evenly.

"Why didn't you tell me you owed him money?"

"Because... It's nothing to do with you. I had it under control." He huffs softly and I scowl at him. He shrugs and turns his head, until he's facing the room where my mother is. In the heat of the moment I'd forgotten about her. And night is falling...

I walk over to him, planting myself between him and the door. "Now, I don't want to be rude, but I have chores to do. Here—" I move to the fireplace and pluck the florin from the pot there, adding it to the three he paid me for the henbane. When I go back to him I stand closer, forcing him to step back to keep the distance between us. "I'll have to get the rest to you later."

He shakes his head. "Don't worry about it. Look, if you like, I can stay, in case he—"

"No!" I cut him off, praying the volume of my voice hasn't woken my mother. "Silas, I meant it when I told Unwin my mother was ill. She's resting, and I don't want to disturb her, so. . ." I hold the money out, but he ignores it.

"You don't have to lie to me, Errin."

"What do you mean?" I freeze.

He speaks slowly, carefully, as though to a child. "Look at this place. The clothes hanging up over there are yours; I recognize them. The bluish smock is what you were wearing when we first met. The green is the one you had on when—" He stops, biting his tongue while I clench my fists with embarrassment. He carries on hurriedly. "There's one cup to be washed, one bowl and spoon too. There's one pallet, next to the fire. One of everything. So unless your mother is *resting* through there –" he nods at the locked door "– nice and far from the fire, and she keeps all of her utensils and her clothes in with her, then I'd say it's pretty obvious that you live here alone."

"I don't—"

"Stop it." He starts to pace, his boots too loud against the floor, and worry begins to tingle along my shoulders.

"It's not that. . ."

51

"What kind of mother would allow her daughter to wander the woods by herself?" He ignores my protests. "What kind of mother would allow her daughter to brew poisons in her home? And sell them to keep the roof over her head? I was standing right beside you a moment ago, Errin, when the landlord came looking for rent and expected it from you. Neither you nor Unwin mentioned your mother until you needed an excuse to turn him down. In fact you never mention a mother. You've told me about your father and your brother, but that's it. And I've seen no one else come and go from here, save you, since I arrived. I *know* you're alone here. I've always known. I'm not asking you to tell me anything else, but stop lying to me about that. It's pointless. You know I won't take advantage of it."

He speaks that last part softly and I look away to hide my hurt. Yes, I know he won't take advantage of it. He's possibly the only man in the realm who won't take advantage of a distressed young woman, even when she's throwing herself at him.

Then his words sink in: *I've seen no one else come and go from here, save you, since I arrived,* and my skin prickles once more. He's been watching me. Why? When? Clearly not during the full moon, or at least not closely, or else he'd know there was someone else here. Something else.

I'm about to argue, out of habit, when I bite my tongue. Though I trust him, as much as I trust anyone these days, I'm painfully aware he already has enough to hold over my head. And despite his assurances that he won't take advantage, it's one more thing he knows about me while I still know nothing of him. He already has too many advantages over me.

"Don't tell anyone." I switch tactics, pleading gently. "If anyone knew. . ."

His head jerks with what I assume is surprise. "Mum's the word," he says eventually, before smiling slyly at his own joke.

"Look." I move around him, towards the door, plastering a chagrined smile across my own face. "I'm grateful for your . . . help, Silas, but I do have a lot to do. If I'm supposed to evacuate, then. . ." I trail off, shrugging.

I can feel him staring at me, but I can't think of anything else to say and he doesn't speak either. The moment becomes a real, tangible thing in the room and it closes in on me. I'm still clutching his money, and hold it out again, but he doesn't move and I put it down on the mantelpiece. Finally he shrugs, walking past me towards the door, ignoring the small pile of coins.

"I'll see you soon, Errin," he says as he opens it, the sky purple and red beyond it.

"Stay out of trouble," I warn him, summoning a smile.

He has barely started to close the door when there is a loud crash from my mother's room.

In an instant he's back over the threshold, his head tilted, appearing to look at me from inside the hood. Then he closes the front door and strides across the room. I throw myself in front of the bedroom door as he reaches for the key in the lock.

"Don't," I say as I realize why she banged, what time it is. I haven't brewed her tea.

He looks down at me and then I'm painfully aware of how little space there is between us. I can't look up at him.

"Please don't. Please go," I beg.

Silas shakes his head and takes me gently by the shoulders, moving me out of the way. I close my eyes briefly as he opens the door.

She is sitting on the bed, her water cup on the floor beside the door, the contents spilled. Her grey hair is wild around her head, her eyes focused on Silas as though he's prey, and my heart lurches.

Silas seems not to notice, approaching her quietly and crouching beside her. "Hello," he says softly, and then, in an action that shocks me, he pushes the edge of his hood back a little and shows her his face. I catch a glimpse of cheekbone, high and sharp, the tips of pale lashes. "I'm Silas, a friend of Errin's. You must be her mother."

There is a bone-shaking moment when I think she's going to lash out at him. But instead she gapes, her mouth an "O". I wait for her to move, and when she leans back against the pillow, her eyes drinking in his face, I rush into the room to examine her.

Her eyes are still red, still feral. Nothing has changed.

When they move to me, they narrow and I step back. "I'll get you some tea, Mama."

"I'll keep an eye on her while you make it," Silas says. He's lowered his hood again, hiding all but his mouth, which gives nothing away. I look back at Mama to see her gaze fixed on him once more, settling down, watching him, but not in a way that suggests he's prey. "Has she eaten?" he asks.

"Yes. Before I left for the meeting I gave her some bread and stew. She won't want to eat until tomorrow, now. She never does."

He nods, and I watch the two of them, looking from one silent figure to the other, neither of them paying any attention to me. It's stupid, so stupid to leave him with her, but I do, tottering back to the main room and stoking the fire, filling the pipkin with water, adding valerian and chamomile to the nettle leaves, along with the last of the honey and a good dose of poppy. When I look back at the doorway he's still beside the bed, and she's still gazing at him with a docile expression, her face slack, and human. There's something sinister about the tableau: a hooded figure kneeling beside a prone woman, and for a moment I forget which of them is the dangerous one. I hurry the rest of the preparations, straining and stirring sloppily and making a mess on the countertop. I have a brief flash of my old teacher tutting at me, and my lips quirk into a guilty smile before I remember Silas and Mama in the other room and I rush back to them.

I almost drop the cup when I see that he's holding her hand, her frail fingers resting limply in his gloved ones. He gestures for me to pass him the cup, and I watch as he blows on it carefully before holding it to my mother's lips. She sips obediently and he smiles at her in encouragement. I move back to the doorway, watching him lift the cup up to her and her fingers curl over his to hold it. A sour pain blossoms in my chest and I realize I'm jealous of how easy he is with her. My feelings for Silas have always been complicated, but this is a new low: jealous of my own mother because he is holding her hand.

And because she's letting him. I'm jealous because it seems that all of her hatred is reserved for me. For Silas she can be calm, even when the sun is setting and the beast is stirring in her. By rights she ought to be clawing his face off, not watching it as trustingly as a baby bird watches the sky for its mother. Perhaps it's me who she wants to hurt. Perhaps there is no curse; it's that she hates me for being the one she's stuck with. We are all the other has left, and yet she'd happily rip my throat out if she could.

Flashes of our life at home, of the four of us sat around the table a year ago, Lief and Papa enthusiastically debating some method of cow husbandry while Mama and I rolled our eyes at each other.

Of me, in the kitchen on my thirteenth birthday, unwrapping my gifts: a real apothecary's apron with a dozen pockets; a set of glass vials; a notebook to record my experiments. Lief giving me seeds wrapped in twists of paper. My father guiding me outside, hands over my eyes, to a patch of land he'd dug and hoed for me.

Of Lief and me lying in the newly scythed fields and staring at the stars after the May celebrations the year I turned twelve, watching bats swoop low, picking insects out of the air, my jaw aching faintly because of their calls, calls I couldn't hear but could feel. Then Mama and Papa appearing with hot cocoa and slabs of buttery, crumbly cake. Of the four of us lying back on blankets, looking up at the sky, tracking a barn owl ghosting across the moon. Of Papa's arm, or Lief's, around my shoulders, keeping me upright as we walked back to the farmhouse, exhausted but happy.

Of waking in the night to see my ten-year-old brother slumped at the end of my bed with a small shovel in his hand, almost asleep on his feet.

"What are you doing?" I'd asked.

"Go back to sleep," he'd mumbled. "You're all right, I'm here."

But he's not here now. He's not here now.

A wave of grief hits like pain and threatens to knock me off my feet. I lean against the door frame, watching as Silas puts the cup down once she's finished. He pulls the covers up, tucking them around her chest, and I have to fold my arms over the agony inside me.

Another flash: of Mama reading to Lief and me, before he moved into a room of his own; of Papa standing in the doorway listening, a glass of brandy in his hands, his eyes soft and fixed on Mama, of her faint blush under his gaze, her lips curving from the joy of his attention.

Of Lief and me tucking her into bed the night after my father died. Of the two of us looking at each other over her shaking form, and then, without speaking a word, getting into bed either side of her. Of her arms wrapping around me, Lief in turn holding us both. Of the smell of my father on the pillow. By the time the sun rose his scent was gone, replaced by our tears, salty and bitter.

I walk away and wait for Silas to leave her, locking the door behind him. When I turn to him his arms are crossed, his fingers tapping them swiftly.

"What's wrong with her?"

I take a deep breath. "After ... the Sleeping Prince invaded Lormere, she ... I think she went after Lief. That's all I can think of, that she tried to get to Lormere to find him. She'd been strange since he went there, quiet and distant, but I put that down to Papa's death, and the move here, taking their toll. I had to prompt her to eat most of the time, but she was better than she is now. She'd wash and dress herself. Then when we received word that the Sleeping Prince had taken the castle, and had... That was when she stopped. Everything. One day I went to the well to get water and when I came back she was gone. I found her in the woods. She's been like this since."

"And the scars, on her arm? Did she do that to herself? Is that why you give her that herbal tea?"

I shake my head. "No. She was scratched when I found her. An animal, maybe?" I try to keep my voice even, try to sound reasonable. "Thorns? Who knows? She won't say. I cleaned them up and thankfully there was no infection, though as you saw, they scarred."

There is a long pause, and my heart beats too hard, too fast.

"Can you not... Is there no help for her, a place she could go, a convent or the like here?"

I almost laugh. Yes, there are places; this is Tregellan. If you have the money, then your loved ones can be sent to a convalescent home by the sea. But if you don't, then it's the asylum, or the vagrant's prison.

Besides, she's not mad. She's a beast. There is no place for that.

"No. There isn't. Not for us."

We both lapse back into silence, me squeezing my dress through my fingers, him staring at the door. Then he speaks again. "What else was in the tea you gave her?"

"Chamomile and valerian. Poppy. To help her rest," I add hurriedly. "I don't think she sleeps, not really. I don't think she does anything other than grieve. The tea at least buys her a few hours of rest."

"What about you?"

I turn back to him. "What about me?"

He seems to look at me, chewing his lip before he speaks. "Are you— Do you— How are you?"

"I'm fine."

His voice is painfully kind when he next speaks. "This isn't fine, Errin. This is far from fine. Surely you can see that?"

Suddenly I can't stand the sight of him and I want him gone. I don't want to think about all the ways in which this isn't fine; of course I can see it isn't fine, I'm not stupid. It hasn't been fine since Papa died and it won't be ever again.

I don't want to think about Papa, and I certainly don't want to think about Lief, don't want to think about him in Lormere, in prison, or trying to fight golems, don't want to think about them cutting him down. *No. He's alive.* I feel it begin to bubble up inside me, something like a scream, or a geyser, something I can't think about because if I do... I wrestle it back down, pushing away images of Lief's eyes staring blankly, of wounds in his chest, of his head... His head— *No, Errin. Enough.*

That doesn't stop my throat and eyes from burning, and I charge to the front door in three steps. When I throw it open in a clear gesture of dismissal, he sighs. His hood hangs low over his face and suddenly I hate it, want to rip it away. What is he hiding? Who is he?

"Leave," I say harshly. "Leave, Silas, please. And don't come back here."

He seems to look at me for a long moment, chewing his lip, before he nods and walks past me, stopping on the doorstep and turning back.

"I think I could help you," he says softly.

I want so much to believe him. Instead I close the door, even as he stands there, and sit down by the fire, shivering in a way that has nothing to do with coldness. Loss washes over me, breaking like a tide, my insides feeling hollow, my eyes smarting, and I fist my hands and rub them angrily.

Enough. I don't have time for this; self-pity's a luxury that I can't afford.

Like bread. Or pride.

Enough, Errin. There's work to do. Get up.

I start to rise but find myself leaning against the table, unable to straighten up, some invisible weight crushing me;

the pain in my chest strains against my ribs and they feel brittle suddenly, and fragile, and not able to keep me together. My eyes fill with water and the room blurs around me.

I am alone. I'm so alone. Everyone is gone.

No, I tell myself. *Do you want to end up like Mama? Do you want to go mad and run wild in the forest? Stop this. Stop this now. Lief will come back. He will. He has to. Then it'll be fine again.* The feeling of breathlessness grows and grows and I'm gasping, my hands curled into claws, my heart beating so fast it's going to explode. I turn hot and cold, sweating and then shivering, trying to breathe, while bone-deep dread courses through me. I sink to the floor, pressing my forehead to the dirt. *Enough*, I repeat, over and over. *Please.*

Little by little, the vice around my ribs opens, my heart begins to slow and I can see, and hear, again. I stay down, breathing in and out, not caring about the soft stink of the rushes, or the mud on the ground. It's enough to be able to breathe again.

I survived.

And I hope I have the strength to do it when it happens again.

Chapter 5

Eventually I manage to stand, and set about my chores, half furious with myself for wasting the last of the daylight, my body feeling tender and used. The cheap candle stubs flicker violently as I move about the room, trying to work away my fear, all the while feeling as though I'm not wholly here, in my own body.

I shake out the tunics and blankets that are hanging to dry – forever hanging to dry and never likely to – rubbing dried lavender into them before moving them closer to the fire. I sort through the rushes on the floor and throw the worst of them out. I cover the windows as best I can, plugging the gaps in the shutters with old rags; then I make a pot of thin soup.

I sit on the bench with my bowl in my lap, examining the room. It looks as forlorn as it did before, worse even, for the sparse rushes, and the empty spaces. None of the furniture is ours; the table, the bench, the pallets, and even the battered rocking chair were all here when we came. All that belongs to us is the old chest in the alcove by the fire, its contents, and the battered pipkin.

I toy briefly with the idea of making some stock potions or tinctures, items that I could use on the road, or sell. But for the first time ever I don't have it in me, to weigh and measure and lose myself in my craft. I don't have it in me to do anything. I look down at my watery soup and feel a lump form in my throat. Oh for the sake of the Gods. . .

So, even though it's still early evening, I stoke the fire and crawl into my pallet, pulling the blankets up and over my ears. I'll get some sleep while I can. Tonight is the second night. Tonight she'll start speaking to me.

For the last three moons, the man has been in nearly all of my dreams. He's tall, at least as tall as Silas, and slender as him too. And as with Silas, I don't know his face; I never see it. Sometimes I catch the glint of an eye, or have the impression of a smile, but always as a fragment, in that strange way dreams have, where you know something without knowing it. If I think about it, I suppose it's no coincidence that the dream man appeared in my life shortly after Silas did.

But it doesn't matter, because whoever the man is, his presence is familiar, comforting. He talks, but as soon as he's spoken the words vanish, leaving behind a feeling of well-being. I know him. He's my friend.

He takes my hand sometimes, rubs my shoulder

encouragingly. Once, he stood behind me as I worked at a bench in the old apothecary and wrapped long arms around me, fingers splayed over my waist with a possessiveness that thrilled me. I woke up from that dream with my heart racing in a different, forbidden way.

Tonight, I dream of home. Once again I am in the apothecary, mixing a cure. These are the dreams I love and hate the most: love because I'm back where I belong, and doing what I love; hate because they are just dreams, as lost to me as my father. Tonight the man stands over me, nodding and smiling his encouragement, as my hands reach to add a pinch of this, a sprinkle of that to my remedy. He calls the recipe out to me and I obey him, doing as he says, and I sense his pleasure in it. I'm dressed in my favourite blue tunic, the pockets of my apron heavy with ingredients, and I'm concentrating fiercely. I know that this mixture is the most important thing I will ever make. It will heal my mother; it will bring my brother back to me. This is the potion to change everything. And I can do it. Only I can do it.

The man says something and I look up in time to see a flash of white as he turns away. I look back at my potion to see it bubbling over, ruined, and now the man is shaking his head at me, his frustration so evident that I can almost taste it. Then the banging starts; the Council are at the door, calling me a witch, a traitor, screaming that they know I've been making poison, that they'll hang me. Burn me for it. I see torchlight flickering in the windows; the glass starts to bubble and melt under the heat. Hundreds of fists bang on the apothecary door, calling for my death, and the man says nothing, his back to me, shoulders drooping in disappointment.

Of course when I wake the banging isn't a lynch mob, but my mother. The fire still burns steadily. I can't have been asleep for more than a couple of hours, and I sit up, breathless, still half caught in the nightmare, watching the shadows play around the room like children dancing. My hands are shaking, my fingers still curved as though around a spoon.

The banging changes, becoming deliberate, and it sends a chill down my spine. Like the opening music of a performance, she beats in time, one-two-three, one-two-three. And like a play, she has her opening lines, and it's those I wait for in the dark.

"Wake up, little one," my mother says in a parody of affection. "Rise and shine, my daughter, my sweetling, my baby girl."

"Stop it," I whisper, covering my ears with my hands. I don't know if she ever remembers what she says and does when she's like this. I hope not, please, I hope not.

"Errin," my mother coos from behind the locked door. "Can you hear me, my dear, my darling? I'm lonely, Errin. I miss your father. Oh, how I miss him! And Lief. Do you remember your brother? Your beautiful, clever brother. Was a mother ever so blessed to have two such bright, brilliant children? Won't you open the door, my child? Won't you sit and let me hold you, let us cry together for our lost boys?"

I feel my lip tremble, fresh tears prickling in my eyes.

"I can hear you, my beautiful girl." She scratches at the

door. "I can smell you. Listen, my daughter, the Sleeping Prince is coming. He's going to come here with his army. I don't want him to take you too; I don't want him to take both of my babies from me. Come to me, child, let me protect you. Come to your mother, Errin."

I hear the faint sound of pawing against the door and swallow.

"You don't have to be alone, little one."

"I don't want to be alone," I whisper, the words spilling out unwanted, barely audible even to me, but the beast hears them.

"Then open the door, Errin. Open the door."

The tears make tracks down my cheeks as I stand, kicking the blankets away and making the wooden floor squeak.

"Good girl." There's a smile in her voice. "That's my good girl. Come to me."

When the sound of me pouring myself a cup of water reaches her, I stop being her good girl.

As she rages I do my best to ignore her, trying to focus on drinking my water, each gulp mercifully silencing her for a second. The first moon this happened I came so close, so very close, to opening the door and letting her do as she would, for nothing could be as bad as listening to her tell me Lief and my father were gone because of me. She spent hours telling me how she hated me, how she'd never wanted me, how my father had wept with sorrow when I'd been born and begged her to drown me. Then it changed, and she told me she loved me, that we only had each other, and that was all she ever wanted. She told me she'd been chosen, and I'd been chosen too, and if I'd open the door...

Then, as I do now, I stuffed bits of rags soaked in wax into my ears, tying strips of fabric around my head to hold them in place. It doesn't drown her out completely, but it muffles the worst of it. When the banging becomes violent enough to shake the pipkin on its hook I turn to watch the door carefully, but so far she hasn't had the strength to break it down. I wait for her to exhaust herself, for the violence to tire her, and when it has – and knowing the respite won't last for long – I tiptoe across the room and open the chest. As I do, memories wash over me, pressing against me and crowding my senses.

My father's cloak is in here and I think I can still smell him as I lift it out, the scent of hay and earth still embedded in the thick woollen fibres. As I press it to my face it feels like beard scruff against my cheeks, as if I'd leant in for a goodnight kiss, and loss twists in my heart again.

I paw silently through the chest, moving old books, texts and lists and charts from my old life, a velvet-wrapped pair of bronze scales, too precious to use here, too important to sell, a present from Master Pendie when I passed my third-year tests with full marks.

And at the bottom, buried, as it always is now, is the thing I'm looking for: Mama's huge leather-bound book of tales. The edges of the spine are frayed and worn, the binding peeling away where the spine is separating from the pages. Dark prints stain the leather where our fingers have grabbed for it, the prints of adults and children marking a tapestry of us across the once-pristine cover.

I learned the old stories before I learned to milk a cow, and I take it back to my pallet nest, opening it by instinct to the story of the Scarlet Varulv. It's become a ritual, digging the book out from the bottom of the chest when the moon is full and reading the story version as the real-life beast plots in the next room. The reality of a curse is different from the storybook version, something the whole realm is learning now.

In the story "The Scarlet Varulv", a young girl is lost in the woods and rescued by a beautiful woman, taken to her castle, and feasted and feted. Only to be woken in the night by the feeling of sharp teeth on her leg, red eyes glinting at her under the bedclothes. She runs for her life, finally making it back to her home, where she collapses into the arms of her relieved father. A moon later she goes to bed early, feeling strange. When she wakes the next morning, she finds blood on her nightgown, gristle between her teeth. And when she leaves her bedroom, she finds her poor old papa dead, all the doors still locked from inside. She runs into the woods, hiding amongst the trees, where she bites a lost woodsman the next moon. He escapes with his life, tells his friends and fellow villagers of the attack, and they hunt through the woods until they catch her.

She is tied to a stake in the town square and a pyre is lit beneath her. And as she perishes in the flames, the villagers light torches and carry them to the home of the woodsman, deaf to the pleas for mercy from the terrified family within, their faces pressed against the windows as they watch their friends and neighbours burn their home, knowing they were all inside.

The cursed girl in the book grew russet fur and pointed ears on the nights when the moon was full, but my mother doesn't change, physically at least. As the moon waxes and rounds, she starts to become restless, her gaze darting around the room, hands suddenly reaching out with unnatural, jerking movements. Then the whites of her eyes turn pink, then red, paling again when the full moon passes. On those nights I can't go near her after sundown; though her own skin doesn't split and her bones and teeth don't lengthen, whatever is human in her is swallowed by the need to bite and tear, both with fingers and words.

The first time the beast was on her, I went in too soon after sunrise and she lunged, locking a hand around my ankle and pulling me to the floor. I'd chipped one of my teeth as my face had smashed into the filthy rushes coating the old wood. If it had happened a few seconds before, if the sun hadn't been as high over the horizon, if I hadn't been wearing two pairs of woollen stockings, so many ifs and so much luck... Maybe I'd be like her now too.

In the beginning, before I knew what I was dealing with, I'd tried to find a cure, scouring my old books for any mention of her symptoms. I thought it was a matter of finding the right page, finding the right recipe. I truly thought that this time I wouldn't fail. But the only thing that matched was in a story inside the book I was too afraid to open until I was desperate and terrified, and when I finally did, I already knew that there was no cure.

Then I hoped to quell the beast, to put it to sleep: camomile, hops, lavender, lemon balm. But she burned through even my most powerful sedatives – even when the doses were dangerously high, she'd be banging at the door again within an hour or two.

Finally I became desperate and turned to the nastier plants: poppy, wormwood, even small, diluted tinctures of aconite. I broke the law time and again gathering dark weeds and berries: half terrified I'd kill her, half terrified she'd kill me first. You have to treat those plants the way you'd treat a beast. You shouldn't seek them out, and if you do you must never take them for granted, or trust them; you have to respect them, fear them. I feared her more.

None of them worked anyway. Her eyes followed me hungrily around the room as the full moon approached, her fingers curled like claws, and she sniffed me when I tucked her into bed. After realizing I'd failed, I stopped trying to help her any further than buying myself a few hours of respite. If my apothecary master, Master Pendie, could see me now, he'd be sickened.

She still looks mostly like my mother when she tries to hurt me. She doesn't howl; she whispers my name, begging me to open the door and hold her, imploring me to be with her, to comfort her.

It's the only time she speaks to me any more.

*

70

I turn the page over and come face to face with the Sleeping Prince. I stare down at the illustration of him, his silver hair whipping out behind him and across the page. In his arms is a beautiful dark-skinned woman. He looks out of the page, his face proud and protective, and she gazes up at him. One of his hands rests on her face and she seems to lean into it, eyes half-closed in pleasure.

Until I started my apprenticeship, I didn't know the Bringer was part of the Sleeping Prince's story. I'd heard of him, of course: *Be a good girl or the Bringer will come –* it was a thing parents said. I never knew his origins were tied with the Sleeping Prince's, until one day I was flicking through Master Pendie's copy of the stories while I waited for a potion to brew. It was the first time I'd ever read the story myself – when I was a child, Mama, Papa or Lief had read it to me – and as I grew up I stopped being so interested in the old tales, making up my own stories instead. But that day, I picked the book up and I read it all. Including the part where the Sleeping Prince became a father and never knew it. I understand why my family left it out; I would have had nightmares for weeks, dreaming of girls – maybe even myself – being led to the Sleeping Prince by his cursed son, to have their hearts torn out. It was horrifying, after all that time, to discover the tragic story had an even darker ending.

Even after I knew, though, I found it hard to believe that the smiling, shining prince from the book would ever eat a heart. I'd look at how he holds the rat catcher's daughter as though she were made of glass; surely he'd cradle a heart and cherish it. His warm, amber eyes would watch over it. I couldn't reconcile them, the pictures to the words, and I still can't, not properly. Even though I know it's true, and not a story at all.

I wonder now if we'd paid more attention to the story we might have been able to stop it. The Bringer was spotted in our woods with a dark-haired girl, and no one thought anything of it. We'd put it down to a pair of lovers running from Lormere – it wouldn't have been the first time – and we'd paid it no mind. Until it was too late. It was an old superstition. Every century the son of the Sleeping Prince would rise from his grave and roam the land for a heart to feed his father; nonsense, surely, an old wives' tale. We'd all but forgotten the Sleeping Prince and his son were, or ever had been, real.

When dawn comes I go through the motions of making my mother's breakfast, her tea, and cleaning her. I sweep out the stained rushes from her room and change some of the blankets on the bed. She lies back when I'm done, staring up at the ceiling, and I leave her, locking the door.

As I make to leave I hear voices getting closer, and I panic, reaching for my knife. Then I remember that the evacuation is today, and peeping out of the window confirms it. Old Samm walks past, dragging a small cart filled with bulging hessian sacks, grumbling at a green-clad soldier at his side. If this were a different kind of place I might push the slats aside and wave, but I don't. I don't want to draw attention to myself, don't want the soldiers here, telling us we need to go too. I have to hope that Unwin accepts my story about my mother being ill and doesn't try to force us out. It doesn't matter so much if they come for us once the full moon has passed; I can sedate her and blame the illness, say she's still weakened. If I can get us through the next few days, I'll have three weeks to try to find somewhere else deserted enough to hide us, south maybe, to the mountains near the Penaluna River.

I need to go to the well and collect enough water to last us, so I don't have to keep going out. The less anyone sees of me, the better, and the more likely they are to assume we've left too. And I need to go into the woods. I remember what Unwin said about people being killed on sight and shiver.

It doesn't matter, because I don't have much choice. I need herbs, and also whatever berries, nuts and tubers I can find. I need to make sure we have enough food to last for at least the next few days, and potions and remedies to sell on the road. Mostly I need enough poppy tea to make sure that the beast is kept at bay. I'll just have to stay well away from the border, and out of sight of anyone else.

The woods feel unwelcoming as I ghost my way through them, keeping low and to the shadows. I know where to go for the poppy pods, and for nightshade, and I head there first, moving slowly, my ears alert for any sound. At the sight of a squirrel dashing into the branches of a pine I startle, then, without thinking, throw my knife at it. I'm too slow; I miss the squirrel and it disappears, but the crash of the knife handle against the bark is loud in the deserted woodland and I stop dead, listening intently, terrified I'll hear shouts and footsteps running towards me because of my haste. I wait long moments before I feel safe enough to go and collect the knife, grateful for my luck as I sheathe it. Still, the missed opportunity grates; I wish my father had taught me how to hunt. I really would kill for some meat to make a stew with.

Then I remember that I'll need to be sparing with the fire so I don't attract too much attention, and I hope I have the same luck evading the soldiers and Unwin as the squirrel had avoiding me.

There is no sign of anyone as I gather the last of the poppy heads, and I'm making my way towards a patch of nightshade when I hear a low, rustling sound. It takes me a moment to place it, and when I move I realize what it is – a cloak dragging through leaves. Instantly I drop into a crouch, lifting the hem of my cloak and moving as silently as I can to duck behind a holly bush, clutching my knife, my heart speeding inside my chest.

If it wasn't for the fact I've spent the last three moons learning how he moves, I might not have recognized Silas as he strides through the forest. His long legs are full of purpose as he crosses the path before me. Some twenty-five or thirty feet ahead of me he stops, tilting his head back to scan his surroundings without removing his hood. My mouth falls open, and I wonder if I've gone mad, because it's as if I'm rewatching the first time we met, here in these woods.

When another cloaked figure emerges I nearly cry out, but the sound never reaches my lips, dying as soon as Silas spins and, spotting the newcomer, breaks into a wide, joyous grin. I almost cry out again when Silas, who I've always thought hated to be touched, throws his arms around the hooded figure as though they're long-lost kin. They embrace for a long while, slapping each other lightly on the shoulder, before pulling back and looking at each other, still clasping each other's forearms as they speak softly. I can't hear what they're saying, but I can see that they are happy to be in each other's company, and again the bitter tang of jealousy rises up in the back of my throat. He's never seemed so pleased to see me.

They turn to leave together, heading towards Almwyk, and I don't hesitate to follow, forsaking my own tasks in order to trail them. Who is this person, that Silas would risk being seen – being killed? Is this part of why he's here? As they walk I see the stranger is shorter than Silas; he has to move a little faster to keep up with the length of Silas's stride, and my stomach twists as Silas flings an arm around the stranger's shoulders, leaving it there casually as they continue on. They stop and start, pausing to talk earnestly before moving on, and I have to keep ducking behind bushes and hiding behind trees to keep from sight. I lose them in my care to not let them know I'm following, and panic when at last I reach the spot I saw them, to find no sign of them.

I'm scanning the ground, looking for disturbed leaves, or even boot prints, when there is a strange swooping sound and a thunk behind me. Gooseflesh flares across my skin and my pulse begins to race, but it takes my brain a second longer to understand what the sound is. The sight of a second arrow burying itself in the tree trunk by my head confirms my fear.

Soldiers.

I forget Silas and his friend, drop my basket, and start to run.

I move between the trees, zigzagging at random to make it harder for the soldiers I can hear crashing towards me, whooping and screaming, their bloodlust high as they give chase. I didn't think they'd be so close to the town, expected them to be deeper in the forest, defending the border there. I don't stop to see how many, don't consider trying to surrender, knowing by the time I lower my hood they will have shot me. Instead I fly over roots and skid on dead leaves, bolting blindly towards where I think home might be. I crash through bushes, twigs snapping off and catching in my hair, branches whipping my face and body.

Another arrow flashes past me and the side of my right ear burns. I raise my hand to it and it comes away bloody. *No, no, no.* I race onwards. My cloak catches on a fallen tree and I fall headlong over it, the impact of the ground making my teeth ring. When I look up it's in time to see a rock land ten feet away. If I'd still been running...

I roll and then scramble to the left, making for a dense thicket of larches, praying all the time that Silas, or someone, anyone, will come, as I hear the men gaining on me.

When I break through the larches I almost crash into more of them, a wall of ten or so green tunics, swords raised, charging towards me, ignoring me, running past me, and I turn in confusion to see that my pursuers weren't soldiers at all but a group of men, fifteen or so, dressed in black and bearing down on us, spears and swords held in their hands as they hack at the line of soldiers between me and them. Their faces are covered with scarves, their armour mismatched, but there's no mistaking the malice in their intentions.

One of the soldiers darts back to me, grabbing my arm and pulling me away from the melee. The sounds of battle echo through the trees, screams and shouts, metal clanging on metal. The air smells metallic too, and when I risk another glance back I see fire on the tips of some of the spears, fire raining down haphazardly from arrows. One of the soldiers is struck, and falls motionless into the dead leaves. I gasp, and then the ground is rising up towards my face and I have to throw my hands in front of me to stop myself from crashing for a second time into the mulch of the forest floor.

"Get up, miss," the soldier barks, "unless you wish to die here."

"I'm sorry," I gasp, struggling to my feet. Then I look up and my jaw drops in shock. The soldier addressing me wears a blue sash, and he grips his sword so tightly that I can see the corded tendons in his wrist, stark beneath the raised scars made by the touch of hot metal. Last I saw him, four moons ago, he was a boy, like Lief. His dark cheeks were smooth, his brown eyes wide with fear and hope as he asked my best friend to go to the harvest dance with him.

The man before me wears a dented iron helmet, there is stubble on his chin, and even the planes of his face have altered, sharper and stronger somehow. His eyes are bright, but not with hope; with alertness, darting left to right over my head.

"Is it you?" I ask, unable to believe this lost link to my past is right in front of me.

Recognition blooms across his face and a smile begins to form. "Errin?" he asks, and I nod.

Then that terrible whirring sound again and he stumbles forward, landing on his stomach with a surprised groan.

Protruding from the back of his leg is a flaming arrow.

Chapter 6

"Kirin? Kirin, no!" I scream, my hands outstretched towards the arrow already burning itself out. It's then I realize my knife is still in my hand, that it has been all along, gripped so tightly the casing of the hilt has left welts across my palm.

"Keep moving, Errin, don't stop," Kirin Doglass says as he pushes himself back to his feet with a grunt and pulls me away, the action behind us getting louder, closer.

Arrows still fly past us, landing in the earth, and I keep my head ducked, both of us stumbling left, then right, in a bid to stay out of their paths. He half hops, half limps, his teeth gritted, his eyes on the trees ahead. I don't look back, though I'm desperate to see if the soldiers are holding their own. The sound of sword against sword now echoes through the forest, and panic rises in me. What if they lose? I shake the thought away and move to Kirin's side, putting my arm around his waist, helping him stagger through the now-endless forest, hardly daring to believe it when I see the end of the woods.

Only when we're clear of the treeline does he slump to the ground, his jaw set, his eyes burning in his pallid face, his pierced leg before him.

"We have to keep going," I say urgently, glancing behind me, sure at any moment we'll be overrun.

"Can't."

"There might be golems."

"No," he gasps.

"You don't know—"

"Errin." It's a command. "I need you to pull the arrow out." His teeth are gritted.

"No. That's not a good idea. While the arrow is in it acts as a plug; you need to leave it until you get to a physician."

He sighs. "Fine. Check to see if it came out of the back cleanly, will you?"

"I think it did. Look," I say, and his jaw tightens.

"I can't."

"Kirin, it's there—"

"Errin. I can't," he says through clenched teeth. He pulls the helmet from his head and drops it beside him, then unfastens his cloak, ripping it from his shoulders and balling it atop the helmet. His short, tightly coiled hair glistens with sweat. He keeps his head turned away from his leg.

I sheathe my knife and do as he asks, my stomach giving an odd lurch when I get closer to it. At least six inches of wood have cleared his flesh. Up close it's horrific. The metal tip is remarkably clean.

"Yes," I tell him, swallowing.

"Is the head attached still?"

"Yes."

"With rope? Wire? Wax? Can you see how?"

"Wax, I think. Possibly glue?" I lean forward and look. "Wax. From good candles."

He sighs softly. "Thank the Gods. Could you snap the head off?"

"Why?"

"I need to look at it. Check it for poison."

"If I disturb the wound, I might tear it."

He shakes his head. "Please, Errin. I have to know. It should come clean and easy." He sounds terribly calm about it, but his hands are shaking, his face grey and strained, and my stomach drops again.

I think back to when I was an apothecary in training, the times I watched physicians clean festering wounds, or dig shards of metal and wood out from injuries so my preparations could be used to treat them. I can do this.

I rip the length of his trousers along the seam before I wrap my left hand around the shaft and brace it against the back of his knee, ignoring the sharp intake of breath it causes. Then I grasp the tip in my other hand. I'm not a healer, I've never had to break a bone to reset it, but I can imagine it must be a little like this, this terrible responsibility, and the knowledge you are going to cause someone pain with your bare hands. My stomach lurches again as I look at the arrowhead. If it didn't come off on impact, it has to be stuck on firmly. There's no way he won't feel this.

Taking a deep breath, I close my eyes and jerk my right hand quickly, feeling sick as the head snaps cleanly away and Kirin screams.

When I look at him, sweat is streaming down his face.

"Kirin," I say, but he holds a hand up weakly.

"Check the end of the arrow," he says, his voice sounding strained and far away. "Is there any wax still attached? What about splinters, any loose bits of wood, or cracks?"

"None. I'm sorry, Ki—"

Without warning he grips the shaft of the arrow just above the fletching and pulls the arrow out. Then he collapses, rolling face down on the mud, lifting himself a moment later to vomit.

I leave him to it, pulling out my knife again and opening out his discarded cloak, cutting a strip from the top of it, where it's cleaner, and tying a tourniquet below his knee. The flow of blood slows immediately and I rip a second strip free, using it to clean the wounds. They're neat, thank the Gods.

"You're lucky," I say as I saw at the thick wool, hacking off two more strips to make pads, and a third as a bandage. "And stupid."

"Sorry," Kirin says, spitting on to the dirt.

"You should never do that. Ever. You had no idea of what might have happened. You might have bled out in moments."

"I'd rather die here than in a medical tent." He takes the

two pads from me and holds them to the wounds while I wrap the other strip over them, holding them in place. When I'm done, I look at him, and notice he's wearing an amulet, dull in the wintry light. Real gold, then. I see the three stars on it and bite my tongue.

"What are you doing here, Errin?" Kirin asks, wiping his mouth on the remains of his cloak and staring as though I might disappear at any moment. "Where's Lief?"

The sounds of fighting are quieter now; whether it's the distance or one side winning I don't know. "You really need to have that wound seen to properly. It could get infected."

"Errin, where is he?"

I push aside the familiar feeling of tightness in my chest, and I tell him as simply as I can what I know: that Lief was in Lormere when the Sleeping Prince attacked, that we've heard nothing since. But that I think he's still alive.

Kirin doesn't look relieved by my words though. In fact his entire face falls; he looks ancient, tired and ruined; it seems as though the bones beneath his skin are shifting and making him someone else, someone new. I see him age before me, losing the last of his boyishness, the spark in his eyes dulling.

"Errin," he says, and I know that tone; it's exactly the same one Silas uses whenever I talk of Lief. And I'm tired of it.

"Don't," I say, before he can tell me how unlikely it is my brother lives. "You know Lief. You know him as well as I do. Do you honestly think he would have let himself get into any situation that might have got him killed?"

"Then where is he?"

"I ... I don't know. Maybe he's hurt somewhere, or trapped. But I know he's alive, Kirin, I feel it. He wouldn't leave us. He'll be on his way back, as soon as he can. I know he will."

"I've heard the reports that have come out of Lormere, and—"

"So have I. And I've asked every refugee I've seen and none of them has heard of a Tregellian being caught up in it all." I don't let him speak, talking loudly over every attempt to protest. "My theory is that he got injured escaping from the castle and is holed up somewhere, recovering."

"Then why hasn't he sent word?" Kirin's tone is maddeningly gentle.

"Maybe he has. Maybe he's tried but he hasn't managed to get through yet. And the border is closed now. We might not hear from him for ages."

"I don't think he'd leave you here," he says quietly, his eyes full of pity. "Not if he could help it. Errin, you have to face facts. It's almost certain Lief is dead."

"No." There's a horrible buzzing in my ears, as though I've rested my head against a wall full of wasps.

"I don't want to believe he's gone either," Kirin begins.

"Then don't," I snap at him, raising my hands to cover my ears like a child.

We both fall silent.

"Do you live in Almwyk? In one of those shacks?" Kirin asks after a moment.

I lower my hands, which did nothing to shut him out anyway, and nod, forcing words past the scream that's become a knot in my throat. "Yes. Lief found it for us."

I don't miss the frown that crosses his face, but before he can speak the sound of shouts reaches us.

"You shouldn't be here," he says, trying to stand. "Come."

And though I'm angry with him for being so doubtful, I tuck my arm under his right one and help haul him to his feet, ignoring the whimper he makes when his left foot presses into the ground.

"When did you join the army?" I ask as we make slow progress towards the centre of Almwyk. Back in Tremayne, he'd been apprenticing, as I had, but with the blacksmith. It had been his dream, to have his own smithy. He would have been due to apply for his guild licence this harvest.

"I'm doing my duty," he says, his voice curiously flat.

"Your duty? Since when has it been your duty to be a soldier?"

He stops beside one of the abandoned huts, his breathing laboured, and looks down at me, soft brown eyes now hard, his mouth a line. "I was drafted," he says finally. "Every fit man between eighteen and forty has been. The call to muster was mandatory for the fit and able, across the whole of Tregellan."

I blink while I take in this news. "How? How can they make it mandatory?"

"Arrest and imprisonment for those who refuse. Confiscation of land, property and goods. Family be damned.

If you don't fight, you'll be arrested, and your family evicted from their home."

"But that's wrong. That's not our way. It sounds like something the Lormerians would do."

Kirin raises an eyebrow. "It's an old law. It was never repealed. Every household must provide at least one man for military duty when ordered by the ruler of the land. Last time it was used was during the war with Lormere. The Council has revived it. The Justices are enforcing it."

"Can they do that?"

"Clearly." Kirin's voice is dark. "Though if you can prove you're religious, you can be exempted."

"But no one is, any more," I say slowly. "What about everyone else? The older men? The women? Master Pendie? Lirys? Ulrik?" I reel off the names of people I care about.

"Anyone useful has been sent to Tressalyn, including Ulrik." His mouth twists as he mentions his old mentor. "They want all able hands preparing for war. The older men have been sent to the great forge to make weapons, even some of the women. Pendie is still in Tremayne, though. Still running the apothecary. Lirys is at home too. Most of the women have been left at home to keep the farms and businesses running. For now."

"For now? Are they going to ask women to fight?"

"If it gets bad enough." He looks at me thoughtfully. "Wait, don't tell me you'd want to?"

"You think I couldn't?"

His mouth tightens before he tries for a smile. "Oh, I

know you could. I think it should be a choice, that's all." He pauses. "An educated one. Not telling people it's for glory. Because there's nothing glorious about death—" He stops himself, too late, and looks at me, paling. "Sorry," he says, and I wave his apology away. "Anyway, you're an apothecary. They'd want you for that."

"I'm not licensed."

"If this carries on, it won't matter. I was a blacksmith; now look at me." He gestures at his bloody uniform.

"What's it like?" My voice is quiet. "Is it likely to get bad enough for women to be called to fight?"

"I don't know," he says slowly. "In Tremayne, things are fine, on the surface, at least. There's no rationing yet, at least not that I know of. No attacks. People are preparing, stockpiling food and fuel, clearing out cellars to hide in, but there's no real sense of panic."

I hear something in his voice that makes me think there's more than that. "But?"

Kirin shrugs and takes a step without thinking, immediately yelping and gripping my shoulder painfully, taking long, deep breaths. I wait until the colour has returned to his face before I bend down to look at his leg. Blood is soaking through the cloak bandage, but not much. I nod for us to keep moving, putting my arm back around him.

"When you leave Tremayne, you see the rich heading towards Tressalyn with carts full of valuables," he continues. "You see lines of men – boys – leaving to be soldiers, their mothers, and sisters, and wives, and children crying as they walk away. And you smell the refugee camp at Tyrwhitt long before you see it. And here, there's men in the woods and a new report every day or so of where he is and what his golems have done. Lortune, Haga, Monkham...

"Truth to tell, we're all hoping that it won't come to a proper battle at all. We simply don't have the men, even with the drafting. We've been at peace for one hundred years; we're not ready for a war. Especially not a war against bloody golems. How do you kill stone? We have no siege engines, no nothing. You can't send men against rock. We can barely fight other men."

I look over my shoulder to the woods, where his comrades still haven't emerged. But then again, neither have the others. "So, who were they?" I jerk my head at the forest. "Are they refugees, or the Sleeping Prince's?"

"Oh they're his, all right." I notice that he doesn't name the Sleeping Prince. "Human raiding parties. It doesn't take people long to turn on their own if they think it'll keep them alive. The Silver Knight commands the human army, recruiting the dregs, and the traitors, to raid and kill the Lormerians who try to resist, or fight back. He's started sending parties into the woods to try to break our army's lines. Testing us. This is the third lot here, so far. They never get out of the forest though. Or back to him."

"The Silver Knight?" It's the first I've heard of him.

"The Bringer. He leads his father's mortal army."

"Of course." I shiver. United at last.

"We have companies all the way along the border, from

coast to coast, patrolling and keeping them back, and so far..." He trails off, frowning. "Obviously this can go no further." He looks at me warily.

"My lips are sealed."

"If I had to guess, I'd say he was toying with us. I reckon if he planned to invade, he'd do it. But this? Sending small parties to harass us, engaging in back and forth with the Council? He knows we're running scared, and that we can't beat him. It's a game to him. Lortune was locked down straight away, and the first we heard of it was the message he sent to the Council to say it was done and he'd declared himself uncontested king."

"So you think he won't invade?"

"Not yet. His main focus now seems to be destroying the temples and killing the devout in Lormere. He's taken against the Lormerian Gods in the worst way."

"Why, though? Why is he targeting holy people?" I'm not religious, few here are, but the idea of burning down temples and butchering nuns and monks makes me feel queasy. It's like hurting children. They're harmless, mostly.

"Burn all the food, and people will starve, weaken, and turn on one another. Destroy the temples and their acolytes, and the people will have nowhere to turn, no sanctuary, no charity. No hope. Especially somewhere like Lormere. They're already distraught because their living Goddess has vanished; it's child's play to him at this point." He pauses, disgust coating every word. "What he does, to the pious... It's awful, Errin."

"What does he do?" I don't want to know, but the question is ready on my lips before I can stop it. And from the speed Kirin replies at, he knew it too.

"He cuts out their hearts. Men, women, seminarians, novices, altar servers. He doesn't discriminate, doesn't care how old they are, or how young. He has the hearts cut from the bodies, and he puts them on display in the town squares. He has men guard them so they can't be claimed. The birds can get at them, and the rats. But not the people. The bodies are thrown in pits, and they're denied the Eating. He's outlawed that too; there's a price on the Sin Eater's head. A good one. She wasn't loved anyway, from what I've heard. Given the price she'll fetch, I reckon he'll have her before Midwinter Day."

I stop moving. "Why? Why is he doing this?" I'm sickened by it, by the bestial, savage cruelty of it.

"Because he's a monster. Because the Lormerians are mice who spent years cowering under their royals and their Gods, afraid of their own shadows. They couldn't have made it any easier for him if he'd strolled up to the doors of the castle and knocked. They haven't done a thing to fight back. They're too scared, too busy praying for salvation. And because he's trampling across Lormere unheeded, our Council has had to make sure he won't get the same chance here." He glances down at his uniform and his fire falls away, leaving him looking more like the boy I used to know. "Why are you still here? You should have been evacuated this morning, shouldn't you? We were told all civilians would be gone today. Which hut is

yours? Come on, I'll speak to your mother now; we can try to get you out this afternoon."

"Don't be stupid," I say swiftly. "You need to get back to your camp. Your leg needs proper attention."

"Surely you can patch it up. Isn't that what you were training for?"

"You need a physician to look at it, not an apothecary. Why don't I meet you somewhere later on? We can arrange what to do then. Come, I'll see you back to the road."

Kirin leans forward and peers into my eyes. "What are you up to, Errin Vastel?"

"Nothing."

"Liar. I know you. You're hedging me. What's going on?"

"If you must know, Mama is sick." I feed him the same line as I fed Unwin. "I can't move her yet. As soon as she's better, we'll go. But I don't want to risk her on the road, or in a camp, as she is." It's as close to the truth as I dare. "We're keeping a low profile until then."

"Maybe we can move her to the barracks. It's a safe distance from the woods. We'd be on hand to keep an eye on her while she's recovering. I'll come now and we'll—"

"Your leg." I talk across him and he scoffs, raising an eyebrow at me. I force myself to look into his familiar, friendly eyes. "I'm scared of wounds left alone," I say quietly. "You know why. It doesn't take long. . . A puncture wound. . ."

"Oh, Errin." Kirin looks wretched, and I feel horribly, horribly guilty for playing that card. "I'm sorry. I'll go now and have it patched up. Then I'll come for you. Gods, if I'd known you were here I would have come sooner and got you out, you know." He shakes his head. "Why would Lief turn down the farm for this?"

I stare at him. "What? What are you talking about?"

"The farm, we all... Wait. You don't know, do you?"

"Know what? Tell me," I insist when he shakes his head.

He swallows, unable to meet my eye. "Ulrik told Lief we'd help; half the town was ready to pitch in to save the farm. We'd buy it, then he could pay us back." He looks at me with pity. "Your father was respected, loved even. We wouldn't have let anything bad happen to one of our own, but Lief refused us, said you didn't need charity and that he'd found work, and a new home for you all. Then you were gone, and no one knew where to."

"I—" I can feel my mouth is hanging open as I turn alternately hot and cold. "He wouldn't... He wouldn't do that. He wouldn't take us from our home to come here."

"We thought you'd all chosen it. A fresh start, away from bad memories."

"I didn't know any of this." The buzzing returns and I have to shake my head to clear it. We had a choice and Lief chose this? "I didn't know at all. I thought... I thought no one cared."

"You thought Lirys – or I – didn't care?" The hurt in his tone is plain and it shames me. "What about Master Pendie? What about the Dapplewoods? Ulrik? How could you think that?"

I shake my head, unable to speak. Why would Lief

do that? Why drag us halfway across the country to live in Almwyk when we could have stayed at the farm? He loved the farm, he took the loss harder than even Mama, so why choose to leave it? What about "family first"? If we'd stayed there, Mama would be... He would be...

"Errin, I know how much you loved Lief. We all did." Kirin's words break into my thoughts and I look at him. He opens his mouth to speak again, but then stops abruptly, looking over my shoulder.

Two soldiers are jogging to us. Both stop and raise their hands in salute before one gasps, staring at Kirin's bound calf.

"Are you hurt?" he asks Kirin.

"I'm fine, Kel."

The soldiers look at me with undisguised curiosity.

"You're lucky to be alive, miss," the soldier, Kel, tells me. "When we saw you come running towards us we thought you were a ghost at first. What were you doing in the woods?"

"She's a camp follower," Kirin says swiftly, and the two soldiers exchange a knowing glance. "With the healers, she was collecting willow bark for her stores. I've already questioned her and extracted her word that she'll not stray there again," he adds tartly. "So what happened?"

"We saw them off. Killed three of theirs, but they killed two of ours, and wounded two more. Three more." Kel nods respectfully. "We didn't know what had happened to you, but Cam said he saw you go down."

"I'm fine. Cam, send word to bring the bodies of our men back to the camp for burning. Leave the enemy as a warning to others. Kel, wait over there for me. I'll need aid getting back."

I look up at Kirin in surprise at the power in his voice. The two soldiers salute and turn away, throwing me a coy glance before they do. I wait until they're well out of earshot before I speak.

"They listen to you."

He clears his throat and refuses to meet my eye. "I'm a second lieutenant."

"Congratulations," I say, and he snorts. "Are there camp followers?" I think of the women who follow after the armies in stories. They're not usually healers. Not in a traditional sense, anyway.

"We have a few." He ducks his head.

"Oh." My skin heats at the implication, and then I feel foolish for behaving like a child. I live in Almwyk, for Oak's sake. "Well, I suppose it must be a comfort. . ."

He glares at me. "I'm betrothed, thank you," he says shortly, and then swallows so violently it's audible.

"What?" I say. "Really? So the harvest dance. . .?"

When a shy smile curves his cheeks, I move without thinking and launch myself at him, flinging my arms around his neck, remembering too late that he's injured. He overbalances and moans, gripping my cloak to keep himself upright, panting slightly with the pain, his face greying once more. When I pull away I see Kel studiously ignoring us.

"Kirin, I'm sorry. I'm so sorry, are you all right?" He tries to scowl but can't keep the grin from his face at the same time.

It makes him look grotesque. "Congratulations! I'm so happy for you both." I can't stop smiling. I'd forgotten what it was to smile like this. My cheeks ache with it and it feels wonderful.

He holds me at arm's length, his whole face glowing. "I know it's stupid, with all this. But. . ." He shrugs. "We're to wed in spring. Lirys will want you there."

"It's the best thing I've heard in ages," I say, and I mean it. More than once I saw them together from the window of the apothecary. The idea of them as a couple and happy fills me with hope.

"Go to her," he says. "Go home. Your real home."

A rush of longing twists my insides. To go home . . . to Tremayne . . . to my apothecary. All my life, it's all I wanted. . . Could I? I could confide in Master Pendie, look into a proper cure, or some way of controlling Mama. . . Of all people, he would understand. I could take up my apprenticeship again. My dream flashes through my mind: me back in the apothecary, the man standing beside me. . . Then I remember the mob at the door, only this time I imagine they're not there for me, but for Mama. Torches burning as they demand I give them the beast to put down.

We can't go home. We can't be around normal people ever again. It's too late.

I look up at him, smiling sadly. "Go, be a soldier. And see to that wound. We'll talk soon," I tell him.

"Stay out of the woods," he warns. "Come to the barracks if you won't tell me where to find you. Stick to the camp follower line."

"Yes, Second Lieutenant," I say smartly.

He gives me an unsoldierly salute and then turns, and Kel walks to his side at once, taking my place and helping him move stiffly away. The moment he's gone from my sight my joy for him and Lirys starts to wane, and my thoughts turn back to my brother. What was he thinking? What was he planning? More than ever I want to see him, to ask him what the Holly he was playing at, dragging us here, leaving us here?

"Lief, where are you?" I say aloud as I approach the hut. "Come home. If for no other reason than so I can punch you for doing this to us. Just ... come home."

But all of my thoughts are pushed away the second that I enter the hut and see the door to my mother's room, unlocked and wide open. I fly into the room, my heart in my mouth, relieved that my mother is still safely tucked in bed, until I hear the sound of a throat being cleared behind me. And when I turn, every single hair on my body stands on end.

His hair is silvery-white, and short, framing a face that could be cut from marble, it's so pale and smooth. He looks carved, made, not natural. But the worst thing is his eyes, golden-amber and unblinking as they take me in. The skin around them is smeared with something black, coal dust or tar, and the gold burns out from it. Those eyes don't belong in a human face. They belong in the pages of a book. In the face of the Sleeping Prince.

I freeze, terror rooting me to the spot, vivid, icy fear

paralysing me even as my mind screams at me to run.

His eyes are wide, his hands reaching for the cloak thrown over the end of the bed, and suddenly I can move again. I don't stop to think. I pull my knife out and lunge, thrusting the blade towards him to drive him from my mother.

He catches my wrist easily, squeezing until I drop the knife and cry out.

"What the bloody hell are you doing?" he asks, outraged, his voice husky and deep.

I realize to my absolute horror that I know his voice. That the man in front of me is my friend. The man I've been calling Silas Kolby.

Chapter 7

No. I try to wrench myself out of his grip but his long fingers are like a vice around my wrist. I panic and stop pulling, instead using my weight against him, throwing myself into him, trying to knock him down.

But it doesn't work. Instead he grabs at my other arm and pulls it behind my back, catching both of my wrists in one of his hands. He moves behind me and pulls my back against his chest, so there's no room to move, to lash out.

"Help me!" I scream, twisting in his arms and stamping my feet, bending backwards and forwards, throwing my head back into his chest, anything to get him off me. "Someone help!"

"Errin, shut up."

The sound of my name on his lips feels like a punch to the stomach. My blood boils so violently I'm surprised he can touch me without burning.

"How could you?" My lungs fill with air and I scream again, scraping my throat raw. "How could you?"

He claps a gloved hand over my mouth. "Stop it," he hisses insistently into my ear, but I continue to struggle, screaming into the glove, trying to bite him. I understand then that I'm done for; he's overpowered me. But I can't stop thrashing, can't stop trying to fight, my body moving without my command as I writhe in his arms. *It can't end like this. Please, please, if I can—*

I look to my mother and it's as though a bucket of cold water has been thrown over me. I stop struggling immediately, staring at her.

Her eyes are fixed on the flaking whitewash of the wall opposite the bed, and I see that he could kill me in front of her and she wouldn't blink. He *will* kill me in front of her and she won't raise a hand to stop him. And just like that, all of the fight goes out of me and I become limp in his arms.

He spins me round to face him, still holding my wrists in his long white fingers, his head tilted as his terrible golden eyes sear into mine. I start to tremble, my blood running cold. *I don't want to die like this. Gods, please, I don't want to die here, now. I don't want this to be it. And Mama . . . I don't want her to die like this.*

I force myself to speak. To beg.

"Please let us go," I say, my voice cracking. "I beg you. Please. I won't tell anyone I saw you. I won't say anything. Please let us go—" Then my control breaks and the words come out as a sob. "Please, please. Have mercy on us. . ." I'm shaking so hard now that I can't speak; all my courage has left me. I'm afraid I'm going to wet myself; I'm afraid it's going to hurt. I'm ashamed that I begged; Lief never would have. I can't remember what you call a prince. "My Lord." I try to bow as best I can. "Please, Your Grace. . ."

"What?" he says sharply, his words sounding as though they're coming from far away. "What the hell, Errin?" Confusion colours his cheeks, suddenly making him look vulnerable, human. Then his face falls, and he blinks at me, once, twice, before letting go of me so fast that I stumble. Before I've had time to right myself and pick up my knife, he's grabbed his cloak, flinging it angrily around his shoulders and pulling the hood up, covering his hair. I can still see his face, though. His eyes.

He glares at me fiercely, his golden eyes narrowed to tiny slits. "I'm not the Sleeping Prince, Errin."

My chest heaves as I watch him, poised to move if he does, his words ringing in my ears until all the meaning is lost from them. My heart still beats triple time. I watch him warily.

"Gods. . ." His eyes are bright inside the rings of black, feverish. He looks . . . he looks distraught. "Really? You truly thought—?" He runs his hands through his hair, knocking the hood back, before his forefinger starts to tap his thumb, the motion so fast it blurs.

And that small, familiar movement takes the edge from my fear, making me feel ashamed, because it's a gesture I know so well. It's anxious, fretful, nervous, Silas. I've seen him do it dozens of times.

I know then that I want to believe him. I want this to be a simple misunderstanding. But I can't believe him. Not yet. Not completely. Because there's too much that doesn't add up, and I'm still shaking, and my lungs are still pumping as though I've been running for miles.

My gut is still telling me to run.

I look at him – really look at him – at his strange eyes and his hair and his face. For three moons I've watched his lips, but now I can see the small bump in the bridge of his nose, his forehead, his white eyelashes and eyebrows. His hairline is a deep widow's peak. His skin is an opaque white, not like flesh. I can't see the veins beneath it; there are no impurities, no freckles or spots. No shadow on his jawline. His eyes are the colour of honey, liquid and amber, and I find myself caught in them.

"I'm not the Sleeping Prince," he says again, jolting me from my thoughts.

"All right," I say, after a long moment.

"Do you believe me?"

I can't nod.

"Do you?" he demands.

"Be fair," I say quietly. "This is the first time I've ever seen you without the cloak. And you look. . . You must know what you look like. What would you think, in my place?"

He looks away from me and bites his lip before his eyes meet mine again. "I can explain, a little, at least. If you'll hear me?"

I nod, and some of the tension leaves his eyes.

Until he looks me up and down.

"Why is there blood on you?" he asks in a strange voice.

I lift my hand to my ear, but the blood has dried. "Oh." I try to keep my voice level. "I ran into some trouble, in the woods." I look at him, watching for any sign that he knows something about it, that the men who attacked me might have even been there for him.

"When were you in the woods?"

"Now. I ... I saw you there. A moment before I was attacked."

He frowns and a line forms between his eyebrows. I watch as the shape of his eyes changes with it, and I realize I have no idea how to judge what he thinks from his face. I don't know him at all.

He looks at my mother, who gives no indication she knows we're there, and then grasps my elbow gently to lead me from the room. I flinch at the contact, and he lets go immediately, the corners of his mouth tightening: I follow him as he stalks out of the room, bending to pick my knife up first. He locks the door and nods at the bench, as though I'm the guest. My heart still thumps too hard as I turn my back on him, but I sit down and fold my hands in my lap, trying to look calm. By turn he looks anything but calm. His eyes rake over me, his fists clenching and unclenching by his side.

"What happened? Were you attacked?"

"No," I tell him, raising a still-shaking hand and starting

to pluck twigs and dead leaves from my hair. "You said you were going to explain. So explain. Let's start with you telling me how you got in here. And why."

He looks down. "The front door was open."

"No it wasn't."

"It was once I'd opened it." He attempts a smile but I keep my own expression stony, waiting.

When he says nothing, I rise, collecting a cloth from the washing line and the pipkin, the water inside cold. Carefully I begin to clean my bloodied ear. "You have about thirty seconds before I start screaming for the guards again."

"I wanted to make sure she was all right," he says quietly. "After yesterday."

"Why?"

He ignores the question. "I wasn't trying to intrude."

"Entering a house that isn't yours and then opening a locked door is the definition of intrusion," I say. "So if you weren't *trying* to intrude you should have left the door closed and not come in."

He looks at me and nods. "I'm sorry." His head lowers like a boy caught with his hand in the jam jar. In the wintry light his hair and skin glow, making him look like a ghost.

"What are you?" I ask without thinking.

"I'm not a 'what'." His head snaps up to look at me, his golden eyes flashing with outrage. "I'm a person, same as you. Not a thing. And not the Sleeping Prince."

"Sorry," I say, looking at the floor. "I've just ... the only time I've ever seen anyone like you was in the stories about ...

him." Sitting opposite the Sleeping Prince's double makes it hard to say his name. "It's different."

"Not to me."

"Well, it is to me," I say. "Just ... Silas, think about it. For three moons I had no idea what you looked like, no idea about you at all. You won't tell me anything; I have no idea where you come from, or what you're doing here. You both showed up at the exact same time, and until recently no one else knew you were here. You have unlimited money; you have secret tasks. And I saw you in the woods before I was attacked, Silas. You were there, minutes before. With someone. I saw you meet them and then I lost sight of you. Then I come back here and see your hair, and your eyes. Can you blame me for what I thought?"

Silas looks at me and shrugs, before shaking his head.

"My family is originally Tallithi, generations back," he says quietly, his voice oddly bitter. If I didn't know any better I'd think I'd hurt him. "I inherited my astonishing good looks from them. Moon hair, the Godseye. That's what they call it, in Lormere. Tallithi features, you can look them up in any of the history books. It's less common to see someone with one or both now, I'll grant you that. But it's because we stay out of the way. We're conspicuous enough as it is." He crosses his long legs like a schoolboy and rests his elbows on his knees. "Obviously, since the Sleeping Prince's return, it's essential for me to keep my appearance hidden. People might overreact."

I swallow, my skin heating, and the two of us fall silent.

I lower my head and look at him subtly through my lashes, trying to reconcile the man I've known for the last three moons with the one before me now. He's absolutely not what I expected him to be and it makes me feel embarrassed. I look up to see him watching me closely in return, as though I've caused the new dynamic in the room, not him.

"What are you thinking?" His words startle me.

"I just. . . You're not how I imagined you."

He reddens and says "Oh" in a way that makes me blush too.

"What's the black stuff for, around your eyes?" I ask hurriedly, trying to brush past the odd moment.

"It helps keep them shadowed. In case anyone came close enough to peer up there."

I feel my skin heating again. "Of course." We lapse back into an awkward silence, him toying with the fingers of his gloves, me looking anywhere but at him.

"What about your family?" I ask him. "Are they. . . Do they look like you? I just. . . It'd be good to know, in case I bump into anyone else like – I mean – with your colouring."

He looks down into his lap, his hands fidgeting before he speaks, his voice measured. "Well, my father's dead. He had an accident while working." There's the briefest of pauses between his words, and I feel my eyes widen with the realization that we share this common sadness. "My mother lives with a group of women near the East Mountains. I lived with her, until recently. Then I came here."

"From Lormere?"

"Yes." He looks away, and then back at me. "I left before the Sleeping Prince arrived." I hear an edge to his voice.

"You don't have a Lormerian accent."

"If I had it might have saved you thinking I was that . . . thing." He looks at me sharply and then looks away.

"You don't get to be cross with me, Silas. It's not fair. You know it isn't."

He nods.

"Is your mother safe, in Lormere?" I ask after a moment.

"Yes, she's fine. They all are. Thankfully the temple they live in is remote, and well hidden."

"She lives in a temple? Is she . . . Has she taken orders?" He blinks and then nods hesitantly, and Kirin's terrible words about what the Sleeping Prince is doing to the holy people come back to me. "Oh Gods, Silas. You have to get her out of there."

"She . . . can't leave yet." He looks down at his hands. "She's fine, though. The person I met earlier was a messenger from her."

"Silas, this is serious. If he – if the Sleeping Prince finds them, he'll. . . He shows no mercy."

"She's bound to the temple, Errin. She can't leave." I open my mouth to speak but he interrupts. "I know, Errin. Believe me, I know what he's doing there. But . . . she has a job to do. There are things that need to be moved from the temple before he has chance to destroy it. It's important."

"Things? Things that are more important than her life?"

"She would say so, yes. Records. History."

I shake my head. I know it's common in Lormere for widows to join convents, but he has to understand the danger of it now. This is his mother, for the love of the Oak. Nothing in the temple can be worth what the Sleeping Prince will do to them if he finds them.

"Silas—"

"It's why I'm here. This is my link in the chain. I'm helping her get the artefacts and documents over the border while we still can."

"Are you out of your mind?" I say. "Are all of you insane? What if you were caught skulking around? What if someone saw you without the cloak? They would think exactly what I did. No artefacts are worth this – the risk is too great – can't you see that?"

"It's less risky for me to be here than it would have been to stay there. Trust me." He bites his lip as soon as the words have left his mouth, and looks away again.

And I realize that all of my doubt in him has gone. That he has my trust again. Even if he and his mother are lunatics.

"What will you do once the evacuation happens?" I ask.

"Nothing. I have to stay." I get the strangest feeling that there's more to come, so I keep still and quiet, silently urging him to speak. "I'm here to wait for something else that is likely to end up here, sooner or later. Something not from the temple."

"Like what?"

Silas shrugs elaborately. "Nothing that would mean

anything to you. It's a religious thing. There's no point trying to explain."

There's a pinch in my stomach, alien and unwelcome, and I don't understand it. "But surely it's unlikely this *thing* will get here now: the borders are closed, and the woods are full of soldiers and Lormerian raiders."

He nods again. "I know. But that doesn't change the fact I have to stay here, for now. Until we're sure."

We're both quiet, thinking. "When you came here, to wait for this something, did you know the Sleeping Prince was coming?"

He looks at me. "Yes," he says.

I open my mouth to ask another question but he holds up a hand to hush me.

"My turn. When you thought I was him, you stopped fighting. You were going hell for leather and then you stopped. I thought you'd fainted. Did you want me – him – to?"

My skin colours. "I was trying to trick you."

His golden eyes flash. "I haven't lied to you, Errin. Don't lie to me."

I can't look at him as I speak. "She sat there, Silas. I ran into the room to defend her. I would have died trying to save her but she didn't do anything. She stared at the wall while her daughter, her only living child, was struggling before her. I didn't want to die. But I couldn't fight. Not after that."

Silas's face is deadpan; he blinks at me and then gives a short nod. Suddenly he gets to his feet, unfolding his tall frame and standing over me.

"Here," he says as he rummages in his pocket and holds out a small brown glass bottle with a dropper in the cap. The kind of bottle an apothecary would prescribe medicine in.

I stand up and take it, opening the top and squeezing to draw a tiny amount of liquid into the dropper. It's milky looking, delicate, and I take a cautious sniff. It smells of roses. There are maybe seven drops in the bottle, and I replace the lid.

"What is it?"

"It's for your mother." He looks into my eyes, holding my gaze. "It'll help her with her problem, I think."

My blood runs ice cold. "What do you mean?" I whisper. Does he know what she is? Does he recognize it?

His face, still so new to me, is carefully blank. "Put it in her tea tonight, instead of the poppy. One drop only. Do you understand? One dose, of one drop, per day. No more."

"What is it? What does it do? What is it for?" I want to grip him by the front of his cloak and shake him, my fists tightening with the desire to do it.

"I have to go. I'll come back when I can. And I'll knock." He smiles.

"Silas—"

"Ask no questions and you'll be told no lies." Then he's gone, the door clicking neatly closed behind him.

I look down at the vial in my hand.

The rest of the day is mercifully uneventful, though that doesn't stop the low-level panic that rises in me when I think of everything Kirin told me. But when I manage to push images of arrows and blood and hearts from my mind, it turns to Silas. White haired, golden eyed. More mysterious now than when he was hooded.

When dusk falls I make my mother some tea, and add one drop of Silas's potion to it. I half-expect it to smoke as it lands in the tea, or to make it change colour, but nothing happens. When I sniff it, I can't detect it, and my mother doesn't seem to notice the taste as I feed it to her, her red eyes on me the whole time. Once she's locked in for the night, I pull the chest in front of the door, and with the shadows on my side, I sneak to the well and bring back as much water as I can carry, using half of it to make a vat of soup large enough to last us through the next day.

When it's done, I return to my blankets, pulling Mama's book with me. I flick straight to the story of the Sleeping Prince, my eyes seeking out a drawing of him. Though I know it's a book, and the illustration might not be accurate, I can't help comparing it to Silas's face. They're so similar. I look back at the pictures, staring into the golden eyes on the page. They stare right back at me as I fall asleep.

The man is holding my hands in his, turning them over, entwining our fingers so we're linked, pressed palm to palm. He takes my right hand and opens it out, rubbing his thumb over the base of mine, then traces the lines, my lifeline, my heart line. He draws along the length of my fingers with his, his touch delicate as he makes circles on my fingertips. My chest feels tight, my skin tingling under his attention, and I feel dizzy. Despite that, I can't help notice his hands are smoother than mine. Mine are covered in nicks and scratches, webbed with scars like fine lacework where I've slipped cutting up plants, or sliced myself on barbs and thorns. My nails are short and jagged, and when I see the contrast with his I pull my hand away.

"Are you ashamed?" he asks, and I keep my head bent as I shake it. "You shouldn't be," he adds, gently taking my hand again. "You hold life and death here in these hands. Kill or cure, that's your gift. These are your weapons."

I look down at my hands, and as I do he takes both of them, raising them to his face. The tip of his hood brushes the back of my wrists, and I'm about to ask him why he wears it, when his lips press against my skin and my stomach lurches inside me. It feels as though I'm falling. Then it's over, and he's letting go, and my hands feel cold without his touch.

"What are you working on?" he says finally, standing up, and as he walks away the room comes into focus around me. Not my old apothecary chambers but the hut in Almwyk. In the dream it looks even worse: there are cobwebs covering the ceiling, and I can hear scurrying along the edges of the room. The rushes are rotting, stinking sweet and slimy under my feet, and I stand, horrified.

"It doesn't matter," he says, as though he can read my thoughts. He picks up the vial from the table and looks at it briefly. "You'll have a proper apothecary again soon."

111

"Home?" I say without thinking, and his lips curve into a familiar smile.

"Home."

"But. . ." I turn to the door to my mother's room. It's dark, black in the dream; everything about it screams danger and forbiddance.

"She's quiet tonight," he says. "Why? Your work?"

I smile in reply. Something stops me telling him I gave her a potion I didn't make.

The man shrugs lightly and walks to me. He folds me gently into his arms, pulling me into his lean body, and my heart swells. I think of what Kirin said and I smile. Home.

The dream ends abruptly, though the feelings linger, and I lie still, listening for whatever pulled me from it. With the windows covered I have no idea how close it is to dawn, but a glance at the fireplace shows me long enough has passed for the fire to go out. I strain for sound from my mother's room; surely that's what's woken me? When I hear nothing, I move, silent as the grave, to the window and pull the cloth back. Greyish, lavender light seeps in around the edges of the slats and my mouth falls open. Dawn. It's dawn.

I'm astonished that I slept through the night – that my mother slept through the night – but astonishment turns rapidly to fear, and then I'm flying across the few steps to her door and grabbing the key, fumbling in my haste to unlock it. What if she's – what if . . . I don't know what was in Silas's potion. How could I be so stupid? I didn't even ask if it was safe, if it had anything dangerous in it. Oh Gods, the dream, it was a warning, it was a warning to me that she. . .

I fling open the door, forgetting to be careful, not thinking it might be a trick, or a trap. She's in the bed, her mouth open, head tipped slightly back, and I run to her, my stomach roiling.

"Mama!" I choke out the word and grasp her bird-thin shoulders, shaking her. "Mama!"

There is a sickening, sickening moment when she doesn't respond and I forget how to breathe. Then her eyes open and she looks up at me and the relief is so great that I crumple on to the bed, still clutching her shoulders as I slump beside her. She blinks slowly and I look at her eyes. They're clearer than they've been for moons, barely pink at all, and her pupils aren't dilated or contracted. Moreover there's no malice in her gaze, and I gently lower her back to the pillow.

"I'll get you some breakfast," I say shakily, and for the first time in three moons, she nods. It's faint, and it might not have been deliberate, but I see it. I back out of the room, unable to take my eyes off her. What is in the mixture Silas gave me?

Chapter 8

It's a lie if I pretend that I always wanted to be an apothecary. My earliest ambition was to be an alchemist. I knew all about the three branches of alchemy from Mama's books: the aurumsmiths, who could create gold from base metal and so would never be poor; the philtresmiths, who could concoct the Elixir of Life and so would never be ill; and the vitasmiths, who could animate a homunculus, or – more terribly – a golem, and so would never be alone.

I never pretended to be a vitasmith – it would have been a fantasy too far, even for me. The lines between the Sleeping Prince, the children's storybook figure, and the actual Crown Prince of Tallith, have blurred over the last half millennium, but both versions of his story say that he was the first and only alchemist to be able to give life to the not-living. But I never wanted that power; even as a child, something scared me about things being alive that were never meant to live. Sometimes I pretended to be an aurumsmith – usually when I wanted something and was told no – but the kind of alchemist I most played at being was a philtresmith.

To be able to create the Elixir was much rarer than the ability to create gold – in fact, Master Pendie later told me that the last known philtresmith died more than seventy harvests ago in the Conclave, and that the Council held a state funeral for her. As a matter of fact, that was the last time the alchemists left the Conclave en masse, and the last time the Tregellian army was active, drafted in to protect the alchemists from kidnap attempts by Lormerians.

But I didn't know that when I played at it, and I spent hours mixing ingredients together – mud, milk, whey, berries – and declaring it the Elixir of Life. I fed my mixtures to Mama when she had a headache, to Papa when his back hurt, and even tried in vain with Lief, when he fell into nettles, or tumbled from the roof of the barn.

Eventually poor Papa explained to me that it was impossible to *become* an alchemist, that you had to be *born* one. Alchemy born, descended from the Royal Twins of Tallith, the ability passed down the bloodlines. But then he told me that, although being an alchemist was beyond my reach, there were potions and mixtures I could learn that would also heal, albeit without the miraculous effects of the Elixir of Life. So I switched my attentions to medicine, and it turned out I was a natural with plants, and a gifted apothecary.

When you train to be an apothecary, you learn about composition and creation, construction and deconstruction. You learn to isolate elements and how to put them together, how to balance them to make the perfect cure. One tiny leaf too many, one drop too much of something, can make the difference between medicine and murder weapon. I spent moons being given whole potions and deconstructing them, testing them by scent and colour, for acid and alkali and their reactions to the humours. I broke down the elements of the entire one hundred cures listed in the Materia Medica and listed every single ingredient in each one precisely. In the dream, the man asked what I was working on, and it's this. My mind was clearly telling me to do it. If Silas knew anything about apothecary he'd know I'd be able to do the same to the vial he gave me. I might not be able to make it, but I'll be able to tell what's in it. And that might be enough to point me in the direction of a recipe.

I decant one precious drop into a glass dish and put the rest of the bottle aside for my mother, depending on what I find. Then I cross to the unlit fireplace and sweep out the ashes, before lifting up the bottom of it. When we first came here there was no bottom to it; it was a pit in a dirt floor. I begged Lief to find a tray and grate for it, saying I didn't think it was safe to light a fire without it. But I wanted the space beneath it to hide some of my apothecary kit, things that were useful to a fully fledged licensed apothecary, not an amateur potion peddler. I was supposed to sell them to raise money for rent, my beautiful Materia Medica, all of my glass dishes and pipettes, notepads and measuring glasses, but I couldn't do it. I knew my father wouldn't have wanted me to. So I hid them. And now I need them.

I smell the contents of the bowl and pull a notepad towards me. I write down "rose" as my base point; my nose is good and I know I smelt it. I leave the bowl and pull my old charts out from my chest, searching for "rose". I find it in thirty-eight of the known cures. Thirty-eight is too high; I need to narrow it down to be able to do my work properly. Salt is bound to be part of it – it's the great purifier – but that doesn't narrow it down either. There's something else, something like the smell after a taper has been blown out, a hint of smoke, but not so sharp. Looking back at the charts, nothing springs out at me, and I frown, sniffing again. Roses, salt, something smoky. I pull the Materia Medica towards me. I can do this.

But it turns out that I can't, at least not as quickly as I'd thought. At lunchtime I take bread and soup to Mama, my eyes roaming over her, looking for signs of further improvement, or relapse. If it weren't for the pink tinge to her eyes and her cobweb hair, you'd think she was healthy, recovering from a fever or injury. She looks like the lie I told to Unwin and Kirin. She sighs as I plump the pillows around her and I pause, turning sharply to her, but she closes her eyes, dismissing me. I leave a mug of water by the side of the bed and I'm about to lock the door when I stop and stare at her hands. Her fingers flutter on top of the blankets, one-two-three-four tapped over and over again on her stomach, like Silas when he's agitated, and an old memory flashes across my mind.

All four of us sitting at the table, my mother's fingers silently marking a tattoo on the tabletop while Lief and my father droned on and on about the pros and cons of a particular seeding method. I see it again, her drumming lightly on the counter, staring out of the window at the rain that lashed down and prevented her from going to have tea with a neighbour. She does it when she's bored. Like Silas's tapping, it's involuntary; I suspect neither of them know they do it.

My mother is bored.

I don't stop to wonder what it might mean. I race into the main room and scoop up the book of stories from the bed. I take it to her and place it in her lap, not daring to breathe in case I ruin whatever this is. Her eyes open and she looks down at the book, and then up at me. There's no recognition in her gaze, and I feel my cheeks start to redden, embarrassed by my sentimentality. How is it possible I can still think—

A cold hand closes over mine and I gasp. But before I can snatch it away and run, her fingers curl around mine, as light as the petals on a rose. For three seconds she holds my hand, and then she drops it, her eyes falling shut again.

My skin tingles and my eyes burn as I leave the room, turning the key with finality. I lean against the door and breathe, in and out, until I'm sure I'm calm. Then I make myself a cup of tea and sit back at the bench staring at my experiments, too many thoughts in my head, a small seed inside me beginning to grow. And try as I might to ignore it, I can't.

It's too early to say that what Silas gave her is what caused this change, even though I know, somehow, in my blood and bones, that it is. That it has to be. Whatever miracle his potion is, it's reaching her, and bringing her back. And if I can figure out what it is, and make more of it, keep making more of it, we might . . . We really might be able to go home.

If she's conscious again, she'll be able to help me manage her condition. There's a chance we could return to Tremayne, not to the farm but. . .

I could pick up my apprenticeship again. I could go back to the apothecary, Master Pendie might still make me a partner, and then we'd have enough money to rent somewhere, on the outskirts. With a cellar. Forget Unwin, forget refugee camps, forget trying to find somewhere far from other people to hide her. Home. Even if war comes, we'll be safer there, behind the city walls.

I will crack this, so help me, Gods from every pantheon, I will crack this.

It's my mantra throughout the afternoon: if the beast can be controlled, then maybe we can go home. I only stop working to check on my mother and the book, but that's as far as I go with chores. Dirty dishes stay dirty, the windows stay covered, and I'm still wearing my blood-covered smock from yesterday.

It doesn't matter. Nothing matters but this. I will find out what is in this potion and then I will copy it and everything will be all right. I sacrifice another drop to this goal.

Every time I think of going home, back to the apothecary, to my real life, the same thrill I felt when Kirin first mentioned it runs through me. Back with our people, surely it will get better. Surely if anything can heal the wounds left by Papa, it would be going home. And Lief would know to look there if he ... when he...

I squeeze the glass pipette I'm holding so tightly that I crush it, tiny cuts peppering my hand. I barely notice them though, the knot in my chest tightening again. I freeze, blood welling up on my palm, but I don't care, disgusted with myself. Guilt holds me in its claws and pins me down and I stare at the vial, at the work I've done.

And then I remember Kirin saying we could have stayed in Tremayne all along; the bewildered pain in his voice that we turned down his help and left without saying goodbye. For the first time I feel a stab of anger towards Lief. He put us through the move here, put me through Chanse Unwin's leering, through countless sleepless nights for his pride. He went to work in a hostile country, leaving me alone with a grief-stricken mother who couldn't bring herself to eat, because he didn't want charity.

We're here because he had too much of an ego to rely on his friends, *our* friends. Mama's illness, my making poisons, all of it, none of it needed to be. Stupid, stupid Lief. How could he? And now he's... *No. He's fine. He's Lief. He'll find us.* And when he does I will make him sorry for everything. He can take care of Mama while I go back to work. See how he manages.

I find myself shaking and close my eyes, breathing deeply. When I open them I look again at the vial. Half of the mixture is gone. The table is strewn with abandoned efforts and tainted liquid. Back to work, I tell myself.

I spend the rest of the day and long into the evening trying to isolate the remaining components but can find nothing I recognize. I test for alkali and acid, and I distil the tiniest amount and try to separate it that way but get no real result. I pause to heat some more of the soup and take it through to my mother with her tea. She eats it with relish, leaning towards the spoon as I lift it to her mouth, and again that thrill of hope blazes in me. I add the fourth drop of Silas's remedy to her tea, studying her as she sips it docilely. I leave her laying peacefully, her face relaxed, and I take the book of tales back out with me before I lock her in. After a moment I drag the chest in front of the door, just in case. It doesn't hurt to be cautious. Then I return to the table, to my charts and my vials. I've missed this.

I cover the windows and work by candlelight, trying to find lilies and anise and common rue and every single other plant I can think of, or find in my books, until I've soaked up all of the remedy from that fourth drop. I've tested against the humours strips, both phlegmatic and melancholic, but there's no reaction to either. I still don't know what is in Silas's elixir.

The only unusual ingredient that elicited any kind of reaction at all was lady's mantle, and even that might be an anomaly, the result was so low. I've been working it so long I'm sure I can smell a hint of sulphur in it, and something metallic. What is it?

I scan the tabletop, the mess of paper and droppers and charts and dishes sprawled across it. I take the bottle Silas gave me and look at it. Two drops left. Tomorrow is the last night of the full moon, so for now I just need one drop for her... And I know I'm getting closer. I must be.

I take the gamble, squeezing out another drop. I test again for lady's mantle, allowing the elements strip to leach away some of the miracle liquid. Again the strip darkens, barely, not conclusive, not at all, and I throw it to the floor. Useless.

I push away from the table, forgetting to be quiet, and freeze when the scrape of the bench splits the silence open. But the hut stays mercifully still. I force myself to take a break, eating the last of the soup straight from the pipkin without bothering to heat it, then washing it up and hanging it back over the fire. I need to step back, that's all. I'm too close to it. The question is, do I keep trying here, or do I try begging Silas to tell me what it is?

Making up my mind, I stand and reach for my cloak. I'll have to be so careful not to be seen, by either soldiers or Unwin, but if Silas can do it then there's no reason I can't.

When I open the door, Silas is standing there, hand raised to knock.

He looks me up and down and then edges past me, into

the hut, and I close the door, hearing him suck his breath through his teeth as I do. He pushes his hood back and turns to look at me, his eyes sending a punch of shock through me. I'd forgotten, already, how they burned.

"You've been busy," he says, his voice flat. "You're wasting your time. And the potion."

"Then save me from wasting more and tell me what's in it."

His expression becomes closed, his gold eyes dimming. "Be content, Errin, with what you have. I've already broken several vows by giving it to you. I can't tell you any more."

"She slept through the night, Silas," I say. "She looked at me, this morning. She touched me. And if it's because of your potion, if it can bring her back, then I need to know what it is. Silas, I need it. Please don't dangle this in front of me and then take it away. I've lost too much."

I turn away, feeling an itch in my throat and burning behind my eyes. Hopelessness bubbles up and I have to clench my jaw to stop from crying.

"Errin?" he says, and I shake my head. "I'm sorry," he says softly. "I wanted to help."

Then a hand, tentative, on my shoulder and I freeze.

I hold my breath; the weight of his hand feels like a ballast and I have to fight to not lean into it. I've never been able to figure out how I feel about him; sometimes he infuriates me, other times ... I know that sometimes his voice does strange things to my stomach if I'm not braced for it. I know I've spent far too much time looking at his mouth, and not because it was the only way to read his feelings before I saw him uncloaked. I'm sure that the mysterious man in my dreams is my mind's attempt at creating a more responsive version of Silas, which is so humiliating.

Because I know the real Silas has no feelings for me. Not like that.

Four weeks after we began our strange working relationship, I went to his cottage to deliver an order, a harmless camphor and mint rub. Nothing special.

I was tired to the bone; between my strange dreams and my mother's first transformation, I was sleepwalking through the days. I'd been consumed with trying to take care of us both and make sure no one in the village had seen our weakness, going to the woods and gathering, making endless potions to try to break her malaise, treating the scratches on her arms, foraging for food and trading where I could. From dawn until midnight I worked, never stopping, pushing Lief and Papa far from my mind, knowing I couldn't afford to break down too.

But as the moon approached I'd noticed her eyes following me around the room, her fingers curling into claws. And then I'd accidentally locked her in overnight, and saved my own life. I'd already endured two long and increasingly traumatic nights broken by her cursing and scratching and slamming, only for her to fall silent and lifeless when the sun rose. I'd been poring over the old stories in the book from the moment we knew the Sleeping Prince had returned, so I'd known the name for what it was that she was becoming, with red eyes and a vicious tongue. I'd recognized it.

I hadn't fully believed it until she'd knocked me to the ground and chipped my tooth.

So when I took Silas his ointment, I wasn't in my right mind. It's not an excuse; I was scared, and exhausted, and grieving. In the last two moons my entire world had changed, and so when he'd offered the smallest kindness, I'd ... I'd misunderstood.

He invited me into his cottage, as he always did, and as ever he held out his hand for the small jar, and I did the same for the coin. I noticed from our very first meeting that he always wore his gloves and his hood, and that he went to pains not to touch me. So I was surprised when his fingers reached under my chin to tilt my face up towards his.

"You look tired," he said, the rumble of his voice stirring something inside me.

"I've been busy." I tried for a smile and his fingers tightened on my jaw.

"What happened to your tooth?" He peered at the chip in my front tooth and I closed my mouth, trying to keep it covered when I replied.

"I fell."

"Into a door?" His voice was dark and angry.

"No, Silas, a floor. A real one. After a real fall."

"At home?"

"Yes." I pulled my face from his hand, unnerved by his questions and by my own strange response to being so close to him. I was aware of him in a way I hadn't been aware of anyone before, and I was aware of myself too, aware of how tall he was, how angular compared to me. How close he stood. I could feel the warmth of his breath on my face when he spoke. I could smell him, a faint scent of mint and old incense.

He chewed his lip, his head tilted. Then he spoke again. "You would tell me if someone hurt you, wouldn't you?"

At that I burst into tears. I couldn't stop myself, couldn't cope at all with this small kindness. He was still mostly a stranger, a customer, but he was the first person to be nice, or what had passed for nice, to me in moons. I threw myself at him, burying myself in his chest and sobbing. Then, miraculously, he folded his arms around me and held me. He kept his arms loose, but he held me until I stopped shaking, letting me weep on to his tunic. He stroked my hair throughout, his fingers tangling in it, smoothing it, gently separating out the knots. It felt so good.

"Are you all right?" he asked, his voice a rumble against my ear.

I looked up, into the shadowy depths of his hood, as he waited for my answer.

I kissed him.

I'd never kissed anyone before, but I kissed him, moving suddenly to press my lips against his. For one, two, three beats of my heart we stayed like that, my mouth on his. I thought that his lips moved against mine gently, so soft they might have been the brush of wings. I thought he was kissing me back.

Then he pushed me away with such force that I almost fell.

126

"No," he said, wiping his mouth as though I'd dirtied him.

I turned immediately and tried to run but he pulled me back, holding me at arm's length.

"Sorry," he said, breathing hard. "I'm sorry I pushed you. And that I shouted. But you can't... You mustn't... Don't, Errin. Please."

In my life I'd never known such shame, and I nodded mutely. He let me go, and I ran home and made myself some poppy tea. The following morning I woke with a headache, a pain in my heart when I thought of him, and a note under the door asking for some willow bark salve.

We've never spoken of it, and until he took my hand in front of Unwin, we hadn't touched.

I shrug slightly, dislodging his hand, and he removes it immediately. My shoulder feels cold in the place it rested.

"Did you want something?" I say flatly.

"I was on my way to meet my contact. I wanted to check on you. Both of you."

"Thanks to you, we just had the best night we've had in three moons," I say, and his face falls. "I've used most of it up trying to understand it, and I can't. I admit I can't; I need your help, and there's only one drop left. Tell me what's in it. Please."

"You can't make this, Errin. Nor should you want to."

"Why not?"

"I wish..." he begins, then shakes his head. "I can try to get you some more. That's all I can do."

I look back at him. "How much? Could you get enough to last me a year?"

He makes a strange face, his lips pulled back, his cheeks paling.

"I'll pay you for it, I'm not asking for favours."

"It's not that. I can't—"

"You can't tell me," I cut across him. "Of course not. It's probably a secret, right, Silas?"

"You're not being fair."

I shake my head at him. "Don't talk to me about fair, Silas Kolby."

He looks at me, his expression wretched, but I can't feel sympathy for him. I turn away from him and wait until I hear the door close softly behind me. Then I return to the table. One more try.

Later, when I fall asleep, I dream of the man again. This time, we're not in the apothecary, or my hut, or anywhere I've been before. It's a small, stone chamber, simply furnished. It's cold and dank, and something about it makes me believe we're underground. The man sits on a wooden chair, leaning over a table stained with dark patches. He's hunched over, looking defeated and weary, and I feel sad for him.

"Come here, sweetling," he says, sensing me, and I go to him. He wraps his arms around my waist and rests his head against my stomach. "What a mess," he sighs. "What a mess."

He reaches up and pulls me down, so I'm curved over

him, then presses his lips to my throat. My eyes flutter closed and he kisses his way along my jaw. When he stops I feel dizzy.

"I have you though, don't I?" he asks, his mouth on my ear, his tongue flickering over it lightly.

I find myself nodding.

I'm woken by banging sometime later, and bitter disappointment and cold air cool the sweat on my brow as I sit up, disoriented. My first thought is that the potion doesn't work after all. Last night it was a coincidence that she was quiet.

Then the knock comes again, faintly, three raps.

On the front door. Not my mother's door.

Every single terrible possibility in the world crosses my mind: that it's Unwin; that it's Kirin and his soldiers; that it's raiders, or thieves. My best hope is that it's Silas, but given what happened earlier, that's fairly unlikely. I scramble out of the bed and freeze, muttering, *Please go away* over and over, under my breath. Silence, and then the knock comes again, more insistent, louder, and my heart sinks. Soldiers, then.

The latch rattles and I dart forward, realizing too late that the door isn't locked. As it swings open, I see a figure holding a large bundle in its arms.

"Help," Silas says, staggering to my pallet and dropping a body on to it.

Chapter 9

I close the front door, then move to where Silas is crouched next to what I think is a man. His face looks like a slab of raw meat. His nose is smeared across his face, one cheek slack, his hair blood-soaked. He's unconscious, and I press my fingers to his wrist. To my surprise I feel a pulse, faint as the brush of a moth's wing, and I count the beats, concerned by how weak they are, how far apart.

"I didn't know where else to go," Silas says, sounding pained, and helpless. "I'm sorry."

"I need water." I don't look at him, continuing my assessment of the man's injuries. He's lucky to be alive. I don't think he's likely to stay that way. "I know it's risky, but. . ."

"I'll get it."

While he's gone I reach for my knife, cutting along the lines of the man's tunic and exposing a battered, muscular chest that's as bruised as his face. Gently I press along his ribcage, trying to feel for fractures, but can find none. I pass my hands over his left hip, then down the leg, exploring the knee and ankle firmly. Satisfied that it's unbroken, I begin along the right.

"Got it," Silas says, racing back into the cottage and slamming the door shut, making me wince and turn to my mother's door. We both pause, eyes wide and waiting.

"I'm sorry," Silas says, and I shake my head.

"Forget it. The water needs to be boiled." I nod at the bucket in his hands, noting the severed rope, and wince inside at the questions the soldiers will have when they try to use the well tomorrow. He carries the water straight to the fireplace, sloshing some of it into the pipkin. I hear him build a fire, the rustling of light papers and the faint cracking of flames. Then he's standing over me again, watching me finish my examination.

"We need bandages," I say. "Take one of the clean blankets from the washing line. Tear it up into long strips."

He fetches one and sits near me, tearing with a violence that puts me on edge. For a while the ripping of fabric is the only sound, and eventually I start to speak, to fill the gaps around that awful noise.

"His nose is broken, and I think his right cheekbone too," I begin. "I suspect his ribs are fractured: two of them, maybe more. His legs seem to be unbroken, though his right ankle is badly swollen, so I can't be sure. It looks to me as though he's been beaten severely."

131

"Will he live?" Silas asks.

"I don't know," I say. I move to the table and rummage in my kit for willow bark and arnica balm. "Add some salt to the water," I tell Silas before I continue. "Do you know him? Is he the person you were going to meet?"

Silas's gaze is fixed on the injured man, his mouth open. His hood wasn't up when he arrived; his hands are trembling. He's losing it; whatever wherewithal he had to get the man here, it's leaving him.

"Silas, I need your help," I snap at him. "I need a stick. A sturdy one. About this long." I hold up my hands six inches apart.

He looks at me, his expression blank, and I realize he's useless to me right now. So I haul myself up, wiping my hands on my already stained dress, and sneak out into the darkness. It's a clear night, and above me a hundred thousand stars wink conspiratorially at one another. The moon is full, pale and heavy in the dark high over my head, the world lit up bright as day, though it's as if all the colour has been leached out of it. It's not even midnight yet.

I find what I'm looking for quickly, an oak branch that's thin and straight enough to use as a splint, and I turn back to the cottage. I freeze when I see a shape, light glancing off something on the outskirts of the trees behind the hut, before it moves deeper into the shadowy forest. I remain still and narrow my eyes, scanning the treeline for movement, a flash of chain mail or a blue sash, the covered face of a raider, or whoever attacked Silas's friend. I wait, counting heartbeats, until sixty have passed and I've seen nothing else. Then I run, as fast as I can back into the hut, closing and bolting the door behind me and leaning against it, taking a moment to calm down before I head back to my patient.

Silas is standing at the table, staring blindly at the vials and mess on it, and I hold the stick out to him, telling him to strip the bark. He startles and begins to do as I've asked, and I set about cutting the man's trousers away, lamenting because the fabric is fine, tightly woven and sewn with small, neat stitches. Whoever this man is, he's come from somewhere with money. I peel and tear the fabric, stiff with dried blood and muck, away from his skin.

"Can you save him?" Silas asks, so quietly that I have to look at him to be sure he's spoken.

"I don't know." I begin to splint the man's leg, binding the stick to it with the bandages Silas made.

"Please try. I'll do anything. Anything." Silas's gold eyes fix on mine, too bright, and I nod, once, before turning back to my patient.

I've always been good with plants. On our old farm there was a small patch of land that my father gave to me for my thirteenth birthday, good, fertile ground; he marked the plot out with a tiny fence he made himself.

"That's for our Errin," he announced to us all as we looked at the bare earth. "So she can grow her herbs and save us a fortune at the apothecary."

That was a joke; the four of us were rudely healthy. Until

the day my father fell we'd never called on the apothecary for any reason other than for me to request an apprenticeship.

The first I knew of his accident was when my brother raced on to the village green. I was sitting with Lirys, half listening to her telling me some story about Kirin when Lief arrived, bone-white and shaking.

"Come," he said, and terror stabbed at my heart as I lifted my skirts and followed him.

We raced all the way home in silence.

At the farm he ran through the kitchen, leaving a trail of muddy prints across the stone floor. I remember thinking how cross Mama would be when she saw it; how she'd scold us both and make us clean it up. I didn't know she'd already cleaned it once, washing Papa's blood away.

I followed the trail through the farmhouse to my mother and father's room.

"What happened?" I gasped, bracing myself against the door frame. Mama sat beside my father, holding a cloth to his leg. The room smelt of metal and alcohol and fear.

"Bloody bull," Papa said, trying to raise a smile on his ashen face. "I was moving him from the east paddock and he went for me."

"He gored you?" I asked.

"No," Lief said. "Father outran him. But he went over the fence too fast and landed on a pitchfork. It gouged his leg."

"Show me," I said, walking towards the bed and gently pulling my mother's hand away.

The blood didn't gush out like a fountain, or pulse with

the beat of my father's heart, and relief flooded me. Nothing vital had been ruptured. It pooled in the wound instead, the gash becoming a reservoir.

"We need to clean it."

Mama nodded and took a deep breath. "What must I do?"

"We need fresh water," I said. "Lief, boil the kettle, keep it boiling. Wash one of the copper bowls out with boiled water, then fill it, add salt, and bring it here. Mama, if you bring the brandy and clean cloths, and fetch your sewing kit. Clean the wound, clean it thoroughly with the water. Only the saltwater."

"And the brandy?"

"Give it to Papa. As much as he wants."

"What will you do?" she asked.

"I'll be in my garden."

I'd been learning under the apothecary for two years. Five days a week I entered his fragranced rooms and learned about herbs and plants and cures. More than once I'd argued good-naturedly with him over advice written in the Materia Medica and some of the methods he used to treat patients, but Master Pendie was a kind man, and he'd forgotten more about medicine than anyone else knew.

Papa was so proud of me. "You have my grandmother's brains," he'd say. "She was clever enough to get herself out of the castle when the people turned on the nobility. She was clever enough to get herself and my father away and hide and build a life, right here in this farmhouse. Good to know you're a clever girl too."

*

Papa gave me a garden and it was there that I went, running my hands through my plants, cataloguing them and choosing the ones I'd need to help me. Comfrey to stop the bleeding. Guinea pepper would be better but I had not yet managed to make it take in my garden, and I didn't want to waste time running to the apothecary for some. Agrimony and comfrey should suffice in its place, yarrow as well, to be sure. Lavender, chamomile and prunella to purify the wound.

With my arms full of leaves I ran back to the house. My brother stood in the kitchen, tapping his foot on the floor as he glared at the kettle.

"Is it not done yet?" I asked.

"Mother has some," he said. "This is the second lot."

From upstairs we heard a shout of pain and both winced.

"He won't be able to work for a while, will he?" Lief said.

"No, he'll need to rest until it's healed."

"You'll need to help me, then."

"What do you mean by that?" I put the leaves on the table, moving around the kitchen for oats, muslin and more clean bowls.

"I mean no gallivanting off to the village to gossip about boys when there's work to be done here."

"My work is in the village, at the apothecary, remember?"

"You'll need to take some time away, then, won't you?"

"You're not my father, Lief."

"No, I'm not. Our father is upstairs bleeding because you were too lazy to put the tools away."

136

I stilled, turning to look at him. "He never asked me to."

He met my gaze, his eyes glittering with anger. "First, you shouldn't need to be asked. And second, he tried to ask you this morning but you pretended not to hear."

"I didn't hear!" I protested, guilt prickling at me, though technically it was true, I hadn't heard, because I'd been rushing to get to the village. "Are you saying this is my fault?"

"Here." He slammed the copper kettle on to the scarred wooden table. "I'm going to check on him. Family first, Errin. Remember that."

He left me standing there, numb, before I remembered I had a job to do. I ground up the comfrey and the agrimony and the yarrow, mixed it with oats to make a poultice, adding hot water and a little milk to bind it. I wrapped the whole thing in muslin, wringing it out and then racing up the stairs with it.

The room smelt of fresh blood when I returned, and Mama stepped aside for me while I examined the wound. Now clean, it was deeper than I'd thought. He must have fallen with most of his weight on it.

"How much brandy has he had?" I asked Mama, and she nodded to the bottle. A third of it was gone. "Hold this inside the wound. It will be messy but it will stop the bleeding. Once it's stopped, we can clean it again, then it'll need stitching."

Mama nodded and took the poultice. Papa cried out again when she pressed it into the wound and Lief picked up the bottle and held it to his mouth.

"I'll go and mix the next part," I said, and Lief nodded tersely.

Back in the kitchen I set the kettle to boil again, adding the lavender, chamomile and prunella to my mortar and grinding it all together. I poured in a little water, and when it became a paste, I added a glob of pig grease to make my salve. Pig grease is best for using on men.

My father had passed out by this point, either from the pain or the brandy or a combination of the two, and it made my job much easier. When Mama pulled the poultice away, the flow of the blood had slowed, and I breathed a sigh of relief.

"I need you to help me now," I said to my mother. "I need you to pull the skin together so I can stitch it."

Though she turned a faint green colour, she nodded, and I threaded the needle she had brought me. But no sooner had I pierced the skin for the first stitch than she had run from the room, her hand to her mouth.

"Lief?" I asked, and he came, sitting on the other side of the bed.

Slowly, we stitched our father back together.

As I was smearing the salve on his leg, I looked up to find Papa watching me.

"How do you feel?" I asked.

"As though I fell on a pitchfork and then was sewn back together by my daughter. And I believe I might be a little drunk," he slurred gently.

"Nothing unusual, then?" I said, and he smiled blearily.

I rose and kissed him on the forehead and he gripped my hand.

"You're such a good girl," he said. "I'm so proud of you."

I didn't feel much like a good girl with Lief's words still ringing in my ears.

The following morning Papa seemed well. He was sitting up in bed complaining of a sore head, of all things, as I checked the wound and smeared more of my salve on it. I left him in the care of Mama while I reluctantly helped Lief with the chores. One of the cows kicked me, and though it left nothing more than an angry bruise, it put me in a foul mood for the rest of the day. Lief and I ate separately, both of us seething because he'd demanded I make the supper and I had refused.

"But it's your job."

"Because I'm a girl?"

"Yes."

I glared at him. "You'd better not let Papa hear you saying that."

"I've never seen Father cook a meal, have you? That's Mother's job."

"Well, today I was a farmer and that's a man's job. Which means today I am a man and I'm cooking nothing for you."

"Fine. Don't. I'll eat bread and dripping."

"I hope it chokes you," I hissed, and left him to it. As a rule we got on well, aside from the usual brother and sister spats, but the tension of our father's injury and a hard, thankless day's work had left us both in foul temper, and neither of us was willing to back down.

We didn't speak for four solid days, and each one felt like a week as we worked side by side to milk the cows twice daily, clean up after them, turn them out into the fields, and take the milk to the dairy. I had some revenge forcing Lief to turn dairy maid while Mama stayed with Papa, but it wasn't much consolation. I checked on my father's wound twice daily and it seemed to be mending well. He complained of some stiffness in his leg, but that was to be expected, and Mama offered to massage it.

The sixth night after it happened, I couldn't sleep, despite how exhausted I was. I tossed and turned, too warm in the sweltering summer heat. I was lying atop my sheets, spread out like a star, trying to cool down, when the door opened.

"Errin, something's wrong," Mama said softly into the darkness.

When I entered their room it smelt bad, sour with sickness, and I gagged. When I laid my hand on my father's forehead he was burning up. He was moaning lightly in his sleep; his skin looked waxy in the dim light, damp with a sweat that had nothing to do with the summer. Then he shook, suddenly and horribly, his shoulders spasming and jerking, and my mother ran back to him, trying to hold him still.

I knew then what it was, but I didn't want to believe it because I didn't want it to be real and I didn't want it to be too late.

"How long has he been like this?"

"He said he was too hot at dinner. He couldn't swallow;

he said his jaw hurt. Then this started, in his neck. I could feel the muscles shaking."

Papa jerked again and I closed my eyes. "We need Master Pendie."

Mama sent Lief at once. And while he was gone, for the first time ever, Mama and I sunk to our knees and prayed to Gods that we'd never believed in.

Master Pendie did what he could, applying willow bark and more lavender, asking for belts and ropes to hold my father down. Each fit became more violent, and the apothecary told us to pour honey down his throat, to keep giving him sugar and cream and butter. We spent all night ferrying food and water back and forth, trying in-between attacks to make him eat to keep his strength up. By dawn he was exhausted but still shaking, his body impossibly thinner than it had been when the sun set.

"He has the lockjaw," Master Pendie said when he returned.

"How do we heal it?" Mama asked.

Lief and I looked at each other.

"We can't," Master Pendie said wretchedly, turning to me. "I'm sorry. I truly am."

He left poppy tears for us to administer to my father. Lockjaw is a painful way to go, but even with the sedative his body still trembled.

My mother was catatonic, refusing to accept it. She spent the day in my room, staring at the wall, and muttering old forgotten prayers to old forgotten Gods, with me silently holding her hand, saying my own prayers inside my mind. Lief remained with our father.

I had gone downstairs to fetch myself a glass of milk. It was late, the moon was high and the world was still. I didn't hear Lief come in behind me; it was only when I saw his reflection in the glass of the window that I realized he was there. When I turned and saw his face, I knew.

"How do I tell her?" he said. "How do I tell her he's gone?"

Chapter 10

Silas works with me for the next hour, painstakingly cleaning the man inch by inch, uncovering multiple lesions and bruises. He doesn't flinch, or gag, working stoically and silently, helping me wash, treat and then dress the wounds as best we can. Ugly, vicious bruises have turned the skin across the man's chest and stomach dark purple, and that's not a good sign. His skin is cold to the touch, and doesn't get any warmer, no matter how much we pile the fire. When we wash the blood and dirt from his hair I see it's white like Silas's, and when I peel back his eyelids to check his pupils, his irises are gold. I look at Silas but he says nothing.

Finally, with nothing left to tend, we stop, covering him with as many blankets as we can.

"Now what?" Silas says, his already husky voice raw with tiredness or pain.

"Nothing. I've done all I can. Now it's up to him. If he's bruised inside..." I trail off, and Silas nods sharply. "The arnica and the willow bark will hopefully bring down the swelling on the outside. We'll know more if – when – he wakes up."

Silas rests his head in his hands.

I stand and check the bucket, using the little water left to make two weak cups of tea. I hold one out to him. He takes it, wrapping both hands around it.

"What happened?" I ask. "Who is he? Is he ... is he related to you?"

"Yes. He's a distant cousin. But I knew him well. He..." Silas stops to sip his tea. "Do you have anything stronger?"

I raise my eyebrows at him.

He takes another sip. "He's been the go-between. He's the man you saw me with yesterday. We have a chain, across Lormere. People stationed at various points passing items along from my mother's temple, until they get over the border to me, and I move them on to safety. He was the border runner, crossing the woods. He was the best. It was him I was supposed to meet earlier, but he didn't show up. I knew something was wrong and..."

I'm ready to interrupt and ask what kind of items he's smuggling, but then a chill creeps up my spine. Attacked in the woods ... I rip the blankets from his friend and start to examine him again, looking for the long, jagged scratches that had covered my mother's arms.

"What are you doing?"

"Nothing, just . . . checking."

"For what?"

I don't answer, relieved when I can't find anything. "And there was no sign of what – who – might have done this?"

Silas shakes his head. "I'm sorry to bring this upon you," he says. "I know you have your own troubles."

"Where else would you go?"

He shakes his head and hunches over, his arms resting on his knees. I find myself staring at the top of his head, noticing his hair is double crowned. It makes me think of Lief, whose hair was the same, and I remember when my mother cut it and the whole left side of his hair stuck out for moons until the weight dragged it flat. After that he grew his hair long and never allowed it to be cut. I wonder if Silas knows he has a double crown. I wonder if he cares.

I stand and pick up my cloak, draping it over his shoulders.

He flinches as it drops around him. "I'm not cold," he says.

"That's not why," I whisper back.

Our eyes lock and I forget how to breathe. That's how it feels; suddenly my chest doesn't remember how to rise and fall, and my lungs don't know how to fill themselves. I don't realize that he's standing too until I feel his breath on my cheek and it kick-starts my own, shallow and rapid as white-hot heat burns through my skin. I look up at him and want to reach out and smooth away the crease between his eyebrows. There's a moment when he looks like the Sleeping Prince from the book, with his high cheekbones and his

145

generous mouth. Then he doesn't look like a prince at all, but a sad, lost man, and it's the easiest thing in the world to step forward, reach up and wrap my arms around him, linking my hands behind his neck and pulling him against me.

He stiffens briefly, then relaxes, but makes no effort to touch me in return. It's as though my embrace is nothing to do with him. My skin heats with the familiar flush of shame and I unclasp my fingers and pull away.

Then his long arms fold around me and pull me back towards him. His head nestles into the hollow between my neck and shoulder, his face pressed to the skin. I feel the warmth of his breath on my neck.

It goes on and on, long past the moment we should have let each other go. He clings to me as though I'm the last safe port in a storm and I try to be that for him. My feelings flit between concern and something else, something that makes my heart skip tellingly. I'm dreading the moment this ends, because some instinct tells me that when he's gone from my arms, something vital will be missing from me.

When he sighs I lean my head against his and he turns his slowly, until his mouth brushes my jaw and I hear him inhale sharply, his fingers tightening for a split second on my waist. He stays there, his lips an inch from mine, and I tilt my head until the corners of our mouths rest against each other. I close my eyes, waiting for him to move, to kiss me, but he remains tantalizingly still, holding me to his chest, where I can feel his heart pounding as violently as mine.

And then he pushes me away. Again.

"Errin," he says, and my ears ring with the rejection. "I can't, please."

"I won't, I'm sorry," I stammer.

"I thought I made myself clear before?" he says quietly, and I nod, reddening again as a new wave of humiliation hits me. "It cannot be," he says, his voice pleading as he walks away towards the door, and my traitorous heart lurches when I see him reach for the latch.

"Stay," I blurt, and he pauses, head tilted, his back still towards me. "It's late."

"I can't." He shrugs the cloak from his shoulders and places it gently on the bench. "I'll come back, when the sun comes up."

And then he's gone, leaving me alone with a dying man.

I tidy away the bloodied water and throw the cloths on to the fire to burn, watching them hiss and pop. The man's eyes are shadowed, his complexion dangerously wan. When there's nothing more for my hands to do I take my cloak and pull it around me, sitting on the bench. And I wait.

"Silas?" It's spoken so quietly that I don't realize I'm awake, hadn't known I'd fallen asleep. When the voice comes again, I open my eyes and look at the man in my bed. Who returns my gaze, one eye swollen shut, but the other fixed on me.

"Silas?" the man says again, and I scramble from the bench to his side.

"Hush, rest," I say. "I'll get him. I'll get him for you."

I'm halfway to standing when the man weakly raises a hand.

"You know him?"

"Yes, he brought you here. He—"

"I need you to pass on a message."

"I'll get him—"

"No!" The man coughs, and his spittle flecks the blankets, dark and glistening. He closes his eye and I worry it's already too late. Then he speaks again. "Tell him she's already passed."

"She's passed?" Who? Who's passed? Does he mean Silas's mother; is she dead?

"She's the reason he's here, he'll understand. Tell him she's gone to Scarron—" The man pauses to cough again and it's a thick, wet sound. Blood bubbles from the corner of his mouth, and I know then that he's not going to recover. I take his hand and the faintest smile graces his bloody lips. "She left there before . . . before *he* came. She's safe, for now."

"All right," I say, taking his hand. Not Silas's mother, then. Someone else.

The man takes a sharp breath. "He needs to find her." There is a rattle in his throat. "And get her to the Conclave. Fast. He doesn't have much time."

"The Conclave?"

"Everyone. . . It's the safest place. He has to get her there. They have to stay there. The prince is coming. He knows about her. . ."

"I'll tell him. I promise."

Then he dies. He just dies. One moment his eye is bright and focused and the next . . . I see him die; I see the change. Indefinable, but something in him is gone, something permanent. I remember then that I don't know his name; I never asked, and Silas never said. And now he's dead, in a stranger's house, miles from home.

I close his eye, hoping it will make it look as though he's sleeping, but it doesn't. There's a slackness to him that makes it clear he's dead. I sit back on my haunches, staring at him. I've never seen anyone die before. I saw my father, but afterwards. I didn't see it happen.

Long, strange moments pass and I feel numb, removed from it. I try to think of something to do but do nothing, staring at the dead man. It's only when something in the fire shifts and crackles that I snap out of it, standing up. I need to tell Silas the message, to get her, whoever she is, to the Conclave.

I'm reaching for the latch when I stop, a wave of understanding flooding me. Silas knows where the Conclave is.

Before the last war, our alchemists lived openly in the towns, but after Lormere defeated us and demanded we hand them over, as though they were property or assets, we hid them away in a secret community known as the Conclave. It's recorded on no map, and outside of the Conclave only two anonymous members of the Council in Tressalyn know where it is. Or so I believed, until tonight.

On rare occasions the Conclave can be visited, by prior

appointment, but the visitor must consent to being placed in a drugged sleep before arriving and leaving, so they can't find their way back. They're guarded by an elite force during the visit, they must not speak to the alchemists except by invitation, and no more than two persons can visit at any one time. Prince Merek visited once, and even he – especially he – was put to sleep and guarded.

There aren't supposed to be alchemists living outside of the Conclave, let alone in Lormere.

He said his ancestors were Tallithi. His eyes and hair. . .

And like that, it all slips into place. The white hair, the golden eyes. Tallithi family. Not any Tallithi, royal Tallithi, the alchemist line. Silas is an alchemist. A Lormerian alchemist.

I lean against the table heavily, knocking the vial over, the last precious drop sliding along the side of the glass.

And then I have to grip the table with both hands to keep from collapsing under the weight of revelation.

A mysterious remedy that cures my mother of being the beast, wakes her from her grief, and that I can't hope to replicate. Given to me by an alchemist.

I don't need Silas to tell me what's in his potion. He's right, I'll never be able to make it.

It's the Elixir of Life.

Chapter 11

I reach for the vial and hold it up to the light. The Elixir of Life. Can it be?

Which means not all the philtresmiths are dead. Some still live, capable of making the Elixir. And I need more of it, for Mama. It's the only way to silence the beast.

I peep through the window slats, looking for signs of life or movement out there, then back at the dead man. Dead alchemist. Do I dare...? Yes, I decide. We're all running out of time. At least under cover of darkness I stand less chance of being seen by Unwin, or soldiers. And Mama will be fine; she doesn't know anything happened tonight, and it's not as if the dead can hurt her. As soon as I have my answer, I'll be back. I fasten my cloak and then bend over the man. I pull a blanket over his face.

"Sleep well," I say softly.

*

The night is too quiet. There should be creatures rustling and snuffling, making me gasp and start when their weight snaps the fallen twigs and rustles the dead leaves. There should be owls hooting softly, or nightjars calling. Rats, mice, deer; living things should be out living, but instead the world is utterly silent, and if it wasn't for my heartbeat skittering loudly inside me I'd worry I'd gone deaf. Where are the soldiers who are supposed to be patrolling? Why can't I hear them laughing nervously and joshing one another to keep the night at bay? The lack of sound makes me feel too aware, my senses reach out into the darkness for anything that will anchor me, any sound or scent or thing to see.

I use the moonlight to guide me as I try to keep to the shadows. It hangs lower in the sky now, and its light has turned the world monochrome: everything is black and white and grey and silver. The village looks painted, like a model, not at all real, and I have the uneasy sense that I'm not here. Almost every window in the village is dark as I scurry through; only the House of Justice is lit, candlelight visible in one of the upper windows.

I'm about to turn down the track that leads to the cottage Silas is staying in when a flash of silver in the distance catches my eye. A shadow moves along the treeline; is it a soldier? Then I freeze.

From the woods a huge figure lurches into view, seven feet tall at least, its outline misshapen and hulking. A scream is born and instantly dies in my throat when I see its head.

It has no face.

The place where eyes, a nose, a mouth should be is a craggy, bulging mass atop a shape that's barely humanoid. But its lack of eyes and ears doesn't stop it from raising its head, as though sniffing the air, before its body turns towards me.

Then another steps out beside it and a gust of wind rattles the treetops and carries the creatures' odour to me. Wet mud, rotting leaves, and sulphur; sweet, heavy, cloying decay. I turn then and run. I don't look back as I move, running from Silas's house, running past the House of Justice, running through the village, determined to put as much space as I can between myself and them. I run to the outskirts of the village and throw myself into a hedge, crawling through the brambles and tugging my cloak from them until I'm sitting in a tangle of undergrowth, my heart racing so fast I don't know how it still beats at all. I curl up, my heart thudding, my eyes shut, panting and shaking.

My heart is beginning to slow when something touches my shoulder and I inhale, ready to split the night apart with my scream. A hand covers my mouth and then Silas is beside me. He's not wearing a shirt; he's naked from the waist up, and barefoot, his skin torn and bleeding from scratches where he's followed me into the bush. As he twists around, peering out from our hiding place, I see markings along his spine, discs, fading from fully black to three quarters shaded, then half full, to a crescent, and finally an outline, a perfect circle of black ink on his skin, crossed through the centre with a line.

I tear my gaze from the tattoo and peer out through the twigs, waiting for the creatures to appear. He follows my gaze, his head tilted as he strains for the sound of movement, the moonlight reflecting off his silvery hair. I start to shrug my cloak off.

"What are you doing?" he whispers.

"Cover yourself."

He looks down. "Sorry. I was getting ready to sleep."

"No. Your hair," I hiss. "It's shining."

His eyes widen and he helps me take my cloak off, pulling it as best he can over his head and shoulders.

We wait, silently, each moment allowing the fear to slip away. After a long while, he nudges me and jerks his head; then he begins to crawl out from our hiding place.

I follow. My arms are scratched by the thorns, but the cold numbs the pain, and then he's touching me, gloved hands on my arms as he hauls me out.

"I think they're gone," he says, scanning the space around us.

I look around too, the hairs on my body still standing upright. "Wait, did you see anyone out there, near the woods? A soldier, maybe?"

He shakes his head.

"I thought I saw someone, before I saw the golems come out."

"I saw two golems." He peers around again. "You're sure you saw someone?"

"No. Yes. I don't know."

Silas frowns. "We have to get inside."

He moves like mist, light-footed and sure, and I follow him, aware that my own movement is not as muted as his. Where he glides I crunch, but he doesn't hush me, staying close as we slide around the House of Justice. The light inside is extinguished now, the moonlight our only guide. At some point the hood slips from his head, my cloak too small for him.

"Hair," I whisper, and he stops. I help him tug the hood up and over, obscuring the telltale glow.

"Better?"

I nod. Then that smell, coating the inside of my nostrils with decay, with sulphur. Our eyes lock as we realize what it means.

"Run!" Silas hisses, suddenly pelting away from me, the cloak flaring behind him as he grips the hood to his head. I freeze, shrinking back against the wall of Unwin's home, watching as one of the large lumbering shapes looms seemingly from nowhere and pursues Silas. Everything about it, from the way it smells to the jerking, lolling way it moves, is unnatural, and I have to fight down wave after wave of nausea, because this thing should not be possible.

Where is the other one?

My eyes stare wildly into the night. I am struggling to draw a full breath. I make a break for it, trying to stay quiet, trying to keep to the darker places.

Only to almost barrel into it.

Up close the stench of wet rot makes me gag. It swings

soundlessly towards me, reaching out with huge hands, and I stagger backwards, twisting and bolting towards the forest, this time hearing the footsteps heavy behind me. I have to bite back my screams. I don't want the other one to know where I am and cut me off. Where are the soldiers? Where is Silas?

In the woods I run, zigzagging, panic ringing in my ears. I remember the mercenaries, the arrows, the swoop and thunk, the way the arrow snapped like bone when I wrenched the tip from it, and I swing myself into the low boughs of the nearest tree, hauling myself up. The closely set trees and bushes at the forest edge make it difficult for the golem to follow, and that buys me the seconds I need to climb ten, fifteen feet above the ground. I perch on a branch, my limbs locked, as it passes beneath me. As the smell reaches me I shudder.

It doesn't have eyes. It doesn't know where I am. If I stay still, and quiet, I'll be all right. I'll be all right.

It pauses, lifting its head and stilling like a statue, and terror almost makes me lose my grip. Then with surprising speed it lumbers away, moving deeper into the trees. I can hear the crushing of shrubbery as it passes. As soon as it's out of sight I scramble down, falling the last few feet, scraping my hands, my knees shaking horribly, but I don't allow myself time to stop, instead half running, half staggering back out of the forest and towards Silas's hut.

I throw myself through the door and into the empty room.

I burrow into a pile of blankets until only the top of my head is exposed. I have to keep my eyes open and staring, because every time they're closed, even for the split second that blinking takes, I see the golem standing beneath me, the space where its face should be featureless.

It feels like hours have passed before Silas appears in the doorway, panting hard. Then he's next to me, cupping my face with one hand, the other pushing his hood back, and I have never been so glad to see anyone in my whole life.

"Are you all right? Were you followed?" His voice is low, and urgent.

"I lost it, in the woods."

"I did the same..." He stops suddenly and turns towards the door and we both listen, my heart punching against my ribcage.

"I think we're safe," he says after a few moments. "No candles. No fire. And no sound. We don't want them to come back." Then he turns to me, startlingly close. "Why were you out? Is Ely—" He stops. "Oh." All the fear, the urgency, flees him. He slumps back, and nods. "Right. I see."

Ely. The dead man's name was Ely. "I'm so sorry. I tried..."

"I know. I know you did." He sighs deeply, rubbing the bridge of his nose with long fingers, his neck bent.

"He woke up, briefly."

Silas's head snaps up. "Did he speak?"

"Yes."

His eyes fix on mine. "And?"

"He said enough. I know what you are."

A shadow passes over Silas's face. "*What* I am. We're back to that, are we?"

I speak slowly, choosing every word with care. "He told me what you are, and what you're looking for."

"Did he." It's not a question.

I nod. "He also said to tell you *he's* coming. And that *he* knows."

Silas's face is blank. "Well, now you know everything," he says flatly. "What are you going to do with this information?"

I've already made my decision. If I tell him the girl is in Scarron, he'll leave. He, and Ely, have made it clear that their duty to his mother's order is their priority, regardless of the danger it puts them all in. Even if that means dying. He'll go and find her, then he'll disappear into the Conclave. And if I lose him, I lose any hope of helping Mama, or getting my life back.

This is the only way, for me and Mama. I don't have a choice. I can't make the Elixir, I understand that now. But he knows someone who can. And if he won't bring it to me, then. . .

Family first.

"I want you to take us with you," I say.

"To. . .?"

"The Conclave." His jaw drops so fast it's almost funny. "You didn't believe me," I say slowly. "You thought I was trying to trick you into giving yourself away."

He stays silent, mutinous.

"I'm not tricking you. Ely told me. You are an alchemist. The reason you're here is because you're waiting for a woman, or a girl, someone who is in danger from the Sleeping Prince. She's why you're here; she's what you were waiting for while

158

you moved artefacts for your mother. Once you've found her, you have to get her to the Conclave." I'm not sure how much of it is true, until I see the little colour Silas has drain from his face. "Ely told me where she is. And he told me the Sleeping Prince knows, and he's coming."

"Where is she?"

I shake my head. "You take us to the Conclave too. You know where it is. We'll be no trouble; you know I can take care of us. We need to be somewhere safe, and hidden. And..." I pause. "More Elixir." His face becomes stony and I speak quickly. "It's the only thing that ... It's the only thing. When I have that, I'll tell you where she is."

"You're blackmailing me?"

"It's not blackmail. I'm asking for your aid in return for what I know."

"I trusted you." He says it quietly, his eyes wide and filled with disbelief.

"Silas, I just want your help. And I'll help you in return. We can help each other."

His golden eyes narrow. "Did you think about asking for my help, instead of making threats?"

"I did," I say, my tone harsher than I meant it to be. "I asked you twice. First for the recipe, then if you could sell me more of it."

He makes a strange face, his lips pulled back, his cheeks paling.

"I'll pay you for it," I say hurriedly. "I'm not asking for favours."

"It's not that. I can't get you the quantity you want."

"Then take me to someone who can."

He gapes at me, shaking his head. "I thought we were friends."

I glare at him. "Friends. Of course. And if I'd told you what your other *friend* said, and then asked for your help, would you have helped me? Or would you have left straight away?"

He looks pained. "Errin . . . you can't possibly understand. If the Sleeping Prince finds her. . . . There isn't time for this. I have a job to do, and this is much bigger than you—"

"Then this is how it has to be." I cut him off.

Silas shakes his head. "If Ely knew where she was, then someone must have told him. I'll find out from them."

"You don't have time. Ely said you don't have much time. We have to work together or we both lose."

The look Silas gives me is loaded with disgust. "Are you really going to do this, Errin?"

I nod, feeling sick to my stomach. "Yes. I have to."

He turns away, facing the window, and his shoulders slump. He keeps his back to me as he speaks and my nausea grows. "So be it. I'll take you to the Conclave. I'll get you more Elixir. Anything else you want?"

"I just want us both safe. Once we're there, I'll tell you why I have to do this. The real reason. I don't have a choice, Silas. If there was another way then I'd do it, but there isn't. It has to be like this."

He scoffs as he turns, the moonlight catching his profile,

his curling lip. "I really thought we were friends. I thought we were more than that."

"More than friends? When you flinch if I touch you?" I struggle to keep my voice down. "Of course, it all makes sense now. The girl. The waiting. Why didn't you say you had someone already? Though she can't think much of you if you don't even know where she is." I know I need to stop talking but I can't.

He whirls around to face me. "Is that what this is about? Is this your revenge because you and I... You think this is about a girl? This is all jealousy?"

"Of course not," I laugh, but there's no humour in it. "You've been nothing but clear about your feelings for me. You're not interested."

"No, I'm not," he spits at me, silencing me. "Because I'm a monk, Errin."

Chapter 12

I stare at him, the impact of his words finally hitting me.

"You're a monk?" I repeat, stunned.

He pulls my cloak from his shoulders and tosses it to me. In the light that glows weakly through the cow horn window, his skin has a faint golden sheen, the paleness washed temporarily away. He bends to pick up a tunic from the floor and the bones of his spine appear like stepping stones in-between and beneath the tattoos, vanishing under a thin layer of muscle when he straightens and pulls the tunic over his head. He looks like a creature from a story, from another world, carved of ice and gold.

"Yes. I am a brother of the Order of the Sisters of Næht."

"I don't understand." I mean it in so many ways. He's too young to be a monk, and too... Monks don't carry knives and stalk forests. Monks don't purchase poisons. Monks aren't

Lormerian alchemists with tattoos. Monks have tonsures, and bad breath. They're old. Silas . . . he's not a monk.

His left eyebrow arches. "What's to understand? I took a vow, I'm bound to serve the Sisters of Næht." ·

"Do you believe in the Gods?"

"No, of course not."

"But then—" I stop, putting it all together in my mind. The Sisters, his alchemy, his smuggling. I test my theory again in my head, and then make my guess. "The Sisters of Næht are alchemists, aren't they? Lormerian alchemists living in secret. It's a cover."

He shrugs, crossing his arms, saying nothing.

I recall what he told me about his parents. "Your mother is an alchemist?"

"No. She's like you. Normal." He says it as though it's a bad thing, and it hurts. "My father was the alchemist. Alchemic blood breeds true."

I take a deep breath, thinking it through. "So you're not really a monk; it's a disguise."

He looks at me, his golden eyes fixed on mine. "No. I am a monk. I took a vow of fidelity to the Sisters of Næht. I swore to live my life in service to them, putting them above all others. I vowed to take no wife and sire no child whilst in their service. I am a votary, in word and deed." He looks down at the floor and as soon as he does I allow my own face to fall.

"Oh." My voice is quiet. "How?"

"How did I become a monk?"

"All of it," I say. "How did all of it happen? Or can't you tell me?"

I didn't mean it to sound barbed, but his eyes flash, eyebrows rising. "It wouldn't hurt you to be a little more gracious in victory. What more do you want? Blood?"

"I meant..." I fall silent when he turns from me again to the window, dismissing me, as he lifts one of the slats, peering out. When he next faces me, his expression is wiped clean. "I want to understand," I say softly.

"The knowledge you're withholding from me is more important than anything else I could tell you. Understand that."

I take a deep, shuddering breath and place my hand over my slowly cracking heart. "I'm sorry for this. I truly am. I wish... I wish it could be another way."

His smile is one of bitterness, and it cuts me to the bone. "If wishes were horses then beggars would ride."

My skin burns and I lower my head. "I'm sorry," I say again. "I have to think of my family. My mother. I have to do what's best for her. Surely you can understand that, given what you're doing for yours?"

He remains silent, chewing on his lip, his arms still crossed. "You know of Aurek and Aurelia, don't you?" he says after a moment, his tone a little less frigid.

I look at him, shaking my head slowly. Then a picture comes to mind. The Sleeping Prince stands atop a tower, a girl, his sister, beside him, Tallith golden and gleaming below them. And I remember the caption that accompanied it, hear the voice of my mother reading it.

The twins, the mirror of each other on the outside, grew apart as they grew older, becoming as different as day and night. Aurek, the golden prince and heir to the throne of Tallith, aurumsmith and vitasmith, and his sister, Aurelia, philtresmith, no longer moved and thought as one.

Aurek. In all that had happened I'd never thought of him as simply Aurek, the golden one. This is the real man, not the Sleeping Prince, the fairy tale. Prince Aurek of Tallith. Cursed to sleep so long the world made him a myth. I'd forgotten that. I'd forgotten he had a sister too. Aurelia. She's hardly mentioned in the story, overshadowed by the plight of the Sleeping Prince and the rat catcher's daughter. But Aurek and Aurelia were the original alchemists, the blessed children whose gifts brought unrivalled prosperity and health to Tallith, until the Sleeping Prince was cursed. Then Aurelia left Tallith for places unknown, though she eventually married and had a family; it was she who carried the philtresmith line.

"Yes," I say. "The twins. The Sleeping Prince, and his sister."

Silas nods. "And you know the tales of Aurek and his . . . appetites?"

I shake my head and Silas looks surprised, and then embarrassed, his eyes sliding to the side.

"Aurek was fond of . . . courting maids and seducing them. He got many of them with child—"

"I know about the Bringer." I interrupt him, and immediately regret it when Silas's face turns stony again.

"We don't include him," he says coldly. "His story isn't part of our lore."

I fall silent. Long, awkward moments elapse; then finally he takes a deep breath and continues. "Aurek decreed that because these children had his blood, they were to be taken from their mothers and raised as noble children in the palace. By the time Aurek fell asleep, he'd sired eight children."

"And all eight were taken from their mothers?" Even with my current feelings towards my mother, I'm still horrified.

"It seems they were paid off, handsomely." His mouth twists with apparent distaste. "And there would have been no point defying Aurek's wishes. He was as cruel as he was lustful. After the curse caused Tallith to fall, and it became apparent Aurek wasn't going to recover, Aurelia left and founded the commune in Lormere, along with a few former servants who were loyal to her. They brought the children Aurek had sired. They were vulnerable, as his acknowledged offspring. Even though at first they seemed not to have his abilities, their name alone would have fetched a high price. Aurelia chose the East Mountains because of how isolated they were. She had no idea Lormere would be a fledgling kingdom in its own right within sixty years of them arriving."

He pauses, licking his lips to moisten them, and I wait to hear if there's more.

"The rise of the House of Belmis, and their obsession with securing alchemists to work for them and further their hold over the land, caused many to leave Lormere. They married normal men and women, in Tregellan, and were largely left alone by your former royal family, save for paying a tithe in gold. They went back into semi-hiding after the war with Lormere."

"Because of the Lormerian royals' demands?"

His face darkens. "Precisely. The House of Belmis had always been a little too interested in alchemy, and Aurek and Aurelia."

My eyes widen and he continues. "When the Tallithi first settled in Lormere, they brought the tales of the twins with them: Aurek, the vitasmith who could give life to the never living. Aurelia, who could heal any wound, cure any ill. Over time the story was passed down by word of mouth, and the people forgot they were twins, and they forgot they were mortal. Rumours spread of Aurek's enchanted sleep; that he didn't rot, or even age. That he was uncorrupted and would one day rise again. He was styled as a God, and Aurelia with him. Then later, as lovers. That's where the tradition of the royals marrying brother to sister came from. The misunderstood history of Aurek and Aurelia, the Golden Twins of Tallith.

"They made them into Næht and Dæg, Gods who'd blessed the House of Belmis and given them the right to rule. As a bitter kind of joke, Aurelia's daughter, who was our leader by then, formally named it the Sisters of Næht. She could never speak out to say that the House of Belmis was lying without giving herself and us away, but she couldn't let them have it all."

167

"Why, though?" I ask. "Why were you so against working with the House of Belmis?"

"We wouldn't have been against working with them. But we are against working *for* them. Parts of alchemy are dark. The Tregellian royal family, and then the Council, have always been understanding of this. The Lormerian royal family wouldn't be. They'd want the gold. And if they knew about it, the Elixir." He looks away, staring into the distance.

"Who makes the Elixir? Is it the girl? She's an alchemist, a philtresmith? Is that why she's so precious?"

Silas looks at me. "Do you really expect me to tell you? You're blackmailing me, Errin. I'm going to take you and your mother into the Conclave, and have to explain how and why to my people. To my mother. I'm going to have to confess to breaking my vows to help you. I'm going to have to tell my people why I put them at risk, for you. I'm in a world of trouble on your account already. You've had enough from me. Be satisfied."

I've never felt so low. "Silas ... I don't have a choice. Mama—"

"Spare me," Silas cuts across me. "I don't need the details."

Tears sting my eyes and I look down at the floor, the pain in my chest growing, weighing me down. "I'm sorry," I whisper.

He leans back against the side of the hut. "If I'm honest, I'd probably do the same in your shoes." Then he snorts. "I did, actually, if you remember. When we first met."

I look up at him but his eyes are closed, and I feel a spark of hope that he might forgive me, or at least understand why I'm doing this.

"I suppose the wheel has come full circle." He opens his eyes. "Getting the Elixir will be hard, I have to warn you. The supply that currently exists is all there is, for now. The vial I gave you was my personal one."

I raise my brows at him.

"We all have one, in case we're injured. It heals physical wounds quickly." He pauses. "I couldn't find Ely's. I checked his pockets before I brought him to you. He must have lost it."

"And you'd already given yours to me." A new wave of guilt floods me. If he hadn't tried to help me, he might have saved Ely with it. I remember then, coming back from the woods and finding him at the table, near the vial, his eyes wild. "It was right there," I say. "On the table. One drop left."

He falls quiet. "I know. I won't pretend I didn't consider it."

"Why didn't you?"

He looks me straight in the eye and says in a voice like iron. "Because you needed it. It's not in my nature to betray my friends."

My skin burns crimson, and I know then that things aren't right with us, and might not be, ever again. I tear my eyes from his. "Thank you," I say softly.

After a moment, he continues, his tone a little kinder. "Recently we've started to carry a vial of deadly poison, in case we're captured. So thank you."

"Me?" I glance down at my hands. "Surely you could make your own poisons?"

"The Elixir isn't like your apothecary creations. The basic principle of mixing ingredients is the same, but the technique differs, and of course with the Elixir we don't have much need for apothecary. We used to have those arts, but for various reasons they were abandoned. We don't experiment any more. Besides, alchemists aren't too fond of poison. Or at least we weren't."

"Well, I'm glad I've been of some use." I twist my cloak in my hands.

He moves quickly, kneeling before me. "You could be of more use. Tell me where she is. I'll still help you, I swear it. Please, Errin. Don't make our friendship into this."

His words burn. But though it makes me feel sick to do it, I shake my head. "Silas, I told you, I'll tell you when you bring my mother to the Conclave and have them take care of her. I'll take you to her myself."

He nods, his head dropping, defeated. "Tomorrow. I'll send a message tomorrow."

I nod. "Thank you. And ... I have instructions, about Mama," I say. "And her illness. They'd have to follow them. To the letter. And keep it secret."

He snorts, then walks to the window and peers out again. "We're good at secrets. She'll be fine there." She would be too; we'd be back well before the next full moon. I feel a small weight lift off my shoulders, but when I look at him I see the opposite has happened. His shoulders are slumped, and he leans against the frame with such an air of weariness that my heart goes out to him. I've done this to him.

I struggle to stand, but as I push the blankets away my foot tangles and I gasp, starting to fall. He darts towards me and catches me, my face mashing into his shoulder before he sets me upright.

"Thank y—" I look up, and his face is right next to mine.

He squeezes his eyes shut and takes a deep, shuddering breath. When he opens them, they're full of resolve and fire.

"It's not fair," he murmurs, his expression pained. "I'm trying so hard to be your friend." I daren't move.

"I meant my vows when I took them." He takes his hands from my shoulders with finality.

"I'll go," I say, unable to look at him, but he moves, stopping me from reaching for the door.

"I can't let you," he says quietly. "I can't run the risk that they see you leaving here and come looking."

"I have to. Mama is alone."

"And if the golems are still out there and you lead them back to her? Think, Errin. She's as safe as she can be there. It'll be dawn in a couple of hours. Wait it out. For all our sakes."

I sink back down into his blankets and hug my knees. I know he's right. While it's dark it's too dangerous; twice the golems almost caught me. If I lead them to her, or to him, then it's all been for nothing.

He looks over at me, his expression watchful, his posture tense and ready to move. His scrutiny makes me blush again.

I wish I could stop throwing myself at him; how many times does he have to push me away before I get it?

"I'm sorry, about..." I lower my head. "I'm sorry. I know you can't. I'm sorry."

"Errin," he says softly, and I look up at him. "If I could, I would. For what it's worth." He smiles sadly, and I see the dimples in his left cheek for a brief moment. "If it were different... If I were different. I wish I'd been honest with you from the beginning," he continues. "I wish I could have told you, then perhaps... I thought we could be friends. I thought it would be enough."

"It is," I say. "It has been. I'm just..." I tail off, not knowing what I am. "Are we... Can we still be friends, do you think? After this?"

"Gods, I hope so," he says in a rush of breath, his eyes blazing into mine before he looks away. "I'd be very sorry to lose you now," he adds, his voice so quiet I have to strain to hear him.

I make a decision. "She's in Scarron," I say before I can change my mind. "The girl. Ely said she was in Scarron."

Silas's mouth falls open. "Thank you. Thank you so much." He moves across the room and presses his lips to my forehead like a benediction, his kiss searing my skin. "I'll send a message to the Conclave first thing, telling them to expect us. I'll tell them to ensure your mother's release and I'll take you both to the Conclave myself, then go to Scarron."

"I could come with you, to Scarron."

"No, thank you. It's best if I go alone. I don't know if she's expecting us."

"Why didn't you know where she was?" I ask. "If she's so important to your people, how did you come to lose her?"

"She didn't live with the Sisters."

"Why?"

"Bad blood," he says, after a long moment. "It's complicated. We can talk when I get back."

Though I don't like it, I nod. There will be plenty of time, I suppose. And if I'm in the Conclave, he won't be able to keep much from me.

"Thank you," he says softly. "You don't know what you've done."

I feel proud of myself for the first time in a long time.

Chapter 13

After that, there is nothing more to say. We sit in silence, though a more companionable one, both of us listening to the sounds of the night, and eventually he drifts off to sleep, his breathing slowing, deepening. I follow his lead, and eventually I sleep, dreamlessly, for the first time in moons.

When I wake the sun is already up, the light milky and pale as it streams through the slats in the window. "Oh Gods, Mama," I say, scrambling to my feet. "I slept too long."

Silas sits up, alert immediately. "Go. Give me an hour to get a message off to the Conclave and then I'll come and bury Ely. In the meantime you should pack. We'll leave as soon as everything is ready. We'll have to walk, unless I can steal some horses. Can your mother manage it?"

"No. Not walking." I peek between the slats to check

the coast is clear. "She's too weak. If you can get a horse or something for her. I can walk. But she won't make it."

"I'll see what I can do."

I smile back at him. "An hour, then?"

He nods.

There is a bite in the air, the promise of winter on it as I creep home, still feeling hopeful. I try to imagine what the Conclave might be like, where it might be. Somewhere hidden, perhaps in the north. After talking about Scarron I hope the Conclave is by the sea. I let my memory fill with the scent of seaweed and brine that I know from the northern town. I could be happy by the sea, if I could find a way to complete my apprenticeship. I could act as apothecary to them, maybe even teach them some things, to thank them for their aid. I could help them, if they'd let me.

My hopeful state is tainted a little as I approach my cottage, the woods behind it looking less friendly to me now, even in the daylight. I remember the golem, the thud of its footsteps behind me, the way it reached for me. I quicken my pace towards the cottage, anxious to be inside.

But as I reach for the latch, the door opens and Kirin is there in his uniform, his mouth a grim line of bad tidings.

"Errin, thank the Gods—" He tries to speak but I shove past him, bursting into the cottage, stopping dead when I see the captain in his red sash and Chanse Unwin standing over Ely, now uncovered and unmistakably dead. The table is still strewn with my apothecary work, my diary, open on the page that details all of the potions I've made. All of the poisons I've made. The box that contains my remedies is revealed, the labels on show: *nightshade, hemlock, wolfsbane, oleander*. The vial of Elixir is in the middle of the table.

I look at them, at the questions on the captain's face, at the smirk on Unwin's. Then I look at the door of my mother's room. Open.

"Errin," Kirin calls again as I run to her room.

"She's gone," Unwin says behind me.

I whirl around.

"I evacuated her to a facility in Tressalyn." He pauses and grins. "A specialist one. For madwomen."

"No." I lunge at him but Kirin appears from nowhere, catching me around the waist and saving Unwin from my attack. "Where is she?" I scream from behind Kirin.

"Madness seems to run in the family," Unwin sneers.

Kirin bundles me into the room and closes the door. Through it I hear him speak to Unwin.

"Leave." His voice sounds cold.

"This is my house," Unwin snarls, but whatever Kirin does stops him from saying anything else.

"The village has been requisitioned by the army," another voice, presumably the captain, says calmly. "You're here at our grace now. And it might be best if you leave."

"No chance," Unwin replies. "I want to know how long she's been keeping a madwoman locked up. Look at this. A body on the floor, poison on the table. She's a criminal and I'm the Justice here. You hand her over to my custody."

"That will be all, Unwin," the captain says, and I hear the sounds of a scuffle. When the front door closes, I step back from the bedroom door and wait.

Kirin opens it. I walk out, slowly, expecting to face the captain, but he's gone, and I turn to Kirin. His face is pale, sweat on his brow, and he's leaning to the right. I'd forgotten about his wound. He must have wrenched it when he stopped me from getting to Unwin.

"Are you all right?" I ask. "You should be resting; you were shot a few days ago."

"Never mind me. What have you got yourself into?" he asks quietly.

"Where's my mother?"

"He had soldiers take her before we arrived."

"And you let him?" I scream.

"Where were you?" Kirin shouts right back at me. "Where were you last night?"

"Please tell me where she is," I beg.

"What's wrong with her anyway?" Kirin continues. "They found her locked in her room this morning. She looked close to death. She didn't even flinch when they lifted her out of bed. Is that you? Are you drugging your own mother?"

My hand rises to my mouth and I sink to my knees. I imagine soldiers here, taking her out of bed in her tatty nightgown, looking at her gaunt body, her vacant eyes. Oh Gods.

"Why were you here?"

"Unwin reported it. Said he'd told the occupants to

evacuate with the others and he thought refugees might have broken in. If I'd known it was you ... I sent some of the lads here with him. By the time I came to check myself, it was too late. They'd taken your mother and found ... everything."

I bury my face in my hands. No. Oh please no.

Kirin pulls my fingers away, forcing me to look at him. "Errin, you can either talk, or I'll have to arrest you myself. There's enough evidence on the table to see you hanged, even without the body. Talk."

I struggle out of his grip and walk back into my mother's room, sitting on the end of her bed. He follows, remaining in the doorway.

"After we realized Lief must be trapped in Lormere, she ... she shut down. She wouldn't eat, wouldn't clean herself, wouldn't go to the privy. I had to do everything for her. We had no money, Kirin. I had to get it somehow. I started making potions to sell, to pay the rent and buy food. It was the only way. And I ... sedate her, sometimes. Something happened to her, in the woods. It changed her." Once I start speaking I find I can't stop. "I tried to cure it; then I tried to treat it. Nothing worked, and it made her angry and dangerous. She attacked me." I open my mouth and show him my tooth. "That was her. And there was more. Kirin, you have to tell me where she is. If they don't take proper care of her, she'll attack them too."

He shakes his head.

"She's like the Scarlet Varulv," I blurt. "She'll hurt people. She'll pass it on if I'm not there to treat her."

"Errin, this isn't funny."

"It's the truth."

He looks at the table, at the mess still there where I tried to deconstruct the Elixir, then back to me, shaking his head, his eyes full of sorrow. "Errin. I had no idea it was this bad."

"I know, but I can control it. We have somewhere to go, with people who can help her. So tell me where she is and—"

"Stop," he says. "It's over. She's safe now. And you'll be safe too."

"What?" I still. "What do you mean?"

"You'll be taken care of. You shouldn't have been left alone. But we'll take care of you now. I'll make sure of it."

I stare at him. "I don't need taking care of. I've found us a new home. And we'll be safer there than anywhere, trust me."

"Errin, you need help. Both of you."

"I'm not mad. Kirin, look at her arms. There are scars there. It happened. It's real. You have to believe me."

But he doesn't. It's written all over him, the way his eyebrows are furrowed, the sad twist to his mouth.

"Errin, I need you to listen to me. I'm going to take care of you. There will be questions – serious questions – because of some of the things you have here. And the fact there was a body. But anyone can see you didn't hurt him, couldn't have hurt him like that. I'll speak for you, and I'll write to Master Pendie to ask him to attest to your character. We'll explain about your father, and about Lief. And that you've been here, alone, with your mother, these last four moons with no money. It'd be enough to send anyone a little mad.

But you mustn't say things like that, especially now, given the Sleeping Prince. You'll be in real trouble. Let me handle it, all right? I'll sort it out. It will be fine."

It breaks my heart, his words, the kindness, the worry in them and his tone; to have him act like the brother I'm missing. But he doesn't understand. I need to get to Silas. He'll know what to do; his people will have ways to help. They're powerful. They'll be able to help me get my mother back. And once we're in the Conclave it won't matter about the log book, or poor Ely. We'll be hidden from everyone.

I look at Kirin and nod my head, making myself look small and sorry. He smiles at me gently, and walks across the room to sit beside me on the thin pallet. He puts a brotherly arm around me and I lean into him briefly.

"I'm sorry," I say. "I'm sorry I've let you down."

"Don't—" he begins. Then I elbow him in the stomach and run. I slam the door behind me and turn the key in the lock. I'm at the front door before he starts banging, across the threshold and racing through the village. I hear the shouts of soldiers behind me as I dash towards Silas's hut, but I don't stop, speeding past every hut and cottage until I get to his.

"Silas!" I call, throwing the door wide. "Si—"

No more than half an hour can have passed since I left him. He said he'd come to me in an hour. There had been a nest of blankets on the floor. But now there is nothing. Not even an old candle stub. The hut is completely empty; it's as if he was never here. It's all right, I remind myself as fear makes my stomach clench; he must have packed and taken his things with him, to send the message. He's probably on his way to meet me—

"Oh, Errin," a voice says slowly, dripping with triumph. I spin and find myself face to face with Chanse Unwin.

"I knew you'd come back here, if that wet behind the ears boy soldier gave you half a chance," he says, standing in the doorway, blocking the exit. "He's gone, your lover. I saw him after I left you. Heading out towards the Long Road. Did he not say goodbye?"

No. He wouldn't. He wouldn't do that. He said we were friends. He said we were more.

You don't know what you've done, he said.

Yes, I do. I let him trick me. Because he pretended to like me. I never knew him at all. Gods, he spent moons lying to me, hiding himself from me. Using me.

I am a fool.

I lean against the wall, using it to hold me up as my insides shred themselves. I have to bend, the ache behind my ribs blossoming, filling me, crushing my lungs and making it impossible to breathe. What am I going to do? They've taken Mama, and I . . . I need him. How could he do this?

In the doorway, Unwin laughs. "You must think I was born yesterday," he says, resting against the door frame. "I know every inch of this village. My village. Do you think I didn't know he was squatting in here, like a beast? Do you think it went unnoticed? I knew. I was biding my time."

My eyes narrow. I don't believe him, and my left eyebrow creeps up to let him know it.

"You wouldn't understand my reasons," he roars, his face turning purple. "You don't understand anything, you stupid girl. I was *kind* to you. I looked out for you. I would have taken care of you. But no. I'm not good enough for you. Little Miss High and Mighty from Tremayne." His head tilts as he examines me and my jaw tightens in anger. "Look at you," he continues. "You're not even that pretty."

"If you lay a hand on me—"

"Ha!" He cuts me off with a bark of laughter. "I wouldn't piss on you if you were on fire. Not now. Not now I know you're soiled goods. I told you, I saw it. Last night. You and him, cavorting around the village. Him with no shirt on, chasing you into the bushes. Then you outside my house, helping him cover himself up. I'm not surprised he left. Why keep the cow once you've drunk your fill of the milk?"

The candle in the window of the House of Justice. He was awake, and watching. But he didn't see the golems, I realize. Then he steps towards me, and I move back instinctively. "I don't care what you saw," I say.

He smirks. "I thought about offering to be your guardian, you know. Making you my ward. Thought how fitting it would be to have you scrubbing my floors."

"I'd die before I let that happen."

"And so you shall," he says. "As I said earlier, Errin, a dead body, a box of poisons. A nice, neat diary telling the world what you made, and who you made it for. I'll see you swing, and your precious Silas too, once we catch up to him."

I didn't think it was possible, but my blood runs even colder.

"I just hope they let me kick the stool out from under you."

I turn around and punch him, clean in the face, my thumb tucked over my fingers, like Papa taught me. I feel the crunch of his nose shattering under my fist and instantly pain radiates through my hand, along my lower arm, as the skin on my knuckles splits. Cradling the damaged hand in my other, I bite down on my tongue to stop myself from crying out. Unwin is trying to staunch the flow of blood from his nose, and I watch, waiting for him to look at me. When he does I step towards him and he flinches.

"What goes around comes around, Chanse Unwin. Remember that. I'd be careful what you eat and drink from now on. You've seen what I can make." I hold his gaze until he looks down, like a dog submitting to its master. Only then do I turn and leave.

I manage to make it halfway across the village before my legs give out and I have to lean against one of the cottages. I take deep breaths, cradling my bruised hand. It hurts so much. Yet I'd do it all over again if I had to.

I lean back against the wall, feeling the wet wood against my tunic, and panic rises, the ever-present rock in my chest pressing me into the earth. I don't have any money. I don't have anywhere to go. I don't even have my knife.

What the hell do I do now?

Part Two

Chapter 14

I leave the village using the same path my family and I arrived on four moons ago, making the journey in reverse, this time veering right along the dirt track, cantering through small copses and lowland until I reach the Long Road. The land on either side of the road is scrub, gorse and bracken and thistle, wild land, unclaimed and unused by man.

When we came here the land was green and rich at the height of summer, at odds with the emptiness inside us, the gaping hole where my father had been. Now it's barren and wintry, and there's another hole where my brother, and mother, should be.

Where Silas should be, I think, and immediately humiliation and anger curdle in my stomach.

I look over my shoulder but can see no sign that I'm being followed. Despite that, I urge my stolen horse into a gallop, eager to put a few more miles between me and Almwyk before sunset. When I turn back again, smoke is still rising in the distance on the left and I allow myself a grin.

After the encounter with Unwin I knew I had to get out of Almwyk as fast as possible, knew that the soldiers would come for me. Between the body, the poisons and assaulting Unwin, I'd be thrown in jail at the very least, and this time Kirin wouldn't be able to step in and save me. I'd felt a small pang of guilt at the trouble he'd be in for letting me slip away, but shaken it off. He'd be fine. After all, I attacked him too; he'd have the bruises to prove it.

So I went to the last place anyone would have thought to find me: Unwin's House of Justice. I broke in through a small window at the back of the building, wrapping my cloak around my undamaged hand and smashing the thin window, before clearing the glass and heaving myself inside. I found myself in the pantry; the house was silent, and still, and I moved quickly. I took a clean towel and bound my split knuckles; then I dragged a sack of flour from the pantry into the kitchen, emptying it over the floor, coughing when it billowed up and into my face, laughing as it settled on every surface. Not that it would matter.

I filled the sack with as much of Unwin's food as I could easily lift: bread, cheese, apples, the remains of a ham, a litre of fresh milk, some potted shrimp wrapped in muslin, my mouth watering at the sight of it, despite everything.

Leaving the sack by the back door, I dashed upstairs. The

idea of wearing anything that belonged to Unwin made me feel sick, but I knew I had little choice: a lone woman on the road would draw some attention; a lone woman covered in a bloody dress, wrapped in a thin cloak, would draw a lot. So I threw open his wardrobe, rooting through his clothes, throwing things to the floor, recoiling from the smell of him. There was nothing that would fit me, so I moved on to old chests, digging through years of his life, the trousers and shirts getting smaller, the quality better, before finally striking it lucky with breeches that, though a good thirty years out of date and still too long, would do for now. I rolled up the legs and added a fine leather belt stolen from a hook by the door to keep them in place. A woollen shirt smelling of mothballs over a thin vest swamped my upper body, but at least I'd be warm. Finally I took a fur-lined cloak and pulled my hair into a braid over my head, using my old tunic to wipe the flour residue from my face.

I left everything else where it fell, my clothes included, and raced back downstairs.

In the small library I stole a handful of coins left scattered on the desk, before pulling all of his papers, all of his books, from the shelves and hauling them into the kitchen, where I dumped them on the table, sending the flour spiralling into the air like a spectre. When the pile of his belongings reached my chest, I fetched the most expensive-looking bottles of whiskey I could find in the pantry, using them to soak the pyre I'd made. Finally, I chose the nastiest, sharpest-looking knife from the block by the stove and tucked it into my belt. The whole thing had taken less than twenty minutes.

Then I took the firelighter from beside the stove and touched it to the bonfire. I allowed myself a moment to watch the rush of blue flame as the alcohol burned, then I pocketed the firelighter, grabbed my sack, and fled straight into the forest.

I watched from the edge of the woods as the house went up, slowly at first, so slowly I thought it would burn out before it caught. I almost went back to give it a helping hand. But then a gust of wind carried burning embers to the thatch; I heard the whoosh as the flames took hold. I watched as dozens of soldiers ran to try to put the fire out, watched them dash to the well to get water and curse the missing bucket, all of them standing helpless as the blaze consumed Unwin's home. I almost, almost, forgave Silas then.

I had relied on Unwin going straight to the soldiers to report me, instead of returning home, when I decided on my plan, and I'd guessed well. He arrived when the house was beyond saving. I gave myself a few more precious seconds to enjoy the rage and confusion on his still-bloody face; then I took my chance and darted down along the edge of the forest, creeping my way to the soldiers' encampment, staying out of sight of the soldiers running towards the village. I suppose they thought the smoke was the start of an attack.

When I was sure it was empty, I moved swiftly, checking the largest tents for my mother, in case they were still holding her there, my stomach twisting every time I pulled back a flap to find the tent empty. From the largest one I stole a leather satchel, a water skin, a map of the realm, and a second, opal-handled knife.

I used that knife to liberate one of the few horses in the makeshift stables, a sleek-looking bay with watchful eyes. She didn't balk when I approached her, or saddled her, or even climbed on to her back.

I took my stolen horse, my stolen clothes, my stolen food and my stolen knife and rode as fast as I could out of Almwyk.

For the first two hours on the road I see nothing, and no one. Pheasants call from deep in the grass and there's the occasional rustling of something bigger, but the horse doesn't seem to worry, so I don't either. Instead I keep my head down and my hood up, watching the road ahead of and behind us.

I stay to the sides of the road, riding in the grass where I can, anxious not to leave a trail to follow. As the sun moves across the sky and the shadows lengthen, I start to see signs of the refugees gone before us. We pass a lost wooden doll, its scarred face turned skyward, the painted eyes following us eerily. I see a shoe, a little larger than mine, abandoned, and wonder how it wasn't missed and what happened to its owner. Who could afford to lose a shoe? Other things litter the roadside: paper, broken glass, bits of cloth, leaving a trail for me to follow, and I do, using the remnants to guide me deeper into Tregellan and towards Scarron.

Because unless he too managed to steal a horse, Silas Kolby is heading north on foot, through a country he doesn't know. So I'm going to ride like the wind to Scarron and find this girl first, before Silas does and they disappear into the Conclave for good. The only thing that makes sense is that she's a philtresmith; I'm convinced of it. That's why the alchemists want to find her so badly. Silas said they have limited supplies of the Elixir and my guess is it's because she's cut them off. Because of this *bad blood*. And now that the Sleeping Prince is here, they want to find her and reconcile.

Family first.

So I'll beat him to Scarron, I'll be the one to tell her that she's in danger and that she should hide in the Conclave. I'll escort her there. I'll do his job, and when the Conclave are falling over themselves to thank me, I'll tell them they can repay me by getting my mother out of the asylum, giving us sanctuary, and a few drops of Elixir each moon. A small price to pay for restoring their philtresmith to them.

And then, when Mama is settled, I'll make Silas Kolby regret betraying me.

In the week that I first met Silas, I also turned seventeen, and learned that the Sleeping Prince was impossibly still alive, and had woken, invaded Lortune, taken Lormere castle, and killed the king, all in one night.

It was also the week that we both realized Lief was trapped there.

I told my mother what I'd heard at the well, trying to stay calm, all the while my ribcage constricting until there was no space inside me for air, no room to breathe. She looked at me, then turned her face to the wall. And I left her, walking out of the house, walking into the woods, walking halfway to Lormere before I realized where I was. The whole time, the pressure in my chest didn't let up, becoming a solid weight between my lungs, until I grew used to it. I told myself that he might be all right, that he was probably on his way home even now. That was the thought that made me turn around. On the long walk back I convinced myself he'd be there when I got home, that we'd passed each other in the woods. That we'd laugh about it. That lightning hadn't struck twice. But when I got to the hut he wasn't there. And neither was my mother.

I found her half a mile away, buried in a pile of leaves, her arms shredded and bleeding from deep and jagged cuts. When I asked her what happened, she stayed silent, her eyes both wild and dead.

The following day I ventured back into those selfsame woods to find herbs, plants, anything that might stop the scratches from becoming infected. With the dark forest all around me, shadowed and secretive, I worried about everything, knowing something inside me, and in her, was broken, terrified it couldn't be fixed. There was suddenly so much to be afraid of: poverty, illness, death. More death. Every rustle, every grunt, every bird call caused my heart to try to leap out of my chest, uncaring about the bone and flesh in its way.

My hands had trembled as I tried to peel willow bark away from the trunk, the blade on my beautiful apothecary's knife – the last gift my father ever gave me – now dulled, my nerves ringing with fear. Then I heard the telltale crunch of leaves behind me, the snap of a twig that meant something big was there, and I turned to find a hooded man approaching me, his body lowered in a predatory crouch. As I staggered back, pushing the knife out before me, he came to a stop, gloved hands held out.

"Easy," he said, and his voice had sent shivers down my spine. It was thorny, if a voice can be such a thing, and curiously empty of any accent. "I mean you no harm."

"Stay back," I ordered, jabbing the knife forward to make my point. "Or I'll gut you."

His lips pulled upwards, but it wasn't a friendly smile. There are people who have smiles that force you to smile back at them; Lief was like that. Then there are others, whose smiles make you forget your name. There are smiles of comfort, and solidarity, and sympathy. There are people like Prince Merek, whose smile was a captive at the corner of his lips the whole time he rode through Tremayne, but never allowed to be free; his was a smile you'd have to work hard for. Silas's smile that first time was pure challenge; the curve of his lips was a dare.

"No need for that," he said. "I thought you were someone else. I can see that I was mistaken. I'll be on my way now." He backed away, and I watched him go, my heart hammering in my chest, the tip of the knife shaking visibly.

As soon as he was out of sight, I picked up my basket and followed. I knew it was stupid; I knew I should have turned around and gone home, but I couldn't stop myself. I needed to know where he'd come from, where he was going. During the moon we'd been living in Almwyk I'd grown familiar with the faces and habits of my neighbours, and it was too much of a coincidence – a stranger lurking in the woods the day after I'd found my mother, scratched and in shock, that made me need to follow him. I wanted to know where the stranger with the wicked smile slept.

And I wanted a fight. I wanted someone to hurt because I was hurt, because Mama was hurt. Because Lief might have been hurt and it wasn't fair.

So with my knife still clutched in my hand I followed him silently all the way back to the village, skirting down to the treeline to track his progress. At one of the recently abandoned cottages near the forest's edge, I watched him pull the flimsy window made of the cow-horn strips that all the cottages had clean out of its frame and then climb inside the building, his long arms reaching back out to replace it. Straight away I realized he was in hiding, a refugee of some sort, but certainly no one Unwin or anyone else knew about, and my suspicions grew. I approached the window cautiously, pressing my ear against it.

Then he was behind me, a hand over my mouth, and I dropped my basket, feeling the contents scattering over my feet, on to the ground. He'd known I was following him all along, had snuck out of the front door as soon as he was inside to wait for me.

"Nosy, aren't you?" he said, pushing my face against the

rough wood of the cottage, though with surprising gentleness, allowing his own, gloved hand to bear the brunt of it. His gloves smelt of mint and nettles. "What's to be done about that, then?"

I tried to free myself but his grip was too secure.

"I'm going to take my hand from your mouth. If you scream, I'll silence you permanently," he said. "Do you understand?"

I nodded slowly, and he pulled his hand away, whirling me around to face him and pushing my chin up. As he did I raised my knife, pointing it at his throat. Beneath the lip of his hood he smiled again.

"You're good," he said, and I felt perversely proud of his approval. Then I felt it, something sharp pressing into a space between my ribs. His own knife, aimed at my heart. "But this time I'm better. So lower your weapon. Let's be civilized."

I did as he asked, and to my relief he did the same, pulling his blade away as I moved mine.

We stayed still. I could feel him peering at my face from inside his hood, studying me, but I could see nothing of his, save his mouth, which was drawn into a thin, determined line.

"Who are you?" he asked finally, taking a step back and sheathing his knife, as I did the same. "Why were you following me?"

"My name is Errin. Errin Vastel. I thought . . . I wanted to know who you are."

"I'm no one, Errin Vastel," he said, his lower lip twisting as he pulled it between his teeth.

There was something in the way he said both of my names that made me shudder, as though there was a curse in them, or a spell. There was an edge there, something to be wary of.

"You don't live here," I said. "That's not your hut."

"It's mine for now," he replied. "Why does it matter to you who I am?"

"I just wanted to know. This is the kind of place where strangers are a cause for concern."

"From what I've heard, everyone in Almwyk is a cause for concern."

"If Chanse Unwin found out..." I meant it mostly as a warning, not a threat, but his response came as a hiss.

"But he hasn't. And he won't. No one will. My being here will be our secret, unless you'd like me to tell everyone how we met. In the woods, you with a basket full of hemlock, and nightshade, and oleander." He nodded to the mess at my feet. "It's a hanging offence to gather them without an apothecary licence, isn't it? I don't suppose you have a licence, do you, Errin Vastel? Or am I mistaken and you're the apothecary of Almwyk?"

I reddened, anger and fear vying inside me. Fear won. "No."

"Well then, you keep my secret, I'll keep yours. What do you say?"

What else could I say? I agreed, and I did my best to avoid the cottage he was living in.

But three days later I saw him again, back in the woods.

It was after Unwin's first town meeting, the day he told us that the Tregellian council would be dispatching soldiers to our village to guard the border, the day half the village packed up and left before they were arrested. Whilst they'd made a long, noisy caravan out of the village, I snuck into the woods for what I thought would be the last time before the soldiers came. He'd been waiting for me.

"I need a potion from you, if you can make it," he said without preamble, hopping off the rotting oak stump he'd been perched on. He brushed dead leaves and moss from where they clung to his cloak, casual, as though we met in the woods often, as though we were friends, his head tilted like a bird's as he did. "A tincture of henbane. Strong as possible. I'll give you three florins for it, and I'll tell no one where it came from."

"Why should I?" As soon as the sullen words left my mouth I wanted to bite them back. Three florins was a moon's rent, and then some. Enough to buy food to supplement my foraging. Three florins was another moon alive. I'd expected him to walk away after my rudeness.

I was wrong.

"Because you clearly need the money. And I really need the potion. We need each other. It makes sense."

I stared at him in his hateful cloak, his stupid gloved hands, and I could feel him staring right back at me.

"What's your name?" I said finally.

As he walked over to me I realized fully how tall he was, how lean he was. Last time we'd met, I'd been focusing on staying alive, but now... He reminded me of a silver birch, or a willow; a casual, insouciant grace to him, at home in the forest. He fitted here.

"Silas Kolby," he said, stopping a foot away from me. I held my hand out, and he looked at it, puzzled, as though the gesture was alien to him. My cheeks flamed and I pulled my hand back, only for him to suddenly grasp it, his larger palm enfolding mine in a way that felt more like the sealing of a pact than an introduction.

It had taken a few weeks for me to shake my fears that he'd been the one to hurt my mother, but the nights of the first full moon after the attack proved it wasn't him; he stayed infuriatingly himself, while she... It was pure dumb luck I'd taken to locking her in when I went out, to keep her from wandering and getting hurt again. It was pure dumb luck that I'd turned the key in the door after I'd given her supper, already half asleep and acting out of habit. It was luck that meant all she scratched that night was a door, and not me, while I sat behind it weeping as she called me names. During that first moon, when I slowly realized inch by inch that Lief was in real trouble, and that it was just me and my beast mother now, Silas was the one thing that kept me sane. He had an uncanny knack of appearing when I was teetering on the edge of something dark that I couldn't come back from.

And I trusted him. I really had. I had no idea how much until he betrayed me.

Chapter 15

Far to the west the sun sits low in the sky and I realize that night is coming, quickly and quietly. I slow the horse to a walk, pulling my satchel around and fetching out the map. Five miles riding towards the sinking sun to Tyrwhitt, but even if I could afford to pay for an inn with my stolen coin, it would be the first place soldiers would look for me, so that's out. Tremayne is fifty or so miles north-west after Tyrwhitt, and we have to make it there by lunchtime tomorrow if I want to get to Scarron before dark.

I decide to press on, get as far past Tyrwhitt as I can before the sun disappears completely. Then we'll have to stop for the night, whether I find shelter or not. It'll be fine, I tell myself. It's one night, and I have a thick cloak. It can't be much worse than the pathetic cottage in Almwyk.

"Come on, girl." I press my heels into the horse's flank

and urge her onwards. As the sky turns from grey to violet, we pass the outskirts of Tyrwhitt and I get my first glimpse of the refugee camp in the distant fields. Kirin wasn't exaggerating when he said you could smell it on the wind. It reeks of rot, and rubbish, and human waste.

I squint to see the makeshift shacks leaning against one another, fabric hanging between them to increase the shelter. There are mismatched tents made from various scraps, propped up with sticks. Small fires glow everywhere, but there's little sign of movement and no smell of cooking on the rank air. It looks forlorn and forgotten. I can see no place to get fresh water, or anywhere for the refugees to clean and toilet themselves. It looks like a breeding ground for disease.

Worst of all is the wire fence around the encampment, flecked with rough-cut trios of wooden star and wound with holly, the berries bright in the dying light. They look like drops of blood against the cruel coils of razor-sharp wire, and the sight of it all is enough to make me urge the horse on. Is Old Samm in there? Pegwin? Gods help those poor souls.

We make it another four or five miles past Tyrwhitt before I finally call a halt to the day. I decide to camp away from the main road, and I dismount and lead the horse along a narrow dirt track. In the last of the light I see the horse's ears turn back and it feels as though mine are trying to do the same, listening for danger. We're surrounded on both sides by a small thicket, dense enough to conceal someone, and I decide that it's likely as good as it's going to get.

The track veers sharply to the left and then a small, filthy-looking cottage, not dissimilar to the ones in Almwyk, looms out of the darkness ahead of us. I freeze, holding my breath and watching it, listening, scouring the ground for footprints.

I tie the horse to a tree and pull out my knife, creeping forward. There's no candle or firelight visible through the glassless windows. The shutters stand open to the elements, despite the temperature, and I straighten as I approach.

I circle around, listening, looking in through the corners of the windows, my heart thumping, ready to run. When I reach the front door I see it's ajar. Carefully, half-expecting something to fly at me, I push it open, wincing at the creak. I wait for my eyes to adjust and then I step inside.

The small windows and twilight make it difficult to see anything at first. I move in further and begin to explore. It's somewhat like our cottage: tiny fireplace, dirt floor. But this place has a single large, empty room and, unusually, a narrow wooden staircase leading up to a second floor. One hand still clutching my knife, the other wrapped around the bannister, I climb it slowly, expecting to hear the splitting of wood beneath my feet with every step.

At the top of the stairs is another open space, though this has a lumpy-looking bed near the window, a wooden crate upended to become a table beside it. The layer of dust on the mattress and the tabletop is thick, and the only footprints on the grimy floor are mine. It's creepy, and isolated, but it's indoors, and no one has been here for a very long time...

Making up my mind, I edge down the stairs and start

a small fire in the hearth, pulling the shutters over to hide the glow. I pray the chimney isn't blocked. Then I head back outside, leading the horse behind the cottage, where I tie her up, murmuring an apology for leaving her outside. For her part she doesn't seem to mind, nuzzling at me until I give her an apple and some of the water from my skin. I hate leaving the tack on her, but there's nowhere to hang it, and I didn't think to take a comb or brush to groom her either. I loosen what I can and apologize again, and she watches me with liquid brown eyes, snorting warmly into my shoulder.

Then I return to my temporary home, bolting the door behind me.

I toast some of the bread and cheese, washing it down with the milk, enjoying it more because of where it came from; then I unpeel my towel bandage and examine my hand. I use a little of the water to clean it, then tie it back up. It still hurts, but I'll bet it's not half as painful as Unwin's face. I play the moment again in my mind. I hope his nose heals crooked, and every time he looks in the mirror he remembers me.

When my eyelids start to droop I toy with the idea of sleeping upstairs, but decide I don't want to cut off my exit. Instead I wrap myself in my cloak, leaving my boots and clothes on, using the satchel as a pillow. I watch the fire as it smoulders, red and black, and I close my eyes. *Please let my luck hold. I've had precious little of it lately.* I don't know who, or what, I'm praying to, but I hope they're listening. *Let me get to Scarron and find the girl.* I'm not asking for a miracle.

That's all I need. Just please, please let me find her before Silas does.

I dream of the man, but it's fragmented: he's there, but he isn't. He's always one room away, in a place with more rooms than seems possible. I run down endless halls, longing for and dreading him being around the corner. I hear him call out for me and the skin on the back of my neck tightens and prickles. I don't know if I'm running to him, or from him.

When I wake sometime later, I'm shaking so hard my teeth are chattering. The fire has gone out, and my cloak is hanging off me, exposing me to the cold night. I reach to pull it back over but stop.

Beginning at my ankles, and rising up and along my calves, I feel gooseflesh erupt, my skin prickling. The crawling feeling spreads as every hair on my body stands on end. My eyes dart around the small room, taking in the shadows, looking for the reason why my instincts are telling me something is wrong.

I strain to hear beyond the cottage, listening for the snores of the horse or the rustling of an animal. There. To the left of the house I can hear leaves being crunched underfoot.

As quietly as I can, I walk to the window and peep out through a thin gap between the shutters, gazing in the direction I think is east, squinting to see if the sky is any lighter.

A shadow crosses in front of the window.

I jerk back, my mouth dry with terror. Then another shadow falls.

Before I've had time to think I've darted back to the satchel and slung it around my neck, abandoning the food and my cloak. Then I climb the stairs, praying that none will creak, moving as fast as I can without making a sound. As I reach the top, the door latch rattles.

I tiptoe across the room, standing on the bed and peering out of the window, unable to see who the visitors are. What if they're soldiers? What if they've found me? I stand still, listening, hoping they'll leave. Please leave. Leave.

There is a loud bang downstairs, then another: the sound of the door hitting the dirt floor.

I look out again, trying to gauge the distance to the ground. Too far, I decide. If they heard me, or if I hurt myself, I'd be done for.

Then I look up. The eaves hang low over the window and I wonder... I hear someone poking the fire, footsteps sounding closer to the stairs, and the time for wondering is over. I climb out on to the windowsill, my back to the night, and reach up, feeling beneath the eaves for a beam. An experimental tug reassures me as much as anything could, and I lift myself up, standing on the small frame and leaning my elbows on the roof. Cold air whips behind me and I'm paralysed by fear.

Then I hear a man's voice. "There's an upstairs," he says, the accent Lormerian. Not soldiers, then.

But there's no time for relief. The muscles in my arms

are screaming as I haul myself upwards, biting my lip as I feel the skin on the knuckles of my right hand splitting again. My upper body lurches on to the roof, the sound muted by the thatch. For a wild, terrible moment my feet can find no purchase; I wheel my legs frantically before my fists grip at more thatch, and I swing them up, one foot then the second reaching the beam. Thank the Oak I'm wearing breeches, I would never have made it in skirts.

Beneath me I hear the sound of footsteps, two sets, thundering up the stairs, and it frightens me so much that I nearly let go.

I lie on my belly, the satchel wedged beneath me, holding my breath.

"She went out the window," another voice says, and to my surprise it's female, though as gruff as the man's, and as Lormerian too. "Look, there's footprints in the dust on the bed. She jumped."

"Without breaking her legs? No chance. She could be on the roof," her companion replies.

"You'd better take a look, then."

My stomach drops when a pair of large hands with hairy knuckles appears inches from my face; I can see the chewed edges of his filthy nails in the moonlight. I'm readying myself to kick out at him when the thatch pulls loose and I hear him swear.

"She's not up there. Thatch is rotten; she'd be on the ground with more than a broken leg if she'd tried. You're right, she jumped. Must have heard us and took off."

"She probably heard you coming a mile off, you were making such a racket."

"She can't have gone far; her cloak was still warm. And she left her food. Might be she'll come back for them when she thinks it's safe. We should wait it out."

"She had two bags, remember. The other one's gone. And there's no sign of the horse. I wouldn't come back, in her shoes. I'd put as much distance as I could in." The woman's words are laced with certainty, and her male counterpart grunts his response.

I hear their boots moving away, on the stairs, and I take a single breath before realizing that if they come around the rear of the house and look up, they'll see me, clinging to the roof like a spider. I shuffle to the edge, but the man has pulled away the thatch I'd need to use to get back into the house.

I have no choice but to stay where I am for now.

I hear them leave and wait, braced for the moment they'll come around and see me, or look for tracks, find my horse and know I'm still here.

Then I hear a muffled thud from inside the house and my limbs lock. They didn't leave after all. They waited. They know I'm here; they tried to trick me. I hear the stairs creaking, feel someone below me, waiting in the window. They stand there for a long time and I can feel my heart beating frantically, in my chest, even in my fingertips. Then, mercifully, I hear stairs creak again, and then silence.

Long minutes pass with me gripping the roof for all I'm

worth, my breath shallow, my limbs trembling. The wait becomes unbearable, and I lean closer to the edge, listening. Have they truly left? When I alter my grip on the thatch it pulls free.

I have to jump, or I'm going to fall.

Lief and I used to jump from the hayloft into the barn below after harvest, throwing ourselves down fifteen feet to bounce in the sweet-smelling hay. As he got older Lief would do somersaults, flinging himself backwards into the piles of grass, but I wasn't quite brave, or stupid, enough.

By my guess the edge of the roof is perhaps thirteen feet from the ground. And there's no hay beneath me.

I shift until I'm parallel to the ledge. There is a thick beam that's part of the frame, and I brace myself against it, holding on tight. I need to roll as soon as I hit the ground and then I need to run. Roll, then run. When I lower myself over and my feet touch nothing I panic, even though I knew it would happen, and I grasp a new patch of thatch.

It comes away in my hand and I fall. Before I've even had time to understand what's happened I'm on the ground and I can't breathe, searing pain across my ribs, my lungs unable to expand. . .

Then it recedes and sweet, sweet air rushes into my lungs. It hurts, but I gasp anyway, sucking the air in. Winded. I winded myself. That's all. I thought I'd broken my back.

I roll on to my side, pushing the satchel out from under me and twisting my head to stare up at the lightening sky. Then I take an inventory of my body. I'm jarred and jolted, but nothing is broken, or even sprained. It's shock that keeps me pinned to the ground, even as part of my mind insists I get up and run. That part gets louder, and I sit, stiffly, amazed by the miracle of being all right. I look at the cottage, trying to summon the courage to go to it. Surely, if someone were still there they would have come out when they heard me fall.

I pull the knife from the satchel and approach.

The door is gone, knocked from its hinges. I edge in, staying near the doorway while my eyes get used to the gloom. Then I forget to be stealthy as I cry out and rush to my makeshift bed.

My cloak, all of my food, even my firelighter is gone. The mattress lies bare in front of the fireplace. All I have is the satchel and the maps, spare knife and a mostly empty water skin. Damn them. As I stand up I smell something so unexpected that I stop dead.

Mint, and old incense. Faint, lingering on the air like dust motes.

Silas was here.

I race into the copse and untie the horse, rushing to tighten the saddle and the stirrups. She snuffles my pocket for food and I push her away in irritation. "It's all gone," I say. "So it's no good looking." She whinnies softly and I feel bad – it's not her fault. And it could have been worse; imagine if I'd lost her too, imagine if Silas or the others had found her. I stroke her nose and murmur a swift apology.

Silas was here. Was he with those people? But no, I heard

two voices, two sets of footsteps. If he came, he came after, while I was on the roof.

If it was him. Can I be sure I smelt incense? It was a pretty big fall; I could be mistaken. I leave the horse and walk along the track towards the road, listening all the while and scanning the ground, squinting in the dim light. Four sets of footprints coming down, three heading away. One set of hoof prints. He still doesn't have a horse, then. Unless he left it on the road. No, he wouldn't be that foolish. I turn back to my own mount.

When I climb into the saddle I feel as though I'm made of iron; everything is too heavy. I'm about to nudge the horse away when I pause. Whoever the first two were, they knew I had two bags. They knew I was female. Which means they must have seen me earlier, followed me. Refugees, I decide. Lormerian refugees either avoiding or escaped from the camp. I bet they were holed up near Tyrwhitt and saw me pass, following me on foot. I suppose I should be grateful they weren't soldiers. Still... It means I'm conspicuous. And obviously vulnerable.

I unpin the braid from my head and allow it to fall down my back. Then I pull out my knife and begin to saw at it, at the base of my neck. It doesn't take more than a moment until I'm holding the braid in one hand, my head feeling impossibly light, the morning breeze ruffling my newly short locks. I look at it, dirty and matted, and then fling it into the forest.

From a distance, I might pass for a young man, which

will hopefully be enough to fool anyone watching out for a likely victim, and perhaps even any soldiers I come across. As long as they don't get too close. I look down at my breasts and grimace, pulling the shirt a little looser to try to disguise them. I wish I still had my cloak. As cold air chills my neck, and I guide the horse back towards the road, I wonder if I look like my brother did.

I keep the sun over my right shoulder until we reach the main road, still called the King's Road after all this time, stretching between Tyrwhitt and Tremayne, forking off to Tressalyn. Once on it I try to make myself look as menacing as I can, staying alert for anyone travelling on foot, both on the road and in the woodlands and meadows to the sides. We stop infrequently, and never near villages and hamlets, and I keep the pace easy, but constant. It soon becomes evident that the horse I took is built for stamina and long distances, but the progress we're making feels too slow.

I pass other travellers headed the same way on the road, lone, or in pairs, always hooded like Silas, which makes my breath catch until I pass them and see they're too wide or too short to be him; they don't walk the way he does. Most keep their heads lowered, though one or two look up, and their hollow eyes, the terror in them, draws me up straight. They always look away first, cowering from me, and I know they're refugees from Lormere. I urge the horse to the other side of the road as we pass, to reassure them I have no intention of harming them. But I can't get their faces out of my mind. How empty they look. What have they seen, to do that to them?

As the day lengthens it becomes obvious that I've seriously underestimated how fast I'll be able to travel. By lunchtime, after five of hours riding, we've barely passed Newtown, and still have thirty miles to go. I dismount and walk for a few miles, letting the horse slow and stop to drink from puddles when she needs to. When I empty the last drops of water from the water skin, I consider refilling it from those same puddles, changing my mind when I see how messily she drinks. I'm not that thirsty, not yet. I think of the people I've passed and wonder how they're drinking. When they last ate.

I don't see anyone else on horseback until later in the afternoon, when the roads begin to widen, the ground beaten down by the passage of many. My stomach is churning from the lack of food and my mouth is dry, my head aching from thirst. As we come up behind another band of refugees I steer the horse past them, bundles on their backs, fear hovering around them like midges over a pond. Then, in the distance, I see a group travelling towards us on horseback, approaching at speed. Immediately the refugees drop their bundles and run into the scrub, and some of the riders peel off and drive their horses into the fields after them. I keep going, but my heartbeats are coming faster, my hands suddenly slippery on the reins, the knuckles on my right hand throbbing.

As the riders get closer I can see the green tunics of the Tregellian army and my fear increases. I start to sweat, despite my lack of cloak. The rest of the refugees scatter, leaving me alone on the road as the soldiers draw near.

"Get after them," one of them bellows, his blue sash marking him as a lieutenant, as his comrades ride after the escapees in the fields. "Round them all up. You." He looks at me. "Dismount. Nice and slow."

Shaking, I do as he says, staying close by the horse.

The lieutenant swings out of his saddle and draws his sword, his eyes lit with anger.

"You stinking thief. Where'd you get that horse? On your knees, Lormerian scum."

"I'm not a refugee."

"Shut it." He looms over me, sneering, a hand reaching for me.

I move back, knocking into the horse, and she whinnies in fright. "I'm Tregellian. I'm from Tremayne. I'm Tregellian."

"Course you are." He grabs my hair, forcing me to my knees, and I gasp, scrabbling for my knife.

There's a shriek from the meadow. "Man down!" a male voice screams.

The lieutenant's grip on my hair tightens momentarily and I whimper.

"He's killed him!" the voice cries again. "The bastard's killed him!"

"Stay there," the lieutenant barks at me, forcing me down so my face is inches from the mud. "Stay," he says again, and then my scalp tingles as he lets go, cold air rushing over it.

I don't even pretend to obey. I'm back in the saddle in seconds, right foot not fully in the stirrup when the horse begins to run. Once I have my seat I look back over my shoulder to see no one is even looking at me; instead they're crowding around something in the grass, something unmoving. Soldiers from all around run towards them, some dragging captives with them, terror on the faces of the refugees and, to my horror, something like elation on the soldiers', their eyes wild, their lips pulled back in rictus grins. I look ahead to make sure the road is clear, then back again. In time to see the lieutenant drag his sword across the throat of one of the refugees.

I whip back around, my mouth open in a silent scream. We keep running.

It's many miles before the horse and I begin to slow. My head is throbbing with pain and my neck aches from turning back and forth to make sure we're not being followed. Every time I look back I see again the refugee murdered, the wildness in the soldiers' faces. They were Tregellian soldiers. My people. People of logic and reason and decency. Not like Lormerians.

They treated the Lormerians as though they were animals. They're here because they're running for their lives. They're people.

Pictures of the camp, the mercenaries, the roads empty of traders, the soldiers, flash through my mind. . . I didn't expect this. Kirin didn't say it was like this. Kirin is a lieutenant too.

Maybe he wasn't really a refugee; maybe they were criminals, dangerous criminals, and the soldiers had no choice.

On your knees, Lormerian scum.

I remember the lost doll, the abandoned shoe. I remember the soldier's wild eyes when he reached for my hair and forced me down. It's not right.

I see no one else until we come up behind a small cart laden with sacks and children, and the little ones gaze solemnly at me as I approach. To my surprise, and if I'm truthful, relief, the two mules leading the cart are headed by a woman.

Before I can stop myself, I call out. "Do you have any water, good woman?"

She looks at me suspiciously. The children are wide-eyed, their tiny fat fingers gripping the side of the cart. Then she rummages beside her and pulls a skin out, shaking it before throwing it to me.

I forget to thank her, too intent on ripping the cork out and drinking. I drink until it's empty, and it's still not enough. I realize too late it may have been all she had.

I look over at her and she's watching me, her expression guarded. "Thank you," I say sheepishly, tossing it back to her, noting the way she holds it delicately between her thumb and forefinger before she drops it to the floor of the cart. "Where do you go?"

"Tressalyn."

I'm disappointed, had half-hoped she was travelling to Tremayne so I might ride with her for a while.

"You?" she asks.

"Tremayne."

"There's a checkpoint, you know," she says.

"Where?"

"At the end of the King's Road, before the city gates. A checkpoint to be allowed admittance to Tremayne. Same at Tressalyn. Same at all the towns. Otherwise the refugees would overrun them."

Overrun them? How many refugees are there? "Since when?" I ask.

"Since the Sleeping Prince stopped sleeping and started setting things on fire in Lormere, making them all want to come here. You'll need papers to get past it. No refugees allowed. Without, you'll have to go on to one of the camps, back east."

"I was born in Tremayne," I say. "I'm Tregellian."

She looks me up and down, her eyes resting first on my loose trousers, then my shorn hair. "As long as you can prove it, you'll be fine."

There is a heavy moment where we both regard each other. Then she clicks the reins and the mules turn left for Tressalyn, as I steer my horse right towards Tremayne, and the checkpoint.

I don't have any papers. I don't have anything to say who I am.

And I really don't want to run into any more soldiers.

So I can't go into Tremayne. That's probably for the best, I decide. My priority is finding water and I know there's a river that runs outside it.

I glance at the sky, the sun halfway through its descent, the air rapidly turning chilly, my breath misting before me.

It's taken the entire day to get this far, time I don't have. I'll have to make for Scarron in the dark.

Around two miles away from the city walls of Tremayne I pull the horse to a stop, checking the maps, planning a route that will take us off the main road, away from the checkpoints and towards the river. Making sure there's no one near us, I slide from the saddle, moaning as my cramped limbs are forced to stretch. My stomach rumbles loudly. A whole day in the saddle has exhausted me, used up whatever energy I had. I need some food, or I'm going to collapse. And I need a new cloak. I won't last overnight without one.

I'm going to have to go into Tremayne after all.

The thought of being so close to my old life, to my apothecary, makes me feel faint, my chest tight.

The thought of soldiers on the gates makes my stomach drop.

I'd imagined my return to Tremayne would be triumphant. I'd have everything under control, the shame of our flight forgotten. I wouldn't be wearing stolen clothes, my knuckles bruised from fighting, my scalp tingling from a soldier's assault.

I don't have a choice, I remind myself; I have to find the girl, I have to get Mama back. I can worry about the apothecary, and the war, and everything else after that.

The slashing of a sword across a throat replays behind my eyes.

I take a deep breath and climb back into the saddle.

Then I see it: a thin, barely noticeable track gently sloping

217

uphill on my right. I click the reins and urge the horse along the path, my heart thumping in my chest. As we crest the small mound, recognition punches me in the stomach and I see it.

Our farm.

I make a strangled sound. It hasn't changed. It hasn't been so long since we left, so I shouldn't be as surprised that it still looks the same, as though any moment Lief and Papa could come striding out of the door, or Mama appear in the window. I should be in there now, with my family. Instead half of them are dead, or missing, I'm on the run, and my mother is locked away Gods know where. And it's all my fault.

I have to get her back. This is my mess.

If I can get food and a cloak, we can keep going. I could be in Scarron by sunrise. I still remember how to get from our farm into Tremayne through the clock tower gate. By the river. And I doubt there's a checkpoint there.

Chapter 16

It's not the first time I've been wrong. When I arrive at the clock tower gate, I'm greeted by two soldiers armed with swords, their expressions closed and unfriendly. A third perches on top of the tower, arrow nocked and pointed at me. It's too late to run, and the sight of them sends my stomach plunging, my fingers trembling on the reins.

"Dismount and state your business," one of the soldiers says.

Shaking, I do, keeping one hand on the pommel of the saddle, my legs braced to throw myself up and into it if they try to attack me.

"You're a girl," one of the swordsmen says in surprise. "Well, well. Nice breeches. Let's see your papers, then." I peer at him, trying to think of a reason – any reason – why I don't have them. "You deaf? I said papers. Show us your papers."

"I . . . don't have any. I was robbed on the way here. They were in my bag – my other bag. I lost my cloak too." I try to keep my tone pleasant and reasonable, but I'm struggling, my chest beginning to tighten. I should run.

"Where are you from?" the man asks.

"Here, originally. I was born in Tremayne. But I don't live here any more. Some of my family do, and it's them I've come to see."

He sheathes his sword and tucks his thumbs in his belt loops, and I let out a soft sigh, some of my tension releasing. "Where have you come from, then?"

"Tressalyn," I lie. "I'm here to pass on some news to my family. Urgent news."

"Alone? Just you, riding across the country on a very nice horse?" He's enjoying this, this tiny bit of power that he has. I can hear it in his voice, and see it on his face. He looks over my baggy breeches, my rough-cut hair, my bandaged hand. "Where did you say you'd come from again?"

"Let her in, Tuck. She ain't the Sleeping Prince, and she don't sound Lormerian. It's almost time to knock off," the other guard on the gate says. The man above is now picking his nails with the tip of his arrow, his bow slung over his shoulder, ignoring us.

"What did you say your name was?" the bully, Tuck, asks.

"Er . . . ika. Erika Dunn." There are plenty of Dunns in Tremayne, plenty everywhere; it's a common enough name.

"Never heard of an Erika Dunn." Tuck grins.

"I have," the arrow man says from above us suddenly.

"I thought I recognized you. Ain't you Tarvey Dunn's niece?"

"Yes," I say, trying to hide my surprise. Tarvey is one of the butchers my father used to sell our cattle to, famed for both his excellent meat and for having one leg. And luckily for me, his family is notoriously prolific. "One of many," I add, throwing a smile at the archer.

Tuck scowls. "Be that as it may, rules are rules. No one gets in or out without papers. And no one gets in or out after sundown. Oops." He glances up at the darkening sky and grins. "Maybe I'll be feeling more generous tomorrow."

"Tarvey'll be furious if he knows you turned her away. He's probably expecting her." The archer scratches his leg with the arrow before putting it away.

"He is, yes," I pipe up.

Tuck glares at him, then at me. "Be that as it may. . ."

"Isn't it Tarvey who supplies our meat?" the archer says with perfect innocence.

Tuck throws the archer another filthy look, but he's examining his nails again. With a long sigh and a nod of the head, he finally stands aside, and I walk the horse through the clock tower gate, smiling meekly, my heart still beating violently. I glance up at the archer, who gives me a sly wink, and in that moment I could kiss him.

We've only walked a few yards when behind me I hear the rattling of chains. I turn in time to see the iron gate slam into place.

"What are you doing?" I ask.

"I told you. No one in or out after sundown."

221

"But I have to leave tonight! I'm here to get some things and pass on my news; I'll be an hour at most. I can't stay."

Tuck's grin is smug. "I'm afraid you'll have to. You wanted in, and you got it. I'm sure your uncle can put you up. Want me to come with you to make sure?"

I shake my head and quickly lead the horse away, resisting the urge to turn around and make sure he's not following me as we head towards the town square.

There are more soldiers loitering outside the tavern, one leaning against the main well talking to a woman I don't recognize. There are sandbags piled in one corner of the square, and large barrels on a cart being pulled by a grumpy-looking mule. But that's the only sign of the war; the chaos across other parts of the country is almost completely absent inside the town walls. Two young boys chase each other in circles outside the bakery, and I can see their mother in conversation with the baker himself; others are gossiping and laughing, shop bells ringing, doors closing. The air smells of good, hearty food, meat and vegetables and bread and pastry. It smells of home; Lief and I used to run around in front of the bakery like those boys; Lirys and I used to wait by the well for Kirin. Everything here is coated in memories of what I've lost: my friends, my parents, my brother. My old life.

Across the square, lights flicker in the upstairs window of the apothecary I used to work at, and I stop and stare. It hasn't changed. I feel I could walk up the steps, open the door, pull my apron from the hook and start working.

The boys run past me, screaming joyfully and shaking me from my reverie, and I walk on, keeping my head down. I move through the village square like a ghost, passing the butcher's where Tarvey is likely working, the cobblers my mother used. I stop at the grocer's and peer inside, but when I see there are still customers – people I used to know, in passing – I can't bring myself to go in. I'll get a cloak first and come back. Then I'll find a way out.

I leave the main square and walk down the merchant's lane towards the tailor's. Each window that I pass has candles glowing inside, and families moving, and I'm filled with longing for home – my home. My old life is everywhere. I walk past the deserted blacksmith's where Kirin used to work, and past the salt merchant's house. I used to know his daughter a little, and I look up, halting when I see a circle with a line through it carved into the door. It's familiar, and I frown.

"Errin?"

I whirl around, pulling at my belt for my knife, my hand stilling when I see who said my name.

Carys Dapplewood, Lirys's mother and a second mother to me, stands half in shadow, a basket clutched in her hands. "Is it really you?"

My tongue sticks to the roof of my mouth.

"I saw you in the square," she says, stepping forward. "I thought I was going mad. But I had to know... What are you doing, child?"

"I ... I ... I need a cloak and some food. Then I have to go."

"What do you mean, you have to go? Where's Lief? Where's Trina? How long have you been back? Where are you staying?"

My heart starts to speed up, my throat closes in, and that familiar clammy feeling starts to crawl across my shoulders. I want to reply. I want to run. I'm not ready for this. I stare at her and shake my head.

Where's Lief?

Without saying another word Carys drops her basket to the ground and takes my arm in one hand, the reins in the other. She leads us away quickly, saying nothing, and all the while the weight in my chest grows and grows. We cross the bridge and then I can see it, the Dapplewoods' dairy, butter-yellow bricks and as familiar to me as my farm. Carys lets go of the reins and leads me to the front door, and I panic, trying to pull my arm away. Her grip is surprisingly strong for a woman her age, and I'm too busy trying to breathe to really struggle.

She opens the front door and calls for Lirys. I'm bathed in light and warmth, the smell of roasting meat, and it makes me want to weep. "I'll take the horse to the barn," she says, patting my arm and leaving me.

The sound of footsteps makes my stomach lurch and I brace myself for the blow of seeing my best friend for the first time since my father's funeral.

She stands before me, blonde ringlets escaping from under a cap, her creamy skin flushed from the heat. She tilts her head to the side and the gesture reminds me of

Silas. We stare at each other and I realize I'm poised to run.

"Errin?" she says finally, looking me over. I swallow, my eyes beginning to prickle under her scrutiny. "Is it really you? You look—" She pauses. "Well, I like your breeches," she says. "Are they Lief's? You look like him, with your hair like that. I thought you were him." She peers over my shoulder expectantly, then back to me. "Is he with you? Are you back? Errin? Errin, are you well?"

Where's Lief?

I stare at her, blood pounding in my ears, my too-fast heart drumming a tattoo.

Lief.

At no point during my plans – not when I was blackmailing Silas, not when I hoped to evacuate me and Mama to the Conclave, and not since I've been on the road have I included Lief in our future.

At no point when I've thought realistically about what will happen next has he been part of it. I haven't included him in a long time. I kept telling myself he'd come home one day.

I knew it all along. I just didn't want to.

And now that I'm here, in Tremayne – in our home – I can't ignore it.

He's not a prisoner somewhere in Lormere; he's not wounded. He's not fighting his way back to us.

Pain, iron-clad and locked away, nestled in my heart like a dead thing, radiates out without warning. He's dead. My brother is dead. He's not coming home. It's sharp and it's a spike that drives me to my knees, pinning me to the cold wooden floor, and I can't breathe in, it's too big, it's blocking my lungs.

Then Lirys's arms are around me and she smells like flour and butter and goodness and I howl, my head thrown back against her shoulder like an animal. Through my raging I hear other footsteps, approaching then retreating, but I cling to my friend and she clings back. Each time my fingers tighten hers do too, until we're gripping each other hard enough to make bruises.

Eventually the tears stop and I sag in her arms, spent.

For the first time in four moons I can breathe.

"You need a bath and some food," she says in her lovely lilting voice. "And then bed."

"I can't," I say, harsh as a crow. "I have to go."

"Errin Vastel, you can't leave. We have a curfew and the gates are locked. And even if they weren't, I wouldn't let you. You're home."

And with that the tears come again, but these tears are fat and warm and I can breathe through them.

She sits on a stool beside the bath, watching me with slightly narrowed eyes. In the room next door I can hear the faint murmur of her mother and father eating their supper. Lirys has kept them away from me since my collapse, guiding me through to the warmth of her kitchen, where she dragged the tin bath before the fire and filled it with jug after jug of steaming water. She helped me undress and get into it, tutting softly at the bruises covering me, at my too-thin frame, and then she washed my hair. Finally, she unwrapped my bandaged hand, re-dressing it with real gauze, rubbing an ointment into it that soothed it instantly.

Though it must be killing her, she waits until I'm ready to speak. She doesn't ask where we've been, or why I've not written. She accepts it all, patiently and kindly, prattling lightly, deliberately, about Kirin, and the slow, steady dance they'd been performing all autumn, until he finally kissed her and asked her to be his wife. She talks about him being a soldier, and what a shock it was, but how she thinks it will be OK.

She doesn't think war will come.

I think of the assault in the woods, of the arrow in Kirin's shoulder. Of the golems in Almwyk, and the camp at Tyrwhitt. Of the mercenaries who hunted me in the night and the soldier who forced me to the ground, then slit another man's throat open. I think of Lief, never returning from Lormere. War has come. It doesn't matter whether the Sleeping Prince invades Tregellan or not; it's already here. The worst part is knowing that if I were in her shoes, here in Tremayne, in the place I'd always lived, I'd doubt it too. I would have continued to think Tregellan was a fair, just and safe paradise.

The innocence of her words, the normalcy of them – no curses, no beasts, no alchemy, no mystery – tighten something inside me and I decide I don't want her to know anything about my life in Almwyk either, don't want her to know the worst of what I've done – making poisons, punching people and lighting fires. Stealing. Assaulting her fiancé. I don't want her to see me that way. And I don't want to scare her; I want her to stay innocent.

But I have to say something, can feel her waiting for me to unburden myself.

I don't mention the Elixir or Silas at all. I leave out Unwin's advances, and the men in the woods. I don't tell her about the golems, or what happened to me on the way here. I keep it simple, telling her about Mama's breakdown – leaving out the parts about the beast – and how I was trying to treat her. I'm doing well, until I realize I have to tell her that Mama was taken away, and that I wasn't there to protect her. And that now I'm scrambling to get her back.

"It's not your fault," she says immediately, passing me a new block of soap, and I smell it greedily.

"Of course it is. I shouldn't have left her alone. Gods, Lir, imagine how horrible it must have been. To have soldiers burst in and take her away. She wouldn't have known what was going on. I did that to her, because I. . ."

"Because you what?"

I shake my head. "It doesn't matter."

"Errin, don't say that."

"I'm sorry."

"I don't want your apologies," she snaps, and I'm taken aback. "I wish you could have seen yourself when you arrived. You looked like a corpse. Your hair, the bruises. You look like you haven't eaten a decent meal since you left. How long have you been living like that? Who was taking care of you?"

"I was."

"No, Errin. You weren't." Her voice is gentle but firm, and again she reminds me of Silas, of the pity in his eyes when he first saw the hut. "I'm not stupid; I know you're keeping things from me. How did you earn the money to rent a cottage? What did you eat? What did you live on?"

"I—" I look at her, helpless.

"I can't make you tell me. But I wish you'd written to me – to any of us," she says, shaking her head. "You should have been here. We're your people. We would have cared for you."

Her words spark a memory that makes me ache. When Master Pendie came to offer his condolences, I didn't open the door, didn't want to tell him I was leaving. Mama was upstairs in her room, Lief was off making some inventory of the farm. I stood behind black drapes and watched through a chink as he knocked at the door, then knocked again. Finally, with a sad glance, he left a basket on the doorstep and went away, his footsteps dragging as though he were tied to the farmhouse with invisible ropes and each step threatened to pull him back to it. When I opened the basket I found vials of potions, for grief and sadness and sleep. And a cake. A lopsided, ugly cake, burned on the bottom and raw inside.

He'd made us a cake. It was awful but I ate every bite. We left the following day for Almwyk and I never thanked him for it.

"I was ashamed," I say finally, quietly, speaking to the

rapidly cooling bath water. "I still am."

"Why? You've done nothing to be ashamed of."

I snort. "The debts. Having to sell everything. Having to leave."

"It wasn't your fault. What can I do to convince you?"

"Wasn't it? If I'd put the tools away Papa might not have fallen on them. Which means he'd still be here, and so would Lief, and Mama. Instead Lief and Papa are dead and Mama is locked away in some Gods-forsaken place in Tressalyn, and she—"

Lirys leans forward and flicks water into my face, surprising me into looking up. "Enough," she says in a voice coated in steel. "You're not responsible for your father's death. And you're not responsible for what Lief did, or what happened to him. You know what he was like – Gods know I loved him like my own brother, but he was reckless. You couldn't have stopped him, no one could. And you're certainly not responsible for your mother. None of this is your fault. Stop punishing yourself."

"Lirys," I say.

"Errin," she says back at me in the same pleading tone. "You need to eat. And sleep. I've left one of my nightgowns on my bed. If you can bear to wear a dress now." She smiles.

"I can't. I have to go. I have to find someone. If I can find her, she's the key to getting Mama back."

"And I'm sure you'll find her. But, in the meantime, stay here, rest. We'll talk to Mama and Papa in the morning and decide what to do. It might take a little while, but I know

230

everyone will want to help."

I shake my head. "I don't have a little while. I have to get her back as soon as I can. You can't help with this."

I wish I could explain about the beast, and why time is short.

Lirys, trusting, unquestioning Lirys, sighs. "Well, you still can't leave until the morning. The gates are locked, all of them. And manned. Like it or not, your quest will have to wait. So you may as well get dressed and eat something." She ushers me out of the bath and into a thick robe before herding me up the stairs and into her small, clean room. "I'll bring some supper up to you," she says, closing the door and leaving me alone.

I shed the robe and pull the linen gown over my head, sighing at the feel of such soft, clean material next to my soft, clean skin. I sit on the bed, trying to calculate where Silas might be right now. If he's still on foot, he'll be a good thirty miles away, even if he walked through the night. But if he has a horse... I'll rest for a few hours, I decide. And I'll be at the gates at dawn. We'll ride like the wind to Scarron. I can't afford to let him beat me.

The man is walking through darkened streets, rain and wind lashing down, his cloak whipping behind him, his hood low over his face. He's calling my name, over and over, howling it into the wind.

I don't say anything, watching him, torn again between running to him and running from him.

Then he turns, his mouth falling open when he sees me. He stands there, immobile, while everything rages around him. Slowly he raises a hand and beckons, one gloved finger calling me to him. I watch, still undecided whether to stay or go, and he tilts his head to the side.

"Errin?" he says softly. "Please."

Without consciously choosing to, I begin to walk towards him. His hands reach for me and he smiles. Lightning blazes above us and then I'm ten paces from him, five, then just two. I lift my own hand to take his—

Nothing. They won't meet. There's something between us, stopping us. We push and prod at the invisible barrier, moving up and down it, trying to find a break.

"My brother is dead," I say. "You were right." I drop my head, my fingers sliding down the obstacle between us.

"Where are you?" he says. "Why can't I get to you?"

"Where are you?" I ask.

"Where I've always been."

"I'm in Tremayne," I say, and immediately regret it. Now he'll know I'm nearly there.

The pale blur of his face turns towards the dark sky. "Tremayne," he whispers, the wind stealing the word away the moment it's left his lips. He looks back at me. "Why?"

I turn away from the barrier between us, ignoring him as he calls after me, his voice becoming lost to the storm.

I wake to the sound of soft snores from the floor beside the bed. I roll on to my back and stretch out, sighing at the feeling of the bed beneath me. It's the first time since we left the farm that I've slept in an actual bed and it's so soft, so welcoming. It's like being held, and I revel in it, wriggling into the centre and making a hollow with my body.

Around an hour later I'm still wide awake, staring upwards, annoyed by Lirys's snoring and her ability to remain asleep. The bed – such a luxury after the pallets and floors I've been sleeping on – is too soft. I've tried lying in every possible position but I feel unsupported by the feathers, feel as though I'm sinking into them. I know then that I'm finished sleeping for tonight, and push back the covers, sliding my feet to the cold wooden floor. Using the bed as a guide, my fingers stretched out before me, I walk to the window and crack the shutters to peer out. Dark. Still. No sign of dawn.

Closing the shutters, I creep back across the room and pull Lirys's robe from the back of the door, before opening it and slipping out. The cottage is silent as I pad down the stairs and into the kitchen, the slate tiles chilly beneath me. I light a taper from the stove, touching the flaming tip to the candles atop the mantelpiece and then crossing to the pantry. My stomach rumbles, horribly loud in the silence of the night; I slept through dinner.

Hoping the Dapplewoods won't mind, I help myself to cold chicken, bread and butter, and pour myself a large tumbler of milk, drinking it in three gulps before pouring another. I take my meal to the table and sit in the seat I've sat in my whole life in this house, feet curled under me to keep them warm.

I am tearing chicken from the bone when I hear someone behind me.

Carys Dapplewood walks past, opening the larder and fetching herself a tumbler of milk, before sitting opposite me. I chew the meat and swallow, waiting.

"Lirys says your brother is dead," she says after a while. "I'm so sorry, Errin. He was a special, silly, funny boy. I was very fond of him. We all were."

I shake my head, pushing down the wave of grief. She knew Lief. Everyone here knew Lief. I can't breathe for being reminded of him.

"Your brother, Gods keep him, was proud. You are too. I pray you're more careful than he was." Despite the harshness of her words they're not said unkindly. "I hear tell you plan to leave again, to get your mother. Lirys said she's been put away, because of her mind."

"She has. And I do."

"Do you know where she is?"

"Tressalyn. I'm riding there."

"Via Tremayne? Funny route to take." Carys's look is shrewd.

"I have to do something first."

"So Lirys said. She also said she couldn't get it out of you. That you'd become secretive."

"It's not a secret," I lie. "I have to go somewhere before I can get Mama, that's all."

"Sounds like a fool's errand to me. You're lucky you made it this far without being hurt. I know you're no fair lady but it's still a great risk." I remember the feeling of fingers gripping my hair, how powerless I was in that moment. It makes me shiver. I didn't tell Lirys about it, and the look on Carys Dapplewood's face makes me glad.

"Fortune favours the bold." I smile weakly.

"So does death," she counters immediately. "The craven tend to live much longer than the heroic. You should stay here, go through the proper channels."

"I don't have time."

"Lirys said you'd say that." She sips her milk. "What will you do, once you've got Trina? Where will you go?"

"I have a plan."

"So did your brother," she says, silencing me. "I won't try to talk you out of it. I don't believe anyone ever talked a Vastel out of doing something stupid. But I will say this: you have a home here. No matter what trouble you're in, or how bad things are. We are your family; this is your home."

I nod, a lump in my throat, and she reaches over and pats my hand.

"The door will be open to you, Errin. It always has been. And we'll always be here. Now –" she brushes the sentimentality away with a shake of her hands "– they won't open the gates before dawn, so you're stuck here. But if you don't mind the company of an old woman, I'll stay with you."

"You're not old," I say automatically, but as I study her in the candlelight I see that she is. Lirys is a year older than me and Kirin; she's the same age as Lief. Carys and Idrys tried for twenty years to have a baby, so the story goes, but they weren't blessed. When it finally happened, Carys didn't believe it. Though her courses had stopped, she thought it was her natural time and that her thickening waist was another symptom. It wasn't until her waters broke that she realized she was having a baby at long last.

Now Carys is in her sixty-first harvest and her hair is streaked with greys and whites. The candlelight, so flattering to the young, draws out the shadows under her eyes and cheeks, plays in the lines that bracket her mouth and span out from the corners of her eyes. In my mind, she looks as she did when we were children – a little grey, a little careworn, but fierce, quick of tongue and temper, but the kindest woman you'd ever meet. I lift my tumbler and drink, and she does the same, yet I notice when she puts it down her hands remain slightly curled in on themselves.

When it's time to leave I have more milk, and chicken, bread and cheese, and apples for my horse, as well as half a plum pie. We debated whether to wake Lirys so I could say goodbye, but I fretted about the time, and Carys didn't push me.

As well as the food, she somehow got hold of new clothes for me. I'm now dressed in a neat blue tunic and better-fitting black breeches. I don't know whose they are and I don't care: they're not Unwin's, and I tell Carys to burn the old ones. In the hour before dawn, Carys neatened the edges of my hair, and she has also lent me her old winter cloak, a rich dark green lined with rabbit fur. With clean hair and clothes and, best of all, freshly forged papers claiming I'm

Erika Dapplewood, which Carys tucks into my pocket whilst tapping the side of her nose. I feel hopeful as I swing up on to my horse, who also looks refreshed.

"We'll see you soon, Errin," Carys calls softly from the doorway. "Promise me that."

"I promise," I say, turning the horse out of the yard and along the lane.

I let my eyes roam over sleeping Tremayne as I pass through. It looks so idyllic, safe and untouched. And I'm torn because I want very much to come back here and carry on with my life. But I don't know how I could, because of Mama. More than that, I don't know if I could after everything I've seen beyond the city walls.

That's the trouble with knowing things: you can't un-know them. Once you let yourself look at them, or say them aloud, they become real. I look ahead to the gates, noticing the guards are different this morning. They give my papers a cursory glance before allowing me to pass, and I glance back one last time at Tremayne, my heart torn as we exit the town.

I urge my horse to pick up the pace a little and then we ride, towards Scarron and the sea. I'll find the girl, and get my mother back. Then I'll make a decision.

Chapter 17

Scarron is a tiny, isolated fishing village that sits at the most north-westerly point of Tregellan, on the mouth of the estuary where the River Aurmere meets the sea. The river begins somewhere in the mountains; there are supposedly over a hundred waterfalls in them, made by the Aurmere rushing back to the sea. Rumours of pirate caves and hidden treasure abound; they even say there is a fountain of youth in there somewhere. I used to think it was a myth, but given the way stories are coming to life these days I might go and look for it if I ever get the chance.

Once the river has escaped the mountains, it runs between Tregellan and Tallith. Seventy miles long and getting wider and wider until it spills out and joins the sea. It's known for being rough, dangerous to cross, the currents violent and merciless. On clear days, you can see clean across the Aurmere to Tallith City, or what's left of it. The castle sat high on the cliff-side over the harbour and the ruins of its seven towers are still there, crumbling slowly into the sea below.

The people who live in Scarron are fisher-folk, and they are hardy, possibly the hardiest people in all of Tregellan – they have to be, to fish the waters there. Their skin is tanned by the wind, their faces lined prematurely, carved by salt and sea and air. Scarron is the kind of village people are born in and die in. Rarely does anyone leave. Still more rarely does a new face arrive. So unless the girl is in hiding, like Silas was, I should be able to find her easily; she'd be known as the "new one" for the next fifty years if she stayed here.

I've been to Scarron once before, with my mother, around eight years ago. She took Lief and me away from the farm for a few days, and it was here we came. We arrived after dark, so we didn't see the sea until the next morning when we raced from the inn to the beach. But we could smell it; all night long we could smell it, the briny, greenish air rushing in through the open windows. I dreamt strange dreams then, of a woman with fish scales and green skin smiling at me with a mouth full of pointed teeth, beckoning me into the water. I wanted so much to go to her. When I woke I was gasping for air as though I was drowning.

I loved Scarron. I loved its handful of wind-battered cottages in a higgledy-piggledy row along the harbour front. I loved the harbour master, a jolly man with a booming voice who was happy to show Lief and me how to tie knots, and bait lobster pots, and dig for mussels. Everything sparkled by the sea, everything was scoured clean by the wind and better for it. And it was so far from everything. It was completely itself, like Almwyk; practically a country of its own, except better, more honest and wholesome. I can see why the girl went there.

The landscape changes again as I ride further north, and I pull my cloak tighter around me to combat the colder air. The trees become sparser, more evergreens, bent from bracing against gales and storms. I stop every couple of hours to eat and drink and get the blood flowing in my hands and feet. I feed the horse her apples, and then a little of the cheese; I drink my milk and chew happily on the fresh bread Carys packed for me.

I alternate between riding and walking a mile or two to keep my muscles supple. After we pass through Toman, I stop seeing soldiers, and even the ones there don't demand to see my papers. The hamlets beyond Toman become progressively smaller, housing fifty, sixty souls, almost all farmers, not large enough to appear on my map. I ignore the curious stares of the villagers as I ride through. They seem unworried, untouched by what's happening to the south and east. I keep my eyes peeled for any sign of the army, but as in Tremayne everyone here seems unconcerned, and for some reason it makes me angry. Not much more than a hundred miles away, young men are being shot at in the woods. Refugees are being run off the roads, rounded up and dumped in hellish encampments. And war hasn't even truly begun. How can the people here stand it? Don't they know?

The edges of the sky turn gold, clouds like bruises against it, then the sky begins to darken. I dismount, walking slowly ahead of the horse, keeping us on the road. A few lights appear in the far distance and we plod towards them as the world turns blue, then purple, then black around us.

By the time we reach the outskirts of Scarron most of the lights have gone out and the hamlet is quiet. As in all fishing towns, most folk are in bed now, to be up in the very early hours to take their boats out to sea. With fear nibbling away at my confidence, I dismount and lead the horse through the small circle of cottages, the clopping of hooves the only sound in the night.

No, not the only sound. It's so natural I hadn't noticed as we'd approached, but all at once I can smell it, and then hear it. The sea: a distant rushing roar. Something in me fills with longing and I want to run to it. But I don't. I continue to walk, reasoning there will be time, not tonight but maybe in the days and weeks to come. With luck. With a lot of luck.

I don't know this girl's name. I don't know how old she is, or whether she's alone. I didn't think about whether there was an inn here; I didn't plan to need one, and I can see no one to ask. I can't even smell a tavern. It's as if the whole village has gone to sleep.

I lead the horse through the neat square, one ear cocked

for sounds of life, and then I hear something much sweeter to me: the familiar deep ring of iron meeting iron. I head towards it, a small shed near a tiny, leaning cottage a little way away from the rest, and tie the horse to the fence outside it. I knock on the door and then wait. The clanging continues. When it stops I knock again and then push the door open, to find myself staring into the twinkling eyes of a man whose face is entirely wrinkled. In one hand he holds a hammer, in the other a bent, rusty hook.

"You're not from here," he says, looking me up and down.

"No. I'm not. I'm looking for someone. She's—"

"The Lormerian girl?" he interrupts. "Dimia?"

The name sounds familiar. I bite back a smile of relief. "Yes. Dimia. Could you tell me where I might find her?"

He gives me a shrewd look. "You a relative?"

"Friend." It's not wholly a lie.

He looks me up and down, then shrugs. "She expecting you, then?"

"No."

"It's very late, dear. I don't reckon she'll want callers at this hour, and besides that, I can smell a storm brewing. Why don't you get along to the tavern and get yourself a room."

"I can't stay. I need to see her tonight. It's very important. It's about the war."

"The war?"

I stare at him. "In Lormere."

"I thought that ended years back."

"No, there's a new one. With the Sleeping Prince."

242

He shrugs again. "We don't know nothing about a war here, love."

"That's impossible," I say. "The Council have mustered an army; surely some of the men here have been drafted? There are checkpoints all along the King's Road, refugees, the city gates are closed at night in Tressalyn and Tremayne. Everyone in the east is in upheaval; there are soldiers everywhere. The Council must have sent word?"

"Ah, we don't bother that lot, and they don't bother us."

"But . . . what about when you take your fish to market? What about people who come here?"

"No one comes here, not at this time of year. And the nearest market is back in Toman. We stop going after harvest, bring back what we need for winter then; the road gets too treacherous when winter comes. We'll get the news in spring, I shouldn't wonder."

He sounds supremely unconcerned by everything I've said and anger starts to rise up again, red and pulsing. "Look, I really need to find Dimia tonight. It's more urgent than you know."

"There's a storm coming, love. You'll need to get indoors."

"Please. I'm begging you. Just tell me where she is."

He blinks at me, and then shakes his head in disappointment. "Walk back through the square and take a sharp left at the harbour. Follow it along until you see the path up to the cliff. Take that, and when it forks back inland, you'll see her cottage at the end of that track. You can't miss it, it's the only one out that way."

243

"Thank you." I nod and begin to close the door.

"Wait," he says, following me out. "You can't take that horse up that way. It's too narrow."

"Is there somewhere I can leave her?"

He thinks. "May as well leave her here. She'll be safe enough in the lean-to out back, out of the storm. I'll lead her round, soon as I'm done here."

I look at the horse, then at him, weighing it up. "Thank you," I say finally. "I'll be back for her soon."

"No hurry," he says. "You got a lantern?"

"No."

"There," he says, gesturing at an oil lamp hanging on the wall. "Take that." I lift it down carefully.

"Thank you."

"No need for that. Any friend of Dimia's is welcome here. You be careful. That storm'll come in fast and angry. Watch your step." With that he turns back to his hook, and I leave him to it.

Following his directions, I walk into the tiny village square. I count nine cottages around the well, with the blacksmith's cottage down the path, the row of five along the harbour front, and Dimia's. There is no House of Justice, no inn, one small store, which is clearly someone's home as well. Is it possible no one here knows about the Sleeping Prince? Is it really true that no message has been sent, that they've been overlooked, or forgotten? I think about it all the way along the cliff path, listening to the sea beat against the rock below me, watching the storm clouds roll in and obliterate the stars.

I pick up the pace before they can cover the moon, turning right at the fork, heading back inland.

The cottage appears quite unexpectedly, looming out of the darkness. It has no upstairs, but is large. I count two windows on either side of the door, more along the sides. I put my lantern down behind me and stare at one of the ones at the front, trying to make out any light around the edges of it. Then – yes – there. A slim orange bar running down part of the wall.

I push my hood back and smooth my hair, regretting that I didn't go into the inn and at least wash my face. Too late now, I decide, pushing open the small wooden gate and making my way through the bare garden. A spot of rain lands on my nose, then my cheek. I hope she's feeling hospitable.

I brush down my dress and then, taking a deep breath, I knock at the door.

Chapter 18

The door flies open, and a girl stands there, silhouetted against the light from the room. She glances at me, then does a double take, looking at me again with narrowed eyes before peering over my shoulder into the night. And I look at her.

Long black hair. Green eyes.

She's not an alchemist. She can't be the one who makes the Elixir.

She peers back at me, frowning, seeming just as confused and disappointed as I am.

"Who are you?" she asks.

"My name is Errin. Errin Vastel."

Her lips part, a strange look crossing her face. "Did someone send you here?" Her tone is brittle, crystalline. Her eyes bore into mine as she waits for my answer.

"No. Sorry." I pause, trying to collect my thoughts. "Are you Dimia?"

She stills, and hope rises in me that perhaps she isn't. "Yes," she says quietly. "I'm Dimia."

"Oh." I can't disguise the sting of disappointment that pierces me, and she raises her eyebrows at me before glancing back into her home. "Wait – are you alone?"

"Am I what?" Her eyes narrow again as they return to me.

"Do you live alone?"

"What kind of question is that?"

"Sorry, I don't mean . . . I'm looking for someone." Dimia's face remains warily puzzled, and my heart sinks. "I can see you're not her," I say.

She shakes her head slowly. "No. I don't believe I am."

"It's just . . . I spoke to a man in town and he said the Lormerian girl lived here."

She hesitates. "I'm from Lormere."

"And if I said 'the Sisters' or 'the Conclave' to you, would it mean anything?" She shakes her head. "Are there are no other Lormerians here in Scarron?" I try.

Another shake of the head.

My eyes sting as tears of frustration prick at them. I should have known. I should have realized, even if she was here she'd be hiding, like Silas was. Not living in a cottage, known to everyone. It was far too easy, to be simply told she was here by the old ironworker. Unless... Silas said that normal people live with the alchemists. Could this girl be lying to protect the philtresmith? Some kind of servant, or

247

cover. "Are you sure?" I say urgently. "Are you sure you're alone? Are you sure you don't know what I'm talking about?"

The look she gives me could freeze water. "I'm not a liar."

"I see," I say. "Well, if you happen upon someone who does know what I mean, tell her to find me in the tavern. She's in danger. The Sleeping Prince is after her."

I'm not prepared for her reaction. "What? What did you say?" she demands. She clutches the door frame. Already pallid in the lantern light, she pales so much the freckles on her nose, cheeks and forehead stand out in sharp relief. "Where is he? Does he go to Lormere? Is he there already?"

I nod, watching her carefully. "He sits on the throne of Lormere. He has done for three moons."

"No. . ." Her voice is jagged.

"The whole of Tregellan is braced for war," I continue. "There are soldiers in all of the main towns, checkpoints on the roads and city gates. People are dying in Lormere. Hundreds of them. He's targeting the religious in the hope of finding the Sisters. And the girl."

"I told you, I don't know what that means. I don't know any Sisters. I've been here since before harvest—" She stares beyond me, into the night. A flash of lightning makes both of us jump, bringing her back to herself. "Three moons," she says. I can barely hear her words over the growl of thunder that rolls across the sky. "What of the queen? Has she allied with the Sleeping Prince? What news of the prince – the king – of Lormere? Does he hide? Is he rallying his men? Are they fighting? Is he in this Conclave?"

"He's dead. The king is dead. He was killed the night Lormere fell."

"Liar." Dimia looks at me, her eyes burning into mine.

I'm about to rage at her when I realize that she's not being rude. She's begging me. "I'm so sorry," I whisper. I know what real grief looks like.

She closes her eyes. Her hands clutch her arms as though she's holding herself together. Then she turns from me, walking into her house, leaving the door open. She crosses to the fireside and picks up a goblet, draining the contents. I watch as she refills it.

"You'd better come in," she says thickly.

As soon as the words have left her mouth the heavens open, so I do, entering her small, neat cottage and closing the door behind me. When I turn back to her, her shoulders are shaking and, without thinking, I cross the room and put my hand on her arm.

She jumps as if I'd stabbed her, spinning away from me with her hand extended, her face horrified beneath the tear stains.

"I'm sorry," I stutter, holding my hands up to show I meant no harm.

A sudden loud tapping makes us both turn around; the rain has become hail and is lashing the windows, leaving streaks across the thick, greenish glass. The room lights up again, thunder rumbles, and I shiver. She turns away, leaning against the mantel, and I take the chance to look around the room. One goblet, one armchair, a book left face down on the seat; she was reading when I arrived. The doors to the other rooms are open; from where I stand I can see a small kitchen, and a bedroom, a patchwork blanket over a narrow bed. I move as though to peer out of the window and see the last room stands empty. There's nowhere for anyone to hide. No one else lives here. Just Dimia, and she doesn't have the Godseye, or the moon hair. She's telling the truth. I walk back to her.

"I know it doesn't mean much, coming from a Tregellian, but I liked your king," I say softly. "I saw him where he came here."

"Merek liked Tregellan. He had plans to introduce some of your ways in Lormere."

For a moment her words puzzle me, and then I realize why. People don't usually refer to their sovereigns by name.

"Did you know him?"

She turns to me. "Briefly." Her cheeks flush pink and she stares into the distance. "I worked at the castle for a while. He was kind to me."

"He looked like he'd be a good king."

She nods, her face crumpling again. "He would have been," she whispers, tears making silvery tracks down her face. "Forgive me." She takes a deep, shuddering breath and closes her eyes. When she opens them they fix on mine. "Tell me everything. What else do I not know of what's happening in Lormere? You said he was hunting the religious."

As I reel off the litany of the Sleeping Prince's crimes, her face becomes more ashen, her posture more slumped.

Lortune, Haga, Monkham. The Bringer turned Silver Knight and the sacking of the temples, the heads on spikes, the hearts on display. The slaughter of the religious, the burning of the food stores. The golems.

Then I tell her about the refugee camps. The people on the roads. The soldiers and their brutality. I feel sick as I recount it, my mind returning to that abandoned doll, that single shoe. Now I think I know why someone would leave a shoe behind.

When I'm finished she drains her goblet in one, her eyes blurring with tears again. "And what is the Council of Tregellan doing to help Lormere?"

"What do you mean?"

"What aid have they offered? Men for an army? Weapons? Food? Medical supplies?"

I shake my head. "The army we have is new; it's conscripted. The men weren't given a choice, they were told to fight, and most are still being trained. Women may have to fight as well, if it comes to it. As for food and medicine, we didn't. . ." She stares at me and I feel my skin redden again. "But some people did escape, as I said. The camps—"

"Camps you described as 'hellholes'?" she interrupts me, and I fall silent. "The Sleeping Prince is killing innocents, and your people have closed their borders. Mighty Tregellan, that is so democratic and civilized, turns a blind eye to the murder of a king and his people. Instead it looks to its own house until the blood splashes its doorstep? Because of the last war, I take it. Because we deserve it, for winning then?"

251

"No, of course not." But even as I protest, I wonder if she's right. Why didn't we act earlier? Why didn't we offer more help? I don't say it aloud, though. "No one was ready for this. The Council has been trying to negotiate with him."

"You can't negotiate with monsters," Dimia says flatly. "Believe me. You can only act."

Suddenly I feel deeply ashamed of my country. I shake my head, unable to meet her eye. "I'm sorry to be the bearer of such bad tidings."

"And I'm sorry I'm not who you were looking for."

We both lapse into silence, and I listen to the rain beating down. It's going to be a miserable walk back to the town. "I'd better go," I say eventually, reluctant to leave the warmth of her cottage.

She looks at me. "You'd do better to stay. It's vile out there. You'll be blown into the sea before you've left my garden."

"That's too. . . You don't know me. I could be anyone."

"So could I. We're even. Sit," she says, nodding to a chair by the fire.

Because I have nowhere else to go, and because I'm tired, and because I'm at the end of my tether, I do, lifting her book and placing it over the arm. She refills her glass and holds it to me, and I take it, sipping the contents. Wine, rich and red, tasting of smoke and dark berries, coats my tongue. I take another sip and hold it out to her, but she waves her hand, so I keep it, cupping it in my palms.

"Why don't you tell me why you're looking for a girl from

Lormere," she says finally. "You said she was in danger. Why?"

It feels treasonous to talk of it with a Lormerian, but it's not as if she can tell the king what I've said. "She's not just a girl. She's an alchemist. That's why."

"There are no alchemists in Lormere."

"That's what everyone thinks. But there are. They have their own kind of Conclave, hidden from the royals." When she frowns I explain. "The Conclave is where Tregellian alchemists live. It's hidden. Secret. The Lormerians did the same thing, except instead of hiding, they disguised their version as a religious order. They hid in plain sight."

"Are you an alchemist?"

"No."

"Then why do you need to find her?"

"I was hoping she could help me. That we could help each other." Dimia looks puzzled. "I'm in some trouble," I add.

"What kind?"

I take another drink of wine, enjoying its warmth. Then I explain, as best I can, about the threat of evacuation, and Mama's illness, though I don't mention the beast. Then I tell her how Silas gave me a potion that seemed to heal her, but when he wouldn't give me more I withheld the girl's whereabouts until he agreed to help.

She raises her eyebrows, leaning against the mantel. "You blackmailed him?"

"No. It wasn't like that. He said he'd help, and that he didn't blame me for trying it. I believed him, and ... and I told him she was here." I pause. "He betrayed me. He waited until I went home to get my mother and our things, and he left without me."

She holds her hand out for the goblet and I pass it to her. "So, he's on his way here too, I take it. To find a girl who isn't."

"I expect so. I don't know which of us will be more disappointed. No offence meant."

She shrugs. "Where is your mother now?"

"She's in an asylum," I say quietly. "While I was with Silas, soldiers came and took her away. And they found... Someone died in our cottage. I didn't kill him," I hasten to reassure her when her eyes widen. "A man was attacked in the woods near the cottage and Silas brought him to me. I was an apothecary apprentice, so he hoped I could save him. I tried, but he died, just after he told me the girl was here. I had to run. So I decided if I could find the girl alone, I could tell her she needed to go to the Conclave and escort her there. I hoped the alchemists would be grateful enough to help me in return."

Dimia offers the goblet to me again and I drink. "Except she's not here. What will you do now?"

I lick the wine from my lips. "I need to get my mother back. They think she's depressed, and grieving, but it's not that, it's bigger than that, and if I don't get her out... She's all I have," I say, my voice breaking. "I've lost my father, our home, my apprenticeship, and my brother this year. I can't lose her too."

Dimia's jaw drops, her mouth hanging open. I can see the

pulse fluttering in her throat as she tries to contain herself. "You lost your brother? Lief?"

I look up at her, stunned. "Did you know him too?" I stare at her. "Did you meet him at the castle?"

"Yes," she says, her voice sounding far away, her forehead drawn into a frown. "Is he..."

I nod, and her hands rise to cover her face, her back bent as though the weight of the world presses on her.

Mama, Lirys, Carys, Dimia. All these people who grieve for my brother.

I'm surprised I have any tears left after last night, but it seems I do.

"I'm sorry," I say when they've stopped, my breath still coming in shuddery gasps.

She has already composed herself and stands stiffly by the fireplace, her expression strained. "Don't be."

"That's why I have to get my mother back. We're all the other has now."

"And he wouldn't have left you," Dimia says softly. "Not if he could help it." When I look up at her, she smiles briefly. "What little I knew of your brother, I know he loved you. And your mother."

I can't look at her. "Thank you." The goblet appears before me and I take it gratefully.

"What if I could help you instead?" she says suddenly. "What will you give me in return?"

The words fall from her mouth so quickly it's as if they've escaped, rather than been spoken. "What?"

"You said you were training to be an apothecary?"

"I was. I'm not licensed, but I'm good. I can make cures. I can make poisons." Her eyebrows shoot up at this and I shrug. "I had to," I say.

"Good. I can use that."

"Use it how?"

"When I fight the Sleeping Prince."

I look her up and down. She looks like a baby deer, all thin limbs and wide eyes. She looks as though she'd snap in a high wind. "*You* plan to fight him?"

She pauses, apparently giving the question real thought. "Yes," she says. "I do. Someone has to. Your people won't, unless he brings the war to you. Merek is dead. If not me, then who? Besides, he won't be the first monster I've faced."

"What do you mean? What monsters have you fought?"

She ignores my questions, looking instead to the window. "We won't get out of here tonight. The track will be too dangerous."

"We?" I ask hesitantly.

She nods. "I told you, I'll help you if you return the favour. Be my apothecary. Make cures that will heal the soldiers I muster. Make poisons we can use on his people – on this Silver Knight and the traitors that follow him."

I stare at her. Who is she? How could she muster people? How could she save the Lormerians? How can she help me? "Your people? How are they your people?"

"The people of Lormere." She waves her hand. "My countrymen. Seeing as yours won't do anything to aid them,

I will. For Merek. And your brother. I'll rally whoever I can in Lormere, and anyone else who's willing, and I'll find a way to fight him." In the glow of the fire there is something regal about her, something in her eyes like iron. She means it.

"Do you know how to fight a war?"

"No," she says, flushing in the firelight. "No. I don't. But I'll find people who do. And I'll have you. Maybe all it will take will be poison in his wine goblet, like in the story. Isn't that how he became the Sleeping Prince, in your stories – your histories?"

I nod, frowning.

"Good. It's a start. So, what would you need from me, to complete my end of the bargain?

I take a deep breath. "I need to get my mother out of the asylum in Tressalyn, and I need to get her somewhere safe. And isolated. I need to get the potion for her." I pause. "And I need to stay away from the Tregellian army for a while."

She blinks rapidly. "I can't help you with the potion. But I think I can help you get her back." She walks over to the mantelpiece and reaches into the chimney. I hear the chinking of coins before she draws the bag into view. It's fat with coins, bulging. A king's ransom. "I'm assuming I'll be able to persuade someone to release her into the care of her dear long-lost cousin?" I nod, dumbstruck. "Good," she continues. "As for isolated, this cottage is quite apart. And it's by the sea. I imagine that's useful for healing."

My eyes widen. "You'd let us live here? In your cottage?"

"I doubt I'll be using it while I'm at war. We're quite far

from Lormere here." She smiles wryly. "You could use the kitchen as a workroom to create the poisons and healing potions I'll need, whilst you care for your mother. Of course, once the battles begin I'll need you a lot closer to our base camp. But that's some time away yet. I'll need time to find and organize my people. If she's not better by the time we need to fight, you can engage a nurse for her while you're gone. You won't be out on the field, so you needn't worry about that."

"She won't be better. She won't ever get better. Her illness is very unusual. If anyone found out what it was. . ."

Dimia hefts the bag so it clinks again. "I'm sure we could find someone discreet enough for the task. You'd be surprised, I think, what people will do for money." She looks at me, her eyes searching mine. "Or perhaps not. What do you say? Do we have an agreement?"

"Why?" I ask. "Why would you do this? I'm a stranger to you; why would you do this for me?"

She opens her mouth, staring beyond me to the rain lashing against the window. "Because you remind me a little of myself."

Then I turn to the rain too, watching it slide down the windowpane. "What did you do, at the castle?" I ask.

Her eyes slide to the side. "I served. I was a servant."

I'm about to ask for specifics when I stop myself, the pieces slotting into place in my mind. A servant who calls the king by his given name. A servant with a bulging bag of coin. A servant confident she has sway over men, enough to call them to muster. To inspire them to fight. I think I understand now. I remember the knowing look on the soldiers' faces when Kirin said I was a camp follower. I deliberately don't think about her knowing my brother.

"Errin," she says softly, and I look at her. Her face is solemn. "It won't stop. The Sleeping Prince won't stop at Lormere. Your Council knows that. He'll come here next. And he'll do to the people of Tregellan what he's done to mine. Your people slaughtered. Your people's heads mounted atop poles. Your people running." She puts her goblet down and crosses the room, pausing before she reaches for my hands.

"I'm not saying I can beat him. I know the odds, and as you said, he has golems, as well as his human forces. But I have to try. If I can get word to Lormere that they have reason to hope, and fight... You know, in the last war, they were losing against your people. And then ... they rallied. They were given cause to hope and it made them fight harder. I would give them that. Help me do it. And I'll help you."

Kirin said Lormere's greatest weakness was that they didn't try to fight back. And now here is this girl, this Lormerian servant who wants to make it happen. Who believes that she can.

I pull my hands from hers and stand, moving past her to the window. I press my forehead against the cool glass, watching as new drops of rain merge with older ones until they become tiny rivers that run down the pane. Flashes of lightning illuminate the horizon; I can see where the cliffs must begin. Where the land ends.

The philtresmith isn't here, and without her, I have no chance of finding the Conclave or getting the Elixir. Perhaps she was never here at all; maybe Ely was wrong, delirious with pain. How could I be sure he knew what he was saying? The only way I'll know for certain is if Silas shows up, looking for her – and then what? Do I try to follow him, reason with him, beg him again? I huff quietly, my breath fogging the pane as I imagine it. No. That bridge is well and truly burned. The one thing I'm certain of is that I have to get Mama back; she's all I have. She's my responsibility.

I try and sort through it all, taking quiet, deep breaths as the minutes pass, each one like a decade. What choice do I have?

"Well?" Dimia says behind me. "Will you join me?"

I turn to face her. "You'll help me keep my mother safe? No matter what you hear about her?"

Her eyes narrow briefly, but she nods. "I swear."

"Yes, then. I'll be your apothecary."

A dark look crosses her face. "I need you to swear it too, Errin Vastel. No blackmail, no double-crossing, no betrayal."

I blush and hold out my hand. "I swear it. I won't betray you. I just want to keep my mother safe."

Her eyes bore into mine for what feels like an age. Then she nods, clasping my hand between both of hers. "And so it is done." Her words send a thrill through me, as though someone has walked over my grave. "Thank you. Tomorrow, we'll leave, go to Tressalyn straight away. I'll buy your mother's freedom and then we'll bring her back here. But for now we should get some rest," she says. "There is another room that could be used for sleeping, though it's presently unfurnished. I'm afraid I'm not used to living with so much space. Before we leave tomorrow I'll engage a carpenter to see to it for when we return with your mother. But tonight you're welcome to take my bed."

I shake my head. She doesn't insist; instead she gathers blankets and cushions, trying to make a kind of bed.

"Goodnight, then," she says, pausing in the doorway to what I assume is her bedroom. She looks as if she might speak, then closes the door firmly. I shed my cloak and bed down in the pile of blankets she's created for me. In my new home. And I think that out of all of the absolutely impossible things to have happened to me in the past week, this is the strangest.

In the dream I'm dressed in armour, and part of me knows that it's because of the promise I made to Dimia. I look down at myself, at the cuirass covering my chest, the vambraces on my arms. I know it should be heavy, but it's not, and I swing my arms, raising them as though I'm holding a sword.

"What's this?"

The man is standing behind me in the doorway, his mouth a pout, his eyes covered by his hood.

"I beat you here," I say. "I'm with Dimia."

"Dimia?" He smiles.

"She's not the philtresmith. The girl you want isn't here."

"Really?" His tone is careful.

"Well, if she is, she's hiding from us."

"Clever girl. And now what will you do, with this Dimia?"

"Rescue my mother. Then we're going to war."

"With me?"

"With the Sleeping Prince. I'm going to help her."

The smile falls from his face. "Are you?"

I nod.

"That changes things," he says slowly. "That changes things a lot."

Chapter 19

It feels as though I've barely closed my eyes when she shakes me awake the next morning. She's already dressed, her hair loose around her shoulders. I sit up blearily, moaning at the sharp pains in my thighs and lower back, and reach for the cup she holds out to me.

"What time is it?" I ask.

"An hour before dawn, by the light," she says, picking up a bag and reaching for her cloak. "I have to go into the village before we leave."

I watch her as I rise and tidy myself. She walks around the room, touching everything, stroking the back of the chair, tapping the tabletop lightly and running a finger over the spines of her few books. There's a ritual to it. It's as though she's saying farewell, and it makes me shudder. We'll be coming back here, she said so.

Unless she thinks she might not.

Finally she turns to me. "Let's go."

We make our way along the boggy cliff path towards the town using the old man's lantern. As I scramble to keep up with her I feel ungainly and childlike. She's smaller than me, but she carries herself as though she were much taller, her head held straight, her shoulders back, hair flowing over her shoulders, black as a raven's wing.

When we get to town, every house is ablaze with light, the shop too, even though dawn is still an hour away. The fishermen are long gone and their women are up and about, fetching water, gossiping with neighbours, swapping food and stories in the tiny square. They all stop and turn when they see Dimia's light, smiling and waving to her.

The small crowd parts as she approaches, as though she's a ship on the ocean and they are the waves. Everyone greets her and she speaks to the carpenter, a seamstress, and the grocer, all of whom defer to her as though she's a queen. I trail in her wake back to the blacksmith's cottage to collect my horse, not surprised at all when he gives her a funny little bow. A few swift words and he's soon leading a fat-bellied pony around for her, saddled and bridled.

"Not as fine as the horse," he says, linking his hands to help her mount. She gives a delicate shrug, and, in a motion more graceful than I'd expected, puts a foot in the stirrup and swings into the saddle. She looks surprised, then pleased, arranging her skirts around her.

"You take care of her, miss," he says to me. "She's one of us now."

"I can take care of myself, Javik." She smiles, and he beams back, showing gappy teeth and red gums, bowing as he backs away.

"So, how far to Tressalyn?" Dimia says, adjusting her stirrups before turning to me.

"We have to follow the river road towards Tremayne, though we don't have to go through it. If we go around it, we can take the King's Road south."

"How long will it take?"

"A day or two."

"And where will we sleep? I can hardly arrive in Tressalyn and plead for your mother's release if I look as though I can't care for myself."

"Do you have papers?" I ask.

She taps her pocket. "And coin for food and lodging."

I don't want to stay in Tremayne. "We'll see how far we get and then make a plan. There are villages and roadside inns on the way. I have a map."

For some reason, she almost smiles. "You'd better lead on, then."

After eight solid hours of moving, swapping between riding and walking, my back aches, my thighs ache and my arms ache. My head aches. Dimia's face is white and pinched and her knuckles are bloodless where she grips the reins, but as long as she doesn't complain I won't either. Instead we plough on, passing mile after mile of purple and brown heathland, skirting around small woodlands and the odd isolated cottage and farm. The sky at the horizon is orange, the wind is behind us, driving us forward, there's a fog rolling in fast, and my heart lifts because we cannot be too far from Tremayne now, perhaps three miles at most.

I'm dozing in the saddle, rocked back and forth by the rolling gait of the horse, when Dimia's voice cuts through my reverie.

"What's that?" she asks, a bite to her voice that has me whipping around in the saddle. Then I see what she's looking at and my stomach swoops. I grip the reins tightly.

"It's a graveyard," I say finally.

"Where the dead are buried? Can we stop a little?"

"We don't have time," I say swiftly.

"Just a few moments. I've never seen one before."

"Do you not have memorials for your dead?"

"No. They're burned. The royal family and the lords have family vaults that they can visit."

"Are the ashes kept in them?"

"No." She looks perplexed. "They're rooms for contemplation. They're places for the families to go to remember."

"What about the, erm, common folk?"

"They don't have the luxury of remembrance."

They. They don't. Without further comment I lead my horse over and she follows. We both dismount and tie up our horses. Dimia runs her hands over the wood of the entrance to the graveyard, looking up at the roof, then down at the recessed wooden benches in the sides of the gate.

"Pretty," she says.

"It's a lichgate," I tell her, unsurprised when she frowns. "A corpse gate. When they bring the dead to be buried they carry them in here, head first. The priest says a blessing and then they turn the coffin feet first and carry it into the graveyard while someone rings the lichbell."

"Why?"

"To confuse the spirit so it doesn't try to follow the living back out." It's an old superstition. She nods and walks through the gate into the graveyard proper. My insides writhing, I take a deep breath and follow her.

Dimia walks ahead of me, her head turning left to right and back again as she takes it all in. I notice she keeps strictly to the path. Once, when I was little, we came to leave flowers on my grandmother's grave, and I'd been delighted by the mounds of loamy earth, running up and down them, chanting that I was the queen of the molehills. My mother had smacked my legs and yanked me back to her side, her skin reddening with mortification. I hadn't known they were fresh graves; I hadn't really known what a grave was. The memory, though macabre, makes me smile. Mama would approve of Dimia's careful tread.

She pauses every now and then to read the inscriptions on the gravestones. She seems to stop especially at the ones for children, her mouth moving silently as she reads, before moving on.

"It's eerie, isn't it, to know that beneath us there are bones shifting and resting." Her voice has a strange, heavy quality to it and in the oncoming twilight it makes me shiver. I look back to the lichgate to reassure myself the horses are still there. "All lined up, like crops, almost," she continues. "A field of the dead." She looks over to where the first row of mausoleums stand, leaning precariously against one another. "How strange to build monuments to house corpses."

I blink in shock. "It's a monument to their lives, not their bodies. It might seem strange to you, but it seems stranger to me that you burn your bodies. Burn the arms of the mothers that held you. Burn the lips of the fathers that kissed your brow when you cried. You destroy the bodies that gave you life. We give them back to the earth. We treat our dead with respect."

She whirls around to face me. "You know nothing of death."

"I know enough," I snap, forgetting that she holds the keys to getting my mother back. "I've seen it. I've smelt it. I've tried to fight it. What more do I need to know?" My eyes drift towards the row of vaults along the far wall and she follows my gaze. She nods, as if remembering something. Then she turns around and carries on walking.

I follow, my nerves jangling, as she continues on her tour of Tremayne's dead. Every so often we pass a grave with a circle on it, a line across the centre of it. The symbol bothers me, because I've seen it somewhere recently, and then I remember: it was carved into the salt merchant's door in Tremayne.

I pause in front of one of the graves with the symbol on it and pick absently at a blackberry bush snarling out from beside it, piling the last of the fruit in my hand. I know it means something else but I can't quite catch the memory.

Without meaning to – or perhaps I meant to all along – I've wandered to the west side of the cemetery. Here the vaults are of tall, grey stone with the family name carved across the top. A field of the dead, she called it. In this part of the cemetery the description is accurate, I'll give her that. They're like little houses; some have windows, and some have altars inside with shelves for offerings. Almost all have oak leaves or holly leaves, sometimes both, carved across the lintels, a superstitious throwback to the old gods and old ways. The tombs here are well kept, none of the stones are broken, and from the corner of my eye I watch Dimia stare at them all, occasionally trailing a long finger across the carved leaves.

The fog has rolled in now, bringing the scent of smoke from the villagers' fires with it. My hand has folded into a fist, crushing the blackberries so the purple juice runs out between my fingers. My eyes shift to the right and my heart begins to race.

Our tomb is right there, perhaps ten or twelve feet away. The door carved with the names of my grandparents, great-grandparents.

And my father.

I turn from it and gaze at the monument behind me, a winged angel asleep on a stone bed, the crossed circle carved into it: the final resting place of Jephrys Mulligan. I try to concentrate on the dates and words as my stomach churns, willing myself not succumb to panic. Dimia passes behind me, her eyes still fixed on the vaults, and I count to ten in my mind.

I've reached seven when she gasps and I turn slowly to her.

She's staring up at the tomb. Her hand is still outstretched, but frozen in the air. Her mouth moves silently as she runs through the names written there.

"Lief Vastel," she says aloud.

"My grandfather. My father's father. My brother was named for him."

I walk towards the tomb, every footstep like walking through swampland, the effort to lift my legs painful. And there it is: Azra Vastel. My father. His name is carved into the door below that of his mother, who died ten moons before I was born. The words already have a faded, old look to them, as though they've been there for much longer than six moons. I step past Dimia and grip the iron handle. It sticks for a moment, then gives, and the musty smell of the tomb flows out and mingles with the smoky air.

I step inside, waiting for my eyes to adjust to the scant light coming from the dirty windows. I begin to make out the shapes of stone plaques on the walls, the names carved on them matching those on the door. There are blank ones, for me, for my mother, for any children that follow. I realize with a sharp pain beneath my ribs that one of the plaques will have to be inscribed for Lief. He won't have a coffin though. He won't lie here, turning to dust with the rest of his family, given back to nature. He might have been burned, like a Lormerian. Or worse.

I take a deep breath, holding it in my lungs and then exhaling so hard that dust motes swirl around me.

The air shifts; Dimia has followed me in. I turn and she gives me a look of heartbreaking pity. I blink, confused by her concern, until a tear lands on my hand. I'm crying again. Quietly, as though I'm a wild animal and she's afraid I'll bite her, she steps towards me and raises her arms. It's she who stiffens as she wraps them around me, holding me rigidly as if she's not quite sure what to do. The awkwardness of it reminds me of Silas. I pull away from her and she steps back immediately.

"I'm sorry," she says, and I don't know if she's apologizing for my loss or her embrace.

"It's the first time I've been here," I say, my voice echoing strangely off the stone.

She looks around the inside of the vault, taking in the plaques, the small, bare altar, the stone shelf that doubles as a seat. "That's why you didn't want to come. You should have said."

"Is this what your vaults are like? For your nobles?" I ask her.

"No. They're not like this." She shakes her head curtly,

and instantly my upper lip curls in anger. "They're ... cold," she says quickly. "This is simpler, but real. The nobles' vaults have carved effigies of the dead in them. Faces, hands, all picked out in marble. More museum than mausoleum." She smiles wryly. "It's not a place you'd go to grieve. It's a place you'd go to be cowed. They make you feel small, but this ... this is supposed to make you feel as though you're part of something."

She nods to herself in her strange way and steps out of the tomb, leaving me alone with my family. I step forward to touch my father's plaque when she appears in the doorway again.

"The horses are fretting," she says. "And the smell of smoke seems stronger. I think something nearby is burning."

I follow her out. The wind has changed direction, and the faint smell of smoke is now powerful, blowing into our faces, thick and sharp. The sky is darkening, the night swooping in, in the swift, without-warning way it does in autumn. Already out, the moon is newly waning, just losing its fullness, and blue smoke passes over it, trailing a line across it, and the image nags at me.

"We should go." I shake off the irritation. "It'll be dark soon."

"Where are we going to shelter tonight?"

Apprehension tightens my belly, but we have little choice. "Tremayne is closest, two miles, if you want an inn."

"Where the alchemist house is."

"Where I was born, too. And Lief." She doesn't reply. "They close the city gates at sundown."

Dimia looks up to where the sky is starting to turn dark around the edges, like ink bleeding across paper. "We should hurry, then."

We stumble in the growing darkness back to the horses, which are fretting, whickering softly to us as we untie them. We ride out, past the silent graveyard, cantering into the night, the smell of smoke getting ever stronger. Half a mile outside the town walls, we find the source of the fire. There, smouldering crimson and orange in the darkness, is what remains of one of the harvest stores built on the outskirts of the village. The barns where the hay harvests were stored over winter, the lofts filled with apples and pears. Byres and sheep houses and stables where cattle and sheep were sheltered when the snows arrived. Burned to the ground. The air is thick with smoke, the smell of burnt hay and corn. Of roasted meat. My throat catches when I think of the animals that would have been caught inside their barns, frightened and trapped.

Dimia is looking at me with some curiosity. "Do you know who owns it?" she asks.

"The Prythewells. Friends of my father's. They kept sheep and cows for eating. That'll be all their food and income for the winter." I shake my head at the loss.

"It looks as though there is nothing to be done."

I frown at the remains of the buildings. The ruins still smoulder. Surely someone should be here, trying to put them out? If the wind blew hot cinders into the village and they caught in a thatch, then the fire could easily spread, passing through Tremayne like a plague. Where are the people? Where are the soldiers? Shouldn't someone, anyone, be here, salvaging, or even looting?

I turn towards Tremayne as a cold, stark fear begins to bloom inside me. I kick the horse straight into a gallop; I can hear Dimia's pony pounding the dirt behind me. The smell of smoke becomes stronger and the ears of the horse flatten against her head as she stops, despite my urging. She skitters sideways and refuses to move, weaving across the track. Dimia's pony pulls ahead of me. Dimia clings to its neck as it rears, its whinny more of a scream. The whites of its eyes are visible as it tries to throw her.

I dismount to help her, but as soon as I'm down my horse bolts, back the way we came. I stare after her in horror. Then Dimia whimpers and I turn to see her pony rushing back towards me, running after mine. As he passes I reach out and grab his reins long enough for Dimia to slide from his back. Then he's gone too, leaving my fingers red and stinging, burned from the leather whipping across my skin.

Dimia leans against a tree, pale and shaking. "What's wrong with them?"

"I've no idea," I say, though it's not wholly true. My horse was an army mount, trained to fight. Whatever it's running from must be terrifying. And unnatural.

"What do we do now?"

"Find out what's going on," I say with a lot more courage than I feel. I pull my knife out from my belt.

*

We find the first body lying inside the gate, his legs bent at a funny angle, his throat slit. His blood is dark and thick-looking, not fresh. Tuck, the meaner one, has been impaled, his sword pinioning him to the walls he was supposed to guard. When Dimia moans I turn and follow her gaze. The soldier who lied to get me through the gate, the one who winked at me, is hanging over the top of the tower gate wall. One eye is open, blue and staring. The other is home to an arrow, and I turn away, praying that it wasn't one of his own and that it was fast. I didn't know his name.

Dimia slides her hand into mine and I grip it tightly as we enter, stepping gingerly around the fallen men. Ahead of us, inside the walls of Tregellan's second city, fires burn. We walk slowly through the merchant quarter, tunics pulled up over our noses and mouths, eyes streaming from the smoke. The light from the fire is enough to see the devastation as we approach the main square.

Everything is gone. Every shop – the baker's, the chandler's, the general store – all black shells, acrid smoke pouring from them. The apothecary is a wreck, the windows gaping like missing teeth, the door vanished, the insides dark and cave-like. The House of Justice is smouldering rubble, the golden bricks charred and shattered, glass reflecting the remaining flames. The village green is torn up; brown earth scores the turf like scars.

People lie prone in the debris, arms flung out, feet disappearing into piles of stone. The angles of their bodies tell me there's no use in seeing if I can help, for no one who falls in that way will ever rise again. What was it Carys said – death favours the bold? Death has favoured everyone here equally. The green tunics of the soldiers, stripped of their weapons, the rough wool in red and blues of the people who lived here. My friends. My neighbours. I'm scared to look at the faces, turning away before recognition can punch me in the stomach. Dimia squeezes my hand, and when I look at her, tears are clearing a path through the soot on her cheeks.

We walk silently through the square and out towards the smith and masonry quarter. I strain for the sound of voices, hoping desperately someone has been left alive here. We walk past houses that have been gutted, doors torn from their frames, windows smashed on upper and lower levels. Belongings are strewn about the place, as though a giant has come in and picked up the houses, shaking them out before tossing them to the floor. Copper pots, broken pottery, bedding, wooden stools, all smashed, or dented, or crushed underfoot; nothing has been left whole, everything has been ripped out and destroyed with a deliberateness that makes me feel sick.

I peer into the house where Kirin used to live. When I see a shadow lying inside, I turn away, covering my mouth.

"Do you know any of them?" Dimia asks quietly. "Are any of your people here?"

My eyes widen and I drop her hand, taking off at a run, tripping over the possessions that litter the ground. I feel the flesh on my left knee split open and stones embed themselves in my palms but I don't care. I force myself back to my feet, hobbling past the tavern, its shell still echoing with pops and cracks as forgotten caches of alcohol catch alight. My lungs burn from the smoke and the effort, and my thighs and calves scream at me, but I can't stop. They live on the edge, near the clock tower. It's far out. They have to be safe.

And at first their house looks miraculously untouched. But then I see the door, gaping open like a wound, and I see the darkness inside.

"Don't," Dimia says as I walk towards it, but I shake her off, leaving her behind me as I approach the house

When I get closer, my heart hammering in my chest, I see a flicker of light near the kitchen. Hope floods through me, and I move to the doorway.

"Lirys?" I call softly. "Carys?"

The light grows as the owner of the candle steps towards me.

It's not my friend.

A dark-haired man stands before me, his teeth as black as his hair, a knife in his other hand. I scream in rage and raise my knife, and he throws the candle at me, hot wax splashing against my hand and I drop my knife.

"There's a girl here!" he calls, and I turn on my heels and bolt.

"Run!" I scream at Dimia's startled face, and she does, lifting her skirts and starting to run.

I grab her as I pass her and we tear away from the farm, my knee throbbing with every hard step. When I look back

I see other men, bearded, sallow-skinned and armed to the teeth, pouring out of the dairy and the cowsheds, like ants from a nest. Their hands are red with blood and I grip Dimia's wrist tighter, dragging her forward.

I guide us towards the town square, hoping we can lose them in the labyrinthine streets around the merchant quarters, racing down narrow alleys, left, then right, stumbling over rubble and household objects the fog blinds us to. Somewhere behind us voices chase and footsteps echo, urging us to move faster, to not stop.

When we break out on to the square I lengthen my stride, putting all of my energy into getting us across it, into the guild area, where we can climb to the walls and hide. We're halfway across when Dimia shrieks and pulls me to a halt.

Appearing from inside the fog like a nightmare and blocking our path is a golem.

I try to double back, but too late: its colossal hand thrusts forward and grips my arm, its clay fingers crushing my wrist.

"Errin!" Dimia screams as it hauls me into the air, black spots exploding in my eyes, my arm feeling as though it will tear from its socket. It hurts so much I can't breathe. It raises me until I'm level with its head, as if looking at me. As I dangle in its grip, I see the men out of the corner of my eye. They've stopped; some of them watch Dimia and some watch the golem. I get the distinct impression they're keen to stay out of its reach, even as they try to edge around it towards Dimia.

"Go," I shriek at her, and the golem swings around, taking me with it. Then I'm soaring through the air, the moon above me. Stars burst behind my eyes as I hit the side of a building, something in my back snapping with a faint pop. A second later pain explodes with such force that I can't even scream, choked by the agony of it. Then I can't feel anything, lying on the ground, staring up at the night.

Everything goes black.

When I wake I'm still on the ground. I blink rapidly, too stunned to move. From the corner of my eye, I see a flash, then Dimia comes into view waving a large wooden pole, the end alight. She stands a little away from me, thrusting it at the golem, which is trying to get past it, reaching for her. There's no sign of the men, and there is a moment when I wonder if I've been knocked deaf, the quietness is so loud. The golem has no mouth, and Dimia makes no noise either; the only sound is the sizzling from her torch when it touches the golem's clay hide, and the scuffles of her boots against the ground when she dodges its attack.

She thrusts the flaming pole into the golem's hand, making it stagger backwards out of my sight. Then it charges forward, she darts aside, and I roll out of the way.

Except I don't. I don't go anywhere.

I try to wiggle my toes, then move my knees, my hips. I don't know if they move, I can't feel them. I can't feel my legs. I can't feel anything. I should be in agony. It threw me into a building.

That snapping sound, it was my spine.

It broke my back.

Chapter 20

I hear shouts from my left and I whimper, helpless as boots run past me, scrunching my eyes closed, but then forcing them open, trying desperately not to cry, or scream. I will my legs to move but there's nothing, I can feel nothing.

"Go for the hand," Dimia cries, and then the crowd moves into my view, men and women with torches like Dimia's, all thrusting at the golem. Dimia fights with them, her teeth bared, pushing the pole at its hand, which appears to be on fire. She wanted to fight, I think wildly, and here she is. There are people around her, joining the fray. She has her army.

I don't think I'll be her apothecary though.

For the third time, I see her push the flames into the golem's outstretched palm, and this time it stiffens. Dimia and the others step back warily. At first nothing happens. Then, without warning, the golem keels over and moves no more.

Dimia stares over its body at me. The she drops the torch and runs to my side. "Errin?" she says, reaching for me.

"Don't," I say, trying to smile at her, to reassure her. "Don't move me. My spine is broken."

"No." She stares at me. "No."

I take a deep breath, and realize I feel calm. "Listen," I say quietly. "My mother's name is Trina Vastel. She has the same illness as the Scarlet Varulv. You can look it up. The potion that helped her is called the Elixir of Life. The alchemist I was looking for, the one I thought you were, can make it. If Mama has the Elixir on the nights leading up to and following the full moon, she's fine. Without it, she'll hurt you. So if you can get some... Please find her. Please help her."

Dimia nods, tears falling freely.

"And you were really good at fighting," I say. "I didn't think you would be, but you did it. You killed it. I wish—"

Gloved fingers close over her shoulders and she's moved away.

Replacing her is Silas Kolby.

"You stupid, stupid girl," he says, looking at me, his mouth pulled into a grimace. "Why did you leave without me?"

"You left me," I say, looking into his amber eyes. "Unwin saw you."

"And you listened to him?" Silas looks down at me, his eyes bright. "I never would." He shakes his head. "I never would," he repeats.

"We have to get inside," a female voice says.

He nods without looking away from me. "I'm going to lift you."

"You can't." The same woman speaks again. "Silas, her back is broken. It would be cruel." She lowers her voice. "She's not going to make it."

"Yes, she will."

There is a pause; the air seems to ripple.

"You can't mean..." The woman appears in my sight line, dark-skinned, dark-haired, carrying a small thin sword in each hand, and her mouth is a line of disapproval. Her eyes widen as she looks down at him, determinedly not looking at me, and I realize with a jolt that I recognize her.

"Yes, I can," he says.

"Silas, she's not one of us."

He turns around, and though I can't see his face, the way the woman recoils tells me all I need to know about his expression. When he turns back, there are tears catching on his white eyelashes.

"It's all right," I reassure him.

"It will be," he says. He doesn't blink, staring fiercely ahead as he carefully slides his arms under my broken back. I can't feel his arms as he scoops me up and holds me close to his chest. I've never been a fan of pain, but this is worse. This nothingness. I feel as though I might fly away at any moment.

"Let's go," he says, and his voice is firm.

I look up at him as we move, but he keeps his eyes fixed ahead, his mouth a line of concentration. From the corner of my eye I see Dimia walking next to him, looking down at me, and I smile, faintly, but it's enough for her to do the same. My gaze slides to the buildings either side of us; we're back in the merchant quarter. We pause outside one of the houses and I look up to see the crossed circle again, realizing we're outside the salt merchant's house. Again that niggling feeling comes. I recognize it and I try to remember where I know it from. A book? My lessons?

Then we begin to move again, passing through a doorway and the air instantly becomes cooler, as though we've stepped into a dairy or cool room. Except it's dark, the way lit by torches, and I can feel Silas's gait change as he shortens his stride. We're moving downwards.

"Where are we?" I whisper.

"Hush. Just rest," he murmurs back, I feel the rumbling in his chest as he speaks. I want to tell him not to dismiss me, but I'm suddenly exhausted. I hear doors being unlocked, then locked again, so many I lose count. I let my eyes drift closed, let the numbness wash over me.

I think I must have lost consciousness, because the next time I see anything, I'm not in Silas's arms any more; I'm on my back, staring up at a rock ceiling. I can't feel what I'm lying on, but from the height of it I guess I'm on some kind of table. The room is lit by candles, sconces mounted on the walls. There are stalactites hanging from the ceiling, thousands of them like needles, white and glinting. We're underground.

Of course, you could travel the whole kingdom and never

ever find it. No wonder they drugged guests before bringing them here.

We're in the Conclave. Beneath Tremayne. It was here. That's what the symbol means. Alchemists. On the doorway and on the gravestones. It's part of Silas's moon tattoos; a circle crossed with a line at the centre. It's an alchemic symbol. It was right under my nose all along.

"Out." Silas orders unknown people from the room and I hear them leaving. The woman who protested earlier is at the back. I can see her if I look to the side, her shoulders high and rigid. Only Dimia remains, looking nervous, her eyes focused on something behind me.

"You need the Elixir," she says softly. "Without it you'll—" She stops and presses her lips together.

I look at her. "But you said you weren't an alchemist."

"She's not," Silas says from my left, and I look towards his voice.

There is another table, next to the one I'm on, and he's behind it, placing a tripod on a piece of slate. My heart starts to speed up as he places a small metal bowl under it, balancing a second one, ceramic, thin, almost iridescent in the candlelight, atop it. I watch him arrange tongs, glass jars with powders and leaves in, two earthenware jars, twists of paper that hiss against the scarred wood of the table when he puts them down, pipettes and spoons, ceramic stirrers. My mouth falls open and I stare at him.

"It's you?" I say. "You're the philtresmith?"

He nods, but doesn't look at me, continuing to set up

his laboratory. None of it looks especially alchemical, it's the same equipment I know from my apothecary work, but there is something about seeing it in this place that makes it strange to me and a thrill of something like fear prickles along my scalp.

"It was you all along?" I ask and again he nods. "But the girl—"

Then his amber-gold eyes find mine and silence me instantly. It feels as though he's seeing into me, reading me, and though my skin burns, I don't flinch or look away.

He breaks the contact first. "What can you feel?"

I close my eyes, trying to work through my body. "Nothing," I say, my eyes flying open, my voice coming out as a sob.

He takes a deep breath. "Can you try moving your toes?" he asks.

I focus on it, on making them wiggle, and he looks at me fiercely, then shakes his head. "Fingers?"

I try and he exhales, looking at Dimia, who nods.

"Did they move?" I ask, hope rising in me.

"Your little one did," Dimia says.

"Again," says Silas, and I do it. When he nods, the relief is dizzying.

"Good. This is good," Silas says, but his gloved hands rise to cover his face, contradicting his words.

When he pulls them away he looks down at them, then takes a deep breath, and it seems that with that breath the room grows smaller, closer, as though he's drawn it inside him. The air becomes charged and expectant and it settles over me like a veil, making the hairs on the back of my neck stand up beneath the scratchy wool of my tunic. I can feel that.

"Are you ready?" he asks. "It might not work. I've never... Not with something this big. But it's worth a try."

"Thank you," I whisper.

He nods and begins to work, uncorking bottles and opening twists of paper, examining the scales. When he looks down at me again I smile, and he clears his throat.

"Let's begin then." He opens a square of wax paper marked with a circle, a line bisecting it, and I gasp.

"What?" he asks, alarm striking through his usual rasp as he looks at me, spilling white grains from the packet onto the table.

"Is that salt?"

"Yes." He scrapes the fallen salt into his hands. "Why?"

"It was bothering me; I kept seeing it. I realized when we came here it was alchemic. But I didn't know until just now that it meant salt. The great purifier."

He huffs, then tips the white crystals into his scales, balancing them against expensive-looking bronze weights before he nods in satisfaction. "It comes from here, the salt. Crystals that form when water drips through the rock. That's what glitters up there." He points towards the sparkling ceiling, before tipping the salt into the pestle and beginning to grind it. "*Sal Salis*. It's different from sea salt. You wouldn't want to use it to season your food. Trust me, I learned the hard way." He's pushed the sleeves of his tunic right up, bunching them around the tops of his arms. I can see the muscles there flexing and tensing as he works and, despite everything, I find it strangely hypnotic to watch them bulge and then ebb as he turns the salt to powder before adding it to the bowl.

"Start the fire, please," he says, shaking me from my trance.

Dimia appears by his side at the bench, smiling at me as she strikes the flint. I feel the sting of envy when I see her working by his side. I want to be part of this.

I stay silent as he tells her what to pass to him, watching as he adds it to the ceramic bowl, trying to keep up as he points out herbs, plants, powders, things I know, things I've never seen before, things I didn't know existed. Marigold, morning glory, angel water, spagyric tonic, bay leaves, mandrake, convolvulus, yew bark, wheat. The names whirl around my mind and I try to remember them all.

As the mixture heats, a strange, herbal smell starts to spiral out from it, and I wrinkle my nose.

"It's going to get a lot worse." Silas leans away from the table and walks out of my sight. When he returns, carrying two earthenware jars, he peers into the bowl as he places them beside it. "Almost," he says, as much to himself as to Dimia and me. He pulls the jars towards him and I see both have symbols baked into their side.

The first has a triangle with an upside-down cross stretching from the base, and from this he pulls a bright yellow rock. From the second, marked with a crowned circle, he pulls a red rock. He stands each in a tiny, shallow copper plate marked with the same symbol as was on the jar and places them in front of the tripod.

"You need to go now." He looks at Dimia and she nods reluctantly, shooting a glance at me.

"I'll see you soon," she says, walking over and touching my hand. I think I feel it. I smile at her, and then she's gone. I turn back to Silas.

He pulls a taper, a small dull knife, a glass pipe-shaped instrument and a crystal vial with a flat metal base towards him and arranges them in front of him. The way he does it is so precise, so deliberate, that I'm furious I can't sit up, can't see it properly. All at once it hits me that what I'm seeing is real alchemy. From start to finish. Not the end product following a drugged sleep, but possibly the last philtresmith in the world, making the Elixir from scratch, before my eyes.

Silas exhales, loudly, breaking into my wonder. With lightning speed, he plunges the taper into the flames beneath the white bowl and uses it to set both the red and yellow rocks alight. Instantly the room fills with a metallic, sulphuric reek and I wish I could cover my nose. He lifts the white bowl in his gloved hands and strains it into the crystal vial. He puts the thin end of the pipe instrument into the neck of the vial and holds it over the smoke from the red rock, and I watch as it flows in through the wide bowl, along the thin stem and into the vial, where it crystallizes and sinks to the bottom, forming a layer of deep, blood-red liquid. When the red reaches the halfway point he stops, and repeats the process over the yellow rock. The yellow layer is heavier than the red, sinking to the bottom of the vial.

When there is barely room for a single other drop he pulls the vial away, removing the pipe and stoppering it. Ignoring my gasp, with his left, gloved hand he smothers both rocks, yellow, then red, until the rocks and his glove smoulder gently.

He shakes the bottle, seemingly oblivious to the pain, and I watch as the liquid inside it turns pale pink.

His mouth becomes a resigned line, his forehead puckering, before he opens them and looks right at me. Keeping his gaze locked on mine, he peels his gloves away and lays them on the table. Eyes blazing, he looks down at his hands, and I do the same. Then I gasp, forgetting about my back, forgetting everything else.

Every finger on his left hand is black. His thumb is still palest pink, as is the whole of his right hand, but his left palm is the same colour as an abyss.

I can't take my eyes from it, from the *wrongness* of it.

He makes a soft sound in his throat and I see him looking at me, as I stare at his hand. I try to find words – any words – to ask what it is, but they've all gone. Instead my mouth is open, my brow furrowed in something like horror.

He sees it and something snaps shut in his own expression. He drops his gaze and turns back to his work, opening the vial and carefully tilting it, until a single drop of the potion sits on the tip of his left thumb. Then he puts the vial down on its iron base.

He lifts the small knife and cuts into the flesh of his left thumb at exactly the place where the drop of Elixir sits. For a fleeting instant the blood that oozes from it is red, before it pales to bright, pearlescent white when it touches the Elixir. He tips his thumb and the white drop falls into the vial, settling as a delicate ivory sheen on top of the pale liquid.

I look back at his thumb in time to see it turn black. I watch the skin change; I watch the darkness spread across the remaining unmarked skin on his hand. It feathers down on to his wrist, stopping in time to become a horrifying mimic of the glove he's removed, and my stomach turns

He walks over to me, the vial of Elixir in his healthy hand, but it's the other one I fix upon. He places it, bare, blackened, behind my head, the coldness of the cursed skin a shock against mine, and lifts my head, pouring the contents of the vial into my mouth, every drop. It tastes faintly of metal and I look up at him, both repulsed and full of pity.

His eyes when he looks back at me seem ages-old and fathomless. "Swallow," he says, and I do.

He lowers my head and moves away, returning with a second vial, and when he brings that to my lips I smell poppy.

I drink that one down without hesitating, suddenly wanting oblivion.

The last thing I remember is him scooping me up again. His gloves are back on, tattered and burned, covering the damaged flesh beneath.

*

I dream, but once again I know I'm dreaming, for beyond it I can feel aches in my body; somewhere in my lower back it feels as though the bones are grinding together. Knowing it's not real doesn't feel important though, the knowledge slipping away from me as soon as I've realized it. I find myself standing at the edge of a room, high-ceilinged, with large glass windows and a flagstone floor. It's nowhere I've been before, of that I'm certain; it's a place of privilege and opulence. But the most remarkable thing about the room is the man made of silver, on a throne carved from gold.

The man is the Sleeping Prince.

I wait for terror to grip me, to shake me and tell me to run, but it doesn't. I can't make out his features properly, other than his golden eyes; they are indistinct, shifting. He looks up and seems to see me. He smiles softly, his expression approving. I'm wearing a long, red dress – a gown, really – velvet and soft to the touch, like the skin of a peach when my fingers rub it. He holds out a hand towards me and I go to him, still unafraid. He takes my face in his hands, tucking my hair behind my ears.

"You're here," he says, and his voice is like sunshine, like honey, it's warm and rich and moreish. "I'm so very glad."

Where Silas's voice is spikes and edges, every word a warning, this man's voice is smooth, velvety and beckoning. He has golden eyes, like Silas, and the same white-blonde hair, though his is long, and shining. He has the same high cheekbones, the same unnatural pallor. He even has the same playful lilt to his lips.

"I thought you were Silas," I say. "All this time, I thought you were him."

"Who's Silas?"

"My friend. He's... He saved me."

"Did he? How?"

"Your monsters broke my back."

"Ah, that was you. I had no idea. How terrible of them. I'll punish them for it."

"He made the Elixir. It mended my spine."

"How interesting," the Sleeping Prince says. "So the philtresmith is male? How very interesting. Tell me, sweetling. Are you still in Tremayne? You and your friend."

"We're hiding. From you."

"You can't hide from me, my love."

He lowers his lips to my brow, kissing my forehead, I can feel them curving against my skin as he smiles and it sends a jolt of warmth through my body.

He leans back, looking at me with hungry eyes, and mine begin to close in anticipation of his kiss.

Instead he thrusts his hand into my chest, tearing the dress, shattering my ribcage until my heart is in his fist, still beating. I begin to lose consciousness as he brings it to his smiling mouth, licking it experimentally.

"Needs more salt." He smiles.

Chapter 21

I scream as I wake, hands rising to my chest, clawing at it, convinced it's gaping and open.

Then I roll over and heave, my stomach cramping as I retch, though nothing comes up. I lean back against the pillow when it's passed, enjoying the stiff, scratchy feeling of cool fabric on my too-warm skin, waiting for my heart to slow.

A soft, gloved hand rests on my forehead and I open my eyes to see Silas standing over me.

"Salt," I say in a strained voice. Already the dream is fading, though it leaves a nasty flavour behind. And as it does I remember the golem; the crack of my spine. The alchemy.

I sit up.

I can sit up.

Elation floods me and I glance briefly at him before I test my feet, wriggling my toes. I laugh without meaning to as I move my knees, tilt my hips, wave my hands. The bandage has been removed from my right hand and the skin on my knuckles is as good as new. It worked. I'm as I was.

"I'm healed. You did it. You healed me."

He looks at me, his face empty of any expression. "I did."

Then the rest of the night comes back to me and in my mind's eye I see again the blackness spreading across his hand, the skin consumed by it, and I shudder.

Immediately he draws away. "I'll leave you to rest."

"No, please. I'm sorry," I say.

He cuts across me, his eyes flashing, his lip curling. "I don't want to *upset* you." His expression is withering, his voice like a knife.

"You're not. I just..." I try to push the image away, softening my tone. "Silas—"

"Don't. I don't want your pity either."

"No. No, of course not." I swallow, composing myself. "At least tell me if it hurts?"

He exhales slowly, taking two steps back across the room to slump into a wooden chair. "It doesn't hurt," he says eventually; the words full of broken glass scratching inside my chest.

His head is bowed, and I watch him as he picks at the tattered gloves, catching occasional glimpses of the darkened skin beneath. "What is it?"

He doesn't speak for a long time, staring down at his hands, and I wait, wiggling my toes subtly, feeling both elated and guilty by turn. "It's not contagious, if that's your worry."

"It isn't," I say, my voice rising, and I take a breath before I speak again, carefully. "Silas, please. I'm an apothecary. I've seen . . . illness before."

"It's not an illness."

"Then what—"

"It's a curse," he snaps, looking at me. "It's the curse of the philtresmith. All alchemists have a curse. That's mine. The name for it is Nigredo."

"Is it. . . Will it go away? Will it heal?" I try to keep my voice even, shoving down the feeling that someone is walking over my grave.

"If I had some Elixir, yes. Then it would go back to being normal skin again."

"Can't you make more?" I ask.

"I can. But it won't work on me. It never does. If there were another philtresmith then I could use theirs. Of course, they'd have their own Nigredo to deal with then. Unless I made them some of my Elixir. . . Do you see the problem?"

I nod, falling silent. He bends his head and begins to toy with his gloves again, his shoulders hunched over, and I want to go to him, hold him. But I know he won't allow it, so I stay still, allowing the silence to build a wall between us until I can't bear it any more.

"Why?" I ask. "Why does it happen? The curse."

He looks up, slowly, as though he's forgotten I'm here. Then he smiles humourlessly. "Alchemy, Errin. What is the principle of alchemy? What's the ultimate function of it? What do the textbooks on it say?"

"To transmute. To turn base metals to other substances," I say. "But you're a person."

"And human veins flow with blood full of iron. . ." he says slowly, and my mouth falls open in horror. "Each time an alchemist performs their alchemy part of them changes, and there's no telling which part it will be. Fingernails, earlobes, lungs, heart. . ." He trails off.

I open my mouth to ask if he's changed anywhere else but he cuts me off with a vigorous shake of the head. "Just my hand. So far. It'll get worse, I've no doubt. If I keep doing it."

"Then you have to stop." Something passes over his face, something fleeting and indecipherable. "It's not worth it," I say. "You could die. What if next time it's not your hand, but your heart, or your lungs?"

He looks at me. "It saved your life. It could save countless others."

"But you'd have to die for it." He looks away. "Wait. Do all alchemists have a curse? Does that mean the Sleeping Prince does? Every time he makes a golem, does that happen to him?"

Silas shakes his head. "If only."

"Why doesn't it?"

"You know Aurek and Aurelia were the first alchemists? They were born with it; they had the moon hair and the Godseye, but no one knew what it meant. When they were eight, Aurek had a nosebleed, and bled on to a set of iron ball bearings he'd been playing with. They turned to solid gold. With the king's consent, experiments were done, and they discovered that Aurek's blood turned base metals to gold if it touched them, and also, horribly, brought clay to life if it touched that. Aurelia's blood seemed to do nothing at first, until one of the more zealous scientists tried adding her blood to water and drank it. He noticed immediately that his bruises vanished, his gout calmed. More blood was taken, and everyone who drank of it was healed of anything that ailed them."

I wince, disgusted by it, but not surprised.

"I told you Aurek sired many children and they were raised at the palace? Well, they tried to use the children's blood to make gold, hoping they'd inherited the gift, but nothing happened. It didn't work. They tried with smaller and larger amounts of blood, but iron stayed iron, and water remained water. They almost killed one of the children, draining her within an inch of her life. That's why Aurelia brought them away when Tallith fell, to stop people trying to use them."

"Oh Gods," I murmur, sickened by the image of it.

"People tried to use Aurek's blood too. While he slept. They'd prick him and steal his blood, but the poison that put him to sleep seemed to have stopped his powers. So Aurelia hid his body, and brought the children away. She thought that alchemy would die with her, and resolved to live quietly until it did. But then the children discovered they could activate their blood to make it alchemical. Some of them were trying to make a potion to wake their father, and one of them accidentally cut her finger and a drop of blood fell in the bowl. The legend says it bubbled and smoked, and when it cleared there was a lump of gold in the bottom of the pan. They'd found a way to be alchemists, like their father. But there was a cost."

"Nigredo."

Silas shakes his head. "The aurumsmith's curse is called Citrinitas. Like the Nigredo, it affects them physically. But they turn to gold. That's the price. They could make as much gold as they liked, and each time they did, part of them would turn to gold too." He pauses, his head tilting. "I always think they have it worse. At least if the Nigredo stops my heart, no one is going to carve it from my chest to sell."

My hands rise to cover my mouth.

"Aurelia was furious," he says, sinking back into the tale. "She tried to prevent them from making it, but when they demanded the right to choose, she gave in, saying when they turned nineteen they could decide for themselves. She banned all other forms of experimentation though, frightened of what it might lead to. And who could blame her, after what she'd seen in Tallith? The Sisters uphold that rule. Hence our inability to make our own poisons. We can make the Opus Magnum, but nothing else. We never learned."

I mouth the words, *Opus Magnum*, as he continues.

"Aurelia eventually married, and had children of her own, and she offered them the same choice as their cousins." He looks down at his hands. "Aurelia didn't know what, if anything, the curse would be for them, but it soon became apparent it was different to the Citrinitas. We don't know why it happens, something in the blood differing from Aurek's and

298

Aurelia's, some impurity. All modern alchemy starts with the same base potion, whether making the Elixir or gold. It's the blood that makes the difference."

"Oh, Silas," I breathe, my head spinning. "So the potion you use to make the Elixir was supposed to be the cure to wake the Sleeping Prince?"

"Originally. You know the saying 'like cures like'?" he asks, and I nod; it's a common apothecary edict. What causes can cure, if the dose is right. "They did what you tried to do with the Elixir. They deconstructed the remains of the poison from the vial found in the rat catcher's rooms. They isolated all of the ingredients: salt, quicksilver, sulphur and so on, and were experimenting with reversing the potion. They thought it would wake him, and if he woke he could restore Tallith."

"And they wanted that?"

"Originally, it was their goal. Raise the Sleeping Prince, and then reclaim and rebuild Tallith. Stop hiding and go home."

Before I can ask him anything else the curtain is thrown open and the dark-skinned woman stands there. Her name comes back to me then – Nia, the salt merchant's daughter. We used to buy our salt for the apothecary from her; she used to deliver it.

She doesn't look at me, looking instead at Silas. "Your mother is here."

He nods. "Thank you, Nia. Tell her I'll be along soon."

Nia raises her eyebrows but says nothing, whipping back out of the room, the curtain swinging in her wake.

"I know her," I say. "I thought she liked me."

"She's funny about outsiders. Interesting, given that she's not an alchemist, but married in."

"Her husband is one?"

"Her wife."

I try to imagine a female alchemist, with the silver hair and an amber gaze. It's how Aurelia must have looked. "So this is the Conclave."

"Welcome."

"I lived above it all my life."

He nods. "You did. Which reminds me, I heard about your mother. We'll get her back. We'll get her here, safe and sound. I mean to keep my promise to you. I always did."

I feel horribly guilty then, for everything; for blackmailing him, and not trusting him. And for asking him to allow my mother in here without knowing what she is. He deserves to know. "You have to let me explain," I say. "I lied to you. About my mother." He looks at me blankly. "She isn't just grieving. The scratches on her arms, I think the Scarlet Varulv attacked her. Changed her."

"The what?"

"The Scarlet—"

"I know what it is," he interrupts gently. "It's impossible; it's a story, Errin."

"Yes, well, we thought that about the Sleeping Prince, but that turned out to be a mistake."

"The Scarlet Varulv really is just a tale, I know that much."

"No. You don't know what she's been like. It was she who

chipped my tooth." My tongue pushes my lip aside to remind him of it. "You've seen her eyes, how red they are. And her hands like claws. Silas, when the moon is full she tries to hurt me. Something happened in the woods, and I think – no, I know – it was that. It's the only explanation."

He sighs. "Errin, I saw your mother, remember. I sat with her, twice. I promise you, she's not a storybook monster; she's sad and lost. And I know it's been hard for you in Almwyk—"

"Don't patronize me," I snap at him.

"I'm not. Truly. I know it must have been hard for you to deal with her behaviour on top of everything else, and naturally you'd look for explanations for it, especially when she didn't respond to your treatments."

"Forget it." I swing my legs off the bed and he holds up his hands.

"Wait. I'm sorry. I'll listen to you, please." When I don't make any further movements, he continues. "Look, we'll get her released and bring her here and then we'll see, all right? We'll get her out before the next full moon and then we'll see what we can do. If the Elixir helps, so be it. I'll make it for her."

I look down at his gloved hands as the full weight of what he's offering – what I'd asked for – hits me. His life for my mother's.

"I can't let you." I speak so quietly I don't know if he hears me.

"I made myself a promise once," he says suddenly, looking at me. "When I was growing up, I saw my father crippling

301

himself to save lives. Every time there was a knock at our door, I was terrified that it was someone begging for help. Well, two years ago, he got a call for help, and as always he went to make the Elixir. The Nigredo stopped his heart."

My hands rise to my face, covering my mouth, which is gaping open behind them.

He looks down. "It didn't kill him straight away. I made the Elixir to try to heal him. It . . . it was my first time. It didn't work; we were too late. The Elixir can cure anything, but it can't restart a dead heart. After that . . . the knocks came for me. And I found that like him, I couldn't say no. How could I when my refusal would mean certain death, or at the very least, a lot of suffering? So I made a decision. No marriage. No children. No relationships. I swore my loyalty to the Sisters. That way I'd never put my wife in my mother's position; she'd never have to watch me kill myself to save others. And there would be no children to worry I was going to die every time I made the Elixir. Or to have to take my place when I did."

"Silas. . ."

"When I saw you lying there, broken, I didn't even stop to think. Even if it meant the Nigredo taking my heart, I would have done it. And gladly." He stands and crosses the room, somehow taking an age to walk the three steps to where I am. He kneels before me, his hands resting on my knees. "I couldn't lose you, Errin. I couldn't have stood it."

"What are you saying?"

He looks up at me, swallowing. I watch the lump in

his throat bob, then meet his gaze again. "I don't know," he whispers.

Slowly, I reach for his hands, peeling the gloves off, holding them, touching the black skin, folding my fingers through his. He closes his eyes and I look at him, at the white lashes resting just above his sharp cheekbones, his skin flushed, his lips parted. I realize his hands are shaking, and I squeeze them gently. When his eyes open, his pupils are wide, dark discs at the centre of the gold, and my heart skips, fluttering like a bird. When he tilts his head, my stomach swoops.

"Silas, your – oh." We whip around and Dimia flushes bright red in the doorway. "I'm sorry, I'm so sorry; it's your mother."

"What about her?" he asks, sounding as frustrated as I feel.

"I'm waiting for you."

Behind Dimia a woman appears. She's tall and thin, and there is something hawk-like to her face. She's dressed in a long robe with bell-shaped sleeves, and though the robe is black, with a short cape, when she puts her hands on her hips I glimpse the gold lining of the sleeves. She wears a headdress that leaves her face exposed; her neck and the rest of her head are covered by a tall hood that fans out as it leaves her forehead, the top of it shaped like a wave. As she turns to look at Dimia I see the hood is shaped the same all the way around, triangular in design.

She stares at us, glancing back and forth between us. "I

warned you," she says, fixing her gaze on Silas. "I told you that you were too young, but you wouldn't listen. You insisted you knew your own mind."

"Mother, please," Silas says, his hand reaching for mine.

"You swore your life to the Sisters, Silas. So you'll answer to them."

Chapter 22

We follow her through the corridors in silence, single file. Silas walks before me, glancing back every now and then, his expression thoughtful, and Dimia behind. The passageway we are being led down is wider than I would have expected; a small carriage could travel through it. The walls are stone, flecked with salt, lit by more sconces. It must cost them a fortune in candles, but then I recall who lives here.

"Did the Conclave build this?" I ask to break the oppressive quiet, jumping when my voice echoes back at me. I'd thought I was whispering.

"No, it's what's left of an underground river, we think," Silas answers me. "Obviously long gone, but you can see the signs. There are fossils in the floor and along the walls. There are caverns down here we haven't even explored yet, miles of them."

The ground is dusty but smooth, faintly dipped in the centre where many people have walked along it over the years. There are columns of stalagmites that look as though they're made of wax, and I trail my fingers over them as we pass, then rub them together, surprised at how soft my fingers feel.

We turn another corner, into a narrower passage, a large red curtain at the end. Silas's mother reaches for it, holding it back so we can enter.

"After you."

The room is cavernous, furnished with three wooden tables, a bench along each side. The two outer tables are full of people, most white-haired and golden-eyed, though some are normal-looking, dark- and light-skinned, old, young, male, female; generations of alchemists and non-alchemists. At least fifty pairs of eyes turn to watch us as we enter, and none of them looks glad to see us; every face is stony and cold, like the room itself.

Along the centre table, four other figures sit alone. Each wears the same eerie robes as Silas's mother. The Sisters of Næht.

I swallow and feel Dimia step closer to me. I turn to look at her. Her face is pale, her freckles stark against her pallor. To my left Silas lets out a long breath, and I shift so my fingers brush against his once-again covered ones, just for a moment.

"Sit," Silas's mother commands us, and I follow Silas to the centre table. Dimia remains close to us. No one smiles, or makes any gesture of greeting as we approach. Instead their gazes move from Silas, to me, finally lingering on Dimia.

Room has been left at the far end of the central table, and it's here we sit. Out of the corner of my left eye I see Nia lean over and whisper to a white-haired woman beside her.

Silas's mother walks to us, standing by her son.

"We haven't been formally introduced," she says, looking down at Dimia and me. "I am Sister Hope, of the Sisters of Næht. We're joined tonight by Sister Wisdom, Sister Peace, Sister Honour and Sister Courage."

Each ones nods in turn, though there's nothing in their manner that would be recognized as friendly. Sister Peace even goes so far as curling her lip at us.

"I'm Errin—" I begin, but stop when a low hiss rises to my right. I turn to look at the sea of faces staring at us, shrinking back when their cold eyes meet mine.

"We know who you are, Errin Vastel." Sister Hope's voice is stern.

I look at Silas, who is leaning forward, tense and poised, scowling at the room.

"And you, of course, are Twylla Morven, daughter of Amara Morven," Sister Hope continues, though in a much warmer tone. I look around to see who she's addressing, to find her looking at Dimia. "We've been looking for you."

"What?" I say, looking from Sister Hope to Dimia.

"Heir of the Sin Eater, lately Daunen Embodied."

A shiver seems to go around the room at her words, and a memory clicks into place. Daunen Embodied, the living Goddess. The missing one.

"That's you?" I say, trying to reconcile the image of the

girl who fought the golem with what I knew of the pious, virgin girl destined to marry the prince. The dead prince. Oh. Of course she was so upset about his death; she was supposed to marry him. "But you said you were Dimia," I say, and again the alchemists and their companions murmur. "You said you didn't know what I was talking about when I said the alchemists were looking for you."

"She doesn't know?" Sister Hope looks from Dimia to Silas, then to me.

"Don't," Dimia snaps, glaring at Sister Hope. "Don't." She turns to me. "I didn't know they were looking for me, I swear. I didn't lie about that. I'll explain why I deceived you. But when we're alone. Please. Please."

Her hands are clasped before her, her eyes beseeching, and I nod, once.

Dimia – Twylla – closes her eyes in thanks and then turns back to Sister Hope. "Well? Why were you looking for me?"

Sister Hope's mouth twists as though her words taste sour. "That is your mother's right to tell you."

"My mother?"

"She's on her way here. She was before we knew you were here, as fate would have it. She can explain; it's her duty." There is something dark in Sister Hope's expression, something scathing and angry, and it's matched in Twylla's face, a deep line forming between her brows.

Her words have reminded me of my own duty. I look at Silas, raising my eyebrows, and mouth "My mother" to him.

He nods and turns to Sister Hope. "Errin's mother

has been taken to a facility in Tressalyn. She has a kind of depression, brought on by grief. I was helping her. Who is available to secure her release and bring her here?"

"No one." Sister Wisdom, silent until now, speaks up. "What concern is this of ours?"

Silas raises his brows. "It's my concern."

Sister Hope looks at him. "We don't have the resources to send across Tregellan right now."

"Then I'll go myself."

"Silas." A warning.

"I promised her. . ."

"And what are your promises worth, Brother Silas?" Sister Peace says in a low voice. "You cannot keep your vows, clearly."

"Enough!" Sister Hope snaps, making us all jump. Silas looks down at the table and I glare at Sister Peace, who in turn fixes me with a calm, brown-eyed gaze. Not an alchemist. In fact, none of the Sisters seem to be. "Leave us," Sister Hope orders the alchemists on the other benches.

They don't protest, rising immediately and filing out of the room. Nia, at the back, shoots me a glance of pure hatred. What is her problem with me?

"Do you have any idea of the damage you could have done?" Sister Hope turns on Silas, her teeth bared, when we and the remaining Sisters are left. "Bad enough to tell an outsider our secrets. But to tell *her*. You could have ruined everything – you still might have. Only time will tell."

"Father told you our secrets. You were born an outsider

too. I've hardly set some kind of precedent."

"You know that's not what I mean."

"Will someone please explain to me what's going on?" I say finally. "I'm sorry if you're upset by my . . . our . . . I didn't know he was a monk when it started and I meant no harm, truly. No matter what happens, you don't have to worry, I won't betray you. Believe me, I know how to keep a secret. In fact, I should tell you now—"

"What?" Sister Hope turns on me, eyes blazing. "What secrets are you keeping, Errin?"

From the corner of my eye I see Silas shake his head. "I just meant I'm not a coward. I wouldn't endanger you. Any of you. Not for anything."

"What if you were captured? What if you were locked in a dark room, and denied food and water until you spoke?"

"Mother," Silas warns, but I stop him.

"I'm no stranger to hunger," I say. Sister Hope's lips quirk and I have the feeling I've walked into a trap.

"Of course. But what if you were whipped?"

I raise my eyebrows. "I had my spine snapped by a golem a few hours ago, I'm hardly afraid of a whipping now."

Again that twist of her mouth: amusement, distaste, I can't tell. "What if your nails were peeled off with pliers?" she says. "What if your fingers were broken, one by one, with a mallet?" I feel the blood drain from my face. "What if you were branded with hot irons?"

"Stop. . ." I whisper.

"What if they didn't do it to you at all, but to Twylla, or one of your friends from Tremayne, while you watched? What if they did it to my son? Or your mother? What if right now there are people seeking her out, knowing she's the link to break you? What would you do to save your family, Errin? How far would you go?"

"Stop it!" I scream, and the sound rings in the cavernous room.

For a beat no one says anything. Silas looks down at the table, his fists clenched so tightly his knuckles, save for those with the Nigredo, are white.

"I love my mother," I say. "To save her I'd do almost anything. Are you telling me you wouldn't, to save Silas?"

She doesn't reply. Finally, though, it is Twylla who breaks the silence. "We're leaving," she says suddenly, pushing the bench back from the table. "These people have nothing to do with us."

"I told you, you will go nowhere until you've heard what your mother has to say."

Twylla slams her hand down, the slap of her palm against the wood echoing through the room. "I am tired of women like you telling me what I am, and what I should be."

Sister Hope looks at her. "Twylla, soon enough you'll understand what the Sleeping Prince will do to us, will force us to do, if he finds us. What he'll do to *you*. I see why you think me cruel, and I'm sorry for it, truly I am. But her people –" she points at me "– won't suffer as mine will if he finds us. He can't hurt them as he can hurt us. She's a liability and if you knew—"

"Can't hurt them?" I speak before Twylla can, my voice icy. "You saw the state he left Tremayne in. Hundreds of people dead. Men, women, children. I lived in this town my whole life. I trained as an apothecary in the ruins above our heads. Today I saw bodies that I've healed in the past. My friends are missing. Maybe even dead." And as I say it, I understand it might be true. The Dapplewoods, Master Pendie. "You have miles of caves down here where you could shelter children, and the weak. And you do nothing. Who are you, to think you're better than us because you're alchemists? That you're worth more than we are because you make gold?"

"You don't know what you're talking about," Sister Hope says to me, shaking her head. "And this is not your concern. Twylla, please. Listen to us."

I ignore her. "We won't hide. We won't cower in the dark. We're going to fight him," I say, relishing the words.

"And if you won't help us, then you become our enemy too," Twylla adds. "And may the Gods help you if you try to stop me."

She leans across the table, glowing with rage. In this moment I understand how she became the embodiment of a Goddess; I almost believe in it.

There is a scuffling from outside the curtain and one of the Sisters rises swiftly, crossing the room and throwing the shade back.

Standing there, clearly eavesdropping, is a group of

people, alchemists and non. I realize with a start that it's the group that helped Twylla fight the golem. Including Nia.

"Forgive us, Sister. But we want to fight too," a tall brown-haired man says, and the others nod.

"They are our people." Nia steps forward, hand in hand with the white-haired woman she sat beside earlier. "We want to fight."

"He can't be beaten in battle," Sister Wisdom says.

"Perhaps not," Nia replies. "But she stopped one of the golems." She points at Twylla. "We saw it. If we work together, we can thin his ranks, make him vulnerable."

"And we can fight men. We can kill men," I say. "The Silver Knight leads an army of men; we can battle them, to begin with, even if we can't kill him with a sword."

Sister Hope stares at me.

"I can teach them to fight," Silas says, standing. "I can use a sword, and a bow. I'll teach the willing what they need to know."

Sister Hope looks back at him. "Silas, you know there's only one way to defeat him, and it isn't a duel. It's a waste."

"You can't stop them," he says softly, looking from her to me and then smiling ruefully. "You know that."

Sister Hope turns to look at her fellow Sisters, seeming to confer silently with them. "As you wish," she says, looking at the crowd in the door. "Silas, find the girls somewhere to rest until Amara arrives. And I'll ... I'll send a message to the Council. Your mother is Trina Vastel, yes?" She looks back at me.

"Yes."

She nods again, then turns, her cloak gliding over the floor like a snake.

"Errin." She pauses in the doorway. "I'm sorry. I truly am." Then, followed by the other Sisters, she moves past the crowd, now looking sheepish and unsure in the doorway.

"What do we do now?" Nia calls to Silas.

"We'll meet tomorrow after breakfast. I'll form a training schedule." He sounds sure, nodding firmly at them, his lip twitching when they solemnly return the gesture.

When they withdraw, he turns to me and smiles, and it's like a lightning bolt. There is no warning: one moment his eyes are hazy and the next they're blazing, his grin taking over his whole face. I can't help but smile back.

The sound of heavy fabric brushing against the stone makes us turn to see the curtain swinging. Twylla has gone.

We don't speak, instead turning to follow her, catching up with her in the corridor.

"Forgive me. I have a headache," she says in a flat, empty voice. "I'd like to lie down."

"Of course," Silas says. "I'll take you to a room where you can rest, if you like?"

She nods, but doesn't turn around. Silas raises his eyebrows at me and I shake my head, puzzled by the sudden change in her.

The passageways seem endless as he takes us to our sleeping quarters, corridor after corridor, until I'm sure we're walking in circles. I try to count the sconces on the walls on the way through the passageways: one, two, three, left turn, narrow, five sconces, another left turn, a slight descent, right turn ... but it soon becomes too much. Twylla walks a little ahead of us the whole way, her head down, and Silas and I stay quiet, not touching as we trail behind her.

Finally, Silas calls on her to stop, reaching for a torch from the wall and throwing back a curtain to reveal a cavern with two beds resting as best they can against the uneven stone walls, a small table between them. In one corner is a washstand with a ewer and basin. I can see a water closet behind a screen in the second corner, and a large cow-skin rug in the centre of the room. The beds are made up with furs and woollen blankets; on each lumpy-looking pillow is a nightgown.

"I'm a few rooms down. If you call me, I'll hear," he says, looking at Twylla, then back to me. When he leaves the room I follow.

He walks a little further along the passageway and stops, leaning against the wall. In the light from the torches his hair looks translucent, like a halo. When I stand in front of him, I see the flames reflected in his eyes, turning his gaze to fire. His eyes meet mine and he flushes. My body feels warm and heavy. I'm too aware of how close we're standing, of the rhythm of his breathing. Of how alone we are. Then he raises a hand tentatively and touches the ends of my hair, and I have to fight not to lean into his touch, not to frighten him away. "I like this, by the way." He allows a few strands to trail through his fingers before lowering his hand. "When did you do it?"

I smile. "Did you stop in a cottage outside Tyrwhitt, the night after we last saw each other?"

"Yes. I was trying to catch up to you. I saw hoof prints in the mud and followed, but you'd gone."

"Actually, I was on the roof. I heard you at the window."

"You were there? Why were you on the roof?"

"Not long before you came I was robbed. Two refugees broke into the cottage, so I hid there. If you'd stayed five more minutes you could have watched me fall flat on my back."

His eyes widen. "Gods... If I'd known." He reaches out and takes my shoulders in his hands, as though to pull me to him, then freezes, looking at me carefully.

"Well," I say slowly. "I did it after that."

"Why? Because of me?"

I think of the mercenaries, then the soldiers. "No. I'll tell you one day. But not now."

"All right." Then his gaze moves to my lips and I lick them self-consciously.

"Gods," he murmurs, his fingers tightening on me. My stomach clenches in response, leaving a strange ache behind.

Then Nia walks past us, huffing loudly. "Goodnight." She spits the "t" at the end.

Silas snatches his hand from my shoulder and we both glower after her. When he turns back to me he looks thoughtful. "What made you decide to fight?" he says quietly. "I thought you wanted to stay safe, and hidden."

I shrug. "I did. But it won't work. I saw the camp at

Tyrwhitt. All those people, caged like animals. And the way it was changing Tregellan, making people superstitious and cruel... He won't stop, and if he gets a tight grip on things, then ... it will only get worse. Besides, he killed my brother. And my friends. And almost me. It's right that I try to return the favour."

"I wanted to do something from the start. That's why I was sent to Almwyk. I was going mad cooped up in the temple. Sending me to wait for Twylla was supposed to keep me occupied and out of reach." He grins.

"Why did she tell me she was called Dimia?" I ask.

Silas grows quiet. "That's her story to tell."

"But you know?"

He nods slowly. "I do. And I'll talk to you about it afterwards, if you want me to."

I don't like the sound of that, but I know better than to question him. "Ask no questions and I'll be told no lies?" I say.

"You'll be told no lies even if you do ask. But speak to her first."

We both fall silent, listening to the rhythmic drips of water falling further along the passage.

"The apothecary, the monk and the living Goddess went to war," I say finally. "We sound like the start of a joke."

He's quiet for a moment, his brow furrowed. "I want..." he begins, then shakes his head. "Us," he says. "I don't know how to do this. But I want it. I'm sure of that." His face darkens, his words coming fast and earnest. "The second I saw you on the ground, I knew for certain it could only go one way for me, after that." He raises his left hand, trembling again, and strokes my cheek.

This time I do lean into it. "We don't have to figure it all out tonight," I say, then press one light kiss on to his palm. "It's been a long day. We should rest."

I hear the words, sensible, practical, coming from my mouth and want to bite them back. I don't want to rest. I want to spend all night exploring this, whatever it is. But I know it's a bad idea. Right now we need to think about the Sleeping Prince, and my mother, and whatever it is that Twylla's mother wants from her, and how we all fit into it. I need to find out why Twylla lied to me.

And I need to be sure of him. That he won't push me away again.

"There will be time," I say, hoping I'm right.

His eyes search mine, worry pulling the corners of them tight. Then, slowly, he leans forward and kisses my cheek, the touch of his lips so hot I half think I'll be branded by them. "Goodnight, Errin Vastel." He is so close his breath kisses my mouth. "But . . . I've made my choice. And it's you. Us, if you want it."

I want so much to sink my fingers into his hair, to pull his face to mine. To touch, to taste. But I step away from him. "Goodnight, Silas Kolby. I'll see you in the morning."

I can feel him watching me as I walk back. "No," he calls as I go to pull one of the curtains. "Next one. I'm four away. If you change your mind."

I smile at him and enter my room.

Though I wasn't gone long, when I return, Twylla's in her bed, seemingly still fully dressed, save her boots, the nightgown ignored. She has the covers piled over her, and she's facing the wall, the torches in their sconces still lit. I light the candle from one of them then extinguish them.

"I'm not asleep," she says, startling me. She turns over and props herself up on an elbow.

"All right," I say, sitting on my bed and pulling one of the blankets over my shoulders.

"I'm sorry. It must have seemed so rude, to have walked away from you in the Great Hall. I just ... I have a lot to tell you, it seems. I suppose we should begin with why I lied?" she says, and I nod. "It's a long story. But to begin, you should know that Dimia was the name of the girl the Bringer used to wake the Sleeping Prince."

I inhale sharply. So that's why it sounded familiar. I remember then, the men who came through Almwyk asking if we'd seen a girl and a young man. She was Dimia, with the Bringer.

Twylla continues. "He took her from the castle in Lormere. She was a servant there. I heard the Bringer when he came for her. I heard the music he played to lure her." She lapses into silence, her brow furrowed. Then she takes a deep breath. "Dimia was the first name that came to me once I got to Scarron. I was escorted part of the way there by her brother, Taul. Merek had dispatched him and some others to try and find her. And I didn't want to be Twylla any more. I was done with her, and her life – lives – so when Javik asked my name, I said it without thinking. I'd already coloured my hair so I could leave Lormere unnoticed, and it seemed fitting: new hair, new name. New life." She pauses and I feel as though I'm missing huge parts of this tale: Daunen Embodied was desperately important to Lormere. Surely they wouldn't let her walk away from it?

As if she's read my thoughts, she continues. "I left, if not at Merek's desire, then with his understanding. I had to go and he respected that. He helped me. It was his money that paid for my cottage, and that we were going to use to rescue your mother."

"Weren't you betrothed to him?"

"I was." Twylla hangs her head. "I knew your brother," she says. Her voice has changed. "When I saw you on my doorstep, I thought at first he'd sent you. Then when you said you sought a Lormerian named Dimia, I knew that he hadn't."

"Why would he send me to you?"

She pauses. "I was betrothed to Merek, but I had a brief . . . relationship with Lief."

"Relationship? With Lief?"

She nods. "He was assigned to guard me and we became close. It's why I left the castle."

"What happened?"

"It didn't work out as I'd hoped."

"He hurt you?" I say quietly.

She pulls the strangest expression, looking as though

320

she might fly apart, but at the last moment she pulls herself together and meets my eye, her gaze defiant.

"I thought you were him, you know. When you knocked. You have the same knock. Isn't that strange, to think something like that is a family trait. But of course it would be. I'll bet one or even both of your parents knocked in the same way."

Now it all makes sense: why she looked so hopeful and yet so scared when she answered her front door, why she looked so sad at my father's grave. But it doesn't explain why she'd want to help me.

"Were you disappointed?"

She takes a deep breath, looking down at her hands. "My heart was. My head wasn't. Most days I'm at war with myself. My head wins, usually. And for that I'm glad."

"I'm sorry," I say finally, because I don't know what else to offer.

"You're not responsible for it," she says evenly, though her gaze drops. "He spoke about you. And your mother. Told me about your farm. And your father."

It makes me want to cry, imagining Lief miles away, confiding in this strange girl about us.

"Why did you offer to help us? If you and he ... If it didn't end well, why would you help us?"

"I'm not glad he's dead," she says, ignoring my question. "No matter what happened. I don't want you to think that."

She closes her eyes, as though praying, and I watch her in the thin light from the candle. She has an oval face, a neat chin. Her cheeks are freckled, and the corners of her mouth turn down slightly, making her look pensive, even when her face is relaxed. The more I look at her, the more I think she's pretty, which surprises me because I didn't notice it first. Lirys is obviously beautiful; all my life I've been used to how people react to her, how they smile automatically on seeing her, as though her beauty is a treat to them. Twylla's beauty is the kind that sneaks up on you. I wonder if Lief thought the same.

"What do you see?" she says suddenly, and my face reddens. She looks at me, fixing me with green eyes, darker in this light. "Tell me, when you look at me, what do you see?"

"A girl," I say, and she smiles. "What should I see?"

"You look like him," she says. "Before you said a word to me I knew you were his sister. Same eyes, same shape to your face. You have the same smile. You're very like him too." She pauses, then sits back, curling her legs beneath her. "I know you want to know what happened. And I will tell you all of it. I promise. But not tonight."

I nod. "Twylla," I say hesitantly, testing this new name for her. "When he lived on the farm, Lief was... He never thought about anything but the farm. When we lost it, he was heartbroken. So if he behaved badly, then..." I trail off. "What I mean is, when Lief cared, he really cared. He was all or nothing. So I think he must have really liked you, for a while at least."

Her expression clouds over, her mouth pursing. "No, Errin," she says deliberately. "He didn't."

Her eyelids flutter shut again and I take a deep breath. I don't want to know any more; I don't want her to say anything that might make me think too badly of him. "Did – do you have brothers, or sisters?"

"Both. Twin brothers, older than me. A younger sister, but she died."

"I'm sorry."

"As am I."

We're quiet for a moment. And then I speak. "I think the worst thing is the way you lose part of yourself." I roll on to my back and stare up at the dark, speckled roof. "There's so much that only Lief knew about me. So many memories that we shared – mostly of things we shouldn't have been doing – but now I'm the last one who remembers them. Times we woke in the night and stole honeycomb from the jars in the kitchen. Times we used to jump into the hay on the farm. No one will ever know me like that again. And what if I forget things? What happens then?"

I turn to look at her, in time to see her wipe her face.

"I'm sorry," I say again.

She shakes her head. "No, it's a nice way to think." She pauses. "I suppose we should try to sleep now," she says. "Tomorrow is going to be interesting, I suspect." She stares into the distance, then turns abruptly, facing the wall once more.

I clamber off the bed to wash my face. Then I pull off my boots and change into the nightgown, happy to have clean clothes, before blowing out the candle. I can hear her crying softly.

Lying in the dark, I think of Silas, a few caves away. He knew her name was Twylla. And he expected her to come through Almwyk, was waiting there for her. Was that because of Lief? Did he expect her to come there because of him, or merely because it's the main border town between the two countries?

Then I have a horrible thought: is that why he befriended me? To get to her?

I sit up in bed, staring into the darkness. Twylla has fallen silent. I'll ask him tomorrow, I tell myself. And even if that was the reason, does it matter?

No, I decide as I lie back down, it doesn't. It alters nothing between us.

After a few moments I hear another muffled sob and I clench my fist in the blankets. I feel terribly guilty for whatever it was my brother did to her. Sometimes I don't think I knew Lief at all.

Chapter 23

I'm woken by the sound of footsteps pounding past our room. I can hear voices, too loud for the night, and though I can't make out the words, I can hear the shrill pitch, the panic, in them. I sit up, turning to Twylla.

"What's happening?" she asks, rubbing her eyes, and I shake my head, my heart racing.

There is a grating, rumbling sound above us, echoing down through the rock.

"What's that?" she gasps.

I throw my covers back, reaching for my breeches and forcing my feet into my boots. "Get up," I say. "Something's wrong."

As she pulls on her boots, Silas throws the curtain open. He looks from me to Twylla and then back. "We're under attack," he says. "I don't know if they saw us coming back here, or if they figured it out, but they're trying to force the main doors."

"What do we do?"

"You both need to find Amara. She arrived an hour ago. She's in the ossuary. Listen to her. Then meet me in the hall; I'll wait there for you. We may need to evacuate, so be ready."

I look at Twylla, pale and determined in the light from the hallway. "We'll see you in the hall."

"Silas!" someone calls from outside the room.

He turns towards the voice, then back to us, speaking quickly. "When you leave here, turn right and place your left hand on the wall to your left. Keep your hand on it and follow it. You'll know it when you see it. Don't take your hand off the wall until you do."

Then he's gone, leaving Twylla and me staring at each other.

Outside our room, everyone is running in the opposite direction from the one Silas told us to follow. Staying close together, we place our left hands on the wall and begin to walk. Alchemists and their partners, people of all ages and sexes run past us, some armed, some holding children, all ignoring us. Above us there is another boom, and I see a trail of dust fall from the ceiling.

"Hurry," Twylla says from behind me. Without taking our hands from the wall we start to run. The ground begins to slope gently, then more steeply, the turns becoming sharper, the path narrower. The grating sounds far away now; I can hear nothing but our breathing and the occasional drip. As the air gets colder, the sconces are spread further apart, leaving patches of shadow. Each one makes my heart skip. Eventually we come to a door – not a curtain but a door, made of dark, grainy wood. Burned into it are two circles, one overlapping the other. In the centre is a small silver crescent moon.

"This must be it," Twylla says, taking a deep breath as she pushes it open and enters. I follow her, pulling the door closed behind me.

And then I stop. And stare.

I'd expected another small cave, possibly a meeting hall of sorts. But the chamber I've walked into is the size of a cathedral, the ceiling a hundred feet above me and studded with white, glittering stalactites, twice my height, pointing down like a thousand swords over my head. The walls, though, are studded with bones. Hundreds, possibly thousands of skulls stare out of the walls at me, stacked neatly on top of one another. Some of them have symbols on them, the symbols for salt, for fire, for air etched in gold on their foreheads.

More bones, perhaps from arms and legs, are arranged into intricate patterns, hearts, circles and stars, embedded in the walls. On the far left wall a rose has been constructed from a group of pelvises; on the right a chalice is made from ribs.

Above my head a chandelier made out of human bones hangs from the impossibly high ceiling: skulls clutched in whole, clenched skeletal fists, candles inside the eye sockets, lighting the room and simultaneously casting eerie shadows.

Long, sturdy leg bones make up the joints between the skulls and hands. Entire spinal columns weave in and out, holding the structure together, and below them, small bones hold up strings of tiny ones, threaded like beads.

It's beautiful and macabre and I shiver. An underground temple. And a crypt, all at once.

I know, without being told, that every single bone in here belonged to an alchemist. And I know that this temple, this ossuary, was built long before the Conclave hid down here; perhaps is the reason it is underground. This is the work of centuries, young bones and old bones all combined to make this place. It's awful but beautiful, and every time I feel disgust rising, appreciation beats it down as I spot some new, impossible pattern.

I wonder whom the marked graves in the graveyard belong to, but the answer comes to me immediately. Silas said the alchemists married non-alchemists. They can't be part of this place, but their place in the alchemic world is marked, subtly, on their graves.

Down near the altar, Twylla has disappeared behind a screen, and I can hear voices. I follow the sound, walking down an aisle lined with pews. I touch each one as I pass. None of them is the same; all different woods, different sizes. Some are heavily carved and decorated with the symbols of the old Gods, Holly and Oak. Some are simple and plain. All of them are worn, grooved where generations of bottoms have warmed them and worshipped on them; where people have sat and looked up at their ancestors.

The altar is the only space not adorned with bones. Instead a large metal sculpture – two discs, one made of gold, one silver – is mounted above it. The silver disc overlaps the gold, making a crescent, and it reminds me of the moon. The altar is laid with flowers and burning candles. The air smells of incense, and something else, not a scent, precisely, but a weight, a presence. The bones. I can feel them, as surely as if a thousand alchemists were here with me, spying on me.

I find them in an alcove, hidden behind a carved wooden screen. Twylla sits stiffly, facing a large woman dressed entirely in black, like the Sisters, though with none of their eerie elegance. She must be the Sin Eater, Amara. Her eyelids are heavy, giving them the look of being hooded, her face round and waxen in contrast to her daughter's obvious anger. I can see no resemblance between them.

"I thought you worked alone," Twylla says as I take a seat beside her. The Sin Eater looks at me and I nod in greeting, feeling oddly relieved when she inclines her head to me, before looking back at Twylla. "I never thought you'd be friendly with nuns."

"Nuns," Amara scoffs. "They're a reformed resurrectionist cult, and no matter what else I tell you, don't forget this mess is partly their fault, too. We've all played our part."

"I don't understand. What are they to do with us – you?"

Her mother gives her a long look. "They are the Sisters of Næht. I am the Sin Eater, High Priestess of Næht."

Chills run through me as she says the words; it sounds as though a hundred woman have spoken them.

"But she doesn't exist, does she?" Twylla says. "For all your talk of Næht and Dæg, they're not real. They never were."

Amara stares at her daughter, who meets her gaze evenly.

"Actually, they were," I say, my voice too loud in the reverent atmosphere. Amara turns and nods at me to continue, betraying no surprise at my knowing. "Their real names were Aurek and Aurelia."

"Aurek and Aurelia?" Twylla asks. "The Sleeping Prince and his sister?"

"You know the story?" I ask, and she nods.

Then she turns to her mother. "I know all of them. I can read now." She sounds both proud and defiant, and painfully young. "Go on," she says to me.

"Well, the House of Belmis changed it all. Manipulated it to support their rise to power. They renamed Aurek and Aurelia Dæg and Næht to fit their purpose. Eventually they changed from siblings to lovers too."

"Gods, imagine waking and discovering all of this. That your life has become a legend, and a much embroidered one at that."

"You would pity him?" Amara stares at her daughter.

"No." Twylla's voice is icy. "He's a murderer. Nothing excuses what he's done. That's why I plan to fight him. Lormere has had its fill of corrupt royals."

"I wondered what it would take to remove the scales from your eyes," the Sin Eater says softly.

Twylla's lips curl into a snarl. "If, instead of merely wondering, you'd seen fit to *tell* me what I was walking into,

I might have been better able to cope. Instead I swallowed every lie they fed me until it tore me apart."

"I had no choice, Twylla. I am the Sin Eater—"

"Yes, yes, your precious role. I hope it takes good care of you when you're old, because Gods know where my brothers are, Maryl is dead, and I will not aid you."

The Sin Eater sits back, visibly stunned at the venom in her daughter's voice, and I reel too. I have already seen the Goddess in Twylla, but this is a different kind of awesome. This is vengeance, and cruelty: a war Goddess. Fighting the High Priestess of Næht. I shiver again, caught between these two women who seem to have forgotten I'm here.

"I tried to tell you, many times, that our role was more than it seemed."

"You fed me riddles in a room like a furnace. I was a child," Twylla says, in a voice that's deep and raw and broken. "How could I possibly have understood what you were telling me? How could I have guessed what the queen was truly like? Did you know the maids at the castle wouldn't bring my meals to me in case I poisoned them? They wouldn't touch my used plates and knives until they'd seen my guards hold them and not die. Throughout it all, my only friends – my only comfort – were your Gods. I lived like that, every day for four harvests, to find out that everything I believed was a lie."

Twylla stands as though to leave but the Sin Eater grips her wrist, moving surprisingly fast, and holds her firm.

"Let me give you some truths. Decide after that if you can fight your war without my knowledge. Then if you want

331

to walk away, I will not stop you. But you are the last of us and I have to try."

"If you hadn't let Maryl die, you'd have her." There is an edge to Twylla's voice, one I recognize. Grief. Tucked away tightly.

"I tried," the Sin Eater says, letting go of Twylla's wrist.

Twylla turns and I see her profile in the light, carved and cruel. "Am I supposed to believe you? I remember, *Mother*, a time when she was a baby, burning up in that awful room. And you left her to die. And when I saved her, you killed the goat. So do not tell me that you tried."

The Sin Eater looks up sharply. "Do you think me so cold? I knew you'd save her. I knew the moment I left that house that you would run to the village and beg for herbs. Why do you think I left you with her? I couldn't ask the withwoman for the herbs, because I am the Sin Eater – I cannot intervene. But you could. And I hoped in my secret heart that you would."

Twylla's eyebrows rise. "Then why kill the goat?"

"A life for a life, that is the rule. The withwoman knew what you'd done. Everyone she told would have known too. So I had to make a sacrifice. I had to obey my own laws."

Twylla blinks, turning to look out into the ossuary at the bone murals. Without a word she sits back down. The relief on her mother's face is naked.

"Forgive us, Errin," she says. "I'll come to your part in this." She looks back to her daughter. "You never asked why we were the ones who Ate sin. I thought of anyone you would, yet you never did."

"You told me why. I was perhaps six; you summoned me and you told me that we existed before Gods and kings, but it wasn't for them that we did it. That someone had to do it, because there had always been sins."

"You remember that?"

"I had cause to, recently. When I discovered the Gods were a lie. Now you say they're not a lie, but a twisting of truth."

"When we came to Lormere, there were no Gods, no kings or queens."

"When we came there?"

"From across the sea."

Twylla leans forward, as though to better hear what her mother has said, and I stare at the Sin Eater of Lormere, a tickling at the back of my neck as the skin there tightens. When the Sin Eater leans forward too, I do the same, three points of a triangle curving in.

"The truth of it is that the poison in the wine that the prince and his family drank, the poison that made him sleep, that killed his father and later his lover . . . our ancestor made that poison. Our ancestor was betrothed to the rat catcher's son. When he learned the Sleeping Prince had defiled his daughter, he sent for his son's bride-to-be to come with her skills, and her draughts, and kill them all for the shame they had wrought. Under the light of the solaris she did, brewing a deadly poison."

I look at Twylla, who is staring at her mother, open-mouthed. "That's impossible."

"She didn't know there was a child. She laced the food for the feast with her poison. As it was carried up the stairs, she overheard the kitchen maids gossiping about the rat catcher's daughter and her condition. Her family creed was to harm no innocent. So she went to Aurelia and confessed. By the time Aurelia got to them with the Elixir, the king was dead, Aurek and his lover a breath away from dying too. Aurelia tried to save them. But the poison contained blood – her own blood – and had an alchemy all of its own. The battle between Aurelia's blood and the witch princess's raged inside both lovers, until childbirth weakened the rat catcher's daughter and she died."

At some point during this tale I've covered my face with my hands, desperate to block it out. Alchemy, poison, magic. Lormerian superstition. Yet real. I feel a pang at the base of my spine, a reminder of how real it is.

"The rat catcher fled with the child, which lived a normal life, but was cursed to rise from the grave every century to feed his father a heart. The Sleeping Prince lay locked inside himself, the battle ever-waging. And our ancestor threw herself on the mercy of Aurelia for her crime. It is in her name – Næht's name – that we live as outcasts, burdened openly with sin to shame us, so we never forget what our blood did. We who will always carry the sins of others, piling on more each generation."

Her tale ends. The ringing silence that follows her words makes me feel as though the walls are closing in around me; I'm suddenly terrifyingly aware that I'm underground, under

334

tons of rock and earth. If the ceiling caved in now, this would be our tomb, and none would know it. I'm consumed by the need for sky, the need for air. The need for sound.

"The queen knew all of this, didn't she?" Twylla asks. "That's where she got the idea to make me poisonous. From that. From our past. She was laughing at us. At them. Make the descendant of the poisoner the sanctioned killer of traitors."

Amara nods. "Helewys was known for her cravings for tales of alchemy and lore. It was a slight, to them, to the people who wouldn't bow to her. To openly make you a poisoner, given your ancestry. Perhaps she hoped to draw them out through you."

Again they fall silent. A faint rumbling in the distance reminds me that somewhere above us battle still rages.

"So that's why he wants Twylla?" I ask. "Because he knows her ancestors tried to kill him? He wants revenge."

Amara looks at me and then turns to her daughter. "And because she could do it again," she says.

Twylla stares at her mother. "What are you...?" But she doesn't finish her sentence. Instead she begins to laugh. I turn to Amara and she shakes her head slightly, looking back at her daughter. Twylla tilts her chin towards the ceiling and laughs, the sound echoing off the bones. "I can't escape it, can I? I have renounced two destinies. I tried to hide behind the skirts of a queen, and then I fled across a whole kingdom, and yet it still will not let me go. They're the same thing. And I can't run from it."

"Twylla..." Amara says.

"They told me I held poison in my skin." Twylla looks at me, her tone now dreamy, her gaze unfocused as she remembers. "They gave me a potion each moon and told me it was poison. That it made me poisonous to the touch. It was my job to kill traitors by laying my hands on them. Of course, it wasn't me. They were poisoned before I got anywhere near them. It was your brother who proved it a lie, when he..." She stops, and her face clears. "Yet it was true all along, in a different way. Not my skin, but my blood is poison. My blood." Her laughter dies away and silence rings in its place. "So I am to execute him, with poison," Twylla says. "I almost wish the queen were here to see this. She, I think, would enjoy this."

"Not just your blood," Amara says swiftly. "Your blood is part of the poison. Not all of it."

"What poison could work on him now?"

I make a sound of surprise. Of realization. "I think I know," I say. "The potion Silas made – the base that all alchemists use – it's the reversal of the one used to put Aurek to sleep. His children used what was left of the poison and broke it down. They believed if they could reverse it, they could wake him. In apothecary, like cures like, you see. In alchemy too." I pause, trying to put my thoughts in order. "So if we reverse the reversed potion, we'll have the original one used to poison him."

"And we have my blood to add," Twylla says, her voice still distant.

Like when Silas adds his blood to the Opus Magnum. Twylla's blood must react with it too, but not alchemically.

Fatally. "We can poison him again," I say. "Add new strength to the poison already in him."

"Can you make it?" Twylla asks, suddenly keen as a hawk.

I try to remember what I saw. "Yes, I think so."

"I believe the Sisters have a plan in place to try and replicate the poison," Amara says.

"No," Twylla shakes her head dismissively. "I want Errin to work with me. Not them."

Amara sits back, crossing her arms. I swallow. "Of course." I say, then turn to Amara. "I might be the best choice anyway. Silas told me the alchemists are lacking in the apothecary arts. They've never really needed them; it would mean them learning techniques from scratch. But to me, deconstructing a potion is child's play. I can deconstruct the Opus Magnum if I know what's in it. I can remake the poison from it."

Amara gives a curt nod, and I look back at her daughter. "I'll need Silas's help with some of it, or any alchemists, I suppose; I can't remember it all. But I could do it. I could deconstruct the potion and we can remake the original poison from that. Give it to him. Flood him with it. Overcome whatever effects of Aurelia's Elixir are left."

Amara cuts across our excitement. "He must not get hold of any more Elixir." She looks at me pointedly. "You'll have to keep Silas far from him. He must never know a philtresmith still lives."

I wonder how she knows about Silas, and a strange cold fills my insides, making me gasp.

"What is it?" Amara asks.

I shake it off. "Just a chill. He's up there fighting," I say. "We should get him away. You two and he are too valuable. We have to get out of here. There has to be a way, a secret back door or something. Silas will know. We can head back to Scarron." I turn to Twylla, who is already standing. "It's far enough away to buy us some time."

We've taken no more than three steps when there is rumbling directly above us. Stones and dust trickle down from the ceiling and we stop, turning uncertainly towards Amara. On the left wall, a lone pelvis falls to the floor and shatters.

For a long moment the three of us look at one another. Then the rumbling comes again, louder now, more dust falling, the chunks of rock larger. The chandelier shakes and we all look up at it; the rattling of the bones is deafening, and there's something hypnotic in watching them tremble.

Then it stops; a split second of peace.

"Run," Amara says, and we need no further instruction. We fly down the aisle towards the door as the chandelier falls from the ceiling with an earth-shattering crash.

Chapter 24

Shards of bone fly at us, stinging my back as I yank the door open. Without the muffling of the thick door, we can hear screams echoing, booming, rolling like wheels through every corridor in the Conclave, finally reaching us down here.

Two alchemists round the corner, each gripping one end of a large wooden box, forcing us to flatten ourselves against the wall as they make for the ossuary. Their faces are blank with terror. I grab Twylla's arm and we race blindly back along the warren-like passages, retracing our steps, my right hand on the right wall this time. Behind us the Sin Eater's breath is laboured, her footsteps slow and thudding, and I feel a stab of concern.

When we reach a wide, brightly lit passage that I hope is the same one we walked down earlier, I start to throw curtains aside, hoping to find people, or weapons, or a way out.

The grating echo continues, like underground thunder. It seems to follow us and I'm flooded with the conviction that the ceiling really is going to come down and kill us.

A figure appears ahead of us. "This way!" it beckons, and we run towards it, to find ourselves back in the Great Hall. Nia and Sister Hope stand beside the table, both armed with short swords. Another woman, white-haired and fierce, is swinging a mace.

"You have to go," Sister Hope says, herding us towards the curtain at the other end. "Silas is on his way; he'll go with you."

When the curtain is thrown back, both Sister Hope and I move towards it, but it's Amara who stumbles in. Her face is bright red with exertion, her hand pressing into her side.

Twylla turns her back on her. "What's happening?" she asks Nia.

"They're inside. We've sent all the children and the elderly out through a bolthole; everyone else has gone to fight."

"Is he here?" She doesn't need to name him.

Nia nods and my blood runs cold. "With his golems. And his son. He's here to conquer, like in Lortune."

"Gods..." Twylla says, and my stomach clenches. "We need weapons."

"You need to leave!" Sister Hope commands. "Nia, take the girls and get them out."

"I want to fight," Nia protests. "This is my home!"

"It might end up being your grave," Amara pants, her

hand now clutching her arm. "Get my daughter and Errin out. And the boy if he arrives in time."

"But—"

"There's no time to argue—" She's cut off by a huge chunk of stone crashing to the ground three feet from where we stand.

A piercing scream rings out from beyond the hall, and we spin to face it. A second later Silas runs in, his face pale, a dark stain on his tunic.

"Silas," I cry, running to him, relieved when I realize it's not his blood.

"They're almost here," he tells his mother, then looks down at me, one arm reaching around my waist even as he says, "You have to go."

"You need to come too," I say. "If he captures you, if he sees your hand. . ."

"She's right," Sister Hope orders, clasping him on his sword arm. "And you, Amara, go. Out of the snake passage."

"I won't make it," Amara says. "Leave me."

"Amara, you can't—"

"I said leave me," she demands. Her face is crumpling, her breath sharp. Silas and his mother exchange a loaded look. "Twylla, you know everything now. I've told you all of it. What you do next is up to you. It always has been." Amara's eyes bore into her daughter's.

There are more screams and shouts from outside, the sound of footsteps, of metal ringing, but none of us moves, all of us locked in this moment.

"I did love you," Amara says. "I tried."

Twylla's face is blank as she looks at her mother.

Then the curtain is pulled down, and two men dressed in black tabards and clutching bloodstained swords lurch into the room.

"Go!" Amara bellows, and the spell breaks. Silas dives in front of us with his sword extended, and I scrabble for my knife, realizing too late I don't have it, that I lost it in Tremayne.

I start to back away, pushing Twylla behind me. Silas is in front of us, sword ready. The alchemist swings her mace, whirling it into the skull of one of the men, killing him instantly. Sister Hope lunges at his comrade and the two begin to fight. I stand mesmerized, watching Silas's mother wielding a sword better than any man, the steel a blur, her robes flaring out behind her as she turns and parries and lunges. When she cuts the man down with a single sweep, Silas turns to me and smiles proudly.

"Go!" Sister Hope roars, as more men pour into the room. She raises her sword again and charges towards them.

We turn from the fight; my hands reach for Silas's and Twylla's. Then the curtain promising our escape route opens and a man enters, dressed head to toe in gleaming armour. We stop and Silas pulls both Twylla and me behind him, shielding us from the Silver Knight. He draws his sword and swings it in an arrogant, easy loop, and I hear Twylla breathe "No."

Silas tenses. "When I start to fight, run," he murmurs.

"No—"

"I'll be right behind you."

"Si—" But I don't get to finish, because the Silver Knight lunges and Silas has to raise his sword to keep from being cut down. The sound of steel against steel is deafening as it echoes off the rocks, and to the left a cluster of stalactites falls, barely missing the alchemist as she swings her mace.

I grab Twylla's hand, but before we can get to the door, the Silver Knight realizes what I'm doing and moves to block us. Behind us Sister Hope, Nia, and her wife are somehow holding their own against the other men, forcing them to bottleneck in the doorway while they lash out, Sister Hope with evident skill, and the others with sheer dumb luck.

I drop Twylla's hand and run to the table, grabbing at one of the benches. Twylla looks at me as though I'm mad, and screams something, but I can't hear her over the noise. I push it across the floor with all my might. It ploughs into the Silver Knight's legs, sending him stumbling away from the door. At the same time, Silas crows in triumph as his sword makes contact with an open joint on the knight's sword arm. "Now!" I hear him shout, and I seize Twylla's hand again, jerking to a halt when a golem reels into the room, clay hands reaching out blindly. It's smaller than the one that broke me, but still as bone-chilling with its blank face. My back gives a twinge and I'm frozen to the spot.

Then, from behind it, another figure enters.

Dressed in gold armour, pulling a golden helmet shaped like a dragon from his head, white hair spilling down his back, a grin carved across his bloodless face.

The Sleeping Prince.

He tilts his head in that uncanny way the alchemists seem to all have. "We've met," he says, his eyes fixed on me, in the voice I recognize from my dreams. He moves his gaze to Twylla. "The Sin Eater's daughter?" He nods to himself before continuing his survey of us, eyebrows rising when they reach Amara. "And the Sin Eater? How neat." He smiles, a long, lazy smile that spreads across his whole face. Then he lunges forward, to be driven back by Silas.

"Run!" Silas bellows.

I push Twylla past him and the golem swings a massive arm at Silas. We immediately run into one of the black-clad men, leaning over a body. I can't tell if it is male or female; all I can see is dark blood soaking into once-white hair. The man looks up and smiles horribly, raising his sword, and I pull Twylla away from the scene.

The man runs at us and my arm snaps out, yanking a torch from its bracket on the wall and smashing it into his face. His scream is awful as he collapses to the ground, clutching his head. The stink of charred flesh fills the cavern. Still clutching the torch, I reach for Twylla's hand and begin to run, away from the Great Hall, and the burned man, and the Sleeping Prince.

I don't look back. As our feet pound the stone floor, I try to keep track of left and right, throwing open curtains to see if I recognize anything. The air starts to feel cooler, telling me we're deeper now, but that's no good; we need to get close to the surface to have any chance of escape.

"Stop," Twylla says, her breath coming in pants, too loud in the ringing silence of the tunnels. "We're not going to find the way out without help; there are miles of tunnels down here. We'll end up hopelessly lost."

"Better that than caught," I say.

She opens her mouth to argue, but then we hear it. Footsteps, heavy ones, the clinking of metal. Of armour plates. Coming towards us. I feel the blood drain from my face. But this time she's taking my wrist and pulling me. When I see the door I understand the mistake we've made, trapping ourselves in the heart of the Conclave, but the footsteps still echo towards us.

"We have to hide," she whispers urgently. "We have to."

Realizing she is right, I follow her into the temple.

The grandeur from before has been replaced with a scene from a nightmare. With the chandelier fallen, the room is dim, lit by the torches on the wall. The floor is littered with a hundred shattered skulls, eye sockets stare emptily up at us, and broken jaws and teeth cover the battered pews. I look up at the ceiling, where bones now hang freely, and I wonder what the Sleeping Prince was doing above us to bring the ceiling down.

We clamber over the dead to get to the altar, slipping on treacherously sharp shards of bone and slivers of wood, dust clouds swirling under our boots as they crush the bones beneath them. My heart beats frantically; I feel sick with anticipation and dread.

"Where will we hide?"

"I don't know." She looks around frantically. "There must be something. Some cave, or shelf in the rock." She begins to peer behind the screens and I do the same, shifting ribs aside with my feet as quietly as I'm able.

When I hear her gasp I think we're saved, that she's found a way out for us. But she's not looking behind the screens; she's staring down the aisle.

My brother stands inside the doorway, clad head to toe in silver armour, staring back at her. A helmet is tucked under one arm; the other, his right, hangs limply, the armour splattered with blood.

The Bringer isn't the Silver Knight. Lief is.

Chapter 25

His eyes are fixed on her as he walks down the aisle, seeming not to notice the bones beneath his feet. There's something eerily matrimonial about it: her standing in a torn and dusty dress before the altar as he makes his way towards her through a river of bones.

He's alive.

I was right, I think wildly, *he's alive, I knew he wouldn't lie down and die.* But my joy fades as soon as it rises. Because he's here with the Sleeping Prince. Working for him – *with* him. My own brother. This is why he didn't come home.

I watch him, half hoping he's not real, that I'm hallucinating. His lips have widened into a smile that is nothing like the one I remember. Though his mouth stretches and curves, it's closer to grimace than grin. "Hello, Twylla," he says, stopping a few feet from her and putting his helmet down on a pew.

"Hello, Lief," she replies, returning his smile.

His entire face lights up, and it's painful to look at him; his feelings shine as brightly as his armour, and I know in that moment that he did love her, he still does, no matter what she believes. I turn to her and see an identical expression of yearning on her face. I might as well not exist. There is only those two.

I think he must be under a spell, that's what this is, why he didn't come back or write. He couldn't. The Sleeping Prince put him under a spell, and now Twylla will break it. Like in the stories, one kiss and he'll be freed and the three of us can go, get Silas, and find a way to defeat the Sleeping Prince.

Then I realize Lief is here, and Silas is not. Lief was fighting Silas. He must have beaten Silas to be here...

I reach for a pew, my mouth falling open in a silent scream.

I look at Twylla. All the love and longing on her face is gone. "You've done it again, haven't you?" she says.

"I can explain."

"Are we really going to have this conversation again?" she snarls, and both Lief and I flinch away from her. "You can't help being a traitor, can you? How can you be related to Errin? She risks her life for the people she loves. You've betrayed everyone who's ever shown you kindness, time and again, for your own gain."

"I don't expect you to understand."

She shakes her head and looks down at his sword. "Is that Merek's?" When he doesn't reply, she laughs bitterly. "Of course it is. If it's Merek's you have to have it, don't you. His home, his sword, his bride. . ."

"I don't remember you being unwilling," Lief says coldly, and Twylla sucks in a long breath. "I didn't know he was going to kill Merek," he continues, obviously at pains to keep his voice even, and my heart twists sharply. My brother was there when the king was killed. He's been there since the beginning. "I thought he was going to take him prisoner. I never meant him any real harm."

"And you called me naïve."

He shakes his head. "Twylla, I—"

"If you say you still love me then I swear to the Gods I will kill you," she hisses.

"I wasn't going to," he says, and the ring of honesty in his words makes her recoil. "I was going to tell you to hide. Make sure you cannot be found."

"Are you helping us?"

"He wants your head next to Merek's on the Lortune gate," Lief says. "And though we are no longer . . . friends, I don't want to see that."

I see Twylla blanch and my own rage rises, boiling and caustic. "Lief?" I say, and the sound jolts them both. They startle and turn to me.

"Errin." Lief tries for a smile.

"Where have you been? Why didn't you come back? Why didn't you write?"

He looks at Twylla; then his gaze slides back to me. "We can talk about this later."

"You're the Silver Knight? You're with *him*?"

My voice echoes and Lief looks over his shoulder. "Keep your voice down."

I shake my head. "Where is Silas? Did you. . ." I can't say it. "Did you?"

He shakes his head. "He's fine."

"But your master has him now, doesn't he?" I spit, and Lief flushes. "Thanks to you. Tremayne is destroyed! Our village, Lief. Gone. The bakery, the forge. My apothecary. His monsters levelled it, smashed everything they could to pieces. People are dead, Lief. The baker's wife. The blacksmith. Maybe Lirys. People we know."

"I wasn't here when that happened—"

"I thought you were dead," I cut across him, spitting my words at him. "I wish you were, Gods I wish you were. Traitor."

His eyes move between Twylla and me. "What did she tell you?" he asks.

I shake my head and step away from him. "Tell us how to get out of here. You owe me that much. You owe her more."

"Errin, I—"

Then the sound of boots. "Lief?" That smooth, chilling voice calls from further down the corridor, and I freeze like a deer caught in a huntsman's sight.

"Here, Your Grace," he calls. "Hide," he hisses at Twylla. "I can't protect you. Hide."

She looks at me and I nod. After glancing around, she

takes a few silent steps to the screen that we'd sat behind an hour or so before, and my heart sinks. It's not going to be good enough. She's going to be caught.

Suddenly Lief darts towards me and grips my shoulder painfully, forcing me to the ground in a horrible parody of the lieutenant on the road. I let out a cry that dies instantly when he raises his sword and points it at me.

"Play along," he hisses. "For her sake. And Silas's. And your own."

Out of the corner of my eye I see the Sleeping Prince round the doorway, and Lief digs his fingers into my shoulder. "Where is she?" he demands, and I cry out again. "Where did she go?"

"I don't know," I say. The pain, the fear, is very real.

"Liar," Lief says, leaning in. "I know when you're lying. Where did she go?"

"I'm telling you I don't know." Tears stream down my face.

Then Lief releases me, and the Sleeping Prince fills my vision, crouched before me, arms resting on his knees. He looks me over, his head tilted. "She says she doesn't know, Lief," he murmurs. "Is that true, sweetling?"

I nod my head, allowing more tears to fall.

"There, there, child." He pulls me up with him, folding me into an embrace. My face is pressed against his cold armour, metal arms holding me to him. I'm so horribly aware of my brother standing behind us, of Twylla hiding behind the screen. Yet still he holds me. I feel his nose against my hair, hear him inhale. "We haven't been properly introduced," he says, lowering his mouth to my ear. "I'm Aurek. King Aurek now. And you're Errin."

I pull away and he lets me, smiling with an easy charm. Up close his cheeks are sunken and the skin across them is thin and waxen. His hair looks dry and brittle, and there are lines around his mouth, between his eyebrows. He's aging. Rapidly.

"Where's Silas?" I ask before I can think.

This time his smile is brilliant, his whole face lighting up with pleasure. "Ah, Silas. My miraculous nephew. What a gift, what an unexpected joy in a dark time. He's safe, of course. He's my treasure. As are you, sweetling. As is your brother. My new family. You can see him soon enough, if you behave. Though I don't expect any trouble from you. You're the girl of my dreams, after all."

My stomach lurches. I've been so foolish. "So it was you—"

"One of the perks of being a vitasmith. My little joke. You're not laughing, though." There is something hideously childish about his manner. He shrugs. "It was really a joke for me, anyway. Both of them were."

"What? Both of what?"

He places a long finger against my lips to silence me. "Later, my sweetest." He turns to Lief. "When did you last see the traitor?"

"In the Great Hall, before they fled. I thought it was her I was chasing. She's coloured her hair; it confused me momentarily."

"And you truly don't know where your friend went?" The Sleeping Prince scrutinizes me, and it takes every ounce of willpower I have to keep my gaze on his and not let it shift to where Twylla hides.

"I told her to run."

"Oh dear," the Sleeping Prince says. "That was foolish." He frowns and turns away, scanning the room, and my heart skitters wildly.

"Is everyone in Tremayne dead?" I blurt. "Did your monsters kill them all?"

"You're not very respectful." He looks back at me, his eyes raking my face. "I'm a king, Errin. You're supposed to bow to me; you haven't yet. And you're not supposed to address me until I've spoken to you."

"Tell me what happened to them and then I'll decide whether or not to bow to you."

He scowls at me, his lip curling, anger flooding his face. Just as suddenly it's gone, replaced with the same mechanical smile. "Enough questions, sweetling. Plenty of time for that later." His hand darts out and takes my wrist, caressing it with his thumb, smiling when I flinch.

Over his shoulder Lief stands with the oddest expression on his face. He blinks once, as if remembering where he is, and then speaks. "Your Grace, if I might be so bold, I can have the golems search for her, if you wish? Matters upstairs should be finished by now, as well as the business above ground."

"Business." I stare at my brother. "Do you mean murder?"

"You have to scotch the nest to eliminate the threat, Errin," the Sleeping Prince says musically. "We don't expect you to understand."

"Good, because I don't." I turn away from him. Panic stabs at me the second my back is to him, but I gather my courage and look at my brother. "What about Lirys, Lief? She was in Tremayne. Did you know she and Kirin were engaged? And what of him? He was a soldier, Lief. Did you come through Almwyk? Did you know he was there? Did you slaughter him too?"

Lief's fingers flex, but his face stays blank. "If any soldiers died, they died doing their duty. It's what they signed up for: the defence of their country."

"He's your best friend!" It comes out as a sob, and then I'm trapped again in the iron grip of the Sleeping Prince.

"Now, now, lovely," the Sleeping Prince says, leaning his head on my shoulder. "I would have accomplished all of this anyway; it's hardly your brother's fault. In fact, I daresay he's saved more lives than have been lost so far. I haven't killed a tenth of the people I thought I'd have to." I can hear the smile in his voice and it sickens me.

I ignore the Sleeping Prince and address my brother directly. "So now what? You live at the castle in Lormere as his lapdog?"

There is a *tsk* behind me. "He's my heir," the Sleeping Prince says softly in my ear. "Unless I have new children of my own, then your brother is my heir. And should I have more children, then he'll become a grand duke, with land of his own to rule, and to pass on to his own heirs. No more bowing and scraping. My thanks to him for all that he helped me achieve. If you can learn to mind your tongue, you can be a duchess."

"I'd rather die."

"I can make that happen," he whispers. Louder, he continues. "I owe your brother a great deal, Errin. His knowledge of the layout of Lormere castle, his knowledge of the geography and laws of Tregellan. He's been invaluable to me. He also told me your great-grandfather was the captain of the Tregellian Royal Army once. I can see that in him."

I look at Lief, expecting to see him glowing under the praise, but he merely bows.

The Sleeping Prince speaks again. "It's simple, Errin. If you're willing to swear loyalty to me, then I will reward you. I want a prosperous kingdom. My opening methods might be distasteful to you, but the legacy will be worth it. I will unite Lormere and Tregellan and we'll thrive. Will you accept me as your king?"

"No," I say immediately.

His grip on my wrist tightens and I yelp. Lief jerks forward as though coming to my aid, but then masters himself, his face carefully blank.

"Lief, would you give me a moment with your sister, please? I believe your presence is stirring a rebellion in her. Sibling rivalry, I remember it well. Have another look for the girl. Take the golems, and Brach and his crew. She can't have gone far."

Lief makes another bow and turns, crunching down the aisle and sweeping the curtain aside. I'm shocked that he'd leave me here, alone with the Sleeping Prince. That he'd leave Twylla alone behind the screen.

The Sleeping Prince spins me around to face him. "Let me phrase it another way, Errin," he says pleasantly. "I have your brother. I have Silas. In a matter of hours I'll have your mother, too. If you make me angry, I will hurt them. If you defy me, I will hurt them. Do you know, Errin, the one thing your brother asked for was your and your mother's safety. All the rewards I'm heaping on him are unasked for. Isn't that noble? I could have given him anything in the world, and all he wanted was for his family to be cared for. For us to be a happy family, together."

"I told you, I'd rather die."

"And I told you, that can be arranged. But I think you'll come around. You liked me in the dreams, didn't you?" I flush and he grins. "Yes, you liked me. You liked me very well."

"If I'd known you—"

"Ah, that's right. You thought I was Silas. There's another gift I owe to the Vastels. My long-lost nephew, the philtresmith. Had you not told me, in your dreams, where you were, who you were with, I dread to think what opportunities I might have missed."

"No. No. They were dreams. They weren't real." My blood freezes. "No."

He answers with a grin like a nightmare. "I'm a vitasmith. I can create life, Errin. So I did. I used your brother's blood and made two little simulacra. I told him I'd protect them, and as long as I did, you'd both be safe. I called one Errin, that was you. And one was Trina. Trina was my favourite, actually. Easier to play with. Malleable."

My ears are filled with a high-pitched sound as the puzzle clicks into place. The doll in the dream. He showed it to me. He said it was me. It was real. And. . . Oh Gods. . . Sweetling. My mother said it when she was under the curse. Except there is no curse. There is no Scarlet Varulv. It was him all along. He made her like that. He made her do those things to me.

He smiles again as he watches me put it together. "I liked to play with my little simulacra. There was something poetic about doing it during the full moon. Something mystical, like in the stories. I didn't tell Lief; I don't think he'd approve. But I do get bored."

I turn my head, tears falling down my face. All those times my mother went for me. It was him. And all my dreams. He was there inside my head. I feel bile burning in my throat. "Why?" I ask in a small voice. I should be relieved Mama isn't cursed, but this is worse.

"I was *robbed*, Errin." He strokes my face with his thumb before turning it back to him. "Of my life. Of my inheritance. Snuffed out at barely twenty-two years old. I have spent five hundred years asleep. I woke to *nothing*. The legacy my family spent generations building is ash, scattered to the wind. I was promised a kingdom," he snarls. "I was promised the greatest kingdom the world had ever known. And I will have one. If it

357

means cobbling one together from the ruins of Lormere and Tregellan."

His eyes bore into mine, lit with madness, made worse when he begins to laugh. "You should be thanking me. You of all people should be welcoming me. Look at you." He pushes me away, holding me at arm's length as he examines me. "You have nothing. You live governed by rich, ignorant men and women, liberals with no respect for tradition, or history, or hard work. They took your mother away and locked her up. They killed your blood, Lief told me. Your great-grandfather died at their hands. You should have always lived in a castle. I will give that to you. I will restore things to how they ought to be."

I stare at him. "How they ought to be?"

"Mine." He smiles wolfishly. "All mine, under my order, and at my pleasure. I told you, I have to scotch the nest, Errin," he says gently. "That's what you do with an infestation. It's what we should have done in Tallith, instead of calling for the rat catcher. I see that now. Burn at the source."

"You're a monster," I whisper.

"I'm a king. My father told me a king can rule through fear, or through love. Fifty years from now, the people will love me. They won't remember this – and those who do will consider it the necessary dark before the dawn. When they have prosperity, and security, and know their place, they will be content and they will love me for it. But until then, I'll rule through fear if I have to."

He smiles at me lasciviously. "And then I will begin

358

again. I will use Silas, and the chosen few I save, and I will breed new alchemists. I will find the last of the Sin Eater's line and I will mount her head above my throne, I will have her hair woven into a crown, have her teeth strung on a chain as a necklace. And when I am safe I will make these lands glorious, Errin. Like Tallith was. And even you will learn to love me for it. You will give me your fealty. You and I, and Silas and Lief, and whomever else I deem worthy will stay with me in these lands and be a court. For ever."

He kisses me on the forehead, pushing my hair behind my ears. Then he pulls me so close that our noses touch. I can taste his breath, faintly metallic, faintly rotten, decaying, like the smell of his golems. "I have been asleep for five hundred years, save for when I woke to eat the hearts of silly little girls like you. I ate the heart of my own son to give me the strength to make my golems. And if you don't shut your mouth and kneel to me, I will eat your mother's heart, and then your brother's heart. I will find everyone you've ever known: your childhood best friend, your first sweetheart, everyone who was ever kind to you. And I will rip their hearts from their chests and eat them while you watch."

He smiles viciously. "And I will make Silas create Elixir until he's nothing but rot. I will have him make it, and I will pour it from the window in front of you both, and then I will make him do it again. The more you defy me, the worse it will be for everyone."

"Why do I matter to you?" I say, my voice breaking.

"You don't."

"Then why are you doing this?"

"Because I can. Because I slept for five hundred years and now I want some sport." He lets go of my arms and looks at me expectantly. "So make your choice."

I don't look at the screen Twylla is hiding behind.

I kneel.

Epilogue

"Dance with me."

It's the stuff of dreams, to stand in the arms of a handsome prince while he smiles down at you. His hand cups my cheek, his thumb moving lightly across the bone as we dance. There's no music, but we don't need it; this ball is just for us two, intimate and full of promises. He's happy; I can see the light of it in his eyes, the way his gaze rests on mine before it lowers, flickering down to my lips and then back up. His body asks a question now; his fingers press lightly into my flesh when he draws my face to his.

When there's no more space between us I lower my eyelids. Then I stab him in the throat with the knife I stole from my breakfast tray this morning. It's blunt, but I put all of my body into the strike.

He staggers back, his eyes wide, and I curl my hands

into claws, watching blood cascade down over his blue velvet collar, staining his shirt.

He pulls the knife out of his neck and plunges it into my stomach. I crumple to the floor as pain explodes across my body.

No. No.

Blood spills over my hands as I hold the hilt, instinct telling me to tear the knife out of my abdomen, to get rid of the thing that's making my vision blacken at the edges. I'll die if I pull it out. Maybe it's better that way.

I test the handle, and then his hand is wrapped around my jaw, forcing my head back and my mouth open as he pours liquid into it. He clamps my jaw shut. "Swallow," he hisses and I do, screaming when he pulls the knife roughly out of me.

By the time I look down the blood has stopped, the wound is closing, I can see it through the tear in my red velvet dress. I slump to the ground, lying on the floor of the ballroom in a puddle of our mingled blood. He lowers himself to the ground next to me.

"This has to stop," he says finally, close as a lover. "Why do you keep doing this? I've given you everything; you live in a castle, for crying out loud. I'm retrieving your mother; I reunited you with your brother. I feed and clothe you. I ask for nothing from you, save your company. What do you want from me? Because frankly, Errin, this is getting boring."

"I want you to leave me alone."

"Ahhh, but I'm fond of you." He smiles at me.

"Because I hate you."

"You don't." He speaks softly, his voice a caress. "You can't. Look at me, Errin. What do you see?"

I look away and then his fingers are on my chin, forcing my head around. I look at him. His golden, hawk-like eyes, his silver-white hair. His handsome, hateful face.

"You'll despise me for ever because I wear his face," he says. "And as much as you hate me, you can't help but want me a little, because I look like him. Same eyes, same hair. Same smile." His lips spread into a grin – that grin – and I know he's beaten me again. "It kills you. Every time. And that's why I can't let you go. So you will learn to control yourself, or I will deal with it, my way." His expression deadens, becoming as guileless as any predator's and my stomach lurches again.

"Clean yourself up." He stands without offering me his hand. "I think we'll ask your Silas to dine with us tonight. What do you think of that, sweetling?" I stay silent, my heart beating strongly as I wait for the punchline. With Aurek there's always a punchline.

"Of course, he'd have to be carried. And fed. It would be quite unsightly, really. Perhaps you wouldn't mind though. You wouldn't, would you? You took care of your mother when she ailed; it's not so different. Of course your mother still had the use of her arms and legs, though she chose not to use them. Whereas poor Silas . . . he has no choice."

"Stop. . ." I whisper, my mouth filling with the strange taste that heralds vomiting.

"I'd like to see it." His voice is deeper, as though the

idea pleases him. "You, cutting his meat, raising a fork to his mouth. Waiting for him to chew and swallow. Wiping his mouth for him." Each word is like a needle, puncturing me. "I don't know how far the Nigredo has advanced up his legs. Last I knew it was below the knee, but now … it could be up to his thighs. I wonder whether he'll choose to stand or sit for the rest of his life? What would you choose, Errin? Sitting or standing?"

I can't help myself; I vomit. Heaving and gagging as my stomach empties itself on my ruined dress, on the floor.

He takes a step back and I can hear the disgust in his voice. "You're a mess. Go and bathe. I'll have a new dress sent for you to dine in."

His boots stalk away, his footsteps ringing across the ballroom. Then they squeal against the wooden floor as he turns back to me.

"Ah, I am a fool. I can't invite him for dinner. He won't have time. He has to make more Elixir to replace what I used on you. Still, I suppose he won't mind, seeing as it saved your life. Take her to her room," he orders a hidden person in the corner of the ballroom.

The door clicks neatly behind him as he leaves and salty tears join the mess of blood and vomit on the once-beautiful dress.

Silently, the servant appears from his station in the shadows, dressed in a rough grey tabard and matching breeches. He stands over me, his dark eyes full of sympathy. His hair is shorn close to his skull, his jaw set as he offers a hand to help me up. I knock it away. I want no help from a coward who bends his knee to the Sleeping Prince to save his skin.

Like I did.

"Forgive me," he says, stepping back to give me room to stand.

I haul myself up and smooth down the dress. I wonder if it was one of Twylla's, and then I wonder how she is, where she is. I hope she got away, far, far away from here. I look down at the gown and crumple the skirts in my fists. I wonder if she ever danced in this room.

I walk slowly from the room. Even though I'm no longer injured, my mind is telling me to be careful, that I'm still hurt. The guards at the door don't look at me as I pass. The servant trails behind me, his presence an annoyance all the way down the corridor. When we reach the south tower, he makes as if to escort me up to my bedroom. I try to slam the door in his face but he wedges himself in the gap.

"Move," I order, and he shakes his head, holding a finger to his lips and pointing down the stairs.

"I said move." I say it louder, but the servant stands his ground, refusing my command.

"I need to talk to you," he whispers. "Please. I have but a few moments. You'll want to listen to me."

I look at him, then shrug, turning away as he closes the door.

"Well?" I ask, looking back at him.

"Is Twylla still alive?" His eyes are wide, his body leaning towards mine with the earnestness of his question. "Do you know where she is? Please. If you know anything. . ."

"As if I'd tell you, traitor."

"Are you still a friend to her?"

I stay silent, watching him.

"All right. Are you a friend to the Sleeping Prince?"

I look down at the ruined dress.

The servant nods as though I've spoken. "Why did you stab him? You know it won't kill him."

"Because it makes me feel better," I spit, immediately wishing I could control both my tongue and my temper.

As if he knows what I'm thinking, the corner of his mouth twitches as though he's holding back a smile. "Or is it because you're trying to collect some of his blood?"

"What?" The room seems to shrink and I glance around, looking for something to defend myself with.

"I've heard about you. You're an apothecary. I know what Tregellian apothecaries can do. I know they can break potions apart, find what they're made of."

"What does that have to do with anything?"

His eyes lock on mine. "You always try to hurt him in a way that will make him bleed. Always. I think you want his blood to test. To take it apart. To find a way to stop him. And I want to help you."

"I don't have a clue what you're talking about."

"What if I said I knew a way out of here? What if I promised to help you get what you need, and then to get out of here with it? Would that change things? I can get you out of here, Errin. Whenever you wish." He pauses, looking at me from the side of his eye and taking a deep breath. "It used to be my castle."

It takes a moment for his words to sink in, and then I look at him, scouring his face. Yes... Yes, in the tilt of his cheekbones, the curve of his jaw. The curly hair is shorn, and the clothes are simple and tatty, but now I see it: that face looking down from the back of a white horse, so many moons ago. "We all thought you were dead."

"One thing I learned from what happened to the Tregellian royal family is that if there are those at your gates who mean you ill, you have two choices. Run, or die. And a dead king is useless."

"You mean to take back the kingdom?"

"If a Sleeping Prince can awaken, then surely a dead king can?" He smiles without moving his mouth at all. Something in his eyes conveys a big, bold grin. I find myself grinning back.

"Why not indeed, Your Majesty?"

"Call me Merek," he says. "All of my friends do."

Acknowledgements

I find it hard to believe I was lucky enough to have one book published, let alone to be here again, a year later, still supported, guided and talked down from the ledge by the following people:

My agent, Claire Wilson, who has handled all of my "Claire. Claire. Help me" emails with such grace and patience. Half of the reason I haven't lost my mind in the past year is because I am lucky enough to have you on my side. Thank you. And thanks again to Lexie Hamblin, I will miss you, and Rosie Price, who has it all to come...

Team Sin Eater at Scholastic UK, and in particular my splendid UK editors, Genevieve Herr and Emily Lamm. Having one editor who gets what you're trying to do is pretty lucky, having two is just jammy. I am that jammy. Here is a fun story: early on in the editing process they sent me a list of edit suggestions, which I then argued against. Every. Single. Point. And my lovely editorial team (including Mallory Kass in the US) simply replied saying, "OK. We trust you. You know the story best. If you say it won't work, we know you'll find another way."

Every single suggestion they made ended up in the book, one way or another. Every single suggestion they made was the right call. Because as I was editing, I realized I might know the story best, but I was far from the only person that knew it. They could see what I couldn't, and *The Sleeping Prince* is so much better for it. I am so lucky to have these guys as my editors, and that they trusted me. I can never thank them enough for that and I'm so proud of what we made here.

Once again Jamie Gregory made me the most perfect cover, and I should probably offer him my soul or something. Jamie, I would if I had one. Magical Publicist Rachel Phillipps, who can literally work miracles and is one of the greatest people in the world. Thank you for being brilliant. Always brilliant. Pete Matthews, Team Sin Eater project manager and proofreader extraordinaire.

Also thanks to David Sanger, Fi Evans, Sam Selby Smith, the Rights team and everyone else who has worked hard on my behalf behind the scenes. One day I will know all of your names and I will fill pages of acknowledgements with them.

On the other side of the world at Scholastic Inc., millions of thanks need to go to Mallory Kass, who, as mentioned above, has offered the kind of support every writer dreams of, as well as lending me her apartment in New York for a night. And buying me cheesecake. And wine. Thank you. And also to Saraciea Fennell, Bess Braswell and everyone else who has supported me, in a non-wine way.

Thanks to my lovely writing-friends-who-are-now-just-friends, especially Robin Stevens, crit partner extraordinaire. Massive thanks to my bros Sara Barnard, Holly Bourne, Alexia Casale, CJ Daugherty, Catherine Doyle and Katie Webber, for a lot of fun and support and laughter over the past year.

Thanks in particular to the following people who have done at least one or more amazing things for me this year: the Lyons Family, and the Allports too, Sophie Reynolds, Denise Strauss, Emma Gerrard, Lizzy Evans, Mikey Beddard, Bevin Robinson, Stine Stueland, Neil Bird, Franziska Schmidt, Katja Rammer, Julie Blewett-Grant, Romana Bičíková, Jim Dean, Lucy Powrie, Kate Ormand, Leigh Bardugo, Nina Douglas, Sofia Saghir, Chelley Toy, Laura Hughes, Auntie Penny, Uncle Eddie and all, Steven, Kelly and co., Auntie Cath and Uncle Paul. You are all magnificent.

The very biggest thanks of all go to Emilie Lyons: the DCI Eugene Morton to my Sheriff Dan Anderssen. Bem bem bem… Really glad we didn't get arrested in Portugal; let's definitely not get arrested again. I'm also so terribly excited for you to see the All-New Shabby-Chic Melseum.

Finally, Javert.

I did not forget you. I did not forget your name.

Melinda Salisbury lives by the sea, somewhere in the south of England. As a child she genuinely thought Roald Dahl's *Matilda* was her biography, in part helped by her grandfather often mistakenly calling her Matilda, and the local library having a pretty cavalier attitude to the books she borrowed. Sadly she never manifested telekinetic powers. She likes to travel, and have adventures. She also likes medieval castles, non-medieval aquariums, Richard III, and all things Scandinavian.

She can be found on Twitter at **@AHintofMystery**, though be warned, she tweets often.